MW00522827

To Love a Stranger

TO LOVE A STRANGER

SHARON MIGNEREY

FIVE STAR

A part of Gale, a Cengage Company

GALE
A Cengage Company

LIBRARY OF CONGRESS CATALOGING-IN-PUBLICATION DATA

Names: Mignerey, Sharon, author.
Title: To love a stranger / Sharon Mignerey.
Description: First edition. | Waterville, Maine : Five Star, 2021.
Identifiers: LCCN 2021011531 | ISBN 9781432879488 (hardcover)
Subjects: GSAFD: Mystery fiction.
Classification: LCC PS3563.I37152 L68 2021 | DDC 813/.54—dc23
LC record available at https://lccn.loc.gov/2021011531

First Edition. First Printing: September 2021
Find us on Facebook—https://www.facebook.com/FiveStarCengage
Visit our website—http://www.gale.cengage.com/fivestar
Contact Five Star Publishing at FiveStar@cengage.com

Printed in Mexico
Print Number: 01   Print Year: 2022

First, to my husband, Les, my companion for life.
No one could have a better partner.

Second, to my village of critique partners whose advice
and counsel are secondary to their friendship and love.
Robin Owens, Liz Roadifer, Pamela Nowak, Steve Moores,
Dené Cody, Meg Mims, and Shelley Bates.
You are the best friends any writer could want.

CHAPTER 1

Colorado Territory South of Denver
Plum Creek Crossing
September 1870

"Come quick, Papa!" the eldest of Ben Haverly's children yelled from outside the store. "Mama said the baby is coming."

He strode toward the door, sudden worry creasing his brow. Abigail Wallace set down the bolts of fabric she was putting away and followed her employer of a scant week to the front of the store. The anticipated arrival of the baby wasn't until next month.

Little Ben flung open the screen door, ran inside, and skidded to a halt. "She said you've gotta get the midwife and come quick."

Ben tossed his apron on the counter and turned to Abbey. "I didn't figure I'd be leaving you in the store by yourself so soon." He grabbed his hat off a hook next to the door. "You remember how to lock up?"

She shooed him out the door. "I'll be fine. Go on with you."

For a man who already had three children, he seemed a bit flustered, Abbey thought, watching him hurry down the street with his son, little puffs of dust stirred up by their feet. But then, the baby was coming early, and that could spell trouble.

She and Ben had been in the middle of stocking the shelves with a shipment of goods that had arrived yesterday, a task she returned to. Customers came and went throughout the day, and the high regard folks had for Ben and Harriet confirmed she'd found a good place to work until she could resume her journey west next spring. Her thoughts returned often to Harriet, and every time someone came through the door, she hoped for news.

About an hour before the scheduled time to close, two men on horseback stopped in front of the store. They dismounted, tethered their animals to the hitching rail, and sauntered in with a jangle of spurs. Everything about these cowboys was different from the miners and farmers who had been customers so far. Their faces were shaded by their hats, which seemed fleetingly sinister until one of them pushed the hat off his head so it hung on his shoulders by a strap. This one was young, she realized, hardly more than a boy, with black, curly hair and equally black eyes, his skin also dark. His ready smile flashed brightly, and Abbey didn't like that she stared. He was the first Negro person she had seen since leaving Missouri, and she had never imagined one being a cowboy. The other man carried a sheet of paper he had pulled from the saddlebag.

"Afternoon, ma'am," he said.

"Can I help you?" Abbey asked from behind the counter.

"Missus Rafferty?" the young one questioned, surprise in his voice.

Abbey shook her head. "I'm Abigail Wallace."

The other man grunted, a rude sound of disbelief. His gaze fastened on her face, and his mouth drew into a frown. This man was whipcord lean, his leather vest as worn as his hat that kept her from seeing his eyes. Slowly, he folded the sheet of paper and put it in his vest pocket.

"Were you looking for her?" Abbey shivered at the dislike in his expression. "I'm new here, so I haven't met everyone yet. And I don't remember that name."

The younger man cleared his throat, then said, "We've been looking—"

"Sam and me just came in for some supplies," the man interrupted. "Ain't that right?"

"Yeah, Jake . . . uh, it is," Sam stammered.

"You came to the right place." Anxiety feathered down her spine, and Abbey glanced at the door, wishing another customer would walk in. "What do you need?"

Jake took off his hat, revealing piercing, brown eyes. He raked his fingers through his light-brown hair, matted down from the hat. "Coffee, flour, and . . ."

The man had a look about him that Abbey had seen too often from the men returning from the war—a certain tiredness as though they had lost hope for a better life. His thorough examination of her, then dismissing her as though she were nothing reminded her of being at the orphanage when they'd been lined up for people who wanted a child. She had always come up short, and she didn't like this reminder.

Her own experiences made her give the younger man a closer look. He looked over the goods with curiosity, and when he realized Jake's voice had trailed off, added, "A bit of salt."

Abbey gathered up their order, which grew as one or the other of them thought of something to add to it.

"You said you were new around here," Sam said.

"I started to work here a few days ago." Abbey repeated what she had told other customers who had been in the store during the day. "Most of the ranchers I've met live east of here." She looked up and found Sam watching her, his expression puzzled. She broke the silence by asking, "Is yours near here?"

"We work the SR Double Bar," Jake said as though his answer meant something to her.

She hadn't heard of it, but she nodded as though his answer made sense and made a mental note to ask Ben and Harriet about it later. "Is it far from here?"

"A couple days' ride."

"Are you a relative of . . ." Sam glanced at the sign above the counter, which read Haverly's Mercantile. "Mr. Haverly?"

"No."

"I guess you're just getting to know folks, then," Jake said. "Since you just got here."

"Yes. So many new people. So many names to remember."

"I'm sure that could be a problem," Jake said. "It must be like keeping lies straight."

Abbey shot him a look. "I suppose."

Sam set a small sack of hard candies on the counter. "Where are you from?"

"The Shenandoah Valley in Virginia." That, too, was a question she had answered many times. It was as though folks were anxious to see if her former home had been the same as theirs and in possession of some snippet of news. "Where are you from?"

"Georgia," he said. "When Mr. Rafferty offered me a job, I counted myself lucky."

The two men finally seemed to have everything they needed or could think of—Abbey wasn't sure which—and she wrote up the order. They paid for it with coin, a contrast to most of the sales, which had been "on account."

Abbey watched them mount up and ride away, then sucked in a deep breath. With the odd currents between the two men, she had initially decided they were bandits. Clearly not, since they had paid for the purchases. The SR Double Bar, she mused. The name conjured images of a broad valley with tall grass and grazing cattle, surrounded by high mountains. Abbey smiled to herself. It wasn't a name for an orchard, which was why she wanted a homestead in California. She'd grow peaches and apples. Abbey's Orchard. Now, there was a name.

It had taken her two years to work her way this far. She worked and saved her money, no easy feat, then embarked on the next leg of the journey. Two years to get from Virginia to Colorado. California was much closer. Maybe by this time next year, she would be there. She imagined planting the seeds carefully sorted and stored in her trunk.

As closing time loomed, her thoughts became consumed with Harriet and the new babe. Since this was her fourth child, her labor should be short, Abbey decided, anxious to get to the house where her position included caring for the children.

She carefully locked the money and sales receipts in their hiding place. She took off her apron, folded it, and set it on a shelf under the counter as she had done yesterday and the day before. After extinguishing the lanterns, a gloom settled over the store.

She glanced around one last time, making sure she remembered everything Ben had told her. Then she walked through the door and locked it. She had slipped the big skeleton key into her reticule when she sensed movement behind her.

She glanced over her shoulder and recognized Jake, the older man of her last two customers. His expression was grim, and his eyes glittered in the late-afternoon light.

Before she could speak, he clamped a hard hand over her mouth. Surprised, then terrified, she pushed against him, a scream trapped in her lungs. She swung at him, felt her fist connect with his jaw, then she pummeled him with both hands.

Another arm wrapped around her waist and lifted her until her feet no longer touched the ground. He turned her around so her back was pressed against his chest.

"For God's sake, Sam, get her hands!"

"Got it."

The young black cowboy, who'd seemed harmless enough before, grasped her wrists, and her small bag dropped to the ground. He tied her wrists together with a length of rope before she knew what was happening.

The pressure against her mouth kept her from opening it to scream or bite him.

His grip became more fierce, and she felt his fingers and thumb hard against her cheekbones. "Stop it," he said. "You'll hurt yourself."

As if he cared, she thought furiously, kicking at them both.

"Are you sure, Jake?"

"She's gonna scream bloody murder the second I let her go."

Abbey gave another strangled cry and tried to wrench free.

Sam removed his bandanna and folded it into a strip. Jake pinned her legs between both of his and used his weight to press her helplessly against the building. Furious tears burned at her eyes as Jake gagged her. The cloth cut into her skin, and the garlic order of perspiration hung like death in her nostrils.

"Get the horses." Keeping her pinned against the wall, he turned her to face him. His eyes narrowed to slits. "I've got to hand it to you, Miz Charlotte," he said. "I almost believed you."

He reached into his pocket and unfolded the paper he'd put there earlier, holding it up for her to read. "You should have figured your husband would be looking for you."

Even in the deep shadows, she could read the big letters of the handbill.

Reward.
$250.00 Cash Money.
For Information of
Charlotte Rafferty.
Contact Sloan Rafferty
c/o the S.R. Double Bar
Poncha, Colorado Territory

He wedged the handbill into a crack between the door and the frame. "I think Mr. Haverly should know he hired a liar, don't you?"

12

Abbey had no time to absorb that because Sam appeared with the horses. He held one while Jake lifted her onto the saddle as though she weighed nothing. He vaulted behind her and took the reins from Sam. Wrapping a hard arm around her waist, Jake urged the horse into a canter. Within seconds, they had left behind the small settlement of Plum Creek Crossing.

She had survived a war. Though she had been a child then, she knew what was in store for her. Ugly memories surged around her, adding to her distress. It couldn't end like this. Not after everything else she had overcome.

She'd survived being abandoned. She'd survived the smallpox when it swept through the orphanage. She'd survived the long winter after Sheridan's army burned the Shenandoah Valley, sure she'd starve before spring came. She wasn't going to be raped and murdered.

Somehow, she'd survive, just as she always had. *God takes care of those who take care of themselves,* she silently chanted. Somehow, she'd find a way. She always had. She focused on her dream. A home of her very own where she belonged. An orchard. She wanted it so badly she imagined that sweet fragrance of peaches and apples at harvest time instead of the salty taste of the fabric against her lips, the stench of the gag.

The saddle soon wore a hole in her stockings and abraded against the tender skin of her thighs. She couldn't have said how long they rode, but every step of the horse jarred her side. She hoped her ride would never end. Agony or not, so long as they were riding, they couldn't hurt her. Her misery made hanging onto the vision of her orchard more and more difficult.

As evening twilight gave into night, she thought they surely must stop soon. She ached everywhere, longed for the ride to be over. No. Not that. Longed to be with the Haverlys, where she would help with the children and bask in the warmth of family.

13

The night sky filled with stars, and they rode without slowing. Abbey was caught forever within the misery of this moment. She became chilled, and she wasn't sure which was worse—the cold or the stabbing pain in her side that twisted a little more with every step the horse took.

Finally, they slowed, then stopped. Jake swung out of the saddle, leaving her back exposed to the evening chill, the one place where she wasn't cold. She shivered.

"Climb down, Miz Charlotte," he said.

I'm not Miz Charlotte, she thought and would have told him had it not been for the gag. Numbly, she swung her leg over the horse, and instead of sliding smoothly to the ground, she collapsed in a heap at the horse's feet. Both men laughed. Abbey sat up and glared at them.

"Must have been a while since you've been on a horse, Missus Rafferty. What happened to your mare?" Sam bent over her and untied the gag.

"I'm not Missus Rafferty." Her mouth felt as dry as the sandy soil beneath her. "I'm Abigail Wallace."

Sam hauled her to her feet. A thousand pins and needles chased through her legs, the sensation worse than the miles of riding had been. She sucked in a gasp.

"Walkin' will help." Sam steadied her as she took a couple of painful steps.

"Which she damn well knows," Jake said. "We both know this is Charlotte Rafferty, no matter what she says. Don't be lettin' her fool you into thinkin' she's some nice young lady."

Abbey glanced at him, hearing the sneer in his voice. "I'm Abigail Wallace," she repeated.

"And I'm President Grant." He returned to his horse and opened one of the saddlebags. He fished around, then took out a small, cloth-wrapped packet that he unwrapped. A daguerreotype, she realized, as he thrust it toward her. In the dark, she couldn't see anything. Jake struck a match, and light flared over the image of a dark-haired woman.

"Charlotte Rafferty?" Abbey asked. The woman's hair was arranged in dozens of intricate ringlets that framed her face.

"On your wedding day." Jake dropped the match to the ground. He rewrapped the daguerreotype, then put it back inside the saddlebag.

"You must not know her well. If you did, you would realize. I am not—"

"Oh, I know you." Jake sauntered toward her, stopping only when he was close enough that she could feel the heat from his body. "Remember that evening in the hay loft, Miz Charlotte? You were wearing nothing but a smile."

When she realized what he meant, heat flowed up Abbey's neck to her cheeks, equal parts of alarm and embarrassment. She tightened her lips, deciding to ignore the remark. Thrusting her hands in front of her, she commanded, "Untie me."

Jake stalked away from her.

"Please," she added, hating that her command had turned to pleading.

Sam shot Jake a questioning glance. Jake stared, then shrugged. Sam untied the rope, and it fell haphazardly to the ground.

Abbey rubbed her chafed wrists, figuring the only reason Sam had untied her and taken the gag off was they were so isolated no one could come to her aid. That assessment didn't keep her from looking around, from planning a way to escape. Even if these men thought she was the wife of the man they worked for, she wasn't safe.

Abbey smoothed down her skirts, turned, and took a few steps away from the men.

"There's no necessary out here, Miz Charlotte. You're gonna have to make do with a bush. You stay where I can see you."

"I'm not—"

"Charlotte," Jake interrupted. "I know. I know. Stay where I can see you anyway."

Abbey felt the heat climb in her cheeks. "I'm not going to do . . . *that* with you watching."

His expression became absolutely cold. "Relieve yourself or not." With a quickness that startled her, he grasped her jaw with his hand. "You will stay where I can see you."

She wrenched away from his grip and lifted her chin. A dozen angry retorts echoed through her mind, not one of which would get her what she wanted. She stared at him with all the disdain she could muster. He turned away, muttering an oath.

She watched him a moment, then marched into the bushes. She walked away as far as she dared before "relieving" herself, as he had so indelicately put it.

Twice he looked at her, and both times, she ducked her head, angry beyond words the man would begrudge her a bit of privacy.

Don't be ridiculous, she thought. *He knows you'll run the first chance you get.*

When she stood, Jake and Sam were bent over one of the horses, examining its hoof. She watched the two men only an instant before making her decision. This was an opportunity. Who knew when she might have another?

Quietly as she could manage, she slipped farther away from them, cursing her long skirts that rustled with every step. Once she was concealed by the dark, she'd be able to slip away from them, she reasoned. She wasn't sure what she'd do next, but she'd figure it out. "God takes care of those who take care of themselves," she whispered.

Finally, she turned her back on them and made her way quietly through the darkness. Every flutter of sound made her jump. Too little time had passed before she heard Jake curse. She lifted her skirts and ran.

CHAPTER 2

Many times, Abbey tripped over stones and rocks. Each time, she righted herself and ran on. She heard pounding footsteps, but she didn't dare look behind her.

Her chest burned, and she panted for breath.

An open meadow loomed before her, and beyond big trees grew that looked even blacker than the night. She started across the open ground. Within the cloak of the trees and the darkness, she could hide. There she would be safe.

The sound of pounding footsteps faded beneath a deeper, more menacing cannonade. She was closer to the trees, but not close enough. She glanced over her shoulder.

A horse and rider bore down on her.

Desperation fueled Abbey to run faster. Her lungs burned as she sucked in one gasping breath, then another. Her vision blurred and the safety of the trees wavered. Suddenly the horse was on top of her, and she veered to the side. Jake leapt from the saddle and tackled her.

"No!" she screamed. Blood pounded through her head, heating her cheeks.

She fought him with every ounce of her strength. She aimed a knee for his groin, but he pinned her legs with his own. She clawed at his face, and he captured her hands. His weight smothered her, and she labored for breath. Still, she struggled. She wrenched a hand free, curled it into a fist, and socked his nose.

"Damn it, stop!" he yelled. "Charlotte, I don't want to hurt you."

She didn't believe him and vented her fury in a scream.

When he tried to cover her mouth with his hand, she bit him. In the next instant, she saw him swing at her. His fist struck her cheek. Pain exploded behind her eye. Her head snapped to the side. She tried to squirm away from him.

And she knew she would not escape.

Tears of frustration burned at the back of her eyes. Like every other man she had ever known, this one would use his size and strength to enforce his will. All she had for combat was her determination and, God willing, enough cunning to escape no matter how bad the odds.

Deliberately, she let her body sag against the ground and closed her eyes. His grip on her didn't lessen for several moments. Finally, his body relaxed subtly, as well.

Abbey waited. Where was Sam? Her cheek burned, and her eye throbbed.

"Jake?" she heard the younger man call.

"Over here."

"Find her?"

"Yep."

"I thought I heard her scream," Sam said.

"You did." Jake let go of her hands and eased his weight off her. At the last instant, she kicked at him with her knee, aiming again for his groin. When her knee connected with him, he gave a yelp of surprise, but he didn't double over as she had hoped.

He loomed over her. "Goddamn, but you're a witch!" He raised his hand.

She had vowed once no one would ever beat her again. She struck first, then tried to scramble away. She struggled to stand up, then fought him when she felt his hands at her shoulders, and she pushed them away. She aimed another kick for his groin and instead connected with his thigh.

"Damn it, Charlotte." Then he hit her.

She tasted her own blood in her mouth. She looked at Jake, then past him to Sam. Both blurred. She blinked, trying to focus. She wanted to stand but could not make her legs work. The world swirled around her and disappeared into an inky void.

Her last thought as she slid into oblivion was, she'd lost again.

When she awoke, rhythmic jostling stabbed her ribs. With the pain, memories flooded her, some from that long-ago winter at the orphanage with Miss Mary and the children. Some from her terrified run a few hours ago. She pried open an eye and found it was light. Distant peaks, widely spaced trees, and light so bright it hurt. Her misery and throbbing head made time blur. Sometimes it was so cold she shivered, and she feared she was once more living through that awful winter of Sheridan's siege. Once she thought she heard Miss Mary calling her to help with the children, and she cried out because she couldn't find them.

They traveled both day and night, stopping for only a few hours at a time to rest the horses. At night she was cold while the full moon illuminated the wide expanses of nothingness and distant mountains. During the day, the sun beat on them, hot and bright as summer rather than the early autumn it must be since the leaves of trees were bright yellow.

She tried to pay attention to landmarks, but one set of foothills looked much like another. She despaired she would ever find her way back.

Jake ensured she had no chance to give them trouble. He kept her gagged except to eat, bound her feet while they slept, and kept her wrists tied all the time. This wasn't exactly worse than anything she had endured during the war, but she was more frightened than she'd ever been.

As they traveled, she lost all track of time. When the sun came up again, she struggled to remember how many times she had watched it rise since she'd been abducted. This was the second. Or was it the third?

The pace they traveled at became subtly faster, as though horses and riders sensed the destination was near. Her thoughts began to clear. They were taking her back to her supposed husband. Surely the man would know his own wife. She grabbed onto that thought, and a sliver of hope cracked through her apprehension. She imagined him calling Jake and Sam fools for thinking she looked anything like his wife. The thought brought marginal comfort.

The sun grew hot as it rose in the sky. They came to a well-traveled trail, and instead of crossing it as they had done with other trails, they turned on to it. They climbed a hill, and from the crest there was a picturesque view of a winding river, surrounded by a beautiful valley. Abbey took it all in, hoping this was a sign everything would turn out.

Aspen trees bordered the road for a time, the golden leaves quaking softly in the wind. Too soon, they rode into sunshine again and began to descend the hill. When they reached the valley floor, they crossed the river, then took a fork in the road that led up another hill. Sometime later, they went through a gate. An emblem had been burned into the wood sign overhead— parallel lines intersecting the initials *S R.*

The SR Double Bar. Dread warred with relief that the unending journey would soon be over, twisting her stomach into tight knots.

They rode another few minutes before a compound came into view. Abbey's tired gaze catalogued a large barn, a corral, and an assortment of other buildings. She heard someone call, "Riders comin' in."

21

Her attention was snagged by Indians and their horses. They were the first she had seen this close, and they looked as fierce as anything ever described to her. They stared at her until a short, older man appeared from behind the barn leading a half-grown cow. One of the Indians took the rope and vaulted onto a horse. There was some handshaking before the other two men mounted their horses and trotted out of the compound. Since no one else stared, visiting Indians must be ordinary.

The tall man who had been talking to the Indians walked toward them with an easy gait that looked deceptively slow.

She felt Jake stiffen behind her. She instantly understood this was Sloan Rafferty. A wide-brimmed, black hat shaded his face. His shoulders had the heavy musculature of a blacksmith, his legs long, lean, and encased in tall boots.

"Boss, we found Miz Charlotte," Sam said.

The man stepped close to Jake's horse and looked up at them. His sheer presence would have marked him as the "boss" without Sam having identified him as such. Abbey stared down into the coldest eyes she had ever seen, which was odd, she thought vaguely. Eyes so dark a brown should have been warm.

She didn't know what she had expected exactly. Certainly not someone so foreboding as this man. He looked neither young nor old. His cheeks were sharply defined, and a muscle bulged in his jaw as he looked up at her. Nothing about his expression gave away his thoughts.

She waited for what seemed an eternity. He'd tell these men they were mistaken. She was sure of it. She wasn't his wife, Charlotte Rafferty. The woman they had described had sounded vain, spoiled. It took a pretty woman to be vain, and Abbey knew exactly what she was and what she wasn't. She wasn't pretty. She was a survivor.

In another moment, the torture she had endured these last days would be ended. She'd wash, bathe even, if she could, brush her tangled hair, find some salve to treat the swelling she felt around her eye, and rest. That perhaps most of all.

He put his hands around her waist and pulled her off the saddle. Abbey was used to being small in comparison to men, but the span of his big hands around her waist shocked her. Her legs felt as shaky as they had every time she'd been taken off the horse.

His gaze swept over her face, his features still expressionless. She wanted to say something—anything—to end this nightmare but couldn't get her thoughts to form a single word. His perusal of her reminded her of the times she had been lined up with the other children, subjected to the scrutiny of an adult offering to take one or two of the orphans off Miss Mary's hands. She lifted her chin and met his eyes full on, hating the memories he evoked, certain she was being subjected to a test.

"Who hit her?" His voice matched his expression. Stern. Cold.

When neither of the men answered, his gaze left hers and fastened on Sam, then on Jake. Abbey turned around to look at Jake, who had taken off his hat and was studying the saddle horn as though he'd never seen it before.

"Jake." The warning in Sloan's voice sent shivers down Abbey's spine.

"The witch bit me," he said, finally, not quite meeting his boss's eyes.

Sloan moved so fast his actions were a blur. With one hand he pulled Jake from the saddle. With the other, Rafferty struck Jake, snapping his head back. He sprawled onto the dusty ground. He rubbed his jaw. He lay there a moment before standing up and dusting off his hat.

"You wanted her back, and I brought her." He jammed the hat on his head and gathered up the reins for his horse. "You were right. She is more trouble than any woman is worth. I hope you know what the hell you're doing."

He led his horse across the compound, and Sam followed, still astride his horse. Sloan watched them a moment before turning his attention back to Abbey.

Wariness competed with relief and surprise at Sloan's sudden attack on Jake. Never in her entire life had a man stood up for her. In her experience, men were brutal, and Sloan Rafferty was as likely to use his strength against her as against Jake. Abbey knew firsthand that chivalry belonged only to the long-ago knights that Miss Mary had been so fond of. Yet Sloan Rafferty had given her a glimpse of what being under a man's protection could be like.

Sloan turned Abbey away from him and untied the gag. Then he turned her back to face him. He studied her a long time, his examination of her face thorough and intimate.

"So, wife." His voice was as deep and cold as his eyes. "I suppose I should welcome you home."

Wife. A chill crawled through Abbey's scalp. She shook her head in mute denial.

He swept an arm around the compound. "What was it you called the ranch?"

Abbey watched him, cold shock sliding down her spine.

"You've forgotten, wife?"

Wife. She hoped to never hear the word in that tone of voice again.

"Tartarus, wasn't it?" He pulled a lethal-looking knife from a sheath at his waist, caught Abbey's wrists with his hand, and cut through the rope easily as cutting through butter. "Welcome to hell."

"I'm not your wife." Her voice little more than a croak. "My name is Abigail—"

"You can call yourself Saint Peter for all I care." He yanked her to his side. "After you tell me where the Cimarron Sun is, you can go anywhere you want. Until then, you're still my wife. You'll do what I say, when I say, for as long as I say."

"My name is Abigail Wallace. What kind of man are you that you don't recognize your own wife?" She lifted her chin, returning his angry gaze, ignoring the tear she felt well from the corner of her eye.

"Don't play games with me. Once I would have believed the tears." His expression, if anything, became more implacable. "You're Charlotte Flanders Rafferty."

Flanders. The name reached into Abbey's deepest memories, splintering open old hurts. Even so, she shook her head in mute denial.

In a swift movement, he grasped the brooch at her neck and ripped it from her dress. "If you're not my wife, just how did you come to have the cherished Flanders family crest."

Abbey lifted trembling fingers to the torn fabric at her neck. Her gaze dropped from his accusing eyes to the brooch. She stared at the polished black onyx, etched with an emblem of crossed swords, weighing what she might say to convince him she wasn't his wife. Nothing, she finally concluded, that would make a difference today.

Abbey's glance raised from the brooch in Sloan Rafferty's hard palm to his cold eyes.

"My grandmother gave it to me."

He dropped the brooch into her hand. "At least you got that part right, wife." He tipped her chin toward him. "As soon as I have the stallion back, you're free to leave."

"The Cimarron Sun," Abbey said.

"So you've heard of him." He pointed her toward the house. "Go get cleaned up. And if you want any help from Consuela, you might try being nicer to her."

Abbey turned toward the house, a single-story structure of logs and stone. She dreaded what she might find inside, despaired at meeting yet another person who thought she was Charlotte Rafferty. Every step she took cracked open another layer of memory, each one making her feel as though she had tumbled over the edge of a cliff . . .

Ma had taken her to a big plantation house in the middle of the valley. Abbey had been maybe seven at the time, old enough to know that Ma wasn't her mother, old enough to sense the visit to the plantation house was important.

Ma had scuttled to the back door with Abbey in tow. She demanded money and threatened to leave Abbey there if she didn't get it. Being left would have been fine with Abbey. No more whippings from Pa. No more taunts about being a bastard child of a crazy woman.

The big old house had seemed familiar, somehow. The mistress came, yelling at Ma and calling her names. Abbey had slipped away, quietly searching through the big rooms. The grand house matched hazy dreams she had—dreams where she listened to someone sing and where she played on a floor in a room where a soft breeze billowed through lace curtains.

In the parlor, she had found an old woman napping in a rocker. Abbey had felt a peculiar longing, and she crept closer. Suddenly, the woman opened her eyes. She smiled and held out her arms.

"My sweet Abbey, I didn't think I'd ever see you again," she murmured.

Abbey crawled into her lap, feeling as though she had done so many times before. The old woman hummed as she rocked Abbey, the melody matching her dreams. The moment was perfect, and she remembered sitting very still, hoping if she were very good Ma and the mistress wouldn't find her.

The old woman had taken off the brooch and given it to Abbey. "Hide it in your pocket, lass. Remember, no matter what anyone says, you're a Flanders." Abbey had listened solemnly, and she wrapped the brooch in the woman's handkerchief and put it in her pocket.

The old woman had held her, told her how much she looked like her poor, beautiful mother, "May God keep her."

Ma and the mistress had found her there, both of their voices shrill. When Abbey was ripped from the old woman's arms, she felt as though she'd been torn from love itself. Those few, precious moments were etched permanently in Abbey's memory. Once she had been loved by her grandmother, and that knowledge had made all the difference.

Shortly after the war had ended, Abbey had gone back to the big plantation house. Like everything else in the valley, it had been burned. She found a family cemetery and the grave of the woman she believed was her grandmother, especially after seeing the headstones. Martha Flanders Wallace had been the old woman's name. Next to her grave was another, and engraved on its stone were the words: "Francis Wallace. Beloved daughter of Martha and mother of Abigail. God rest her tortured soul."

Abbey began wearing the brooch. As Ma and Pa were dead and no one else was alive who cared, Abbey took Martha's and Francis's last name: Wallace. For the first time in her life, she had an identity. Whether wishful thinking or truth, Abbey didn't know. To her, it hadn't mattered.

Until today.

CHAPTER 3

Sloan watched her walk slowly away. Until she had lifted her chin and given him that resolute look, he hadn't been positive she was Charlotte. Whatever doubts he harbored vanished in that instant. Black eye or not, sunburn or not, swollen lip or not, he knew that expression.

Once, he'd liked the fire in her, and more than once he'd kissed her when she lifted her chin, her dark-blue eyes flashing in defiance. Those eyes. Darkest blue, the color of night shortly after dusk, a shade he had never seen in anyone else. Oh, she was Charlotte, all right.

In all the times he had thought about finding her, not once had he imagined she would pretend not to know him. This was the sort of high drama she would like—trying to convince him she was someone else.

Wherever she had been, whatever she had been doing these last six months, the time had been hard on her. Gone was the elegant Charlotte whose skin was porcelain clear without a single freckle marring her complexion. She was thinner, and he'd felt the outline of her ribs when he lifted her off the horse. He'd never seen her dark hair in such an untidy mess.

She walked as though every step was painful. When she lifted her skirts to climb the porch steps, he saw she was in stocking feet. He couldn't remember a time, except in the bedroom or bath, he'd ever seen her without shoes. He knew better than to believe the vulnerability she conveyed, but it hit him in the gut, anyway.

She opened the door to the house and stepped inside. With that, he went to find Jake and Sam. They were in the barn, unsaddling the horses and brushing them down. Inside the doorway, Sloan slowed his stride, weighing how to best mend fences with his old friend. Striking Jake in front of the other men had been a bad move. Sloan once prided himself on being a man slow to anger. But where Charlotte was concerned . . .

Sloan shook his head in disgust. Where she was concerned, he was a damned idiot. Their paths should not have crossed, would not have if he hadn't been so determined to buy the Cimarron Sun, a stallion that would be the foundation for the finest horses in the Rocky Mountains. Charlotte was an excellent horsewoman, and she had been as alluring to him as the horse. After bedding her, he had done the only honorable thing possible—marry her. She had been bitter with the discovery his was a working ranch rather than a wealthy farm affording a life of privilege like she had always had. Nothing had made her happy except her mare, a pretty, well-behaved paint with the unlikely name of Lady Godiva, and, it turned out, her dalliances with the men who worked for him.

Sloan grabbed another brush and began brushing down Jake's big gelding. Angry as Jake was, Sloan half expected his friend to move the horse beyond his reach. One moment stretched into another as the two men worked side by side, the gelding providing a common purpose.

The familiar routine accompanied the sounds of the brush sliding over the animal's skin, the musky scent of the horse, the bronze band of light stretching from the door toward the stall. Sloan sensed Jake's occasional glance.

"Where'd you find her?" Sloan finally asked, vaguely

surprised at how difficult it was to keep the anger from his voice.

When Jake didn't answer, Sam gave him an uncertain look before turning to Sloan. "We'd been in Denver a couple of days, checking all the usual places. The train depot. Hotels. Livery stables. Didn't find a living soul who'd seen anyone like Miz Charlotte. Hadn't found a single person who knew anything about the stallion. We'd been passing out the handbills all along, and we were making our way south. Then we stumbled across her. She was working in a general store. Claimed she was Abigail Wallace."

"She didn't try to run?" Sloan asked.

Sam shook his head. "Nope. Didn't even seem much flustered when we first came in and I called her Missus Rafferty. Said she was from the Shenandoah Valley."

Sloan grunted. Charlotte's father owned property there. Sloan had seen it—or what was left of it anyway. Like most everything else in the valley, it had been destroyed during Sheridan's siege. Never once had he heard Charlotte say she was from there. Her father had moved the family to Washington, D.C., when the war began, and he had made a considerable fortune in supply contracts for the Union army. After the war, he parlayed his wealth into a huge farm along the Potomac River not far from Mount Vernon.

"So how'd you pick her up?" he asked, dragging his attention from the past.

Sam related going back to the general store after it closed and waiting for her to leave. His description of the struggle she put up sounded exactly like the kind of thing Charlotte would do. Only, why had she kept up with the deception after Sam and Jake grabbed her.

Sooner or later, he'd find out. Charlotte liked drama and thrived on creating trouble. This time, he'd have the cinch tightened, and he'd be ready for whatever surprise she had in store. As soon as she told him what she had done with the Cimarron Sun, he'd send her back to her daddy or wherever she wanted to go.

"The new barn looks good," Sam said when the silence stretched into a long minute.

"Yeah." Sloan looked up from the horse to the new timber above his head, another reminder of what his wife had cost him. The old barn had burned to the ground while he was in New Mexico chasing down a dead-end lead on the Cimarron Sun. The fire had supposedly been an accident, but an itch at the back of Sloan's neck had him convinced the fire had been set.

Sloan glanced at his old friend across the top of the horse. "Nobody bit on the reward for the stallion, either?"

"Nope." Jake gave the horse a final pat and hung the brush on the outside of the stall. He met Sloan's gaze briefly, the dark splotch of a bruise beginning to discolor the skin on his jaw.

Deciding it was a good sign that Jake finally spoke, Sloan said, "I've been thinking . . ."

The glance Jake threw at him was no encouragement to continue, but Sloan fell into step beside him as they headed toward the barn door.

"She had help."

"Stealin' the stallion?"

"Yeah."

Jake came to a slow halt and turned toward Sloan, his eyes narrowed into slits. "If you're accusin' me of anything, old friend, spell it out."

"You know me better than that—"

"I don't know you at all," Jake interrupted, his usual drawl clipped. "Once, maybe. But not since—"

"I was just saying"—Sloan fought to hang onto his temper— "that she had help. Now that she's back, maybe between the

31

two of us we can keep an eye out."

"Let me get this straight. You want me to . . . spy . . . on your wife. After tellin' me you'd kill me if—"

"Yeah. Call it anything you want. I want to know who she talks to. I figure she thinks she'll have more freedom if she can make us believe she's this other woman."

"She almost has Sam convinced she's Miss Abigail Wallace."

"Sam's young. She's not going to tell us who helped her or where the Sun is."

"Not damn likely."

Sloan stared down the valley, remembering it as it had been last spring. He had taken surveyors over the mountains to San Luis, where a spur of the new railroad was supposed to be built. Bad as the timing had been, the money was good, a chance to get the year off to a sound financial footing. While he was gone, his foreman, Joey McLennon, and the rest of the hands had driven the cattle onto the plateau above the valley for their summer range.

While they were all gone, Charlotte had saddled up her mare for a ride one afternoon and hadn't been seen since. Consuela's boy, JJ, swore she had been riding her mare and leading the Cimarron Sun. She had also taken a pack horse and clothes. Sloan figured she had run off, though he had spent a couple of days scouring the valley for any sign of her.

A hint of a smile tugged at Jake's mouth. "You finally came to your senses."

Unwilling to admit Jake was right, Sloan slapped his friend on his back. "I'm glad to have you home. It's been a hell of a summer."

"Winter ain't nothin' to look forward to." Jake came to a halt. "Heard from your brother?"

Sloan shook his head.

"Worried?"

"Not yet." But he was. He and Jonah had split up in Santa Fe. Sloan had followed rumors of his stallion south toward Mexico. Jonah had headed for the high plains of west Texas, hoping to turn up something from the Kiowa or Comanche. If there was good horse flesh to be had, Chief Quanah would know it. Since Jonah was half-Comanche, he was as at home— maybe more—in that world than at the ranch.

"In Denver folks are all riled up about the Indians. It's bad as it's ever been."

"Jonah knows how to watch his back." Sloan prayed he was right. Before they split up, they had talked about the growing hostility between the Indians and the settlers flooding across the West since the end of the war. Jonah's mother, Two Doves, had been unwilling to leave Chief Quanah's band, and his loyalties to the band were reinforced by that.

Sloan knew how uncomfortable she was away from her people—something that had been a problem for her even before his father died. Sloan wanted her to leave the Comanche and come live at the ranch for one simple reason: it was an inducement that might keep Jonah away from Quanah's band of Comanche warriors. Jonah had made it plain that riding with Quanah—dying with him, if it came to that—was better than living in the white man's world, where he was treated like vermin.

Sloan understood, since he was something of an outcast, himself. Still, he didn't want his brother dying in a war he couldn't win. More than once, Jonah had laughed off Sloan's worry, and more than once he had proven he could spot trouble before it happened.

Just then, the door of the house opened, and Consuela, the housekeeper, ran across the porch and down the steps, shouting in Spanish and waving her arms.

Sloan strode across the compound, unable to make sense of

anything in Consuela's hysterical ranting.

"What is it?" he asked, grasping her arms.

"*Mi niña.*" She took a deep breath, then sobbed, this time in English, "She has my baby." She grabbed Sloan's hand and tugged him toward the house. "Come now."

The memory of his wife's scornful voice rang through Sloan's head, echoing the sentiment too many folks held about Indians. *What they say is sure enough true. Nits make lice.* Sloan had been furious to discover Charlotte branded people as good or bad without knowing them. Indian, Mexican, Negro. To Charlotte, they were all inferior.

He had seen her take a crop to his brother. Surely, she wouldn't hurt an infant. Or would she? His long strides lengthened into a run. He leapt onto the porch and pushed open the heavy door.

The door banged against the wall, abruptly silencing a crooning lullaby. On the far side of the room, Abbey whirled around to face him, Consuela's baby held against her breast. Sloan didn't know what he had expected, but it certainly was not the look of pure terror that chased across her face or her protectively cradling the baby in her arms as he stalked toward her.

"What the hell are you doing?" Sloan took off his hat and tossed it on the table.

The baby continued to whimper

"Shh," she commanded. "I just got this little one quiet." She swayed slightly, rocking the infant in her arms.

Sloan had the fleeting image she looked natural holding the baby, as though she had quieted an infant many times. Which was ridiculous. Charlotte had never once raised a hand to help Consuela with any of the children.

"I don't know what the hell you're up to—" Sloan reached for her, and she stepped back, twisting away from him. The baby's whimpers grew into a cry. "Give me the baby."

"Stop this." She lifted her chin toward him, raw fear in her eyes. "You're upsetting the baby."

Consuela flew into the room followed by Jake and Sam.

The baby's cries escalated to a full wail.

"Enough!" Sloan's roar split through the room, momentarily quieting Consuela. The baby cried harder. In a swift move, he snatched the squalling infant and handed it to Consuela. She gathered the baby close, murmuring reassurances and casting his wife a venomous look before leaving the room.

"Charlotte—she doesn't like babies?" Abbey asked. Dear Lord, she thought. These people acted like she planned to murder the wee thing.

"You leave Consuela's children alone," Sloan ordered.

"What was I supposed to do? Leave the little one crying in his cradle?"

"Don't touch them. Don't talk to them. Don't do anything at all to upset her."

"I was just—"

"See if you can't stay the hell out of trouble."

Abbey watched the two men behind Sloan shrug at one another, then slip from the room. Sloan took a couple of deliberate steps toward her. Determined not to let him see how much he frightened her, she stood her ground, kept her gaze fastened on his.

Surely there had to be a way to make this man understand. "I—"

He raised a hand, cutting her off, and, despite her resolve, she flinched.

"I don't want to hear it." His hand dropped to his side. "Charlotte or Miss Abigail Wallace. It makes no difference to me. I want to hear only one thing from you. Then, I'll send you back to your rich papa in Virginia."

Rich papa? Pa hadn't been rich, and he hadn't been any kind of father.

Wondering how far she would have to go to appease Sloan Rafferty, she swallowed. "Your stallion. You want me to tell you where he is, and then you'll let me go?"

Sloan nodded, his lips stretching into what Abbey supposed was a smile but looked instead like a snarl.

With sudden decision she took a breath. "I took him to Abilene." Folding her arms across her chest, she added, "I want to freshen up and get a good night's rest. And tomorrow you can have someone take me back—"

"Where in Abilene?" he asked.

Where on earth would you leave a horse? Abbey wondered. "The livery at the edge of town." That sounded believable enough, she decided, watching him.

"That's where you met the buyer?"

"Um . . . yes," she murmured, looking away from him, realizing she was on the verge of being caught in her own lie. All she had to do was make it believable enough. "His name was, ah, George . . . Washington . . . Smith. From Austin . . . Texas."

"How much did you sell the Sun for?" Sloan asked, his tone bored.

Abbey frowned. The flyer had a reward for two hundred-fifty dollars, so the horse must be worth at least that much. The sum seemed a huge amount, and she wondered if it could possibly be correct.

"Five hundred," she finally said. "Dollars."

"Five hundred dollars!" Sloan slapped his hand on the table next to Abbey, making her flinch. "What kind of fool do you take me for?"

"I—" Oh, my, she'd been right. Too much money by far.

"I paid your papa more than a thousand dollars for that animal. I know you didn't sell him—"

"You're right," Abbey interrupted. *A thousand dollars? How could a horse be worth so much?* "I got more."

"You used to be a better liar, wife." He strode away from her, his hands clinched into loose fists. At the front window he turned to face her, raking a hand through his hair. "You didn't take a priceless stallion to any livery anywhere, and you didn't sell him to any George Washington. Smith, or otherwise."

"And what did you expect me to tell you?" Abbey demanded, advancing on him, hating that she was judged for another woman's sins, hating him. " 'Tell me what I want to hear, and you can go,' " she mocked, her control shaky, her voice even shakier. "Ha! I told you what you wanted to hear. I don't know where your horse is. I'm not your wife—"

"Oh, you're her, all right." He grabbed her by the upper arm and pulled her close. "And your ploys still work." One arm slid around her waist. "Fighting always led to loving." With his free hand he stroked her cheek. "When a man's laying with you, he can't think at all, damn you."

Surrounded by his heat and strength, Abbey's anger twisted through the fear and settled into a seething knot in her stomach. She pushed against his chest. "No."

One of his dark eyebrows rose. "No?"

"I'd rather die first," she said.

"I suppose you'd rather take a tumble with one of my men." She wrenched away from him so suddenly, she stumbled. With quick reflexes, he caught her before she fell. He gazed down at her a moment, his expression bleak, his eyes cold. "If I find you with any of my men, I promise you, wife, you'll wish that Jake and Sam had never found you."

Abbey wrapped her arms around herself, watching him walk across the room, where he picked his hat off the table. She wanted to scream her frustration, wanted to throw things at him, wanted to do something . . . anything . . . to make him understand. Utter weariness competed with her anger, and she decided that, mostly, she wanted him to leave, wanted them all to leave so she could figure out what to do next.

"When you're ready to tell me the truth . . ." He shook his head, then opened the door outside and whistled once—a sharp, piercing sound. He faced her, the door open behind him. "Since you've proven you can't be trusted, and since I've got a ranch to run, I'm leaving Silas to keep an eye on you."

"Silas?" A guard? Her wish for solitude dissipated, igniting her temper. "I won't—"

"You don't have a choice." Sloan gave her a quelling look. A huge dog came inside, looking like the black shadow of a wolf— except his eyes, which shone with golden intensity. "Guard," Sloan commanded, pointing at Abbey.

The dog trotted across the room and sat down in front of her. Relief that Silas was a dog, not a man, seeped through her.

"Just remember what he did to Buck Johnson."

Abbey opened her mouth to ask what had happened to Buck Johnson, then closed it, deciding she didn't really want to know. Sloan walked through the doorway and slammed the door behind him. From some other corner of the house, Abbey heard the baby start to cry, then the soothing tones of Consuela's voice.

She eyed the dog warily, wondering what "guard" really meant. Holding her hand out, she let the dog sniff her fingers. She wasn't sure what to expect, but she wasn't going to spend the next hour standing in the middle of the room trying to figure out if the dog was going to bite her. If he was, the sooner she got that over with, the better.

She took a step away from the dog.

He watched her.

Another step.

The dog didn't move.

Slowly, she crossed the room, pausing next to the cradle where she had found the infant crying. Trailing her fingers along the smooth wood, she moved toward the doorway on the far side of the room, her attention mostly on the big black dog. He watched her, his head cocked to one side. Stopping in the doorway, she discovered the next room to be a large kitchen—a place where the ranch hands evidently ate, as well, since the table was easily large enough to seat ten or more people. Another door on the far side of the room led outside. Of Consuela or the infant, there was no sign.

Abbey felt movement next to her skirts and glanced down. The dog stood with her, peering into the kitchen.

Guard, Abbey thought. She patted the dog's head, then rubbed her fingers up one of his ears. The dog looked up at her, and she again offered her fingers to sniff. Silas breathed against her palm, then licked her fingers.

Some of the tension loosened in her chest, and she sighed. Someone who didn't hate her on sight.

Turning back to the front room, Abbey took in a cradle, a table—smaller than the one in the kitchen—a couple of chairs, and a desk in one corner, which made up the furniture. Across the room, another doorway led to a hall. Abbey tiptoed toward it, not all that anxious to disturb Consuela, wherever she might be. In fact, if she never spoke with any of these wretched people again, she would consider herself blessed.

Abbey opened another door. A huge bed dominated the room. Deciding it was Sloan's room, she started to shut the door when a bump of curiosity urged her to push it further open. Surprisingly, the room was tidy and contained only a few items. A shirt, perhaps two, neatly folded on an open shelf. Propped on the shelf next to the shirts was a daguerreotype, this one larger than the one Jake had shown her. Without conscious thought, Abbey moved toward the shelf. The picture was of three people stiffly posed in front of a tepee. Two men, one of them obviously Sloan, and an Indian woman. The other man, wearing moccasins that came to his knees, was nearly as tall as Sloan. Wondering at the relationship Sloan had to the other two people, Abbey studied the print for a long time.

Thinking of the Indians that had been here when she first arrived, she could see this world was different than the one she had come from. One where Indians and Negro cowboys were ordinary. And Consuela—a Spanish woman. Abbey wondered what the language might sound like when she wasn't being yelled at.

No other personal effects cluttered the room except for an Indian shield whose design was nothing like she had ever before seen and a spear propped against one wall. At her side, the dog lazily wagged its tail as though expecting his master to appear. That thought was enough to make Abbey retreat to the hallway and shut the door.

Across the hall, she opened another door. Another huge bed, but this one competing with a big armoire and a dresser for her attention. On the far side of the room, there was an alcove, partially hidden by a half-closed curtain, where a bathtub sat. She knew she had found Charlotte's room. The furnishings in this room were in stark contrast to the rest of the house—more ornate, obviously made by a fine craftsman. Aware of how expensive it had been to get her own small trunk as far west as Denver, Abbey marveled at the cost incurred to get this furniture to this remote ranch.

At her side, the dog tensed, hair raising on his neck. Curious, Abbey studied the dog, whose posture had been completely different at the doorway to the other room.

"So, you hate her, too," Abbey murmured, patting Silas on the head. He had known she wasn't Charlotte. That, at least, was one small blessing.

Abbey moved further into the room, feeling like a trespasser. None of the furniture had been dusted recently, and the room had a faintly musty smell as though it hadn't been used in a while.

Catching a glimpse of herself in the mirror, Abbey paused, barely recognizing herself. Seeing another reflection in the mirror, she started.

Behind her, a woman stared into the mirror from a painting.

Turning around, Abbey crossed the room to study the portrait. The woman who stared back at her from the painting was dressed in a royal-blue gown that looked positively resplendent. Like herself, the woman in the painting had dark hair and blue eyes. More and more sure this was a portrait of Charlotte, Abbey once again turned around to face the mirror, comparing her reflection with the painting.

Abbey's lip was puffy where it had been cracked open. One eye was black and mostly swollen shut. Lightly, she traced her fingers over the bruise around her eye and over her cheekbone. Another bruise covered the lower part of her face, this one in the distinct imprint of a hand. No wonder Sloan had known someone had hit her. Where her skin wasn't black and blue, it was red and peeling.

Convinced she looked nothing like the woman in the painting, Abbey raised her gaze, critically studying the features.

She turned her head to the side, imitating the posed angle. Beyond the ornate hair style, could she really look so much like another woman? Feature by feature, Abbey compared hers with the painting. The curve of her brow. The slope of her cheek. The cleft in her chin. The shape of her mouth.

The results shocked her.

She and Charlotte could have been twins.

41

CHAPTER 4

Abbey stared at the reflections in the mirror a moment longer, questions chasing after the memories surfaced. Why did she and Charlotte look so much alike? Abbey believed Frances to be her mother. Had she been Charlotte's mother, too? And if she was, why was Abbey's name the only one on the headstone with Frances's name? And if Charlotte was her sister, dear God, why had they been separated?

This cruel woman was her sister? Her twin? Would she ever know? She glanced back to the doorway where Silas, the dog, had stationed himself. The dog knew she wasn't Charlotte, which was some consolation. All I have to do, Abbey thought, is keep acting like myself, and sooner or later Sloan Rafferty will believe me.

She rubbed her temple with the tips of her fingers, at once angry and confused. Wearily, she looked away from the mirror, taking in the rest of the room. Her gaze focused on a hairbrush, comb, and hand mirror set, carefully arranged on the center of the dresser. Abbey studied the handles, noting the scroll work, the silver tarnished as though they hadn't been used in a while, a few dark hairs caught in the bristles of the brush. More than utilitarian items, the set was finely crafted, far nicer than anything Abbey had ever owned.

She trailed her fingers over the dresser, leaving a faint line in the dust. In one of the drawers she found jars of lotions and balms. She opened each one, smelling and testing each with her

42

fingers. All were heavily scented with roses. Abbey loved the smell of roses, but she wasn't about to use anything that would give Sloan Rafferty a reminder of his wife.

Moving away from the dresser, Abbey opened the doors of the armoire, then stared. Inside were more clothes than she had ever imagined owning. Fine dresses for evening wear, day dresses, a riding skirt and matching jacket. Abbey fingered the fabrics, examining the edging laces and piping. From seams to the finishing details, the workmanship was quality. Hat boxes and shoes, several pairs, and a cloak rounded out the contents of the wardrobe.

Abbey wondered if Charlotte's rich papa or Sloan Rafferty had paid for the clothes. Abbey couldn't imagine Sloan buying the dresses, though if the man could pay a thousand dollars for a horse, he could afford anything in the wardrobe.

Everything was evidence of an easier life beyond Abbey's experience. A litany of memories marched through her, memories she never spoke of. Cruelty, hard work, and the terrors that accompanied war colored her recollection, juxtaposed to the life she imagined for Charlotte. Charlotte had known her parents, and she had belonged somewhere. Abbey had been glad when Pa Hawkins had died soon after the war started, and she had felt no loss when Ma died of consumption a few months later. At Miss Mary's orphanage, Abbey was as hungry, and she often worked harder than on the farm. No one had beaten her, and no one continually reminded her she was the bastard child of an insane woman. What Abbey hated most, though, was always feeling like an outsider. Equal to her dream of having an orchard was setting down her own roots, of having somewhere she really belonged.

She shook her head to clear her remembrances. Whatever had happened to her was in the past. Being covetous of another's easier life would do her no good, not to mention being a sin. Besides, no one had ever hated her the way they had Charlotte—not until now, anyway. God helps those who help themselves, Abbey reminded herself.

She tested the fabric of one of the dresses between her fingers, enjoying the texture, dreaming, if only for a moment, of a time she might wear such a fine garment. She smoothed a hand over her own stained and torn dress. With a sigh, she closed the doors and continued her exploration, hoping she would find a sewing basket. At least then, she could repair her dress.

Sweeping aside the curtain that partially hid the bathtub in the alcove adjoining the bedroom, she found a small fireplace and a water pump positioned over the tub. Two pots of soap, one without the scent of roses, and a couple of linen towels occupied one shelf. She glanced around the room, wondering where the pot was to heat the water, then noted the fireplace seemed to be set up more for warming the room than for heating water.

She had hoped to avoid Consuela for a while longer yet. But, for a bath, she'd face down Satan himself. Abbey headed toward the bedroom door where Silas lay. He watched her approach with his intense golden eyes, his muzzle resting on his paws.

"Come on, boy. We're going to find hot water for a bath." He got up and followed her out the room. She suspected the dog would follow her regardless of her wishes, but her calling him and his response to her summons gave her hope that he might forget his master's command to guard her.

In the front room, the baby was once again lying in the cradle, this time napping with his rump stuck in the air, a fist against his little mouth. Abbey smiled and bent over the child, arranging the coverlet over his back. Movement at the doorway into the kitchen caught her eye, and she looked up.

Consuela watched her, distrust in her eyes, and a large wooden spoon in her hand, held more like a weapon than a kitchen utensil. Belatedly, Abbey remembered Sloan's warning. Leave Consuela's children alone. She moved away from the cradle, forcing a smile, reminding herself, I'm not Charlotte. If I don't act like Charlotte, sooner or later, someone will believe me.

"I'd like to heat some water," Abbey said.

Consuela frowned. "For tea?"

Abbey shook her head. "For a bath."

"Why?"

Why? Abbey glanced down at herself. "Because I'm dirty." She tried smiling again. "If you could show me—"

"Why do you want to heat the water?" Consuela asked.

"Because I don't like cold baths," Abbey answered with some asperity. "I'm not asking you to do anything for me. I can do it if you simply give me a pot."

The woman shrugged, her gesture conveying she thought Abbey's request odd in the extreme. Consuela pointed toward the wall where pots in assorted sizes hung.

Remembering the small size of the fireplace, Abbey selected a pan smaller than she would have liked. It would take her a long time to heat enough water to fill the tub. She didn't care—she was going to have a bath.

"And kindling for the fireplace."

Consuela indicated where it was with another negligent shrug to her shoulder. Abbey had the feeling the other woman thought she was crazy. Then again, maybe Consuela had her reasons if she really believed Charlotte could hurt her baby.

Abbey dumped several handfuls of kindling in the cast-iron pot.

"One more thing."

The housekeeper crossed her arms over her chest, and Abbey lifted her chin, determined not to let this woman, who had to be nearly her own age, intimidate her.

45

"I need a sewing basket."

One of Consuela's eyebrows lifted, and her glance shifted to Abbey's dress. Abbey knew just how sorry a state it was in. One sleeve hung from the armhole, the bodice was partially ripped away from the skirt, and there was a ragged tear at the neckline.

"Your dress is beyond repair, Señora."

Silently, Abbey agreed with the assessment. It was, however, the only one she had, so repair it, she would. "Perhaps. I'd still like to mend it."

"You?" Consuela's lips twitched a moment before she smiled, then burst into laughter, a sound that could have been infectious but instead was devoid of any joy.

Abbey flinched, recognizing the laughter for the taunt that it was.

Consuela's laughter faded. "You gave the basket to me, Señora."

Abbey shook her head. "If you don't mind, I would like to . . . borrow it."

Consuela stared at Abbey, as if she had suddenly sprouted horns. At last, she said, "I'll bring it to you."

"Thank you." Abbey's response was automatic. Still, she felt anything but grateful as she left the kitchen. Back in the bedroom, she set about lighting the fire. A small bucket of water sat next to the pump, which was positioned so the water would flow into the tub. Abbey used the water to prime the pump, then began pressing the handle down. The pressure changed suddenly, and, within a few strokes, water gushed from the spout—to her surprise, warm water.

Abbey put her hands in the water, which became warmer with every stroke of the pump. How was this possible? she wondered with a tinge of awe. Hot water for a bath any time she wanted. Without having to heat it up. Nothing sounded more luxurious.

No wonder Consuela thought she was crazy. Charlotte, of course, would have known hot water flowed directly into the tub.

"Hot water. Who would have ever thought?"

Silas cocked his head to the side at the sound of her voice, and Abbey smiled.

"Miss Mary always said there were blessings if a body took time to notice them."

The tub filled in short order.

She unbuttoned the bodice of her dress. After she stepped out of it, she inspected it critically. She could make the garment serviceable again, but it would never be the same. A pang of remorse stirred through her.

It was the first dress she had ever owned that wasn't either a homespun or a hand-me-down. If Miss Mary or the reverend were here, they'd tell her she was paying for her vanity. Perhaps, but that didn't keep Abbey from thinking about the wardrobe full of clothes far finer than her one dress or from thinking Sloan Rafferty owed her another to replace this one.

Carefully, she hung it on one of the pegs on the wall, then finished undressing. Then she stepped into the tub of warm water and sank to her neck in its soothing embrace.

Heaven. Hot, clean water that came with being the first in the bath instead of the last. She opened her eyes. The alcove was surprisingly cheery with its small fireplace and a huge, black dog for company.

Grabbing her chemise and drawers off the floor, she dunked them in the tub with her, washing each. Both were worse for the wear, Abbey noted, as she hung the clean, wet clothes over the chair she had positioned in front of the fire. With any luck, the garments would be dry enough to put back on within a short time.

She settled back in the tub, closing her eyes again, letting her mind empty, letting her body relax.

Sometime later she heard voices at the front of the house. One of them was Sloan Rafferty's distinctive baritone. Abbey listened for a moment, hoping he wouldn't come looking for her, realizing for the first time she hadn't checked to see if the door had a lock. Quietly, she got out of the tub and drew the curtain across the doorway that separated the bathing alcove from the bedroom. Then she returned to the tub where she washed from head to toe. With hot water at her fingertips, she decided to rinse her hair a last time with a bucket of clean water.

Wrapping the linen towel around her body, she returned to the bedroom in search of a comb or brush, other than the fine set on the dresser.

To her surprise, a basket sat on the end of the bed, mute testimony Consuela had been in the room. Abbey opened the lid, searching for thread and needle, finding the basket held everything she needed to repair her dress. Now, if only she had Miss Mary's skill. Abbey had learned to sew out of necessity, but she never had the patience to do it well. She far preferred being outside. She loved gardening the way Miss Mary had loved her embroidery.

Unable to find any other combs or brushes, Abbey ended up using the set on the dresser. She left her hair loose, hoping it would dry enough to braid by the time she finished mending her dress.

Setting the brush and comb back on the dresser, Abbey yawned, admitting the toll of the last several days had caught up with her. Her gaze lingered on the comfortable-looking bed, tempting as Delilah. However strong the temptation to succumb to the weariness was, to give into it would be wrong.

She still had her dress to mend. Then, she needed to figure out a way to leave the ranch. Her glance rose to the portrait as she added a final item to her list. She needed to know what her relationship was to Charlotte Flanders Rafferty.

Abbey went back to the alcove and donned her clean undergarments. Still damp, they felt clammy against her skin, and for a moment she thought about wearing a set she had found in one of the drawers. Remembering the utter disdain everyone held for Charlotte, Abbey decided she was better off wearing her own clothes.

Clad only in her chemise, drawers, and petticoats, Abbey began the daunting task of mending her dress.

She had not been working long when the door to the hallway opened suddenly. Startled, she glanced up, expecting to see Sloan Rafferty or Consuela. Instead, a tall, gangly man with light-brown hair stared at her from the doorway. Instinctively, Abbey lifted her mending to her breast, feeling utterly exposed beneath the man's bold gaze.

"I hear'd it, but I didn't believe it," he snarled, advancing into the room. "How'd you get away?"

Silas rose from his spot next to her feet, a growl in his throat, the hair standing on the back of his neck.

The man backed up a step, his pale face becoming even pastier. "Holy shit. Call that bastard dog off."

"I don't know how." Abbey was grateful for Silas's protection. "And, I have no idea, sir, what you are talking about."

This man, whoever he was, was as unpleasant a person as she had ever laid eyes on. From his fair hair to his pallid eyes, he looked like something that spent most of his time under a rock. From across the room she could smell him.

From the relative safety of the doorway, he raised his fist. "You better not tell anyone. I'd have to kill ya if ya did."

Silas's growl became more menacing, and he took a step toward the door. The man backed up an equal distance.

"Buck, what the hell are you doing in here?" Sloan, looking

huge and threatening and in control, appeared behind the man and grabbed him at the back of his collar.

For the second time today, Abbey found herself grateful for Sloan Rafferty's presence, no matter how irritating a person he might otherwise be.

Buck shrank a little as Sloan pushed him against the doorjamb, his pale eyes bugging like a frog's. He doffed his head in deference to Sloan. "Aw, I jus' wanted to give my respects to the Missus." The bully tone he had used on Abbey reduced to a whine. "Being as to how she's returned from the . . . uh, dead, an' all."

"I pay you to put in a full day's work." Sloan let go of Buck.

"Aw, no, uh . . . I'm going right now." Buck fled, much to Abbey's relief.

Sloan's eyes narrowed when he focused on her. "You won't be planning any rendezvous with Buck."

"I should say not," Abbey agreed crisply. "He's a most unsavory sort of man." Buck. The name snagged in her memory, and she glanced at the dog, who had once again settled at her feet. "He's the man Silas . . ."

"Which you damn well know." Sloan advanced into the room, his footfalls sounding unnaturally loud against the wood floor. His mere presence unnerved her, and to keep from showing it, she met his dark gaze unflinchingly. Once again, she was struck with the absolute coldness of his eyes. A freezing winter night would have had more warmth.

The man repelled her and drew her in equal measure, a state she found most confusing.

First, there was his size and appearance. From his hands to the breadth of his shoulders, he was everything she feared in a man—big, very big, with unquestioning strength. Yet, he moved with a certain grace a less fit man would never attain. His face was all angles and planes, and she found herself wondering if his sharply defined jaw had ever been the rounded contour of a child's face. The only soft thing about his appearance was his hair—a thick, wavy, rich, dark, reddish brown.

Then, there was his attitude. He acted like a protector, which tantalized her and allured her with possibilities she had never imagined for herself. And, he obviously hated her. Not her, Abbey reminded herself. Charlotte.

Abbey openly studied him, deciding he wasn't as old as she had first thought, perhaps less than ten years older than herself. He returned her examination in full measure, and she felt her cheeks heat. Unused to being so openly bold, she dropped her gaze.

"Jake took my shoes." She wished the man didn't tower over her. She had little enough advantage when she was standing. Sitting as she was, and half dressed at that with her dress clutched to her bosom, she had none. "I'd like to have them back."

"You have other pairs. Wear one of them."

"Your wife has several other pairs of shoes," Abbey agreed. "I'd prefer to wear my own."

"What you'd prefer," he said, his words clipped, "isn't worth squat to me."

Abbey lifted her chin, unreasonably hurt even as she told herself he wasn't talking to her. "You've made that abundantly clear. Now, if you'll please leave me alone, I'd like to finish mending my dress."

Dismissing him, she bent her head over the seam she was repairing. Carefully, she slid the needle through the fabric, listening for the sounds of his leaving. From the corner of her eye, she saw him take a single step toward her. With no warning at all, he snatched the dress from her hands.

He shook it out in front of him. To Abbey, the garment looked even shabbier than it had when she examined it. Knowing Miss

51

Mary had somehow worked miracles with clothes in far worse shape than this gave Abbey hope.

"It's a fine thing you're finally interested in sewing, wife. This dress is a rag." He pulled on the fabric at the neckline, ripping it even further.

The deliberate destruction shocked Abbey, and she sprang from the chair. "No!" She grabbed the dress and pulled. "You can't do that."

He didn't relinquish the garment, and it ripped further.

"Please, let go!" she begged.

"You have a wardrobe full of other dresses." He tore the bodice away from the skirt.

"No." The tearing fabric ripped at her soul.

"You don't need this one ugly dress."

"It's mine!" With a last yank, Abbey snatched the dress from his grasp. "Look at what you've done," she cried. "How dare you!"

Impotent anger welled within her as she held the ruined garment. Turn the other cheek, she had been taught. Vengeance belonged to the Lord, she knew. Once, just once, she wanted to take an eye for an eye. A wistful wish so long as she lived in a world where others were bigger, stronger, and had more power.

She gathered the dress against her breast, lifting her face to him. "If your wife left you, it's no less than you deserve. A chicken intended for tonight's dinner would be treated with more kindness than you've given me." She poked him in the chest. "You may be able to keep me here, but I don't have to talk to you. Get out."

He captured her hand and held it with frightening ease. "It's just like you to call the kettle black. This is my ranch. My house." His gaze swept around the room. "My bedroom . . . my wife." He yanked her into his arms, stilling her head with one large hand, using his thumb to tip her chin toward him. "I did

52

warn you what would happen if I caught you with any of my men."

"I didn't seek him out."

"I don't believe you." Sloan's fingers slid into her hair, and his face came so close to hers that she could see the thickness of his eyelashes and feel his breath mingle with hers.

"Don't do this. Please, don't . . ." This was a trap from which she had no escape. This man, and his complete certainty of right being on his side, terrified her far more than Jake or Sam. She should have had more sense than to argue with him.

"Begging?" One of Sloan's eyebrows lifted.

Acutely aware of his hand around her face, his arm at her back, the hard length of his body, she hated knowing she had lost yet another battle. Never had she been more aware of another person. Unable to bear the scrutiny of his dark gaze any longer, she closed her eyes. If begging was what it took to make him leave her alone, then so be it. She nodded.

"That's too damn bad," he murmured, "because, much as I hate you, I've never wanted this more."

His lips came down on hers without warning, warm, as the rest of him was, soft, unlike the rest of him. Abbey held herself perfectly still as tears squeezed from beneath her eyelids. The pressure of his mouth increased, painful against her split lip. She cried out.

Her mistake gave him access to the interior of her mouth. His tongue swept over hers, unfamiliar, rough, searingly intimate. She struggled against him, needing to put some distance between them, needing to breathe, needing to still the alarm that pushed through her chest. He caught both of her hands within one of his and held them behind her back, then backed her against the bed, where she had no balance, no way to move her legs. No way to escape.

The movements of his tongue in her mouth were blatant,

signaling his intent. Raw panic clawed through her with no outlet except the graphic memories that blistered inside her head.

Riders had come to the house in the middle of the night, as they sometimes did. These men, though, were drunk. Miss Mary told Abbey to hide the children in the cellar, to stay there with them. That hadn't kept Abbey from hearing the rough insults of the men and the sounds of a struggle. Peeking through a crack in the trapdoor, she had watched those men repeatedly rape Miss Mary. Abbey should have somehow stopped them, but she had been too much of a coward to face them. And now, there would be no escape—no help for her, either.

How am I going to endure this?

Suddenly, he lifted his head, and she took a great rasping breath of air. Trembling so badly her legs barely supported her, she opened her eyes. Within Sloan's, she saw a confusion that matched her own, which didn't make any sense at all. He shook his head once, then let go of her and stepped back.

The ebbing panic fueled her fury, and she crossed her arms over her chest and glared at him.

"I am not your wife." She took a shaky step forward, then flinched when he reached out to steady her. She knocked his hands away from her shoulders. "Don't touch me."

The last remnants of bewilderment in his eyes hardened into the glittering, cold depths she had come to expect.

"I'll touch you any damn time I want."

Abbey lifted her chin. "You'd resort to rape?" She swallowed, wishing she were as brave as she sounded. "Then you'd best get on with it." Furious with her and appalled with himself, Sloan stared down at her an endless moment. Her defiant gaze—vulnerable as hell—locked with his, her pupils so dilated her eyes looked nearly black. A pair of wet tracks wound across her cheeks and disappeared into her hair. She had washed it and combed it out, and he could see it was still damp. The silky strands flowed down her back, beautiful and far more alluring than the complicated ringlets his wife preferred.

A pulse fluttered at the base of her neck, throbbing so rapidly he was reminded of a trapped butterfly beating itself in panic against a window. That and her accusation of rape shamed him, but not as much as did his complete lack of control.

"I had promised myself I would never touch you again." That was God's own truth. He had no idea why this one woman so provoked him. Get within shouting distance of her, and he acted like the worst kind of fool.

"A man of his word," she murmured, her voice rich with scorn.

Her sarcasm was exactly the sort of thing Charlotte had used against him many times. Yet, for an instant, she hadn't felt or behaved like Charlotte at all. If she wasn't—He refused to consider the complete folly of such a mistake.

From the haughty tilt of her head to the set of her shoulders, this was Charlotte. No matter what name she called herself. There simply was no other alternative.

Without a word, he turned on his heel and left the room. She knew what he wanted, and sooner or later, she would give it to him. Until then, he had only one possible course of action—stay away from her. And, so help him, he would.

CHAPTER 5

"You ain't gonna like it, Boss, but more cattle are missing. Fifteen head," Eli Stodges reported as he sat down for supper a couple of hours later. "An' jus' like with the previous bunch, they was herded south."

Eli was right. Sloan didn't like it. All summer, cattle had been rustled off. At first, just a couple of head. Enough to feed a band of Utes as they came through the area. Those were losses Sloan was willing to abide—an accepted price for living in peace with the Indians who had been part of this land long before the white man's invasion. Lately, though, the thefts had been more than the random slaughter of an animal or two.

He seethed at this latest news.

"Gotta be the Utes," Caleb Holt said. "Damn Injuns."

"Seems like you're always blamin' the Indians," Jake offered, sitting down across from Eli. "One raid, maybe it's the Indians. But five or six? That's too organized." He caught Sloan's eye. "We still the only ones bein' hit?"

Sloan nodded. "Near as I can tell. The Crooked Fork was hit early in the summer, but not lately. And, since Frank Gibbs is selling his place, it doesn't make sense he'd turn to cattle thieving."

"Maybe he's tryin' to build up his own herd."

"You must have been kicked by a mule," Sloan returned, "or you'd remember helping him drive his cattle to Pueblo last spring."

Eli chuckled, his wizened face splitting into a wide grin and revealing several missing teeth. He slapped Caleb on the back. "Always knew you were an ugly, dumb cuss. And you wouldn't be talkin' so free and easy about the damn Injuns if Jonah was sittin' here givin' you the evil eye."

The door to the cabin opened, then slammed shut, and a couple more men came into the kitchen, sitting down at empty places on the benches. With their arrival, Consuela set a platter of fried steaks and a huge bowl of boiled potatoes in the middle of the table. Abruptly, conversation ended as the men speared the meat off the platter.

Consuela served herself, filling the plates for her two older children, Pearl and JJ, who sat at a smaller table near the fireplace. Sloan watched a moment, making sure Consuela had taken not only what she needed for the children, but for herself, as well. She had been prickly as a mama bear in spring, insisting she didn't want to take advantage, and she didn't want Sloan's charity. What she didn't seem to understand was she worked harder than any two men on the ranch, and he didn't know how he'd manage without her.

Satisfied she had taken enough to fill up JJ and Pearl, Sloan dug into his own meal, pondering the thefts. Since the spring thaw, everything he touched had gone to rack and ruin. First, Charlotte had disappeared with the Sun. Sloan, his brother Jonah, and Jake had taken off looking for her, leaving Consuela's husband, Joey McLennon, in charge.

Sloan ill afforded those weeks away from the ranch, and the combined results of his neglect and ongoing mishaps proved to him he couldn't continue to look for Charlotte and the stallion personally—not if he wanted to still have a ranch a year from now. The irony didn't escape him—he might lose the very thing Charlotte had most hated.

While he had been gone, Joey had overseen the first hay cutting, and he'd done his best to save the barn when it caught fire. Last month, he died in a freak accident while driving a small herd of cattle to Oro City. Sloan blamed himself for that, as well. It was a trip he should have taken. Instead, he had been down Taos way, looking for the Sun and Charlotte.

The blame for Joey's death squarely lay on him. Sloan had sworn he'd take care of Consuela and the children. If she wanted to stay at the ranch, she could. If she decided to return to her father's home in Santé Fe, Sloan would take her.

And, all summer long, someone had boldly stolen his cattle. Not the other ranchers' in the valley. Just his. And he couldn't shake the feeling the thefts carried some personal message.

He glanced around the table, studying each of the men, wondering for the umpteenth time if any of these men had helped Charlotte steal the Sun. She was an excellent horse-woman, to be sure, but he couldn't imagine her pulling off the theft of a high-strung stallion without help. Trouble was, he couldn't imagine one of these men stealing from him.

Not Jake. Not Sam, either. If Sloan was sure of anything, it was that. Sam was family. The boy was impressionable as hell, but he didn't have a dishonest bone in his body. Sloan had first met him when he was pounding iron for the railroad. Then, Sam had been a skinny runt, doing whatever he could to eat. When Sloan had earned the money he had wanted for improve-ments on the ranch, he had quit, asked Sam if he'd like a job, and brought the boy home with him. During the five years since, he had become more family than paid cowboy.

Buck wasn't smart enough to spot a stray calf in the south pasture, but finding him in the house this afternoon renewed Sloan's suspicions. Being stupid didn't necessarily make him a thief, but if any of his men were likely to steal, one of them would be Buck.

As for Caleb Holt and Eli Stodges, they had ridden in

together a year ago last spring. They were an odd pair, Eli old enough to be Caleb's father. Near as Sloan could tell, though, they weren't related. Both men had worked hard, more than earning their keep. Like a lot of men, they might be hiding something in their past, but while working for him, they had been honest enough.

Except for the temporary hands who worked for him over the summer, the only other man on the ranch had been Consuela's husband. Joey had been no more likely to steal from him than his own brother. Joey's devotion to Consuela, daughter of a well-to-do merchant in New Mexico who had disowned her when she married a gringo, had given Sloan hope he could make the best of his own marriage. Except Charlotte hadn't had a fraction of Consuela's grit.

Sloan was half tempted to go drag his wife out of the bedroom and make her sit here with the men, sure that sooner or later someone would give something away. Only, he stayed seated, admitting to himself he didn't want to face any more of her barbed accusations or her complete denial she was his wife. She sounded so damn sure of herself, like she always had. And like always, he was too tempted to believe her.

Patience, Brother, Sloan could hear Jonah say. His brother could be as impatient as any man when he had a burr under his saddle. And, there were times he could watch grass grow without any sign of fatigue or boredom. Sloan could use a little of that right now.

He finished eating, only half listening to the men talk, his attention on the woman in the bedroom. He hadn't expected her to come out for dinner, but damned if he was going to go out of his way to feed her, either. If she wanted to eat, she knew where the kitchen was.

Even so, his treatment of her pricked his conscience. A little voice he would have rather ignored reminded him he was at least as much at fault for her not being at the table for supper as she was.

After dropping the scraps into a bucket next to the washtub and setting the plate on the sideboard, Sloan snagged another plate off the shelf. Aware the men were watching his every move, he loaded the dish with meat, potatoes, and gravy. As he left the kitchen, Sloan heard Caleb snicker.

Sloan turned around to face him. Caleb caught his eye, the smile vanishing from his face. A good thing, too, because Sloan was sorely tempted to wipe it off. Maybe, just maybe, he decided, he had something against Caleb after all.

He knocked. No surprise she didn't answer, so he pushed open the door. Silas lay on the floor next to the bed. And curled up on one side of the bed was the woman, looking as though she had simply fallen over while still sewing. In the dim light, the bruise around her eye and the handprint across her cheek were dark against her pale skin. As before, anger surged through him that she'd been hit. He had only a couple of infallible rules, and one of them was no man worth the name struck a woman or a child.

He was too tempted to believe she was who she claimed to be. She had braided her hair into a single rope that hung down her back, a style he had never seen on her.

Sloan watched her for a moment, unable to decide whether to leave the food with her. He had a thousand reasons to hate her but for the moment found doing so beyond him. At last he whistled softly to the dog, let him outside for a run, and returned to the kitchen, the plate of food still in his hands.

Abbey woke the following morning, disoriented by her surroundings. She glanced around the room, memories of the previous day spilling through her like cold water. She didn't know how she was going to manage another day with people judging her, hating her because they thought she was Charlotte Rafferty.

Turning onto her side, she stared blindly into the room. She imagined the routine at the Haverlys' house and wondered how Harriet and the new baby were doing. They had hired her to be an extra pair of hands at the store and in the household. It was a job Abbey had liked, and she had looked forward to spending the winter there. Being mistaken for another woman wasn't Abbey's fault. Even so, she was letting Ben and Harriet down. They were fine, decent folks. She prayed she would still have a position when she got away from here.

Abbey wondered what advice Miss Mary would have for this situation. Pray for guidance, most probably. So far, that hadn't done much good. The guidance Abbey really wanted was a good sense of direction and a way to leave here.

She sat up and stretched, remembering she had awakened once during the night and had crawled beneath the covers of the bed. The dog had been there, watching her with his golden eyes. This morning, he sat next to the bed, his muzzle resting on the mattress, his unblinking eyes fastened on her face.

Abbey reached out and scratched the dog's head, then his ears. He wagged his tail, and Abbey could have sworn he smiled. At least, the dog seemed to know she wasn't Charlotte. Abbey sat up, wondering if she'd be any more successful today than she had been yesterday at convincing Sloan Rafferty she was not his wife.

Getting out of bed, Abbey gathered up the ruined dress and held it in front of her. She critically examined it, then threw it back on the bed with a mutter of complete disgust. Not even Miss Mary would be able to fix it.

She hurried through her morning toilette then approached the armoire, facing a choice she had been determined to avoid. Wearing Charlotte's clothes would likely cause her as much trouble as Joseph's coat of many colors. Taking a deep breath, she opened the doors. The dresses inside looked as fine as they had yesterday, as fine as anything Abbey had ever seen in Godey's book.

She took one dress, then another, from the armoire, holding each in front of her. The colors were rich, flattering. And, Abbey couldn't imagine wearing them, much less getting a lick of work done in any of them. Finally, at the back of the closet, she found a plain dress in her favorite color—midnight blue. An added plus was it didn't smell of roses, as did most of the other garments in the wardrobe. Donning stockings and the unfamiliar dress, she felt more sure of herself. Shoes turned out to be a problem—not even one of the several pairs in the armoire were big enough for her.

One last time, Abbey searched through the wardrobe. Behind one of the hat boxes, she found a pair of soft buckskin moccasins, surely Indian made. Abbey studied the beadwork, remembering the photograph in the other bedroom of Sloan with another man and an Indian woman. Sitting down, she slipped one on her foot. The fit was snug, but unlike the shoes, she was able to wear them. In fact, they were surprisingly comfortable.

Critically, Abbey surveyed herself in the mirror, hoping against hope she had done nothing to further emphasize any resemblance between herself and Charlotte. Toward that end, she had even left her hair in a single long braid that hung down the middle of her back, a style as different from Charlotte's portrait as Abbey could manage.

Her own reflection paired with Charlotte's brought to mind a verse from the Bible that seemed to fit. "I send you forth as sheep in the midst of wolves," Abbey whispered, pausing a moment as she tried to remember the rest of it. "Be ye therefore wise as serpents and harmless as doves."

Somehow, she would find a way to get back to the Haverlys. Turning away from the mirror, Abbey murmured, "It's time to face the lions."

The dog cocked its head toward her.

"Come on, Silas." She knew very well the dog would stay right with her but issued the command. "You're going to show me around."

The front room was deserted, but seeing Sloan's hat hung on a peg next to the door, Abbey concluded he was close by. In the kitchen, Abbey found Consuela sitting in a rocker pulled close to the Franklin stove. At her breast, the baby nursed.

Abbey's glance went to the tiny window where the sunshine streamed through.

"Is that coffee on the stove?" she asked.

Consuela jumped, obviously startled. She looked over her shoulder at Abbey.

"I'm sorry." Abbey came into the kitchen. "I didn't mean to give you a turn."

Consuela frowned, her pointed stare beginning at Abbey's feet and working up. Resisting the urge to check that she was properly buttoned up, Abbey moved into the kitchen. Spying the clean dishes on the drainboard, Abbey took one of the cups and filled it with the hot coffee on the stove. It always smelled better to her than it tasted, but this morning she didn't care. It was hot and bracing. Just what she needed.

Peering through the window, she saw the day was bright, the sun well into the sky.

"It's late, isn't it?"

"*Si.*"

Abbey sat down and took another sip of her coffee. A napkin covered a plate in the center of the table. Lifting the cloth, she found a few cold biscuits.

"May I have one of these?"

63

Consuela shrugged.

Abbey broke the biscuit in half, then nibbled at it. Cold or not, it tasted wonderful. She sat in silence, sipping her coffee and eating the biscuit as Consuela burped the baby, then shifted him to the other breast.

Abbey had dozens of questions but doubted the other woman would answer any of them. So, she let the silence grow between them, a silence Consuela didn't break, though she began to fidget with the hem of the baby's gown.

"Is Sloan—Mr. Rafferty—about?" Abbey finally asked.

"I don't know where he is."

"Or when he'll be back?" The seeds of a plan began to germinate. Surely the man would listen to reason. All she had to do was talk to him without losing her temper. And that shouldn't be so difficult. She was known for being a most even-tempered and agreeable person. Once he understood a mistake had been made, he'd send her back to Plum Creek Crossing. Simple.

Consuela smiled faintly. "You understand."

Abbey understood all too well. If the man was unavailable, she couldn't talk to him. She stood and went to the sink. Pumping the handle of the water pump until water flowed through it, she rinsed out the cup and set it on the drainboard where she had found it.

"Fiddlesticks," Abbey muttered, again peering outside. "I'll go crazy with nothing to do but wait for the man." She turned to face Consuela. "Idle hands are the devil's workshop."

"*Señora?*" Consuela raised an eyebrow as though Abbey had suddenly begun speaking another language.

"I'm used to being busy. The time will pass faster if I have something to do."

"Something to do?" Consuela repeated.

"That's right." Abbey punctuated her answer with a nod.

"There's always the milking."

"That's a splendid suggestion." Abbey smiled. A chance to be outside. Presuming Silas thought his guarding duties allowed her outside. "Where is the milk bucket?"

Consuela pointed to it. "You're, uh, not worried about getting calluses on your hands?"

"From milking a cow?" Abbey held her hands out in front of her. "My heavens, no. I already have . . ." Her voice faded as she realized she had been given yet another insight into Charlotte's character. Or lack of it. "I suppose there were a number of chores Charlotte didn't like."

Consuela dropped her gaze.

"Do I really look so much like her?"

"Because you *are* her." She studied Abbey much as she had a few minutes before.

Abbey took a step toward Consuela and held out her hands. "I have calluses. Maybe proof I'm not Charlotte."

"You've been away six months. You could have been working hard since then."

Abbey stared at the other woman a moment. "There really is no way to prove I'm Abbey, is there?"

Consuela shrugged. "If Sloan thinks you're Charlotte—a man would know his own wife."

"He should," Abbey agreed. "The milk cow—she's in the barn?"

"Where else would it be?" Consuela countered.

"Indeed." Abbey took the bucket and opened the door that led outside. "Come on, Silas."

As before, the dog followed her. Abbey closed the door behind her and stood on the porch a moment, absorbing the crisp morning air and a stunning mountain valley spread out in front of her. A peak jutted into the sky in the distance, irregular patches of snow gleaming from its crevices. Below the peak, foothills, splashed with the brilliant yellow of autumn leaves and the dark green of spruce and pine, rippled toward the valley floor. Cottonwoods marked the progress of a river. Much of the rest of the valley was pasture land, dotted with the dark-brown hides of grazing cattle. She had the oddest sense of coming home, a feeling she immediately shook off since she was a prisoner here until she could figure out a way to leave. Still . . . she was moved by the vista before her as she never had been before.

She stared a long time, memorizing everything about it, hoping her orchard homestead in California would be as alluring as this.

Stepping off the porch, she headed for the barn, which looked brand new. A fresh coat of red paint covered only half of one side as though the painter had run out of time or supplies. The dog trotted along beside her. She paused a moment at the wide doorway, waiting for her eyes to adjust to the gloomy interior. The smells inside were the familiar musky scents of hay and animals. The scent of new lumber was stronger inside, as well. Abbey looked around, noting the pine had not yet darkened with age. She passed a couple of empty stalls, evidently used for horses, and made her way toward the milk cow at the back of the barn, watching her with unblinking eyes.

"Well, what do you think, Silas. Is this a cow who's going to be happy to have her udder emptied? Or, is she the kind that will kick me or the milk bucket just for spite?"

She glanced at the dog, who had stayed right with her.

"Hope she's not nervous about dogs, since you and I seem to be a pair."

A milk stool sat on the outside of the stall, which Abbey picked up. This had been one of her chores more days than not for most of her life, and it felt good to be doing something familiar. This could be accomplished without any fuss.

Before entering the stall, she began talking to the cow, getting it used to the sound of her voice. What mattered was a calm, confident tone. Touching the cow as she had many others, Abbey settled on the stool and wrapped her hands around a pair of the teats. So far, the cow seemed more interested in the relief that came with milking than giving a stranger trouble. Abbey hoped it stayed that way.

She leaned her head against the cow's flank and gave herself into the timeless rhythms of milking. The barn itself was quiet, but in the distance, Abbey could hear the occasional bawl of a cow in the pasture and the voices of men somewhere else in the compound.

And one of those men was Sloan Rafferty. How had he ended up with a wealthy wife who was so unsuitable for life here?

A tiger-striped cat jumped up on the top of the stall, meowing as if to announce its presence. Abbey smiled. Some things were the same no matter where a body was. Milking and cats went together here and in the Shenandoah Valley. Abbey watched the cat, who returned her stare, then set about washing itself.

Little by little the bucket filled and was about two-thirds full when the cow suddenly moved. Abbey had been expecting that, and she neatly lifted the bucket out of the way.

"Nice move, Lady Bell, I'm still smarter than that—"

"Not by much," came a man's voice, "since you ended up back here. And milkin'. Who would have thought?"

Abbey glanced up at the man standing at the end of the stall. With his drawl, she thought for a moment the man was Jake. He wasn't. Nor Sam. Nor Buck. Another stranger. At least this man didn't look as sinister as Buck had yesterday.

There didn't seem to be anything to say, so she simply watched the man as she milked.

"Well, Miz Charlotte—"

"My name is Abigail Wallace."

He took his hat off, revealing light-brown hair. He fingered the brim. "Abigail Wallace, huh?"

"That's right."

"Whatever you say."

What an odd response, Abbey thought, returning her attention to the bucket of milk.

"And milkin' a cow, too. Your husband must be right proud, you takin' on such a chore. Who would have ever thought . . ."

"Thought what?" Abbey asked.

"That Charlotte would—"

"As I told you: I'm Abigail Wallace."

"I see," he finally said. "You do have to admit you look like her."

He came a bit further into the stall. Abruptly Abbey remembered Sloan Rafferty's warning about finding her with any of his men. This man hadn't insulted her, threatened her, or manhandled her—which made him almost as good company as the dog. Still, Sloan Rafferty was her key to leaving the ranch, and she wasn't about to upset him unnecessarily.

"You're . . . uh, not mad about ol' Buck, are you?" he asked.

Abbey frowned, remembering his appearance in the bedroom yesterday afternoon and his threats. How this man knew anything about Buck's visit to her room, Abbey didn't know. She hadn't liked the man, and she didn't like the idea she had been the topic of gossip.

"I most certainly am. He's filthy and a bully, to boot."

"I'd guess you'd know. Don't you worry your pretty little head about a thing. I'll make sure he don't bother you none."

"Thank you, but I doubt that is necessary."

She stood, picking up the heavy bucket in one hand and the stool in another. "Which pasture should the cow be put in?"

He gave her an odd look.

"I know," Abbey filled in. "Since I'm supposed to be Charlotte, and since she lived here, I ought to know. Well, I'm not Charlotte, and I don't know."

"The north pasture. I'll let the cow out."

"Thank you."

He reached for the bucket. "This is much too heavy for a pint-sized gal like you."

"I can manage." Abbey felt the cow at her back. "Mr. Rafferty doesn't want me talking to his men."

"He's a hard man when he's crossed."

"Yes. He seems to be. What's your name?"

A flicker of surprise chased across his face. "Caleb Holt, ma'am. At your service."

"I really am not her."

He inclined his head to the side and whispered, "You could tell me the sun rises in the west, and I'd believe you." He followed her out of the barn, leading the cow. "You have a real fine day, Miss Abigail Wallace."

"Thank you." Abbey smiled politely at him, giving him one of Miss Mary's patented dismissive nods and hoping he would take the hint. He did, touching his fingers to his hat and tugging on the rope around the cow's neck. Thoughtfully, Abbey watched him stride across the compound. At last, one person who didn't hate her—Charlotte—on sight. The conversation had undercurrents she didn't understand. Everyone hated Charlotte. So why didn't this man?

CHAPTER 6

Consuela's surprising announcement that Charlotte had gone to milk the cow drove Sloan outside in search for her. He came to an abrupt stop at the edge of the porch when she emerged from the barn with Caleb Holt, the milk cow, and his dog. She smiled at something Caleb said, and unwanted jealousy flared through Sloan's belly, especially as she watched the other man as though she couldn't bear having him out of her sight.

Once she had looked at Sloan like that. Once he had believed the promise in her eyes. Once . . . a long time ago. Silently, he cursed himself. So much for his vow he wouldn't let her get under his skin.

Her dark hair was pulled into a long, shiny braid that hung down her back. The dark-blue dress looked a little big for her, emphasizing she had lost weight. He searched for the familiar contours of his wife's face beneath the bruises and sunburn. For some reason, she had given up her ornate ringlets, but there was no mistaking the dark, glossy brown of her hair—a crowning glory she had taken great pride in. Her features were Charlotte's, from the arch of her eyebrows and the tilt of her head to the way she carried herself.

She continued toward him, absorbed with her thoughts, her brow puckered, her eyes focused on the ground in front of her. She carried the heavy bucket of milk with the confidence that came from having done so before. Sloan frowned, wondering again where she had spent the last six months. He would have

70

bet his wife would have been hard pressed to know which end of a cow produced milk.

She caught sight of him, and her gait faltered. She looked down for an instant, then lifted her chin and met his gaze head on. He recognized the expression—his wife when she had something on her mind and was determined to have her own way.

"Good day, Mr. Rafferty." The deep crack on her swollen lower lip looked worse.

"Don't be formal on my account." He took the bucket from her hands. He hadn't intended the kiss to be a brutal act of possession and still didn't understand how he had let things get so out of control. She had behaved as though he was a stranger and she was an outraged virgin. He wondered how much longer she could keep up the pretense. "When did you learn to milk a cow?"

She searched his face as if the question had some hidden meaning. "I don't know. I think I've always known how."

The admission sounded so much like the truth, he was half tempted to believe her. He looked away from her face and found himself staring at the moccasins on her feet. Surprised, he grabbed a handful of her skirt and lifted it out of the way to better see.

She slapped his hand away and stepped beyond his reach, a look of indignant affront crossing her face. "Mr. Rafferty, I—"

"Why pick now to wear Jonah's wedding gift?" Sloan asked, remembering the scorn in her voice the day Jonah had given them to her and her declaration she wouldn't be wearing anything made by filthy Indian hands.

The anger in her expression faded, replaced by a grim determination he didn't begin to understand.

"If Jake hadn't thrown away my own shoes, I wouldn't have to wear these. And if I've offended you by wearing another man's gift to your wife, that's too—"

"You haven't . . . offended me." Sloan met her gaze. Oddly enough, that much was true. If she didn't remember saying she would never wear them, Sloan wasn't about to remind her. Further, he liked the way they looked on her feet, one more admission that didn't please him.

"These are the only shoes in the closet that fit," she added. "Your wife's feet are smaller than mine."

"I doubt it. You're vain, or at least you used to be. Smaller was somehow better, even if your feet did hurt."

She lifted her chin. "I am not Charlotte, as I keep telling you, and as you keep ignoring. Now, if you'll simply post a letter to my employer, Mr. Ben Haverly or better yet, take me back to Plum Creek Crossing—it's south of Denver—we can clear up this whole misunderstanding."

"And where was this place of employment?"

"Haverly's Mercantile," she promptly replied. "This whole matter can be immediately resolved if you'd simply return me to my employer."

The defiant tilt of her head and her putting forth yet another of her endless plans brought an abrupt end to Sloan's patience.

"Forget it. I already told you how you're getting off this ranch. When you tell me where—"

"—tell you where a stupid horse is that I'd never heard of until a couple of days ago," she finished.

"You catch on," he drawled.

"I don't know where your horse is. I honestly don't."

He didn't dare believe that. If he did, he was on his way to believing she was some misbegotten waif named Abigail Wallace. "Then, Wife, it's going to be a long winter."

"Don't call me that." When he would have walked away from her, she laid a hand on his arm, then immediately snatched it back. "Please let me write a letter to the Haverlys."

"Write anything you want."

Her face brightened for an instant, then fell. "I can write, but you won't post my letters."

He nodded. "As I said, you catch on."

She nodded right back. "It's unfortunate, Mr. Rafferty, that you do not."

Abbey turned her back on him, as close to losing her temper as she remembered being in a long while. Then she remembered the man had generated a similar response from her the last time they spoke. Miss Mary's admonitions about anger echoed through Abbey's head, something from Proverbs about an angry man behaving foolishly. She certainly was foolish to think the man would listen to her simply because she willed it so. She marched across the hard-packed earth of the compound toward the road, bent on one thing only—putting as much distance between herself and him as she could.

At the gate, her progress came to an abrupt halt when Sloan's dog, Silas, stepped in front of her, blocking her way.

Abbey eyed the dog, who watched her with intent eyes that reminded her of the master. "Sit," she commanded.

Silas promptly sat.

Abbey sidestepped him to walk through the gate. Silas got up and again blocked her way, this time using his body to push her back into the compound.

"Silas," she muttered. "You can't be that smart."

The dog wagged his tail.

"Silas, lie down."

He did as she asked, his head cocked to one side, his expression alert. When she tried to move through the gate, he got up and once again barred her way.

Exasperated, Abbey pushed him to the side. As if she had decided to play some game he liked, he pushed back. She pushed him again, and he dropped his front legs to the ground, his rear end elevated, his tail wagging, his expression happy. Frustrated as she was with the situation, being angry at Silas was impossible.

A smile twitched at the corner of Abbey's mouth, and she stamped her foot at the dog. He pounced toward her, clearly inviting her to play, just as clearly determined to keep her from going through the gate when she once again tried to pass him.

"They eat dogs in some places, you know," she said to the dog.

"And, in some places, the price of a wife's infidelity is her death," came Sloan's deep voice from behind her.

Abbey whirled around to find Sloan standing a scant few feet away. The fleeting joy of the moment gone, Abbey searched his implacable gaze.

"Are you meeting Caleb somewhere?" His voice was soft, flat, his eyes anything but.

"I . . . Caleb?" The echo of Sloan's accusation rang through her head. As she realized what he seemed to think, her barely cooled temper sizzled again. "Of course not."

"Then, Wife, where are you off to?"

"That," Abbey responded, "should have been obvious. Somewhere away from you."

"You can go as far as you want when I have the stallion back. In the meantime, stay away from the men."

"You, sir, have a one-track mind."

The conversation had once again come full circle, which he seemed to realize, for he shook his head, muttered an oath, and turned away from her. Abbey watched him go, wondering what she had to do to convince him she wasn't Charlotte Rafferty.

Earlier, Abbey had been so sure simply acting like herself would be enough. The problem was, her own behavior seemed to make others believe she really was Charlotte. How could another person she didn't know be so much like her in both looks and personality?

Abbey followed the fence around the perimeter of the compound, eventually finding herself behind the house where a faint path led through the tall grasses, heavy with the seeds of late summer. Silas walked beside her, staying right with her every step of the way.

As the path led through an open gap in the fence, Abbey expected Silas to again bar her way. When he didn't, she followed the track, not really caring where it went, wishing it led back to the Haverlys' home, wishing even more it led to California and her dream orchard.

Abbey's gaze lifted to the snow-capped mountains in the distance that stabbed the most brilliantly blue sky she had ever seen. The valley between here and the distant peaks somehow matched her dreams of a home. This was perhaps the most beautiful place she had ever been. The morning air had lost its chill but still had a crisp tang of autumn she liked. This would be good apple growing country, she thought, if the season were long enough. Then, she shook her head. However beautiful this valley was, she was a prisoner. That alone was reason enough to want to be somewhere else, anywhere else.

A rustling in the long grass caught her attention, and she slowed her pace. After a moment's search, she found the source of the sounds—two small children, who were following her. They regarded her with open curiosity.

"Hi." Abbey automatically stooped so she was at their height. "Who are you?"

"Joey Junior," the taller of the two said, straightening himself up to his full height. He was nut brown, Abbey noted, from his bare feet to his shaggy hair, except for his eyes. They were a brilliant blue. His clothes were well worn and well mended, showing the inevitable wear and tear of a little boy busy playing.

"Hello, Joey Junior. Is that what I'm supposed to call you? Or can I say Joey?"

He shook his head. "My pap was Joey. I'm Joey Junior. JJ for short." Matter of factly, he added, "He got gored by a steer."

"He's in heaven now," the other child said. Dressed in clothes as worn and as well cared for as JJ's, this child had shoulder length, dark-brown hair and eyes and pale skin. "Huh, JJ?"

"What's your name?" Abbey asked. Her liking of the children was instant, the recognition of kindred spirits. Though she had been more relieved than sad when Pa died, she knew what it felt like to be a child without a parent.

"Pearl Mae McLennon." The little girl held up her hand, spreading her fingers. "I am four years old."

"My, and such a big girl, too," Abbey said.

"My mama, she said you act funny," Pearl added.

"I don't mean to," Abbey returned gravely, realizing these two children must be Consuela's, realizing the children could provide her a wealth of information. Most kids could talk your ear off—all you had to do was prime the pump, then listen while they talked—usually revealing secrets adults would rather were kept. "The baby, what's his name?"

"He's not a he," JJ said. "He's a girl."

"Sarah," added Pearl. "And she's beautiful."

"I think so, too." Abbey straightened to her full height.

"Where are you going?" JJ asked.

"I don't know."

"Then how are you going to know when you get there?"

Abbey laughed. "Now that's a very good question. So, you tell me. Where will I go if I follow this path?"

"Come on." Pearl took Abbey by the hand. "We'll show you, won't we, JJ?"

"I don't think that's such a good idea," he said, then whispered to Pearl as though Abbey couldn't hear him. "You 'member what she did to your doll. That was real mean."

Abbey had no doubt which "she" the boy referred to, and too easily, she imagined what might have been done to Pearl's doll.

"Don't be so silly. She is not the same one." She raised her gaze to Abbey. "You're not, are you?"

"I'm not," Abbey agreed, figuring the conversation had once more turned back to the missing Charlotte. "My name is Abbey."

Pearl shot her brother an I-told-you-so look.

He studied Abbey. "She looks the same."

Pearl looked up as well. "No, she doesn't. I can tell." She tugged on Abbey's hand. "Silas will come, too, won't he?"

"I'm sure he will," Abbey responded.

"If you're not her," JJ asked, "how come you look the same?"

"I don't know," Abbey admitted, following him along the path. Undoubtedly there was a family bible or some other records in Charlotte's room that might answer some of Abbey's questions. Tonight, she would look.

"My mama said good riddance when you disappeared last spring," he said.

"That was afore Pap went to heaven," Pearl said. "Do you always have to die to get there?"

Abbey glanced down at the little girl. "I think so."

She shrugged her small shoulders. "Then, if I want to talk to my Pap, I have to die, too." She lifted her gaze to Abbey. "Would I be put in the same hole as my Pap?"

The question caught Abbey's attention as nothing else could have. She stopped walking and crouched so she was once again eye level with the child. "You don't have to die to talk to him, little one."

"I don't?"

Abbey shook her head. "All you have to do is find a quiet place to sit." She didn't know if any such thing was true, but she didn't like the idea of Pearl thinking the only way to speak with her papa was to be dead.

"He won't answer back," JJ said in a superior tone. "He won't hear you, neither, 'cause he's dead."

"Perhaps you're right," Abbey said, acknowledging the boy before returning her attention to his sister. "If you listen with your eyes closed, you might hear him." She smiled at Pearl. "It's worth a try, don't you think?"

"We're almost there," Pearl said with the sudden change of subject common to children. She pulled on Abbey's hand. "C'mon."

Standing, Abbey saw the field ended in a loosely spaced grove of cottonwood trees, their yellow leaves rustling softly in the breeze. Beneath the trees was a small, carefully tended graveyard. Abbey turned back to look at the path they had walked, a path that showed signs of frequent use.

She followed the children, who stopped in front of a grave still mounded with soil and covered with dried flowers. *Joseph Andrew McLennon* the grave marker read with the dates of his birth and death, the latter a mere eight weeks ago. Next to his grave was another, older one. Matthew James McLennon had died when he was but a few weeks old, and another infant, identified only as Baby Boy McLennon, had died at birth a year earlier.

She studied JJ and Pearl, thinking of their mother, who wasn't much older than herself. Without a provider, life wouldn't be easy for any of them. Abbey couldn't imagine the responsibility of raising three small children alone, much less having given birth to five.

Leaving the children in front of their father's grave, Abbey moved toward the other, older graves. Two Raffertys were buried here, and both had died on the same day in the autumn of 1866. She thought of another family graveyard and wondered if she would ever know how she and Charlotte—the woman whose name she had not known before yesterday—were connected.

"I'm going to pick some flowers for Pap's grave," Pearl said. "Wanna help me?"

Abbey glanced from Pearl to the dried flowers, a few more recently placed and thus more wilted than dried. She remembered picking flowers for her grandmother's grave on that last visit. "Of course," she said.

"There are lots of daisies over this way." They followed a path away from the graveyard, a trail less traveled than the one that led from the house.

Abbey followed Pearl, grinning as Silas and JJ fell into step behind her. Hopefully, Pearl's daisies were within the boundaries Silas was guarding. JJ caught up with Abbey and openly stared at her. His thoughts were transparent—like everyone else, he was seeing her resemblance to Charlotte.

"Your shiner is turning green."

Abbey touched her fingers to the bruise at her eye. She had noticed the same thing when she washed her face. At least it wasn't as tender as it had been yesterday.

"I wonder why they do that," he added. "Turn green."

"That's a very good question," Abbey said. "I don't know."

"How come are you being so nice to my sis and me?" he asked.

" 'Cause I want to."

"Are you sorry for pulling the doll's head off and throwing it into the fire?"

Abbey was sorry—sorry anyone could do such a thing to a child. "I didn't do that. I am sorry it happened."

"I watched you."

Pearl stopped walking suddenly and faced her brother with her little hands on her hips. "That was Miz Charlotte. I told you already."

"I think she's just foolin' us. You're gonna be sorry when Mama finds out. And, if she"—he nodded toward Abbey—"rips off *your* head and throws it into the fire, it won't be my fault." With that he took off at a run across the field, his brown head bobbing up and down among the long stalks of grass.

Pearl rolled her eyes and lifted her gaze to Abbey. "Boys."

Despite the sting of once again being judged for Charlotte's sins, this time by a child no less, Abbey found herself grinning at Pearl's tone.

"He's dumb."

"He's just acting like a big brother," Abbey said.

Pearl nodded. "Dumb."

Abbey laughed, and Pearl smiled, slipping her hand into Abbey's.

"You should laugh when Mr. Sloan tells a funny story," she advised. When Abbey's eyebrows rose in question, Pearl added, "She laughs like this." She covered her mouth with the back of her hand and fluttered her eyelashes, then said, "Tee hee."

Abbey laughed again, and this time Pearl laughed, too, an infectious little-girl giggle that bore no resemblance to a polite titter. They skipped away from the path, and for a moment, Abbey felt joyful, carefree. The sunshine was warm, the sky, a brilliant blue, and a cheerful profusion of yellow and purple daisies spread across the field. Beyond the field, a copse of young trees grew, their formation too regular, too geometric to be natural.

The daisies forgotten, Abbey walked toward the trees, and Pearl skipped along next to her.

"An orchard," Abbey murmured.

"Apples. JJ and me, we've been picking them. Mama says they're ripe."

Pearl was right, Abbey discovered. Though the trees were young and the orchard overgrown with weeds and tall grass, most of the trees had a few apples, enough to produce two or three bushels. Abbey snagged an apple off the nearest tree, polished it on the sleeve of her dress, and handed it to Pearl.

The child sank her teeth into it and broke a chunk away, raising her hand and wiping away a dribble of juice from her chin. Picking a second apple, Abbey bit into it. The tart flavor spread over her tongue, and she chewed slowly, savoring the taste and aroma.

She meandered through the small orchard, munching on the apple. In all, there weren't more than a dozen trees, and of those, two were scrawny and struggling to stay alive. The others, though, were in fine shape despite their neglect. The trees hadn't been pruned, and weeds grew in profusion, some of them more than four feet tall.

Possibilities bubbled through Abbey as she gazed around. If the land and the climate would support apples, what about peaches or even pears? There was plenty of room for another row or two of trees. She imagined a few peach and pear trees. An experiment, to see how they would do. Raising her gaze beyond the confines of the orchard, she saw the valley stretched out before her, banked by purple mountains in the distance. How could a place that felt so right and was this beautiful, not to mention matching the vision of her dreams, be so wrong? She at once felt cheated to have found this final piece of her dream in this unlikely prison and felt hopeful somehow everything would work out. According to Miss Mary, it always did. Of all the verses she had taught, Abbey's favorite invited her to forget the past and look to the future with God proclaiming, "Behold, I will do a new thing. Now it shall spring forth, shall ye not know it? I will even make a way in the wilderness and rivers in the desert."

He eyes filled with tears as she took in everything around her. This wasn't the answer to her prayer for her own home and orchard. This was not her dream where she would belong— really belong. "Look to the future," she whispered. This view was meant to remind her of what she had been working for all these years, since the first time she had heard about homesteading.

The brilliant sky above, the cheerful chirp of birds in the trees, the soft breeze ruffling Pearl's hair as she skipped through the trees—all of it made Abbey's breath catch. It was the sort of day that invited a person to flop on the ground, suck on a grass stem, and watch the clouds float across the sky.

Determined to set aside her melancholy, Abbey did just that. Equally caught up in the moment, Pearl ran toward her with her arms stretched wide. She lay down beside her. Abbey heard Silas sigh, and when she peeked over Pearl Mae's head, the dog had stretched out in the meager shade of one of the apple trees.

Abbey smiled, resting her head back on the warm ground. She stared into the sky, letting her attention drift with the clouds.

An orchard . . . on this ranch belonging to the hardest man she had ever met.

"Who planted the trees?" she asked.

Pearl rolled onto her tummy and raised her head to look at one of the trees. "They just grow here."

"Yes, I can see they do," Abbey responded. She would bet the trees had been in the ground fewer than ten years—a whole lifetime for Pearl. And, somehow, she couldn't imagine Sloan Rafferty could be interested in a few apple trees. Cattle and his horse would occupy his time and attention.

She closed her eyes and inhaled. Though she had just eaten an apple, her mouth watered at the fruity, pungent scent of the ripening apples and the crisp bite of the autumn air.

"We should pick these apples."

"I'll help." Pearl sat up.

Abbey leaned on an elbow and looked around for a basket or something else to carry the apples. "We don't have anything to put them in," she pointed out as she sat up. "All I have is my skirt."

"I'll get a basket from the house." The little girl stood and grinned. "And maybe Mama will make apple pie for supper." She began skipping away, then stopped. "You won't go away, will you?"

"I'll be right here," Abbey assured her. "With Silas." She glanced at the dog, who lay with his head resting on his paws, watching from a pool of shade beneath one of the trees.

"Maybe JJ will want to help," Pearl said.

"Maybe." Abbey doubted he would. Smiling, she watched Pearl run toward the house. Abbey liked the child, enjoyed how carefree she seemed to be despite her papa's death. That spoke well of the adults who cared for her. Abbey wasn't sure she had ever skipped across a field the way Pearl was doing. Maybe, before the day was over, she should try it, if only to see what doing so felt like.

Smiling, Abbey laid back down on the ground and stared into the brilliant sky, letting herself relax into a nebulous daydream where she felt safe, cherished, happy. A daydream where she held sweet babies in her lap like Sarah and Pearl.

Sometime later, a low growl in the back of Silas's throat interrupted her reverie. Raising up on her elbow, she peered through the grass. A pair of men ambled across the field, deep in conversation.

"Shh," Abbey whispered to the dog.

He slunk toward her, his belly brushing the ground, the hair on the back of his neck raised. Abbey recognized Buck and Caleb Holt.

As the two men came closer to the orchard, the low rumble of their voices gave way to distinct words.

"You got it all wrong," one of the men said.

Carefully, Abbey lifted herself up slightly so she could better see. The men had stopped walking and stood facing each other, just beyond the first row of apple trees.

"I left you to do a job," Caleb returned.

"Don't be gettin' yourself into a lather," Buck interrupted. "She ain't talking."

"You'd better pray it stays that way," the other man said. "Rafferty's going to be watching every move anybody makes. What did you do with the mare?"

For an instant, Abbey thought she heard stallion, and her attention sharpened. Then she realized Caleb had said mare, not stallion. Another horse. Not the missing Cimarron Sun.

Buck ducked his head and didn't answer.

"Goddammit, Buck, don't be holdin' out on me now."

From across the field came Pearl's shout. "Oh, Miss Abbey. I got the basket."

Abbey twisted her head and watched Pearl run toward her, her progress hampered by the basket she dragged behind her.

"Miss Abbey, where are you?"

With growing alarm, Abbey's attention shifted back to the two men, who looked around them. Searching. For her. An eavesdropper. Abbey swallowed.

With great show, she slowly straightened from the ground, lifting her arms in a stretch and yawning.

"There you are," Pearl called, heading for Abbey, the basket bumping her legs as she skipped along. "And guess what? Mama said she'd come help carry the basket and make pie."

Abbey smiled at the child, hoping none of her worry about the two men showed. From her side vision, she watched them approach. "I think I must have fallen asleep," she confessed around another yawn and stood up. Perhaps she even had, she thought, uncertain how long Pearl had been gone.

"Well, well, well." Caleb hooked his thumbs in his belt as he ambled toward her. "Miss Abigail, enjoyin' a bit of fresh air?"

Abbey brushed off her skirt. "I am," she admitted. "It is a lovely day. A good one for picking apples."

"I would have thought you'd rather go ridin'."

"That's what Miz Charlotte always did. Riding," Pearl said to Abbey, setting the basket down between them. "My pap said she doted on ol' Lady G'diva more'n Mister Sloan. When I get my horse, I'm going to name it Blue Belle."

"If yer wantin' a ride, I'd take ya." Buck's face slid into a sly grin. He took a step toward her.

Silas moved from behind Abbey, his fangs bared, though he didn't utter a sound. Buck abruptly stepped backward.

"I'm picking apples today." Abbey patted Silas's head in silent thanks. And tomorrow it would be something else. She had no intention of going anywhere with Buck. Ever. Abbey picked up the basket and held out her other hand to the little girl. "Come on, Pearl."

Walking away from the two men, Abbey gave Pearl's hand a reassuring squeeze.

"Miz Charlotte," Buck called.

Abbey gritted her teeth at again being called by another woman's name. Torn between ignoring the man and correcting him, the latter urge won out. She turned around. "I . . ."

At the sight of his drawn gun, her voice faded.

"Someday I'm goin' to shoot that damn dog." With a flourish, he holstered the pistol and straightened the hat on his head. "And, Miz Charlotte, before I'm done, you're gonna wish I'd shot you."

Chapter 7

"C'mon, Buck." Caleb gave the man a nudge in the direction of the field that separated the orchard from the house. To Abbey, he added, "Don't you give another thought to Buck. I'll take care of everything. And don't be worryin' he'll shoot Rafferty's dog."

Buck flashed him a dirty look that was answered by an equally strong, silent warning from Caleb.

Too aware that Caleb hadn't commented on Buck's threat to her, she watched the two men a second longer, then turned away from them. Caleb's statements weren't much of a re-assurance, she decided.

"Don't pay Buck no never mind," Pearl advised with childish wisdom as she and Abbey moved away from the two men. "That's what Eli always says."

Taking a firmer hold on the basket, Abbey glanced uneasily over her shoulder and breathed a sigh of relief when she saw Buck and Caleb walking back toward the ranch house. One part of her was furious, but beneath the fury, fear rose, naked and ugly and undeniable. What if she never got back her own self, her own identity? Worse, what if someone else—this child—got hurt because of her?

"Mister Sloan says ole Buck is a bully," Pearl continued.

Abbey set the basket on the ground and began pulling apples off the tree. She handed them to Pearl who put them in the basket, counting each one as she did so.

". . . 'leven . . . twelve . . . fourteen."

"Thirteen," Abbey absently corrected.

"Oh, yeah. Thirteen . . . fourteen."

Over the next little while, Abbey deliberately narrowed the focus of her thoughts to the task at hand. It was the only way to calm herself enough to figure what she ought to do. At last she sighed and glanced down at the child. Pearl had been surprisingly quiet as though she understood Abbey's need to think. Abbey smiled. How could a child understand what she didn't understand herself?

"Lady Godiva. That was Charlotte's horse?"

"Yep." Pearl accepted another apple from Abbey. "Nineteen . . . Only she said it was a mare. One day, Miz Charlotte, she went off riding Lady G'diva, and that's when Mister Sloan got a letter from her. . . . Nineteen . . . tenteen."

"Twenty."

"Twenty," Pearl said agreeably. "Miz Charlotte, she hated the ranch, you know."

"I've heard that," Abbey returned.

"An' she hated us." Pearl's voice dropped to a conspiratorial whisper. "JJ, he said that was just fine 'cause everybody hated her, too." She glanced at Abbey. "But you know that already, huh?"

"Mmm," Abbey murmured in agreement.

"An' she was goin' to her papa. That's what she said."

"Ah," Abbey mused, holding onto the apple she had picked. "I wonder why Mr. Rafferty thought she had taken the stallion."

" 'Cause my pap saw her, and she had her horse and the Sun, too." Pearl took the apple from Abbey and set it in the basket. "He told Mister Sloan, and there was an awful ruckus."

"Mr. Rafferty yelled?"

Pearl nodded. "And throwed things, too."

"I see." The more Abbey heard, the more questions she had. Charlotte had left with her own horse and Sloan Rafferty's stallion. And Buck and Caleb seemed to know something about a mare. Lady Godiva or some other? Abbey wondered. What if the mare was Charlotte's horse?

Abbey turned that over in her mind, wondering if she should tell Sloan about the conversation. Since he seemed determined to misinterpret her most innocent contact with any of his men, she worried he'd accuse her again of some indiscretion. She wasn't sure how much more she could take. Further, talking to him had so far been a futile exercise, so why bother?

The information didn't get him any closer to finding his dratted stallion—what he wanted. And it wouldn't convince him to let her leave the ranch—what *she* wanted.

Abbey and Pearl pulled the last apple off the tree, moved the basket to a new tree, and began picking again. Out of the side of her eye, Abbey watched Silas rise from his stretch of shade beneath one of the trees, his tail wagging. Abbey raised her gaze and watched JJ and Consuela coming toward them. JJ's approach imitated the prance of a horse, and Consuela's stride was as determined as her expression.

Too late Abbey remembered Sloan's warning. Stay away from Consuela's children.

"Hi, Mama," Pearl called. "See what we're doin'? We gotta whole bunch of apples. 'Nough for pie an' applesauce an'—"

"Pearl Mae, it's time you were getting to your chores." Consuela's tone discouraged any discussion. "JJ will help you carry the basket back to the house."

"That's okay, Mama. Me an' Abbey—"

"Right now. Don't you be dawdling, either."

Pearl flashed her mother a dark look. "Yes, ma'am." She lifted her gaze to Abbey and smiled. "Tabby Cat, she has new kittens in the barn. Maybe we can go see 'em later."

Abbey smiled at her. "Maybe," she agreed. If Consuela allowed it. Though the woman looked none too happy, at least she wasn't carrying on loud enough to wake the dead like she had been yesterday. She felt sure as soon as Consuela realized she wasn't Charlotte, they would get along fine.

Consuela reached for one of the remaining apples on the small tree, plucked it, and polished it against her sleeve much as Abbey had done earlier. Consuela took a bite from the apple, her eyes on her children as they carried the half-full basket between them, bits of Pearl's chatter carrying back to them.

"She's a sweet little girl," Abbey said.

Consuela turned her dark-brown eyes on Abbey, her expression suspicious.

Abbey sighed, deciding the only way to deal with Consuela's distrust was to bring it into the open. "So, Charlotte doesn't cotton to babies or small children. Or hard work." She stared down at her own hands, her fingernails short and her palms toughened. "I guess I can understand why you don't like her."

Without answering, Consuela took another bite from the apple and slowly chewed, her gaze focused on the peaks that rose above the valley.

"I grew up in an orphanage," Abbey explained, wishing she knew the magic words that would make others see her for herself. "After the war ended, I worked my way west taking care of children."

Consuela shook her head. "If I let myself believe you're this other woman—"

"Abbey."

"—I'll be a bigger fool than Sloan Rafferty or any other man on this ranch ever was. I'm no fool." She met Abbey's gaze. "And I'll never forget or forgive what you did. No matter what you say or how nice you are to Pearl."

"I'm not Charlotte."

89

"I don't believe you." Consuela threw away the core of the apple. "My advice to you . . . Stop playing your game, tell Sloan what he wants to know, and leave."

"I would if I could."

"If you don't, it's only a matter of time before someone tries to . . ."

"What?" Abbey prompted.

"Kill you."

Abbey swallowed. It wasn't the first threat. Buck had made one yesterday and again today. For another woman to feel that way . . . Abbey's flicker of hope guttered like a wildly dancing flame about to run out of wax.

Consuela looked down, then shook her head. When she looked at Abbey, her eyes were bright with unshed tears. "Not me, though once I would have liked to have seen you dead. I thought about it—what I would say to you, what I would do to you if I ever saw you again. You're here, and Joey's dead." She took a ragged breath and swallowed. "It barely seems worth the effort."

"Charlotte seduced your husband?" Impossible, but it was the first question that popped into Abbey's head.

"You." Consuela's voice hardened. "Not some other woman. You."

Was there no man on this ranch Charlotte hadn't known in the carnal sense? Abbey shuddered in revulsion.

"Not because you loved him or wanted him. You simply had to prove you could have him." Consuela placed a flattened hand against her breast. "When he died, he died loving me. And when you go to your grave, no one will weep for you, no one will cry over your grave loving you. No one."

She swept a scathing glance over Abbey a last time. She opened her mouth as if to add something else, then abruptly closed it and hurried out of the orchard.

Heartsick and hope lost, Abbey watched her go.

Abbey spent the rest of the afternoon in the orchard, crossing the field between the barn and the orchard only twice. Once to find a couple more baskets to put the rest of the apples in. Once to find a saw to trim dead branches from the trees. Work had always provided solace, a channel for her frustration. Today it failed to soothe her in any way at all, and her frustration increased with her fatigue.

Venting her anger at Sloan, at Consuela, at this stupid tangle of events, Abbey attacked the dead branches, cutting them into small pieces that she stacked neatly at the edge of the orchard. Lord forgive her for contemplating violence, but she wanted to shake Consuela, and she wanted to rant at Sloan. Why couldn't they see the obvious? She wasn't Charlotte, no matter how much alike they looked.

She hadn't felt this helpless since she was a child. Then, she'd had no choice but submit to Pa's brutality. War had brought a different kind of cruelty—not so personal, but as devastating. And now . . . events were again beyond her control.

She considered and discarded a dozen different plans to escape. She knew what it was like to be cold and to wonder where her next meal would come from. Being lost in country she didn't know with winter approaching would be stupid. For the moment, she was safe. The first problem was figuring out where she was and how to get back to the Haverlys.

Aware long shadows had stretched across the field, Abbey worked on. In the distance, the sounds of the ranch subtly changed—those associated with a day coming to an end. Occasionally she caught a whiff of cooking onions and meat, an aroma that made her stomach rumble. The biscuit and apples she had eaten today hadn't filled her up. Abbey had no illusions. She wouldn't be a welcome addition to the dinner table. There would be no friendly conversation that included her, no one who cared what kind of a day she had.

She heard Consuela call to the children and Pearl's high voice answer. A door—or perhaps a gate—slammed somewhere, loud enough that Abbey raised her head a moment to listen. All she heard was an infant's cry and Consuela's soothing tones. The sounds reinforced the isolation Abbey felt.

She couldn't hide forever in this small orchard. But she wished she could. She couldn't indefinitely ignore Sloan Rafferty or Consuela or the other men on the ranch. But she wished she could. She couldn't snap her fingers and be back at the Haverlys. But she wished she could. Oh, how she wished it.

The only companion she had all afternoon was Silas, who dutifully followed her from the orchard to the barn and back again. He had been happy enough to play fetch when she threw a stick for him, but Abbey hadn't been able to forget his primary purpose. He was her guard. Unlike the others, he didn't taunt her or dislike her, but he couldn't be dissuaded from his purpose, either. She didn't resent him, but she wanted to.

Abbey stretched, arching against her hands at the small of her back. She gazed around, pleased at what she had accomplished even as she wished the work had been for her own farm.

"Practice for your own orchard." Someday, she would do these same chores for Abbey's Orchard. In some ways, she felt as though she had spent her whole life in anticipation of a future she wasn't sure would ever be hers. Despite Miss Mary's frequent admonishments not to count chickens that were not hatched, Abbey had slipped often into her dreams of one day being surrounded by her own family and firmly rooted onto her own land.

Facing the long rays of the setting sun, she smiled. At least she was farther west than she had hoped to get this year. Farther west, yes, but not necessarily closer to her dreams.

Gathering up the last of the branches she had pruned from the trees, Abbey stacked them neatly with the others. Again, she wondered how long ago the orchard had been planted and by whom. Not knowing how long the growing season was or how vigorously trees grew, she couldn't judge how old they were. The neglect had lasted longer than a single season—of that Abbey was sure.

Abbey glanced down at her dust-covered gown. That she had been working hard all afternoon was all too evident. Maybe, she'd be able to convince Sloan her actions weren't those of his wife. Heartened with that thought, Abbey brushed at the sleeves of her dress and pondered how to carry the heavy baskets of apples back to the house without help.

Movement beyond the trees caught her attention.

A huge bull ambled toward her, closer to the orchard than to the fence that separated the field from the compound next to the house and barn. Where had he come from? Abbey wondered. No livestock had been in the field all day. In fact, there was no sign animals had been left to graze in this field in a long while.

Compared to the placid milk cow, this was a beast of the wild. He walked as though he owned the ground.

Abbey knew enough about cows to realize she didn't want to be on foot around this one. She knew enough about bulls to know they were unpredictable at best. She took a tentative step backwards. The bull's attention focused on her, and his walk hastened into a trot.

Abbey glanced wildly around. She couldn't run. The animal would overtake her before she reached the safety of the fence. She couldn't simply stand here. She did, though, torn by indecision.

To her complete surprise, the animal stopped when it reached the edge of the trees. Warily, motionless, she watched the bull watch her. It snorted, then lowered its head. Abbey took another step backward, bumping the tree behind her. The bull backed up a pace or two and pawed at the ground.

Abbey stepped behind the tree, thought fleetingly of climbing it. The small apple tree wouldn't support her weight, nor would the lowest of the branches put her beyond the bull's horns.

Gored by a steer. JJ's calm voice rang through her memory in counterpoint to her horror at the reality.

Suddenly, the bull charged toward her. Its hooves thundered against the ground, and, in spite of herself, Abbey screamed. She turned and ran, zig-zagging through the young trees. Silas began barking, and Abbey glanced over her shoulder.

The dog flitted around the charging bull. At every step, it looked as though one of the immense hooves would crush him. At each step Silas twisted away, escaping sure injury by inches.

The bull right behind her, Abbey whirled around one of the trees. Breathing heavily, the bull rushed past. The barking dog nipped at its hocks.

Beyond the final row of trees, the bull circled around and again spotted her, lowered its head and charged. With a last look, Abbey ran, putting the largest of the trees between her and the bull. Behind her, she felt the animal's heat, heard its heaving breath as though it were her own. At the last instant, she swerved to the side, and again the bull bolted past her.

Gasping for breath, Abbey tripped over her own skirts and fell. Instantly, Silas ran between her and the bull. Snarling, the dog jumped in front of the animal. This time, one of the hooves caught Silas, and he tripped. In the next instant, the bull butted the dog's prone body and flung it into the air.

Silas landed with a high, whining howl.

"No!" Abbey screamed.

The bull circled around, shaking its massive head. When it

again caught sight of Abbey, it lunged toward her.

"Run!" It was a primal, roaring command that rang through her ears.

And run she did, tears of panic blurring her vision, her breath exploding painfully from her chest.

Sloan, mounted on a huge, dark horse, rushed past her. He brought the horse to a sudden halt, putting himself between Abbey and the charging bull. The animal veered around the horse. Sloan urged the horse into a gallop and chased after the bull, cracking a huge whip as they ran. The bull circled back. Sloan again put himself between Abbey and the crazed animal.

Abbey came to a stop beside one of the larger trees and brushed the tears from her eyes. Her sides heaving, she watched Sloan and his horse gradually bring the bull under control and move it toward the fence where it had less room to maneuver.

Abbey heard Silas whimper.

She lifted her skirts and ran toward him, her gait awkward and stumbling in her hurry. Fearing for Silas, for Sloan, for herself, she kept one eye on the bull as she ran.

Sloan laid the whip across his lap and picked up a length of rope coiled over the saddle horn. He whirled a lasso lazily above his head, at odds with the fast pace of his horse. Gracefully, the loop settled over the bull's head.

Sloan jerked the rope tight, and the horse came to a halt, backing onto its haunches. The bull jerked to a stop. With a snort, it turned on its new foe. Working as one, Sloan and his horse kept the rope taunt. A second later, another horse and rider—Jake, Abbey realized—appeared as if by magic and threw another rope over the bull's head. Caught between the two taunt ropes, the animal bucked, lunged from side to side, and shook its head.

Abbey dropped to her knees, tenderly touching the dog, fearing the worst. Silas labored for breath, and Abbey's own caught in her chest.

Gently she ran her hands down his side, murmuring soft words of reassurance to him. The dog raised his head and whined.

"I know, I know." Her voice broke as she relived the instant the bull had caught Silas. "It hurts. I know it does." Silas laid his head back on the ground and groaned.

Lifting her gaze, she saw several other men join Sloan and Jake. Now that the danger was over, the distance from the orchard to the corral at the edge of the compound didn't seem so far away. The bull snorted. Guiding the bull through the gate was no easy feat. She returned her attention to Silas, who took in a shuddering breath, then stilled.

Returning her attention to Silas, she gently pried open his mouth, looking for blood or other obvious signs of injury. There were none, and she breathed a sigh of relief. She didn't feel any obvious breaks in the ribs beneath the dog's thick, black pelt. When he took in another breath, she felt her own return. Gingerly, she turned him over, crooning to him all the while.

On his other side, her examination revealed no ribs that seemed to be more sore than the others. Sitting back on her heels, Abbey regarded the dog, afraid he might have injured something inside. She smoothed her hand over his soft muzzle, and he licked her hand.

Sloan's horse cantered across the field and came to a skidding stop next to her. Sloan slid off the horse and came toward her, his expression hidden by the shadow from his hat.

"You all right?" he asked.

Abbey met his gaze and nodded. "Silas, though . . ."

She glanced at the dog, who lay with his eyes closed, his sides moving slightly as he panted.

"Silas, up," Sloan commanded.

The dog opened his eyes and twisted his head so he could

look at his master. When he caught sight of Sloan, the dog thumped his tail a couple of times against the ground.

"Up." Sloan repeated the command, squatting in front of the dog. Concern somehow softened his usual harsh expression. He stripped off his leather work gloves and stuffed them in his rear pocket. Gently, he examined the dog in much the same way Abbey had.

"Nothing appears to be broken. Probably just got the wind knocked out of him."

"C'mon, boy." She scratched his ears, running her fingers over the velvety tips. "You can do it."

Sloan smoothed his large hand down the dog's coat, and Abbey folded her own hands in her lap.

Silas sighed and struggled to his feet, turning to Abbey. Bowing his head, he nuzzled her hands. She ran her palms up each side of his face and circled his neck with her arms. The dog rested his muzzle on her shoulder and groaned.

"Good boy," Abbey murmured, scratching the dog's ears.

"I'll be damned," Sloan muttered under his breath.

"What's wrong?"

"Never figured my dog would be a sucker for your soft touch like the rest of us."

Abbey held Sloan's gaze a long, hurtful moment. Without a word, she stood and whirled away, determined to put distance between herself and all the wounding things he said to her.

Before she had run three steps, Sloan caught her by the arm.

"Whoa. Now what's in your craw?"

"Can't you say anything nice?" Abbey asked. "Even once?"

He frowned. "I thought I had."

"Maybe I was petting him because I was worried—"

"And he liked it." Sloan let go of her. "Just like I always did. That's a pure fact." He threw his hands into the air and turned away from her. "Spare me from a woman's mind."

"And spare me from your insults," Abbey returned, her hands at her hips.

He faced her from five feet away. "I wasn't insulting you."

"You've done nothing but since I got here. If there's a way to see the worst, believe the worst, you find it."

He took a step towards her. "You earned it."

"Not me. Your wife."

He lifted his hat, ran his fingers through his hair, and shook his head. "Another damn conversation gone full circle."

Unwanted tears burned at the back of Abbey's eyes, and her throat tightened. "Yes," she agreed softly.

He glanced toward the dog, who stood watching them with his head lowered, as though he scarcely had energy to move. Sloan stared at the dog a moment, then turned toward his horse. Gathering the reins in his hand, he led the horse, taking a few steps in the direction of the house, then turned back to Abbey.

"Thanks for being worried about Silas."

Abbey figured this was as close to an apology as she was going to get, and she accepted it. "You're welcome."

"You coming?"

Abbey glanced back toward the orchard. "I've got apples to fetch."

His gaze followed hers toward the overflowing baskets. His attention lingered for a moment before traveling onto the neatly stacked dead branches and the saw leaning against them. He surveyed the orchard, his face expressionless. Abbey hadn't expected his thanks or even his appreciation, but this complete stillness as he examined her afternoon's efforts she hadn't anticipated, either.

Finally, he cleared his throat. "Leave the baskets. I'll send a couple of the men after them."

He stood waiting for her as though he expected her to join him. After a moment's hesitation, Abbey moved toward him, and the dog fell into step beside her.

"Who planted the orchard?" she asked.

One of his eyebrows rose. "My father. The summer of '66."

The date four years previous confirmed Abbey's hunch the orchard was young. On the heels of that, she realized Sloan's father had died not long after planting the orchard.

"Why the sudden interest?"

"I've always dreamed of having an orchard," she answered. "That's why I've been working my way toward California. I'm going to homestead some good acreage."

He didn't answer, and for that Abbey was relieved. Undoubtedly, he would have some pithy remark, and they'd be off and arguing again.

As they walked across the field, Abbey's gaze was drawn to their shadows moving in unison in front of them. Long, distorted, Sloan's image much bigger than hers. Even so, they seemed to have their heads together as though sharing secrets.

Abbey risked a glance at him. He met her gaze briefly before dropping his own. The silence stretched awkwardly between them, broken only by the evening calls of birds.

Intensely aware of him, Abbey wondered what he was thinking. Recalling his comments about petting, she shivered. Until that moment, she hadn't thought about what it would be like to touch a person the way she had touched Silas. Or to be touched like that. From beneath her eyelids, she ventured another quick look at Sloan. She imagined running her palms across Sloan's cheeks in the same way she had touched the dog's face. By his own confession, he had liked it. Her glance fell to his hands—big with long, square-tipped fingers and pronounced veins. Hands that had been surprisingly gentle when he examined the dog.

Heat flared up her neck and cheeks as she imagined his hands touching her. Much as she wanted to shove away the unaccustomed thought, it lingered.

Sloan and Abbey had nearly reached the edge of the field when a voice called out. The moment of near truce was abruptly ended when she watched Sloan stiffen. She glanced ahead and saw a short, rotund man standing next to a mule tethered at the corral, his cheery face encased in a smile. When his gaze lit on Abbey, the smile rounded into surprise.

Abbey looked from the stranger to Sloan, hoping his reaction would provide her some clue as to the man's identity. As usual, Sloan's expression revealed nothing of his thoughts. He met her gaze briefly, letting her precede him through the gate at the edge of the field.

"Well, now, Missus Rafferty, ain't you a sight for sore eyes." He walked toward Abbey and Sloan. "My, my, my."

Dressed in black, from his Derby to his trousers, and a white shirt, complete with a tie, Abbey pegged him as a professional man, perhaps a doctor.

The man extended his hand to Sloan.

"Preacher," Sloan said.

Abbey's eyes widened, and she took another quick survey of his clothes and cheery, blue eyes beneath bushy, gray eyebrows. A minister. She ought to have guessed.

He took both of Abbey's hands in his.

"Reverend," she murmured.

His eyebrows rose. "Now Missus Rafferty, I'm nothing but a circuit riding preacher."

He studied her face a moment, and Abbey flushed, suddenly remembering her black eye and the hand-shaped bruise on her cheek. His gaze narrowed suddenly and focused on Sloan.

"I know you were upset with her, but I don't hold with hitting a woman."

Sloan's glance fell to Abbey's face. "I don't either." With no more explanation than that, he clicked his tongue at the horse and led it across the compound and into the barn.

Preacher drew one of Abbey's hands into the crook of his arm and began strolling toward the house. "You pert near broke his heart when you run off last spring."

Abbey longed to insist on her own unique identity with yet another person. And she began to realize the senselessness of doing so, especially as he had so readily accepted her as Charlotte. So, she remained silent.

"I was talking to little JJ, and he said you were out picking apples this afternoon."

Abbey let out a sigh she hadn't realized she had been holding, and she nodded.

"That's fine," Preacher said. "Real fine. As I told you last winter, you give up your foolishness, pitch in with the chores and be a helpmate to Sloan, and things will be easier."

"A helpmate." Abbey paused and cleared her throat, which had grown suddenly tight again. A simple word, but one that identified how she thought a marriage should be. Helpmates to one another, bringing skills and strengths that were valued. Like her observation of Harriet and Ben Haverly. "That is what a man and woman should be to one another."

She hadn't intended it to be a question, but he said, "I believe so." He patted Abbey's hand again. "Sloan will come around. And he'll be glad for it." He caught Abbey's glance and smiled, then sniffed the air. "I surely do hope that is some of Consuela's fine cooking I smell." He pressed a hand against his generous stomach. "A man couldn't be expected to ride home on an empty belly. Particularly a man of the cloth."

Abbey smiled. "I'm certain she'll want you to stay for supper." She knew no such thing but hoped he would be welcome. He might be her key to an escape plan.

He fingered the inside breast pocket of his coat. "I mustn't forget; I have a letter for Consuela."

A sudden flare of hope lit within Abbey. "Would you post a letter for me?"

CHAPTER 8

"I'd be happy to mail your letter," Preacher said. "I reckon this means you've forgiven me."

"Forgiven you?" Abbey's heart did a little flip-flop as she realized this conversation was about to turn unexpectedly on itself. Just as most others had. She supposed she shouldn't have been surprised, but she was. She stopped walking and faced him, determined to set him straight and wishing she had told him right away she wasn't Charlotte. "Preacher, there's nothing to forgive. You see, I'm—"

"Bless you." He patted her hand. "It was never my intention to . . . ah . . . butt into your business."

"You don't understand." Abbey wished she hadn't come across another skeleton. She didn't want to contemplate what Charlotte might have done to a minister. In fact, the initial thought that Preacher might be another man Charlotte had lain with horrified her. "I'm—"

"There's nothing to understand," he interrupted again. "It's enough to know that you've decided to let go of the past. And you've come back to your husband. He's a hard man, but he's fair. You'll adjust to married life, I promise you." Preacher gave her hand one more pat. "That you decided to come back . . . Well, now, that's a fine thing."

"I didn't come of my own accord. I was abducted."

"I see." Preacher's color rose a little. "Surely it's not abduction when a lady is returned to her home."

"That's what they keep telling me."

"You don't seem so unhappy as you were," he continued. "In fact . . ." He paused and studied her a moment. "I'd say you've grown up these last months."

Abbey shook her head. "Preacher, how well do you know Charlotte Rafferty?"

He frowned and stared intently at her. "That's a very odd question, young lady."

"My name is Abigail Wallace."

"I see."

From his confused expression, Abbey doubted he saw at all. He scratched the side of his face, his eyes focused on the sun, which had settled into a notch between two peaks and cast brilliant streamers of golden light across the valley.

Sloan emerged from the barn with Sam, Jake, Caleb, and Buck.

"Miss Abbey." Sam doffed his hat.

Jake touched his fingers to his hat and strode past without speaking.

"Miss Abigail," Caleb acknowledged. "Evenin', Preacher. Haven't seen you out this way in a coon's age."

"Miz Charlotte." Buck's sly smile twisted his lips. "Preacher."

The minister's eyes narrowed as he watched the men stride toward the house. When Sloan came to a stop in front of Abbey and Preacher, he asked, "Is this woman your wife?"

Sloan's dark eyes settled on Abbey's face for an endless moment. She swallowed, and heat suffused her cheeks. Knots gathered in her stomach, though she couldn't imagine what he might say that would make things any worse than they already were.

"My wife," he said at last, "insists she is Miss Abigail Wallace, recently of the Shenandoah Valley." He cleared his throat. "Her grandmother's last name was Wallace, and until the war started, that's where she lived."

Abbey felt Preacher's attention shift back to her. His confusion softened into compassion, and something close to relief fluttered through Abbey. At last. Someone besides Silas and Pearl who would understand.

"It will be all right." His tone was that condescending one reserved for the very young or the very stupid.

Abbey's relief fell into seething anxiety. "You don't believe me."

"I know what you told me last winter. If there was any way to leave this God forsaken country and wipe it from your memory, you would."

Abbey pressed her hands together to keep them from shaking. "Are you suggesting," she asked quietly, "that I have a whole lifetime of memories that I made up?" Her voice rose. "That never happened? That I went to bed one night as one person and awoke the next morning as someone else?"

"You believe you're Miss Wallace?" he asked.

"I don't *believe* I'm Abigail Wallace," she stated. "I *am* Abigail Wallace."

Preacher's attention shifted to Sloan. "As Abigail Wallace, perhaps she can accept what she couldn't as Charlotte. In light of all the trouble she caused, maybe this is for the best."

"I am not Charlotte," Abbey stated emphatically, resisting the urge to stamp her foot.

"Now, now." Preacher once again patted her hand as though she were five. "Don't you be getting yourself all in a dither."

"And furthermore, I am *not* married to this man." Abbey yanked her hand out of Preacher's. At best, he thought she was a liar. And at worst, crazy. Crazy, for pity's sake. She didn't dare think about that, or she would be.

Preacher winked at Sloan. "Well, now, that's an easy enough problem to remedy. Seein' as to how you're already married to him, and I'm a preacher man."

"Over my dead body." Abbey stomped away from the two men.

"That young lady still has a temper," Preacher commented.

"Yep," Sloan agreed.

She climbed the steps to the porch, crossed it in two strides, and flung open the door to the cabin, which she slammed behind her. Silas had trotted after her, but he wasn't fast enough to slide through the door with her. He glanced over his shoulder toward Sloan, as if offering an apology, and sat down in front of the door.

"Do you think she is—" Preacher tapped his temple—"in her right mind?"

Until Preacher mentioned it, Sloan hadn't considered Abbey might be daft. Abbey. He shook his head. Charlotte . . . Her.

"Crazy?" He'd seen an insane man once during the war, babbling nonsense and drooling like a baby, and Abbey—Charlotte, damnation—was nothing like that. "She's not crazy."

"Her behavior is its usual, then?"

Her temper, her defiance, her plans—those were familiar. In other ways, she hadn't been herself at all. Charlotte had hated the endless work. Hired hands and servants—those were the people who worked. She didn't lift a lily-white hand. Until today.

"No. She hasn't been herself."

"Whatever she calls herself, she looks like your wife."

"That she does."

Preacher tipped his head. "As I said, perhaps this is for the best."

Sloan doubted that. Personally, he was still waiting for the other boot to drop. He mounted the steps, then held the door open for Preacher.

"Clean up the language, gents." Jake followed Sloan and

Preacher into the kitchen. "A man of God is in our midst."

His announcement generated a chorus of chuckles, not the least of which came from Preacher. "Jake, you old rapscallion. You mean you'd rob me of the chance to save a few souls? If there's no sinnin', I'd be plumb out of work." He took off his hat and smoothed his hand over his mostly bald head. "Men who would cuss in front of the lovely Consuela and her children—why such a thing can't be."

"There's women and children here?" Eli Stodges swiveled his head around and pretended great surprise when his gaze lit on JJ and Pearl, both of whom promptly giggled. "Lands sake, there is. Children. Right there!"

Preacher hung his hat on the peg next to the door and hugged Consuela when she greeted him. His wife, Sloan noted, was conspicuous by her absence.

"Where is she?" he asked.

"Miz Charlotte?" Buck questioned.

"Miss Abigail?" Caleb asked.

"Miss Abbey, she went to her room," Pearl informed him. When Sloan's gaze lit on her, she nodded her head for emphasis. "She did. I saw her. And guess what? She wants to see Tabby Cat's kittens."

Sloan hung his own hat on the peg, tousled Pearl's hair as he passed her, and strode through the house toward the bedrooms. At her bedroom door, he knocked, then pushed the door open without waiting for her to respond.

She stood at the dresser in front of a wash basin, her bodice partially unbuttoned and her sleeves rolled up. Her face and neck were damp, as was the washcloth in her hand. Her sunburn looked better, and the swelling around her eye was down. The bruises on her face looked, if anything, worse.

In the mirror above the dresser, he caught her gaze. She neatly folded the washcloth and put it on the lip of the bowl.

Though she held his gaze, color flushed her cheeks; a rosy hue began at the swell of her bosom.

"Was there something you wanted?"

"You will come to supper," he stated.

Her eyebrows rose. "Of course."

Feeling surprisingly defensive and off balance from her unexpected agreement, he moved toward the dresser. "I figure I'll wash up first."

Turning her back toward him, she murmured, "Help yourself."

Sloan poured a bit more water into the bowl from the pitcher and hastily washed his face, forearms, and hands. Through the mirror, he watched her bent head and slender back. Too easily, he imagined her buttoning the bodice of her dress. He had undressed her enough times that the thought of her dressing should have held no allure of the forbidden. Shouldn't have, but it did. She rolled down her sleeves, buttoned the cuffs, and patted her hair into place, then left the room, all without giving him a glance.

And he cursed himself for being five kinds of a fool for thinking she had looked pretty with her face all damp. For wanting to talk with her, for half believing her tale of always wanting an orchard, for wishing she'd been like this when he married her. Seeing the bull chase her had scared a dozen years off his life. He never wanted to be that scared for Abbey again.

"Abbey," he whispered. "Damn. Not Abbey. Charlotte . . . Charlotte." The woman who had taught him everything he knew about betrayal. He clamped a tight lid on those painful memories and the even more painful recognition that she had used him. That she was probably using him even now. This time he was on guard.

"Charlotte," he repeated.

With a muttered curse, he threw down the damp towel. He

had crossed to the door of the bedroom when a niggle of odd awareness nudged him to a halt. He moved slowly back into the room, searching for whatever it was that had snagged his awareness. What was out of place? Absently, he picked up the damp cloth she had used to wash her face. The aroma of the soap Consuela made clung to the cloth.

Sloan brought it to his nose and sniffed again. All he smelled was the soap, lightly scented with some concoction of native herbs and plants. Not the heady scent of roses Charlotte preferred. Sloan set it down, then returned to the kitchen.

Seated on the end of the table across from Pearl and JJ, Abbey noticed instantly when Sloan appeared in the doorway between the kitchen and the front room. His dark eyes caught hers briefly, then slid past her to the two children. Pearl winked at him, and he winked back.

"JJ, if your mother gives permission, I'll take you riding tomorrow morning," Sloan said.

JJ's eyes lit, and he sought Consuela's gaze. She gave her head a quick nod, and he grinned. "Sure."

"Mister Sloan," Pearl said, "I can ride, too, can't I?"

"No, you can't," Consuela said. "Don't you be pestering Mister Sloan, either."

"Aw, Mama," Pearl returned.

Sloan brushed a hand over her hair. "You pay attention to your ma. When she gives the word, I'll teach you."

"Well, it's gotta be soon afore I get old."

"Old like me an' Preacher?" Eli teased.

A dimple appeared in Pearl's cheek as she grinned at the wizened cowhand. "That's pretty old, huh? Older than eleventy eleven."

"And how old is that?" Eli asked.

"Old. Very, very old," Pearl assured him, grinning when the cowhands laughed at her answer.

109

Abbey found herself smiling at the children, acknowledging her hunch about them was confirmed. The adults in their lives took good care of them. An incredible gift, whether they ever realized it or not, one that gave Abbey renewed hope the misunderstanding of her identity would somehow be resolved.

Most surprising to Abbey was Sloan's interest in and gentleness with the children. He encouraged JJ's conversation, belying the conventional wisdom children were to be seen and not heard. Sloan listened, really listened to the boy as though what he said mattered. No more able to resist Pearl's impish charm than anyone else, Sloan responded to her silliness in kind. His eyes danced as he caught up on the children's day.

With a certainty Abbey didn't question, she was positive Charlotte's dislike of these children had hurt this man. But then, much about the woman's behavior had hurt everyone, not just Sloan. When he caught Abbey's gaze, she glanced away. She didn't want to like him or sympathize with his problems or find him attractive. She risked another glance at him, noticing a dimple that creased one cheek when he smiled. And those cold, cold eyes of his . . . they weren't cold now. Uncomfortable with the turn of her thoughts, Abbey forced herself to pay attention to the other people around the table.

During the meal, conversation centered on Preacher, who, after a quick blessing, relayed news from the other families up and down the Arkansas Valley. He seemed to know everyone, and he also seemed to have some official duties that went beyond being a man of the cloth. Abbey pieced together impressions that didn't make the ranch so isolated as she'd thought.

Evidently, it was a scant half-day's ride from a place called Poncha where there was a stage stop and a post office. A bit farther up the valley in the other direction was another town, Nathrop, that had a flour mill and brand new lumber mill that had supplied the materials for Sloan's new barn. From what

Abbey could gather, there was quite a brisk trade between farmers and ranchers in the area and a mining town farther north called Oro City. The names of neighbors jumbled together in her head, but she was determined to remember the names of the towns.

Gradually, the conversation drifted back to the happenings on the ranch, which included a planned delivery of a few head of cattle to Oro City and the bull's rampage this afternoon.

"When I figure out which of you put the bull in the field this afternoon, you're gonna be looking for another job." Sloan glanced around the table, pinning each man with a hard stare.

"Maybe he just wandered through an open gate," Sam said.

"Not bloody likely," Sloan returned. "The gate between the field and the north pasture was closed, and I found grain sprinkled on the ground inside the field. He was lured there, sure as I'm sitting here."

"Buck, weren't you working in the north pasture this afternoon?" Jake asked.

Buck flushed. "I ain't got nothin' to do with it."

Abbey glanced around the table, then dropped her gaze to her own plate, Sloan's statement echoing through her head. Until now she hadn't given any thought to how the bull might have gotten into the field. The fact someone might have deliberately put the beast with her made her shiver when a chill slid down her spine. Unyielding as Sloan had been, and brutal as Jake had been, only one man at the table had threatened her—twice in fact. Abbey looked at Buck and found him staring at her, his pale eyes defiant.

Despite Sloan's anger and his assurance of retribution, to point a finger at Buck would do her no good at all. Her appetite gone, Abbey pushed her food around the plate.

When Consuela excused herself from the table and went into the front room to feed the baby, Abbey excused herself, as well.

Out of long habit, she began cleaning up the dishes.

Intensely aware of Sloan's scrutiny and Preacher's beaming at her, she did her best to ignore both. The other men finished eating, and all but Preacher and Sloan left the house. Pouring himself a cup of coffee from the pot, Sloan stretched his legs out in front of him.

Pearl and JJ carried their dishes to the sink.

"Time for your lessons." Consuela returned to the kitchen, carrying the contented infant at her shoulder. Her eyes swept over the room, her surprise palpable that the kitchen was clean and ready for the next meal.

"I'll fetch the slates." Pearl ran into the front room. She returned a moment later, carrying the slates and a primer. "Do you want to see me write my name, Miss Abbey?"

"Yes," Abbey responded, remembering many such evenings when she had practiced her letters around Miss Mary's table after supper was finished. "I'd like that."

"I won't be changing my mind," Consuela whispered to Abbey.

"I know," Abbey whispered back. "But if she wants to show her letters, I'm going to look at them."

Aware Consuela disliked her, Abbey still could have done without the reminder. For a little while longer, she would have liked to indulge in the fantasy. To imagine this kind of evening after she had her own place in California. Orphans lived everywhere, and since she was unlikely to marry, they were the only children she was likely to have.

For a moment, however brief, this evening had felt like those in the orphanage—a pleasant mixture of chores and learning. Somehow, Miss Mary had made them all feel important. Abbey wanted that for herself again with an intensity that frightened her.

Her glance strayed to Sloan, who watched JJ's tracing of his letters. What kind of a father would he be? He looked up suddenly, and Abbey felt heat bloom in her cheeks. She returned her attention to scrubbing a non-existent stain from the drainboard.

"So what's really on your mind, Preacher?" Sloan pushed the coffee pot toward him. "You don't come out this way purely for a social visit."

Preacher refilled his cup. "I had a letter from your wife's father, and I figured you'd like some notice that he's planning to pay you a visit before winter sets in."

Sloan stared at his wife's back a moment, remembering the missive he'd sent to Charlotte's family, hoping against hope they'd let him know she had arrived safely back in Virginia. Now that she was here again, he'd need to let them know she had returned. Never mind he'd have to leave out it wasn't by her own choice.

"As you can imagine, William Flanders was considerably upset that his daughter is missing." Preacher took a sip of his coffee. "Now that Missus Rafferty has returned, I'll be able to write him that she is safe and sound. It's unlikely, however, a letter would reach him in time."

She turned around, her mouth open to undoubtedly protest again that she wasn't Charlotte. Sloan shook his head, and she clamped her lips together. Just as her ready agreement to eat supper in the kitchen had surprised him earlier, her restraint now did also.

"Why'd he write to you instead of getting back to me?"

Preacher's color rose, and he cleared his throat. "Well, now, my recent election as probate judge seems to have a bearing on that."

Sloan wondered at Preacher's obvious discomfort. It was no secret he couldn't live off the meager offerings gathered from his far-flung flock. He had carried mail between Oro City and

Cañon City for several years, and as he knew most homestead-
ers and ranchers in the valley; his election as probate judge had
been an obvious, sensible choice.

Preacher fumbled in his breast pocket and brought out a pair
of envelopes. "Ah, Consuela, I have a letter for you."

Consuela stared at the letter, myriad emotions chasing across
her face. Rocking the baby against her shoulder, she carefully
broke the seal and unfolded the sheet before sitting on the rocking chair next to the fireplace. Sloan noted she didn't read it, as
though she feared what might be inside.

The other letter, Preacher withdrew from the envelope and
unfolded. While Preacher scanned the page, Sloan watched
Consuela grip her own letter, and he understood how she might
feel. He was positive he wasn't going to like whatever it was
Preacher was going to tell him.

A moment later, Preacher began reading.

I always had questions regarding Mister Rafferty's
character, and it was with the greatest reluctance I gave my
blessing to the union between him and my daughter. I fear
his inquiry into Charlotte's disappearance may be a ruse to
throw suspicions away from himself. In your capacity as
probate judge for the county, you have a degree of stature
and authority. I pray you'll look into the matter on my
behalf and contact the law if you come across any reason
to suspect my daughter is the victim of foul play. Several
matters in Washington require my immediate attention, but
I shall be free to travel west before the close of September.
Fortunately, the completion of the Union Pacific Railway
makes it possible for me to travel to Colorado and return
home before the onset of winter. I will look you up upon
my arrival.

"Foul play, huh?" Sloan wrapped his hands around his cup. His brother, Jonah, had cautioned him that's likely how Charlotte's family would view Sloan's role in her disappearance if she had not arrived home safely. It was a warning Sloan had disregarded.

"A father's understandable worry, under the circumstances." Preacher caught Abbey's glance. "You should write to your family immediately and let them know you're well." His smile became more guarded. "Perhaps I should write a letter on your behalf."

"I can write my own letter, but thank you."

"What letter is this?" Sloan asked.

Abbey lifted her chin and met his gaze. "My letter to the Haverlys. You already said you didn't care if I wrote, only that you wouldn't post it for me. Preacher has offered to do so."

"Is it ready to go?"

"Not yet."

"I'll see that she gets into Poncha to mail her letter," he said. "There's no need to delay you any further tonight, Preacher."

The minister smiled. "I don't mind waiting."

"And I'm sure my wife doesn't want to impose."

Preacher stood, retrieving his hat. "It would be good for you two to come into Poncha, you know. Folks will be anxious to see you. There is always an open pew for you on Sunday morning."

Abbey doubted that, unless Charlotte had made a vastly different impression on people there. But she wanted to see this town . . . needed to know how to get there.

Preacher made his goodbyes, pausing a moment in the front room to speak with Consuela. Sloan followed Preacher into the front room. Abbey sat down at the table with the children, admiring Pearl's neatly drawn letters and absently listening to both Pearl's chatter and the more serious conversation in the other room. Sloan came back into the kitchen, his expression thoughtful as he approached Consuela.

"Do you want to go back to Santa Fe?" Sloan asked.

Consuela sighed, long and ragged. "I don't know. I always hoped Papa would forgive me for marrying Joey. This. I didn't expect this."

"Family is too important," Sloan said. "If you want to go, I'll take you."

"I can't ask that of you. You could be gone weeks. There's too much here."

"I'll make it work."

"What about the most recent thefts? I heard what Eli told you last night."

"Consuela—"

"And I know you're worried about Jonah. You're not going to rest easy until you know he's safe." An instant of silence followed. "You can't leave the ranch right now, and you know it."

"Hang the ranch."

Consuela choked, a sound that could have been a sob or laughter. "So say you, Sloan Rafferty. I was with you when you buried your father and brother out back. I know how important it is to you—more than the stallion, more than . . . her." She cleared her throat. "My papa . . . he says he'll come for me."

During the moment of silence that followed, Abbey saw the children were listening even more intently than she was. Pearl's legs swung from the chair, and she caught Abbey's eyes.

"My mama, she's crying," Pearl whispered. "I can tell. I don't like it when she cries."

"I'm sure everything will be all right," Abbey whispered back.

"I'll need to let him know soon," Consuela said. "I don't want to travel during the winter with the children and the baby."

After Abbey retreated to Charlotte's room, she searched through all of Charlotte's belongings, looking for a Bible or other records that might provide some clue. Other than some letters from Charlotte's mother, Abbey had found nothing. The letters didn't reveal any of the information Abbey had hoped for—only personal news, mild complaints about how busy William Flanders was, and references to a full social life. Her grandmother had told her: "Never forget you're a Flanders." And William Flanders was Charlotte's father.

What did it mean? Would she ever know the story of where she had come from or why she had been given to Ma and Pa Hawkins? She tried to imagine Consuela giving away JJ or Pearl Mae. Sure as the sun would rise tomorrow morning, Consuela would never give up her children.

Abbey had long ago vowed she would stop wondering about her earliest memories in the big house. Yet, here she was, stuck with the same unanswerable questions haunting her. Nothing she could do about that. As Miss Mary had been fond of saying, "All you can do is take care of right here and right now. The rest is out of your hands." With that thought in mind, she found paper, a pen, and a small bottle of ink.

As soon as she wrote *Dear Mr. and Mrs. Haverly,* she couldn't decide what to say. That she had been abducted because she had been mistaken for someone else sounded too much like one of Miss Mary's fairytales. So, she went to bed, too aware she was a prisoner despite the comfort of a bed that she didn't have to share with two or three others. Nor was she going to sleep hungry as had been too often the case during the war.

Sleep eluded her, though, while she stared at the dark ceiling above the bed, her thoughts racing. This was only her second night at the ranch. In some ways, she felt as though she had been here for weeks. The Haverlys seemed less real, yet it had been less than a week since she had last seen them.

The problems Consuela had so succinctly outlined while

talking to Sloan and Preacher seemed far bigger than her own. Cattle rustled, a horse stolen, and a wife missing. Some other piece of the puzzle hovered at the edge of her awareness, but she couldn't quite place it.

Rolling over to her side, she thought about the day, the people who lived here, what she had learned about the ranch. It was prosperous, enough so for the hiring of hands and for Sloan to afford an expensive stallion. Equally evident was how hard everyone worked, including Sloan.

Her memory of the wealthy men of the Shenandoah Valley was of people who had time for elaborate social gatherings, of a life supported by the backbreaking effort of the slaves and sharecroppers who worked the land. In comparison to the ranch's prosperity, those farms had been far wealthier. The big house that dominated her earliest memories had been the grandest of them all. Abbey closed her eyes, casting her thoughts as far back in her childhood as she could.

Dark green shutters had once framed the wide windows of the second floor, and a wide porch had provided a place to sit during the summer. The images filled her mind of her last visit when all that had remained of the house were its chimneys. The people who lived in that house had benefited from the work they didn't perform. If that was the life Charlotte had come from, it was no wonder she hadn't fit in here.

What if she never found out what the relationship between them was? Abbey wondered. What if . . . oh, dear heaven. What if it was as Preacher had said, and she really was Charlotte?

Abbey sat up in bed, her heart suddenly pounding.

She was from the Shenandoah Valley. And so was Charlotte.

She had a brooch that had been a family heirloom. And so had Charlotte.

She had a grandmother, a woman whose grave she had seen, whose last name was Wallace. And she knew that woman's daughter had a child named Abbey. And she was Abbey. Not Charlotte. Abbey. Wasn't she?

Yer mama's crazy as a coon, came Pa Hawkins's remembered taunt. *And you keep on sinnin', yer mind is gonna be gone. Just like hers.*

Could Preacher be right? What if she *were* Charlotte? What if she had lost her mind?

Could she be like the poor child that Miss Mary had taken in who had no memory of her life until a few days before she came to the orphanage? Was insanity that simple? You simply woke up one day with no idea of who you really were?

Except Abbey had memories. She knew the names of the other children—Molly, Beatrice, Lucy, and Olivia. And the boys—Jack, Obadiah, Franklin, and Daniel. An insane person couldn't make up a name like Obadiah. Abbey had sat in Miss Mary's lap on summer nights and gazed for hours at the stars, learning the names of the constellations. The Big Dipper. Cassiopeia. The Little Dipper. The North Star. She sighed, the scent of the starch on Miss Mary's collar so potent a memory she was sure she could smell it. Surely something that vivid wouldn't be a made-up memory. Would it?

Driven by the need to reassure herself, Abbey slipped from the bed, opened the door into the hallway, and padded into the front room of the house. Scarcely aware of Silas's presence beside her, Abbey went outside onto the porch.

The crisp scent of night filled her lungs when she inhaled deeply, her breath coming out in a loud sigh when she exhaled. Despite the chill, she stepped off the porch aware of Silas silently matching her steps. She came to a stop and tipped her head back.

A brilliant canopy of stars twinkled, so bright, so numerous, that for a moment none of the patterns she had learned so long ago were evident. Anxiety bubbled through her as she searched the sky.

At last, she found the Big Dipper. From the tip of its handle, she located the North Star. Her uneasiness faded as she identified the other constellations she had learned so long ago. She sighed, flung her arms wide, and twirled around.

From the shadows of the porch, Sloan watched her, wondering what she was doing. Too restless to sleep, he had come outside. The night was the sort he loved—cool, clear, and quiet except for the occasional hoot of an owl and the singing of a distant pack of coyotes.

The last thing he had expected was for Abbey to emerge from the house, and his heart sank. At last, he'd have his proof that her odd behavior was a ruse, and he'd dreaded finding out which of the men she had a liaison with.

To his complete surprise, her attention was entirely focused on the sky, as though she had found a great treasure. He could see nothing of her expression, but he heard her sigh, and he could have sworn it was one of great relief. Sloan tipped his head, trying to see out from beneath the eaves of the porch.

In her bare feet and her white nightgown, she looked vulnerable and virginal—the two things he knew for certain she was not. Positive as he was about that, he drank in the sight of her. For an instant, he hoped she'd never remember she had been Charlotte. Daft or not, the woman she had been today had been the one he had yearned for—a partner unafraid of pulling her own weight, a spitfire who knew how to hold her own with him and when to keep quiet, a generous woman who had cared more for Silas than for her own safety.

She sighed again, wrapped her arms around herself, and turned back toward the house.

"C'mon, Silas," she whispered. "Back to bed."

Dutifully, the dog followed her into the house, the door clicking softly behind them.

Sloan stepped off the porch and looked at the brilliant sky. What had she been looking for? He stared at the stars, remembering childhood superstitions and wishes made upon a falling star.

Wishes. Who the hell was he fooling? His wishes hadn't come true, nor were they likely to no matter how much he wanted them.

And then . . . a single falling star blazed across the sky.

CHAPTER 9

Abbey rose early the following morning and finished her letter to the Haverlys. While she dressed, she rehearsed what she wanted to say to Sloan. Only he wasn't at breakfast, nor did she see him when she went to milk the cow, nor was he anywhere in sight as she returned to the house with the milk bucket. In fact, none of the men were to be seen.

"Where do you suppose he is?" she mused, shivering a bit when a chilly gust of wind rustled through the leaves of the cottonwoods that cascaded to the ground in a golden shower.

His dog, never far from her side, nudged her free hand as if in answer, while she carried the milk bucket to the house. Inside, the aroma of onions and beef stock wafted through the air. Consuela stirred a pot on the stove. Abbey set the bucket of milk near the door and covered it with a towel.

"Do you know where Sloan is?" Abbey asked.

Consuela didn't look up from the flour-covered table where she was kneading bread. "Your husband?"

"Yes." Abbey shook her head. "No—he's not my husband. Mr. Rafferty."

"He and Jake left early and won't be back until supper time."

So much for posting her letter today. She stood there a moment, tapping her toe against the floor until Consuela said, her tone sharp, "He is a busy man."

"Of course, he is." Abbey wondered where he had gone, then decided it didn't matter. However tempted she was to vent her frustration, there was no way she was going to do or say anything to further convince Consuela that she was Charlotte. "I'm going to the orchard."

On the way, she detoured by the barn to get the tools she would need to prune the trees, but her attention was on the gate that marked the boundary of her prison and on the dog who remained at her side no matter what. Maybe if she gave him a soup bone, she could keep him occupied long enough to make her escape.

And then what? She didn't know, but she couldn't sit around and wait for a rescue that might never come. Charlotte's father? She doubted he would be of much help even if he recognized she wasn't his daughter. Frustration at the situation simmered through her all day while she thought of and discarded one escape plan after the other. She was resourceful, and she liked to believe she could make it back to Denver on her own, but a few things worried her, chief among them, the weather. Today, the clouds hung over the distant mountain peaks, gray and angry looking. Now and then, when they shifted, she saw they had left a fresh sprinkling of snow. If the tales she had heard about Colorado winters were true, getting back to Denver after the snow came would be nearly impossible.

Though her task with the orchard kept her occupied, most of her attention was focused on the barn. Late afternoon settled into dusk, and Abbey returned to the barn, putting away the tools where she had found them. Consuela was preparing supper and didn't want any help. So, Abbey went back outside, shivering against the chill, which finally drove her back inside. Consuela ignored her so completely she might have been invisible. Even Pearl and JJ seemed to pick up on the tension, and they didn't speak to her, either, though Pearl offered a smile. All the hands except Sloan and Jake came in for supper when Consuela rang the bell on the porch.

After the meal, Consuela disappeared into the adjoining room where the baby's cradle was. She came back into the room, wrapped in a shawl, the baby nearly hidden within her arms and the other two children at her side.

"Mr. Rafferty expects us each to earn our keep." Her gaze went from Abbey to the dishes piled at the end of the table, her unspoken command as clear as the dinner bell. "The children and I are going home."

JJ led the way outside, and Abbey followed them to the door, aware that, even as spacious as the house was, Consuela or the children didn't live in it. They crossed the yard to a smaller, more rustic structure than the house. They went inside, and, a moment later, light flared through a small window, suggesting a lamp had been lit. Abbey envied the companionship.

She turned back to the kitchen and the chore of cleaning up, sure everyone would be surprised she didn't mind the work. If nothing else, it helped the time to pass.

It had been dark for more than an hour when she heard horses and voices outside. She opened the door in time to see Sloan and Jake dismount. Sam met them at the barn and took the horses. Both men walked toward the house as though they had ridden a hundred difficult miles. While they shed their coats, Abbey ladled up the stew still warming on the stove. Sloan barely acknowledged her when he and Jake sat at the table, though he lifted an eyebrow when she set his dinner in front of him. They ate silently and as though they hadn't eaten in days.

Common sense urged her to wait until tomorrow to talk to Sloan about posting her letter. But the sense of necessity that had bubbled through her all day won out.

"I'd like to go to town tomorrow," she announced.

Sloan raised his head, and his dark eyes were their usual cold. She had the feeling she'd surprised him, though nothing in his expression gave away anything of his thoughts.

"I've finished my letter to the Haverlys," she said, "and I'd like to go to town to mail it. The sooner Mr. Haverly confirms I'm in his employ, the sooner—"

He blinked, which somehow demolished her concentration.

She cleared her throat. "And then you'll realize . . . and . . . we can clear up this mess."

His gaze held hers an endless moment. He glanced at Jake, then dipped his bread into the gravy, once more loading his spoon with a bite of stew and putting it in his mouth. He ate that bite plus three more without answering.

"Mr. Rafferty. I'd—"

"I heard you." He set down the spoon and picked up his cup of steaming coffee. "You give me what I want, and I'll give you what you want."

"You can't keep me here forever."

"I can. I will." He set the cup down without drinking. "The thing is, I can't be duped like Preacher, who thinks you've turned over a new leaf."

"He thinks I'm crazy." Sudden frustration erupted over having her plans evaporate like morning mist. She stamped her foot. "I am not crazy."

"Maybe not, but the thing is, we went down the Arkansas today to the German colony." He paused as though that news would mean something to her, which it didn't. "Carl Wursten said the same thing today that he told me when you left."

He watched her as though expecting her to say something. "And that was?"

"You know damn well. You offered to sell him the Cimarron Sun."

"Your wife. Not me." Abbey firmed her chin.

"Mr. Wursten offered his sympathy that my own wife would swindle me out of my own property." Sloan looked at her then,

125

his gaze piercing. "He recommended I take a strap to you."

The remembered horror and humiliation of being beaten made tears spring to her eyes. "You wouldn't dare."

Before the tears could spill, she turned around and ran to her room—not hers. Charlotte's.

In this moment, Abbey hated her as much as everyone else did.

"Mornin', Miss Abbey," Caleb said.

Abbey returned the greeting as she met his gaze over the milk cow. Each morning over the last four days, Caleb had stopped to watch her milk and converse a little. Though he was friendlier than anyone else, except for Pearl, something in his manner had Abbey always on her guard. Even so, she welcomed his company and these moments of conversation. If he compared her to Charlotte, he hid it better than the others, especially Sloan and Consuela.

Sooner or later Jake, Eli, or Sam would show up and carry the bucket of milk back to the house. Fortunately, Buck had avoided her and, in fact, had been missing from the dinner table the last two nights.

"You're lookin' well today," Caleb said. "The bruise is almost gone."

Abbey touched her cheek and glanced around the barn as she resumed milking the cow. For once, Jake wasn't close by. He hadn't said more than hello to her in days, and though he didn't seem to pay her any attention, Abbey was intensely aware of his presence. No matter what she took on as a chore, he seemed to have something to do that kept him in the vicinity—as much of a watchdog as Silas. She couldn't forget the beating she'd taken at his hands, nor could she forget Sloan had all but threatened to beat her.

She toyed with the idea of asking Caleb to take her letter.

Despite his being friendly enough, she didn't quite trust him, but the bigger worry was Sloan would somehow find out and construe the worst. Sloan Rafferty was, she reminded herself, the key to getting away from here, not Caleb.

She continued to plot her escape, but every plan she'd imagined had too many pitfalls. Oh, she might be able to slip out during the middle of the night, but without transportation or a clear idea of where she was—much less, how to get back to Denver—that would be stupid. And darned if she would compound her problems by being stupid. So far, she was no closer to visiting either Poncha or Nathrop, the two closest communities, than when she first arrived. All her avenues of escape seemed as illusive as Sloan's missing stallion.

"You're lookin' all lost in thought," Caleb said.

"I'm wondering how long it will be until Sloan believes me when I tell him I don't know where his horse is," Abbey replied. "If he's so all fired determined to find it, why isn't he out looking for it himself?"

Caleb pushed his hat back on his head. "Every time he leaves, trouble crops up. Cattle get stolen, men get hurt . . . the barn burns down."

"You make it sound like someone has a grudge against him."

"Maybe."

"Why?"

Caleb turned so he could look outside, and Abbey had the feeling he wanted to make sure he wasn't overheard. "Maybe he took somethin' that belongs to someone. Or maybe he killed somebody."

"If that's so, why wouldn't the marshal arrest him?"

Caleb laughed. "This is the West. Oh, there is the law. The real law is the one a man makes for himself. By holdin' what is his. By avengin' what was done to him."

"Are you talking about Sloan? Or you?" Abbey asked.

"Maybe me. All I'm sayin' is maybe Sloan Rafferty had to decide which he wanted more—his horse or his ranch."

That statement surprised Abbey. The ranch operation had seemed solid to her. In fact, she had made a few notes to herself about details she needed to keep in mind when she had her own place.

"Nothin' in life is certain. And, since the stallion hasn't turned up, chances are, it's not to be found."

The statement was matter of fact enough, but something in Caleb's voice made the words seem threatening. "I hope that's not true." Abbey returned to the milking. "He seems real determined that I'm staying put until I tell him where it is." She raised her head and met his gaze. "You don't happen to know where the stallion is, do you?"

His smile slipped a little. "Miss Abigail, what a question. The wrong answer could get a man killed."

"Miss Abbey," called Pearl, skipping into the barn. "You done with the milking? You said we'd go see Tabby Cat's kittens when you were done."

"Almost," Abbey returned, her attention shifting to the child. Three days ago, Pearl had shown Abbey where Tabby Cat had hidden her kittens in the back of the hayloft. Abbey was sure Pearl's mother and Sloan would both be upset to find the child climbing up the ladder alone. Twice, Abbey had moved the kittens down to an unused stall in the barn, and twice Tabby Cat had moved them back to the loft. She made Pearl promise she wouldn't climb the ladder alone.

"Caleb," one of the other men yelled from outside. "Boss is lookin' for you."

Caleb muttered something under his breath, touched his fingers to his hat, and strode out of the barn.

Pearl squatted down next to Abbey's milk stool. "Bucket's

almost full," she announced. "Then we can go see the kittens, huh?"

"Kittens are dumb." JJ came into the barn.

Pearl flashed her brother an annoyed look. "They are not."

"Are, too. And, I asked Sloan. He said somebody's gonna get hurt if those kittens stay in the hayloft." He headed toward the ladder. "I'm gonna get'm down and hide'm from Tabby Cat. If she don't know where they are, she can't put 'em back in the loft."

"That's mean," Pearl stood up. "I'm gonna tell."

From the bottom rung of the ladder, JJ taunted, "Go ahead. See if I care."

Abbey had seen JJ often enough with the kittens to know he was no more likely to hurt them than his sister was. He simply liked knowing he could annoy her with the threats.

"Be careful, JJ." Abbey picked up the full bucket and headed toward the door. She paused to touch Pearl's shoulder. "I'm taking the milk to the house. When I get back, I'll climb up to the loft with you."

"Good." She clapped her hands together.

A little higher than eye level with Abbey, JJ stopped and grinned down at his sister. "I'm not scared of nothin'." He bounced on the rung as if to prove it.

Abbey shook her head as she watched him climb. It was a trip she had made more times than she cared to count over the last few days. And, she didn't like climbing the ladder now any more than she had the first time.

Granted, it was a sturdy contraption compared to the ladder made from twigs and a pair of saplings that a couple of the boys had built for Miss Mary. But this loft was higher up, a good fifteen feet off the ground. The climb up was so steep she couldn't look down without getting dizzy. If climbing to the loft was what it took, though, to keep Pearl safe, she'd do it.

"Look at me," JJ said from a good ten feet off the floor. A couple of rungs from the top, he turned around and sat down on one of the rungs. "See. No hands." He stuck out his hands and feet, balancing his weight on his bottom.

Abbey's throat caught, but she didn't speak. To admonish him would be to invite even more outrageous behavior, and encouragement was obviously the last thing he needed.

"Mama's gonna tan your hide," Pearl scolded.

JJ put his feet back on the rung and grasped the sides of the ladder and turned around to climb the last couple of steps. As he had before, he bounced on the rung.

It gave way with an awful crack.

For an instant, time seem suspended, and Abbey watched in horror as JJ's foot slipped through the jagged break on the rung, then slid down to the next rail. Instead of his foot hitting it, his leg slid behind, and he lost his balance in a wild flailing of arms and legs.

The top of the ladder swayed.

Abbey dropped the bucket of milk and rushed toward the ladder.

The top tipped away from the loft, then pitched back. JJ fell from the ladder. He hit the dirt floor of the barn with a dreadful thud.

The ladder crashed down on top of him. Dust erupted from the floor in a big poof.

Pearl screamed and ran toward her brother.

"No, no, no!" Abbey rushed to JJ. She grasped the ladder, which was far heavier than she expected. With a mighty heave, she lifted it off him and thrust it away, where it banged against one of the stalls.

JJ lay at an awkward angle. Quiet. Pale.

Broken.

A sob caught in her throat. She dropped to her knees, putting her fingers to his throat, searching, searching . . . searching for the beat of his heart. Blind panic flowed through her when she felt nothing except awful stillness in him. She urged Pearl up, who was still crying. "Go fetch help."

Pearl ran from the barn, yelling at the top of her lungs.

"JJ." Abbey pressed a hand against the boy's chest. "Please open your eyes. C'mon, JJ."

Pounding footsteps approached the barn, and Sloan rushed inside, followed by Pearl and a couple of the other men.

"What happened?"

"He fell off the ladder," Abbey choked. "My fault. Oh, God, my fault. I should have stopped him."

Sloan knelt next to the child, touching him gently, calling his name. Suddenly JJ wheezed, and he opened his eyes. Within a few seconds, his dazed expression focused into one of acute pain, and he tried to move.

Sloan held him down with gentle hands. "Don't move, son."

JJ whimpered, an anguished sound that ripped through Abbey.

"What can I do to help?" Frantic in her worry for the boy, she grasped Sloan's arm. "Please, what can I do?"

The surprise and wariness in his eyes mutely told her she was again being judged as Charlotte. That hurt more than Abbey cared to admit. JJ was a child. Just a child.

"Help keep him calm until we figure out how bad he's hurt," Sloan said.

With trembling fingers, Abbey brushed the boy's hair off his forehead, whispering nonsense words of reassurance to him. JJ's eyes focused on hers briefly, and through her tears, Abbey smiled at him, promising him he would be all right. He looked away, making a considered effort to control the quivering of his chin.

Sloan thoroughly checked his arms and legs, returning again and again to the boy's shin. "He's broken a leg." Catching Sam's eye, he added, "We're going to need to splint this. Get what you need from Consuela."

Sam headed out of the barn, and Sloan called to him.

"Don't let her get too upset when you tell her."

"Sure thing, Boss." And Sam took off at a trot.

"JJ, listen to me." Sloan waited for the boy to look at him. "Can you move your head side to side like this?"

He showed JJ the motion he wanted and smiled when the boy imitated the action. "Good." Then he pinched JJ's toes, and when he yelped, Sloan's smile widened. "Doesn't appear you've done any real harm. I'll bet you'll be sore as an old bear in spring."

"Hurts," JJ said.

"Your leg?" Sloan questioned.

"Yes." A pair of big tears slid down his cheeks, which he swiped away with his arm. "Is the bone pokin' out?"

"Nope."

"Then why d-do-does it h-hu-hurt so b-bad?"

"That's the way of broken bones. The pain will go away soon enough."

"When?" JJ asked, his chin quivering.

"As soon as we get it set. It's going to be pretty tender for a few weeks." He patted JJ's head. "We'll splint it up, and you'll be good as new."

Abbey blinked. A broken leg. That wasn't good, but he would recover. She relived the instant when the ladder toppled to the ground. Her attention was drawn to the ladder. Beneath one of the rungs, the smashed bucket lay on its side, the milk soaking into the ground in a sodden puddle. The break on the rung looked strange to her, but what did she know about ladders or how they were made?

Abbey heard Consuela's wail from the house, then footsteps as she ran across the compound. An instant later, she burst through the barn door, paused a brief second with her hand at her breast, then ran the rest of the way into the barn.

Tears streaming down her face and babbling in Spanish, she dropped to her knees, her hands fluttering over JJ.

Sloan caught one of them. "He's going to be fine."

Consuela sniffed and leaned over her son.

"Honest, Mama. Please don't cry." JJ tried to smile.

"How?" Consuela asked, looking around the barn. "What happened?"

"He fell off the ladder," Abbey answered.

Consuela swiveled toward Abbey as though just then seeing her. "What was he doing on the ladder?" Without waiting for an answer, she added in a rising voice, "I should have known. My son breaks his leg and who is right here in the thick of it? This is your fault!" She raised her arm. "Yours!"

Sloan grabbed her hand before she could strike Abbey. "Consuela."

Abbey stood up. Consuela's accusation hurt as only the truth could. "You're right. I should have stopped him. I should have told him to wait. I should have—"

"Stop it," Sloan interrupted.

"I don't want that witch anywhere near my children." Consuela waved her arm at Sloan and lapsed into a volley of Spanish.

"It is not Miss Abbey's fault," Pearl said. "JJ, he was jumping and—"

Consuela turned on Sloan. "You promised me. You'd make sure she stayed away."

"Mama." Pearl patted at her mother's arm, trying to get her attention.

Sloan touched the child's hair, and she grabbed his hand.

"He was jumping," she repeated. "He was."

"You promised me." Consuela held Sloan's gaze. "You know

what she cost me."

Sloan looked at Abbey, his features drawn into the controlled mask that she couldn't read. He glanced at Consuela, then returned his attention to Abbey. "You heard her. I warned you about this."

Abbey's glance fell to Pearl, the one person whose company she really enjoyed, the one person who saw her, really saw her as her own true self.

Sloan's lips tightened. "I mean it, Abbey."

Surprise widened her eyes.

Abbey. He had called her Abbey.

It shouldn't have mattered against the enormity of JJ's injury and Consuela's hatred. But, it did. Firming her chin, Abbey nodded and walked from the barn, Silas silently following her.

Hours later, Sloan returned to the barn, automatically putting things away. His thoughts, however, were on Abbey's admission that JJ's accident was her fault. Abbey. Charlotte.

Hell, did it even matter anymore?

Charlotte hadn't been the sort of person to take responsibility for anything. In fact, she was more the kind to blame someone else.

Abbey had thought it her fault when maybe it wasn't. At least, according to Pearl. If JJ had been jumping on the ladder, he had only himself to blame, and he was damn lucky a broken leg was all he had.

Critically, Sloan examined the milk bucket, which was dented where the ladder had hit it. Picking up the bucket, Sloan carried it to the workbench, where he beat it back into shape with a wooden mallet.

Then he turned his attention to the ladder, pulling loose the broken rung so it could be replaced. The break was clean without the usual splintering of breaking wood. Too clean. Picking up the two halves, he carried them outside where the light was better.

To his complete surprise, the rung had been sawed through from bottom to top. Sloan fitted the two pieces together, noting the jagged break where the wood hadn't been cut. The scant eighth inch that hadn't been sawed wouldn't hold any weight worth talking about—certainly not that of an adult. Or, a bouncing, rambunctious little boy. Would the rung have held Pearl's or JJ's weight if he hadn't jumped on it?

His eyes narrowed, Sloan strolled back into the barn, examining everything that came into sight. Of all the "accidents" over the last few months, this was the most subtle, but potentially as deadly.

Carefully, he examined the remaining rails on the ladder. Near the top, one other had been sawed through, leaving less than a quarter inch of solid wood. Comparing the two rails, he noticed they were slightly off center, about where a person's left foot would rest. If the first hadn't broken, the second one surely would have. Cursing under his breath, he pried the damaged rail off the ladder. Then he saw that the nails that kept the ladder attached to the loft had been pulled out.

Someone had planned this. Someone was supposed to get hurt. Who? Besides the two children, Abbey had been the only one to regularly make the trip to the hayloft. Was she the target?

Abruptly, Sloan focused on the bull in the field the other afternoon. At the time, Abbey had been the only one in the field. Only sheer luck had kept her from being hurt or worse. Sloan looked from the ladder to the loft, then back again, measuring the distance JJ had fallen. He shook his head, thankful the boy had not been more seriously injured. His fall could have easily been fatal.

Sloan picked up the two rungs, the broken one and the sabotaged one. If Abbey was the target, it would be only a matter of time before some other "accident" cropped up or before some more overt attempt on her life was made.

Abbey or Charlotte, it was time to have another talk with her. Sloan left the barn and headed for the orchard, positive that was where he would find her. In addition to sawing off the dead limbs, she had pruned the trees, pulled weeds, raked the ground, and generally returned the orchard to the prime condition it had never been in since his father's death.

When she wasn't working in the orchard, she had managed to sneak in help Consuela badly needed and didn't want. Sloan had caught Abbey hanging out laundry, sweeping the house, digging the last of the potatoes in the garden. As if recognizing how much she was disliked and distrusted, she simply pitched in where needed, disappearing to some other part of the property when Consuela returned.

Sloan didn't understand her willingness to work when she had hated it so much before, but he didn't trust it, either. If she wasn't daft, she had reasons for behaving the way she did—reasons that would likely lead to no good.

Maybe he'd find out more when he heard from Ben Haverly. Sloan figured, if there was any chance she was telling the truth, he should at least ask what the man knew about her. So, he'd sent off a letter, figuring it could be several weeks before an answer came back. He had included money with the letter, as well, asking for her belongings to be sent. He could only hope that might turn up some clue about where she had been all these months and what had happened to the stallion.

Sloan was halfway across the field before he spotted her. She sat with her back against one of the trees, her attention fixed on the mountains in front of her. Silas lay next to her, and she absently petted his head, then scratched his ears. Silas groaned and rolled onto his back, offering his tummy. She chuckled softly and scratched his exposed underside.

The soft laugh made Sloan pause midstride. Not once, ever, had he heard Charlotte laugh like that. Was she crazy? If so, he hoped she never remembered she was Charlotte.

Except that, if his suspicions were true, as Abbey or Charlotte, she could end up dead.

As if sensing his presence, Silas sat up and turned around, then began wagging his tail when he spotted Sloan. A half smile on her face, she looked over her shoulder at him. The smile faded when her eyes met his. Sloan resumed walking toward her, not happy with the discovery that he'd give a great deal to see her smile at him—and even more for her to laugh with him.

She stood, brushing the back of her skirt and straightening her shoulders.

"JJ's falling," Sloan began without any preamble, "wasn't an accident."

Her expression stiffened as if she expected him to accuse her.

"Anybody on that ladder would have fallen. The rung had been cut."

She stared at him, looked away a moment, then brought her glance back to him. "You mean someone deliberately—"

"Yes."

"Who would want to do this to the children?"

"I don't think they were the target," Sloan answered. "If JJ hadn't been jumping, the ladder probably would have held his weight."

"That doesn't make any sense . . ." Her voice trailed away, then she added in a whisper, "I've been climbing the ladder with Pearl."

"I know."

"I wanted her to be safe."

"Somebody wanted you to fall," Sloan said bluntly.

Abbey dropped her chin, her gaze on the ground. "Me? Or Charlotte?"

"Does it matter?" Sloan waited for her to look at him. "You might have been able to handle the Cimarron Sun by yourself, but I don't think so. I think you had help. And I think your accomplice wants to make sure you don't talk."

Her shoulders straightened. "Talk," she scoffed. "That, I think, is exactly what you intend. You've threatened to beat me, and now you bring these suspicions that are perhaps a ruse. If I'm frightened enough, then I'll tell you where your dratted horse it."

"I never threatened you." As soon as the words were out, he remembered the night he and Jake had returned from chasing down another dead-end lead and the advice he'd been given that he ought to beat her. "And, you damn well ought to be frightened." Sloan had the urge to shake her. She was the most exasperating woman he had ever known. He'd learned to hate her, but he had never—not once—wanted harm to come to her. "It was pure dumb luck that kept JJ from having only a broken leg. You could have been killed today."

"You can't be sure I was supposed to be injured."

"What about the bull?"

Her eyes widened slightly. "I haven't wanted to think about that."

"That's more like the Charlotte I know. Only interested in saving herself." He leaned closer to her. "When are you going to give this up and tell me what you did with the Sun?"

"And who helped me steal him?" She lifted her chin.

"That's right."

"I can't very well confess what I don't know." She laughed, the sound completely without light or humor. "Believe me, I'd tell you. You don't want me here, and I surely don't want to be here."

"I may not be able to keep you safe."

Her fingers rose to the faded bruise on her cheek. "When did you ever?"

Her soft, bitter question punched him square in the middle of the chest. That nagging uncertainty about her identity returned, less easily pushed aside this time. What if she was telling the truth? Then, she'd have no way of knowing he would never raise a hand against her.

CHAPTER 10

"It won't be long before the first snow storm." Sam turned up the collar on his shearling coat, his breath steamy puffs in front of his face.

Sloan glanced at the predawn sky laced with wispy, pink clouds as he finished adjusting the cinch on his gelding's saddle. He figured Sam was right. Frost gleamed on the roof of the cabin in the predawn light, and for the last couple of days, the high, thin clouds that were often ahead of a storm had streaked across the sky. The threat of snow was the main reason he wanted to get the last of the cattle off the upper range on the plateau and back into the valley. The rest of the herd had been brought down more than a week ago.

If the weather ran true to form, they would get an early snow storm that would cover the peaks until spring but that would melt here in the valley until the real onset of winter in another month. One last chance to get the last of the cattle down from the high country.

Buck had been sent after the strays a few days earlier, and that had been the last anyone had seen of him. Had anyone but Buck disappeared, Sloan would have been worried. Buck had been complaining for weeks, and Sloan figured, since he had just paid the men, that he had taken off. No great loss, even if it meant getting up before dawn and finishing the job himself.

He climbed onto his own saddle, the creak of leather adjusting beneath his weight. Cold immediately settled into his thighs.

The leather would warm soon enough, but damn, he'd rather be sitting in the kitchen with another cup of hot coffee.

Turning up his own coat collar, Sloan nudged his horse into a walk and followed Sam across the yard. Abbey came out of the house, Silas at her heels, and headed for the stack of wood at the end of the porch. Sloan knew good and well there was already enough wood inside to keep the fire going all day. She was probably putting some distance between herself and Consuela's increasingly sharp tongue.

True to her word, Abbey had fostered no further contact with the children. The situation was one Pearl clearly didn't understand, despite her mother's instructions. Pearl had a dozen things she wanted Abbey to do with her. The gentleness and tact of Abbey's refusals surprised Sloan. He had talked himself back into Preacher's assessment—she was daft and somehow had forgotten Charlotte. Fine by him. Things were better this way.

Once out of the yard, he and Sam headed up a gulch that steadily climbed up a hill. Above the plateau, the Sangre de Cristo mountains rose, the south border of the summer grazing range. Sloan figured, if they weren't hidden by a bank of clouds, they would be covered with a fresh layer of snow. If they were lucky, the strays would have continued to wander downhill—toward the ranch and winter range. If they weren't lucky, they could be scouring the hills all day, finding only a steer or two.

They climbed out of the gulch as the sun peeked over the top of Cameron Mountain to the east. A wind swept off the mountains to the south, another indication a storm was brewing.

"It's sure cold enough," Sloan said.

Sam grinned. "Only as a witch's heart."

As Sloan had suspected, the mountains were hidden by clouds. He pulled his horse to a stop and turned around to look back. He couldn't see the ranch house below them, but much of the rest of the Arkansas Valley could be seen from here. It was a view Sloan never tired of. Flanked by mountains on three sides that provided protection from all but the most severe storms, the valley was beautiful—more, his home.

"I'm a lucky man," said Sam from beside him.

Sloan turned his attention on the younger man. "You don't say."

"Sure." His gaze encompassed the valley. "This is prettier than anyplace else I've been."

"That doesn't make you lucky necessarily."

"It does since I have a job I like and a warm place to spend my time after winter starts."

Sam had been a scrawny kid when their paths had first crossed, and he had been working for food. Somehow, the kid had attached himself to Sloan, who could have no more left him behind than one of his own brothers.

"You need to be dreaming bigger."

"I'm dreaming plenty big and saving my money. Just about have enough to buy that hundred acres Frank Gibbs wants to get rid of." He lifted his hat and grinned. "Dreamt about winning his place in a poker game like your daddy got this place. I'm lucky, but not that lucky."

The statement settled into Sloan. That poker game had changed all their lives and brought with it death. Not once had it occurred to him the current rash of trouble could be related to the siege five years ago. His dad and a brother had died when Charlie Isenholt had returned to claim the patch of land he had lost to Sloan's father a year before the war began.

Then, the only structures on the land were a small, leaky one-room cabin with a dirt floor and a lean-to for the stock that barely passed as a shelter. Charlie, who liked his drink, had complained ranching life was too hard, the land too unyielding, the winters too long. And, at the time he lost the ranch, he'd proclaimed it a good riddance. His story changed after he saw the improvements made with the back-breaking efforts over six years. They had stolen from him, and he had returned to take by force what he considered his. He had died trying.

The first time Sloan had ridden into the valley with his father and his two brothers, it was still part of the Ute territory. Then, it had been lonely and far different from the plains around Fort Bent. They had come to trap and ended up with a ranch that became their home in this beautiful mountain valley. Their big dreams required capital, and so Sloan had left during the war years. He had driven ammunition wagons during the war and laid track for the new railroad after. He had worked like a demon to earn enough money to give them a solid financial footing. His own sweat and the blood of his family were soaked into this land. It was now as much a part of him as winter snow was to the mountains.

Evidently, he'd been quiet for a while because Sam said, "Boss?"

Sloan smiled at the younger man. "Just thinking back. Trying to see any patterns between the old and the new. And, you gave me some things to consider I hadn't thought of."

Sam grinned. "Always glad to be helpful, even though I don't know what the dickens you're talking about."

"You may have stumbled onto something. When my daddy got lucky and won the ranch, it wasn't much to brag on then. He died trying to keep what was his. Maybe that trouble has something to do with now."

Sloan nudged his horse into a walk, rolling the pieces through his mind. Charlotte's infidelity and disappearance along with the stallion. The accident that had killed Joey. The fire that had destroyed the barn. Hell of a thing to think all those were somehow connected.

"We're dawdling," he said. "And those strays aren't going to come to us."

"And here I had a pocket full of sugar, sure they'd come a running if I held out my hand and hollered, 'C'mon little dogie.' "

Sloan laughed. "Might work on some little potbellied calf. But, his mama?"

"Finding them would have been easier with your dog."

"True enough, but we'll have to manage without him."

With each passing week, a gnaw in his middle—the one that warned him of danger—had intensified. Whether because of his brother's long absence or the threats against Abbey—Charlotte, damn it—or something else, he didn't know.

As soon as they reached the trickle of water coming out of the mountains known as Squaw Creek, they headed up the narrow valley. Sloan kept thinking he smelled smoke.

"Smell the campfire, boss?" Sam asked a few minutes later.

"Sure do." The small lake that formed the headwater for Squaw Creek was a favorite for one of the Ute bands Sloan had been trading with for years. Their chief had signed a treaty that would require the Indians retreat to a reservation, a fraction of their current territory, and would open most of Colorado to settlement. With the summer ending, they were all supposed to have stayed west of the Upper Arkansas Valley, but he had a hunch his old friend Nashua had come anyway. Either that, or trappers.

Sloan suspected the Indians because trapping wasn't as good as it had been when he had first come to this valley with his father nearly twenty years ago. Since then, too many miners, too many settlers. Too few beaver.

They topped a rise, and below them smoke lazily curled into the sky. A couple of teepees were pitched near the trees, and a rough lean-to held supplies. Sloan recognized a couple of the horses as being ones he had traded to Nashua a year ago. Dogs yapped, and an old man became visible under a grove of aspen.

"Guess we'd better pay our respects." Sloan urged his horse down the slope.

A few children darted into the clearing, then disappeared in one of the tents. Nashua slowly made his way toward the campfire. Though he hadn't raised his hand in greeting, Sloan knew the old man saw him.

"One of your beeves is on the drying rack," Sam said.

"Looks like."

The hide still bore the brand of the Triple Bar S, and the hide was too big to be the calf he had traded a couple of weeks ago. Despite the brand, the Indians saw range cattle as the same as an elk or a deer—a gift from the land rather than someone's property. The loss of an occasional cow to the Indians was the price of living on the land they considered to be theirs.

There was a certain protocol to coming into any camp, and though Sloan had visited this group several times, he and Sam stopped at the outer perimeter of the camp and waited for an invitation to come in.

It paid to be polite since everyone was more skittish these days. New treaties had been formed, but everyone expected promises to be broken because they always were. As for himself, Sloan wanted to live on his land and get along with his neighbors. That included the Ute.

"Come. Sit," Nashua commanded with a wave of his hand as he settled himself on a log near the campfire.

They dismounted, and Sloan pulled the sacks of peppermint candies and tobacco from his saddlebag. The old man's eyes lit on the tobacco when Sloan sat down, and he accepted the pouch with a murmured thanks. The children hung back as they always did but knew he had a gift for them as well, as he always did. He set the sack of candy on the log a little out of reach. Seconds later, one of the youngsters grabbed it and ran back to the others. Giggling, they opened the sack, and a second later the sharp aroma of peppermint wafted to them.

"Are you heading south soon?" Sloan asked Nashua after the pleasantries were over.

The old man didn't answer until he had finished packing the tobacco into his pipe, lighting it, and taking a long pull. "Soon. We'll leave after this storm." He patted his hip. "The long ride is not so easy anymore."

He offered the pipe to Sloan, who took a couple of puffs on it, then handed it on to Sam. He coughed after his turn, which made the old man grin.

"He looks like a man, but he's still a boy."

"Man enough to help me round up the last of my cattle," Sloan said.

"Ah." Nashua's gaze slid to the lean-to where a cowhide was stretched across a drying frame. "I think you will find them farther up. Not so far as Shakano Lake." He tipped his head toward the sky. "It will snow tonight."

"More than likely." Sloan stood. "I reckon I'd better get going. I'll see you next spring?"

Nashua shrugged. "Ouray wants a treaty. So who knows?"

The old man's statement was bland, but Sloan figured he didn't like the terms, which would consign the tribe to a reservation farther west. If he'd been in Nashua's shoes, he would have figured the Ute chief had conceded too much. It was a fact that most whites didn't like the treaty, either, figuring the Indians hadn't given up enough. They wanted the rich farmland in the Grand Valley and the silver and gold in the mountains. Sloan figured it was only a matter of time before the tribe was pushed even farther west.

Sloan offered the older man his hand. "Have a safe journey, old friend."

Nashua nodded.

"And, if you come across my brother, send him home to me."

Nashua smiled. "Your Comanche brother is welcome at my fire, as you are."

Sloan and Sam remounted and with a wave headed on out.

"Don't know why you put up with them stealing your beeves," Sam grumbled when they were out of earshot.

"Beats being at war with them." Everyone knew statehood would soon come to the Colorado Territory, and since that was so, the Indians were bound to be on the losing end of the proposition. "The first time I came with my daddy into these mountains was about a year after Bent's Fort burned down. He told stories about when he had first come here, and a man could travel for days without seeing another man. Then the gold and silver rush came. That's when he decided to try his hand at ranching. To survive, Nashua will have to change, also."

"They're still stealing your cows," Sam said.

"Yep," Sloan agreed. "And his children won't be starving this winter."

"I don't understand you. You get all upset because somebody has been rustling your cattle, and you'll go to hell and back to find the Cimarron Sun, but you're okay with Indians taking what's yours."

"I figure it's a fair trade," Sloan said. "I live on land that used to belong to them, and they take only what they can eat, unlike the rustlers out to make a profit on my hard work."

The valley grew more narrow, and the brush grew thicker. Within minutes of leaving the camp, they spotted the first of the cattle they sought. They separated, Sam working his way down the east side valley and Sloan coming down the west. It didn't take long to scare the first animals out of the brush. Sloan saw Sam was having similar luck, whistling and calling to the cattle as he worked them into the open ground in the middle of the narrow valley.

Between the two of them, they had picked up nearly a dozen animals when Sloan scared a few crows into the sky, who circled above with a chorus of raucous calls. Sloan guided his horse deeper into the brush, just the kind of place a range cow was most likely to hide herself and a calf. When he came into a small clearing, he didn't see any sign of cattle and was about to turn back when a flash of red next to a rotted log caught his eye. A ragged bit of cloth caught on the brush. He picked his way toward it.

Beyond the log, Sloan found what had drawn the crows—the body of a man. He lay face down, the back of his skull blown away. The blood was the dark, reddish brown of the Colorado earth, but even dried, a mess. Sloan dismounted and turned the man over.

Buck. With an oddly neat bullet hole in the middle of his forehead.

CHAPTER 11

Nearly a month Abbey had been here. A month! She was no closer to convincing Sloan she was not his wife than she had been the first day. She had yet to step foot off the ranch property, nor had she found a way to do so without making her situation worse.

As had become her habit, she walked to the gate, Silas matching her step for step. Just as he had done every single time, the dog blocked her way when they reached the overhead sign with the name of the ranch.

"Just once you could let me through," she murmured. Silas wagged his tail. Then, what, she wondered. Was it a mile or more to a road? From there, how would she know which way to go?

Jake rode toward her, and when he reached her, he pulled the horse to a stop. "Think today will be the day?"

"For what?" Abbey returned, pretending she didn't know what he meant and wrapping her shawl more firmly around herself.

"That ol' Silas will let you through the gate?"

"I keep hoping," she responded honestly.

"We'd all be better off if he did. Except, then we'd have another problem."

Abbey raised her eyebrow in question.

"I'd have to come after you." He patted the horse's neck

149

again. "And we know what happened the last time you ran from me."

Abbey looked the man up and down. "Yes. We do know. Not to me, but to you, as well."

To her surprise, red stained his cheeks, and she looked at him more closely. Shame that Sloan had beaten him? Abbey wondered. He cleared his throat and looked away, giving her a chance to study him. In her mind's eye, he had been ugly, unrelentingly harsh. This morning, he seemed neither, a realization that surprised and displeased her. Another of Miss Mary's Biblical axioms flitted through Abbey's mind. Where thou judges another, thou condemns thyself; for thou that judges does the same things.

Abbey looked away, seeing both herself and Jake in a new light.

"I never hit a woman before." His voice was so low he could barely be heard. "God help me, I never did."

He glanced at her, then tapped his feet against the horse's flanks and trotted away.

Abbey wondered if he had apologized or if he was trying to somehow explain himself. Either way, she wasn't ready to forgive him.

Abbey gazed longingly down the road. Poncha, where was it? How far? From there, which way back to Denver and Plum Creek Crossing? The days were cooler, and she assumed snow would fall soon—another worry if she were to take on a clandestine journey.

Last night was only the most recent of those long on restlessness and short on sleep. Since the day of JJ's accident, Sloan's dire warning that her life could be in danger swirled around in her brain, feeding her imagination to the point she jumped at every small sound. In her dreams, JJ fell repeatedly. To her shame, she was thankful she had not been on the ladder.

That made her feel small and petty and mean. Like Charlotte. Abbey found herself thinking more about that, fearful Preacher could be right. She was daft. Her memories were conjured from her imagination. The empty gnawing in her stomach grew with her worry, a feeling even worse than starvation had been during the winter of Sheridan's siege during the war.

Only an evil, selfish person would be glad she had walked away unhurt instead of a child.

She retreated toward the refuge of the orchard where no one bothered her and where she had no company except for Silas. The dog walked alongside her feeling more like her companion than her guard. Here she felt more like herself, had more confidence in the reality of her memories. They couldn't be stories she had somehow made up.

In the orchard, little was left to be done until spring. She wasn't used to being this idle even if she did long to return to her life. With the passage of each day, her old life became hazier. The fading memory of her time with the Haverlys worried her. Another sign she could be crazy.

She had left her letter to the Haverlys on the table next to the front door, hoping Sloan would relent and take it to town. Except, if he had ever gone, she wasn't aware of it. Nor had the preacher visited again. And the letter remained.

Abbey sighed and turned around to face the house. Across the field, she watched Consuela hang another basket of laundry. Hours earlier, it was a chore Abbey had volunteered to help with when she had finished milking. Consuela hadn't wanted help, and Abbey had found herself at loose ends. Nothing new there.

Consuela had decided to return home to Santa Fe, Abbey knew, and so the routine of her days had changed, becoming even more busy, but with long stretches of the day spent in the small cabin she shared with her children.

Within the last few days, the leaves had fallen to the ground, rustling as she walked through them. A cool breeze whispered through the trees, and more leaves cascaded to the ground, fluttering gold against the bluest sky she had ever seen. Abbey had not imagined she'd be spending the winter in the Colorado mountains. And, if she didn't get back to Denver soon, that appeared more likely.

A flock of birds fluttered suddenly from their roosts in a nearby cottonwood. They swirled overhead, moving as one, diving and soaring and calling to one another. Wondering what had startled the birds into flight, Abbey's gaze returned to the grove of trees.

The tall form of a man emerged from the shadows and moved toward her with an easy, silent grace.

A man—an Indian. He was far taller than the braves that sometimes came to the ranch.

He was on foot but led a horse that seemed to move as silently as he did. His buckskins blended with the shade of the trees and bushes behind him, making his features look even darker. His hair hung in a pair of braids over each shoulder, and Abbey realized his hair was as long as her own. His regard of her was as thorough and intense as hers was of him.

He dropped the reins, and the horse mouthed the grass. The man stopped some six feet in front of her. He seemed familiar somehow, though Abbey was sure she had never seen him.

"For a ghost, you look mighty fine," he said.

From across the field, Abbey heard Pearl cry out, "Uncle Jonah!" She came running toward them, excitement lighting her face.

Uncle Jonah? Abbey thought. The name she would have attached to this man would have been something like Lone Wolf, not Uncle Jonah.

Pearl came to a skidding halt in front of him, then paused the merest instant. He knelt and held out his arms, and she threw herself into them.

"Uncle Jonah, we've been worried about you." Pearl wrapped her arms tight around his neck. "Sloan and Mama, too."

Jonah met Abbey's eyes over the top of the Pearl's head. "Where did you come from?"

"Denver," she answered.

"I hear the south in your voice."

"I was raised in the Shenandoah Valley of Virginia."

He nodded as if that made sense to him. "You must have been a hell of a surprise to my brother."

"Your brother?"

He smiled, the expression making his dark eyes gleam. "Sloan."

Abbey absorbed that, realizing this was the Jonah who was sometimes the topic of conversation at the dinner table. It hadn't occurred to her that he was an Indian. As her bewilderment faded, she recognized him from the picture in Sloan's room.

"What's your name?" he asked.

"She's Abbey." Pearl plopped in his lap when he sat down.

He winced, an expression he hid when he glanced at the little girl. "I see."

Abbey tensed, expecting him to voice the same denial everyone else had.

"My brother's wife never mentioned having a sister—much less a twin." He pressed a hand against his shoulder and shifted Pearl off his lap.

"You know I'm not Charlotte?" A bubble of hope stirred within her chest, the first she had in too many days.

Jonah nodded, looking suddenly very tired. "You couldn't be, unless you've come back from the dead."

153

With that, he slumped over, then fell forwards onto the ground as though he suddenly had no more energy.

"Uncle Jonah," Pearl cried, pulling at his hands. "Wake up."

Abbey knelt next to him, baffled at what had happened. Putting her fingers to the man's neck, she was relieved to feel his pulse beating strongly. She smelled the coppery scent of blood, and she rolled him onto his back. The buckskin shirt was stained, she realized. Loosening the laces at the neck, she opened the shirt and found a crude bandage over his left shoulder. She pulled the heavily stained dressing away from his skin. He'd been shot, the wound angry looking. A fresh, bright-red flow of blood trickled from the crusted scab around the wound.

"Uncle Jonah," Pearl cried, shaking him, then lifting her gaze to Abbey. "He's dead. Just like Pap."

"He is not dead," Abbey returned firmly. She took Pearl by the shoulder. "Run back to the house and get help."

Pearl took off across the field, and Abbey returned her attention to the man. The ooze of blood alarmed her but not as much as his pallor did—a sign indicating whatever reserves this man had, they were nearly gone.

Abbey pressed a hand against the wound, hoping the pressure would stop the bleeding. By the time Jake arrived, still riding his horse, the bleeding had nearly stopped.

"Let's get him to the house." Jake eased Jonah into a sitting position. "You're nearly there, old man."

Jonah opened his eyes. "Younger than you, my friend." A trace of laughter lit his voice despite the obvious pain that creased his brow.

"The red man speaks." Relief flooded Jake's face, and he hoisted Jonah into a standing position. "A pure wonder. When did you get shot?"

"Yesterday."

"Hell's fire, man. You were practically home."

"Not close enough." Jonah grunted as Jake put one of his feet in the stirrup.

Somehow, Abbey and Jake got Jonah onto the horse. Jake climbed on behind him, then took off at a brisk canter. Neighing, Jonah's horse ran after them. They reached the house long before she did.

Jake had taken Jonah to the bedroom across the hall from hers, a room she had always presumed was Sloan's. Now, she understood the significance of the things she had found there on that first day. This wasn't Sloan's room, but Jonah's.

Scolding him for getting shot, Consuela issued orders to Jake for hot water and bandages while she fussed over Jonah's prone form.

"What can I do to help?" Abbey asked, allowing herself to be pushed away from the bed as Consuela undressed Jonah, who appeared to be more unconscious than not.

"Stay away from him." Consuela raked Abbey with an angry glance. "Why would you want anything to do with a lying, filthy redskin?"

"I never said that."

"Of course you did not. You are the innocent Abbey, unable to be so cruel as Charlotte." Consuela turned her back on Abbey. "Leave us. He doesn't need your kind of help."

Once again cut to the quick, Abbey retreated to the kitchen. Jake swept past her with an armload of clean linens and a pot of hot water. There was nothing left to do except keep watch with JJ and Pearl.

Jake came back only once—heading outside to the bunkhouse and returning with a bottle of whiskey.

"He ain't gonna die, is he?" JJ asked.

"You can never know about these things for certain," Jake responded as he walked through the kitchen. "Your mama is a fine nurse, and she's doing everything she can."

JJ turned a baleful gaze on Abbey. "It's probably your fault. You want him to die, like you did Pap." He struggled to his feet and grabbed his crutches. The splint prevented him from running as he went outside but not from slamming the door behind him.

The accusation cut, just as they all did. Though Abbey understood fear, she still wanted to lash out at JJ, but most of all at the absent Charlotte. What kind of woman could wreak so much havoc and heartache on others?

Hours passed, and based on the occasional yells and pain-filled groans coming from the bedroom, Abbey supposed they were digging a slug out of Jonah. With nothing else to keep her occupied, she took on the chores Consuela had abandoned. Bringing in the laundry when it was dry. Scrubbing the hearth.

Pearl stayed at Abbey's side, her endless chattering a reminder to Abbey of how much she had missed the little girl over these last many days.

When late afternoon arrived with Consuela and Jake still involved with caring for Jonah, Abbey began preparations for the evening meal. She wasn't as good a cook as Consuela, but hungry men still had to be fed.

"I'll help you make biscuits." Pearl climbed onto a chair.

"Good. I need it," Abbey told her. "You can also show me how much wood your mother puts in the stove." That was the real trick, Abbey knew. Having the oven hot, but not too hot. She didn't know what Consuela had planned for the evening meal, but Abbey decided she was making stew. She set aside some of the broth, thinking it might be something Jonah would need later.

By the time Caleb and Eli arrived for the evening meal, she was ready for them, and the biscuits were only a little burned. Jake must have spoken to them earlier because they both knew

Jonah had returned.

"I heard cattle bawling up the draw," Eli told her, sitting down to the table. "so Sloan and Sam will be here shortly. We can eat now, then give him a hand. Sure do thank you for makin' supper, ma'am. Sort of figured we'd be having hard tack tonight."

"When did you learn to cook, Miss Abbey?" Caleb asked as he sat down, that vague current of disbelief present in his voice though the question was ordinary.

"A long time ago." Abbey ladled up the stew into bowls and served Eli, then Caleb. "Miss Mary taught me."

"You talked to Jonah?" he questioned as she set the stew in front of him.

"Right before he passed out." She shuddered, remembering the moment when she was sure the man had died right before her eyes.

"You be best to lay low for a while," Eli advised. "That Jonah, he hates Charlotte more 'n anybody."

"That's for sure," Caleb agreed.

Abbey turned away without saying anything. Jonah undoubtedly had cause to hate Charlotte, assuming Eli was right. He knew the truth. She couldn't be Charlotte unless she "had come back from the dead." She didn't like thinking of Charlotte being dead. That didn't keep hope from bubbling through Abbey's veins. Soon, she thought, they would all know she wasn't Charlotte. Soon she would no longer be hated for another woman's sins or thought to be crazy. Once more she whispered a prayer for Jonah's swift recovery, then remembered to add a prayer for Charlotte's soul.

She served the children dinner, sitting with them, but was too nervous to eat herself.

"My mom's stew is better," JJ said.

"I'm sure it is," Abbey agreed without any heat. Despite the insult, the boy ate as though he hadn't been fed in days.

As soon as Eli had wolfed down his meal, he urged Caleb out the door. Outside, she heard the bawling cows.

Not fifteen minutes later, Sloan burst through the door, bringing in a gust of cold air. "Where is he?"

She nodded toward the hallway. Without taking off his coat or hat, he strode through the house, his footsteps reverberating through the floor. Abbey closed the outside door Sloan had left open behind him, then listened to the sounds coming from the room where Jonah had been taken. The murmur of voices didn't have the hushed tones of being around the dying, which relieved her.

She set the pot of stew at the back of the stove where it would stay warm, then washed the dishes. While Abbey was drying them, Consuela appeared at the kitchen door, her hair disheveled and her blouse stained with blood. She looked around the kitchen as though she had never before seen it.

"You cooked supper." Her statement sounded like an accusation.

"You were busy." Abbey nodded toward the stove. "There's stew, and it's still hot. And a pot of broth, also."

"You never cook."

"As it happens, I did tonight." Abbey pushed down the now familiar flare of irritation. Carefully, she folded the towel and hung it on the rack near the fireplace. "Sloan's brother. How is he?"

"His color is better. The wound hadn't festered yet, so with God's help . . ." As Consuela's voice trailed off, she made the sign of a cross.

"You haven't spoken with him?"

Consuela's familiar antagonism surfaced. "It's difficult to talk to a man who is unconscious. Perhaps you would know this if you—"

"Enough! Just this time, please let go of the criticism and the insults."

Consuela advanced on her. "It will never be enough. The pain you have caused, the lives you have ruined. You can never atone for what you have done."

Biting her tongue against the retort that would surely cause problems later, Abbey retreated to her—Charlotte's—room, brushing a hand over Pearl's hair as she went. "Good night."

She came to a stop in front of Jonah's room, straining to listen to the sounds coming from behind the closed door across the hall. Sloan's deep voice she recognized, though the words were too muffled to understand. If Jonah was unconscious, then Sloan was talking to Jake. And they still all believed she was Charlotte.

She entered her room and closed the door behind her, but not before Silas slipped through the doorway. Her room. It wasn't, though she had slept in this bed many nights. Abbey glanced around, seeing Charlotte in each piece of furniture. Charlotte, who was dead if Jonah had spoken the truth. And why wouldn't he?

She wanted the oblivion of sleep, though she expected it would elude her tonight. Hot baths, she had discovered within days of her arrival, were a sure way to get relaxed and sleepy. She should offer the bath to Consuela, she thought. To do so would lead to another round of bitter accusations. And tonight, more than ever, Abbey longed to be known for herself by someone other than the dog and a little girl no one else paid any mind to.

Abbey pulled the curtain across the opening to the alcove, undressed, and settled into the tub, the water warming and soothing her. She closed her eyes and settled her head on the lip of the tub, letting her mind float.

Sometime later the door to the bedroom banged open, rousing her out of the half-asleep state the warm water of the bath had induced. Heavy footsteps came toward her, and the curtain was swept aside.

Sloan came to a sudden halt in the doorway. He stood there so big and dark, the fabric of the curtain clenched in his big fist.

She crossed her arms in front of herself, new anger surfacing at this latest intrusion. She lifted her chin. "What do you want?"

"Stand up, wife."

"I am not your wife." She carefully spaced the words, hating his inflection.

"Prove it. Stand up." The curtain dropped from his hand, and he took a step into the alcove, the room suddenly even smaller with his large presence.

"I will not."

His glower became even more fierce. "It's not like I haven't seen you without your clothes before. I'm damn tired of the outraged virgin act."

She longed to shout back, but no coherent thought formed. She'd spent too much time comparing her own features to those in the portrait, and she knew how much they resembled one another. If their faces were so similar, wouldn't their bodies be, also? Except for the scars . . . and he would undoubtedly have an explanation for even them.

"Have you spoken with Jonah?" she asked.

"Stand up." The command completely ignored her question. Uttered without raising his voice, his controlled anger frightening her as nothing else about the man ever had. "You don't want me touching you."

"Finally. Something we agree about." She gave him a last defiant look, then, shedding her pride, stood. Water coursed down her body. Embarrassed, angry—furious—at him, she held his gaze. The black depths of his eyes were unreadable, but

To Love a Stranger

there was no doubting his expression. He was as angry as she.

His dark eyes remained locked with hers an unbearable minute. Then, his gaze dropped to her breasts, and she resisted the urge to cover herself, to hide. Not even Miss Mary had seen her naked since she was little more than a child. His Adam's apple bobbed, and then his gaze wandered lower. His expression became even more forbidding.

What displeased him so? Even in this, did she so completely resemble his hated wife?

Humiliation thrummed through her veins, and she tightly closed her eyes. Images bubbled up from the past and seared the inside of her eyelids, so she opened her eyes. She knew she was in this small room, knew the boots in the center of her vision belonged to Sloan, but her memory overlaid images of Pa in his muddy boots and the dank shed where he had stripped her naked, then regularly whipped her—not only her, but Ma's children as well. Lashes for laziness, for crying, for being disrespectful—all of it to beat the devil out of them. And those not whipped were forced to watch when he beat the others.

Abbey sucked in a shuddering breath and looked up and found Sloan's gaze was once again fastened on her face.

"Your brother—"

"Is damn near dead."

Tears flooded her eyes, and in that moment she knew she was as evil as Sloan's hated wife because her tears were not for Jonah, but for her own loss. He was her only hope, her last hope. Without him, how would she ever prove she was her own true self?

The pin holding her hair gave way, dropping into the tub with a plop. Her hair tumbled over her shoulders and down her back. The movement seemed to surprise him, and he jerked.

She could have sworn his eyes were filled with pain, regret, and some other emotion she did not recognize. Impossible. The man wasn't capable of regret.

Without saying a word, he walked around her, and she bowed her head, wishing she understood what had provoked this latest confrontation, wishing she knew why he was here . . . wishing she weren't so terribly afraid. In another moment, it would be over. He had said he wouldn't touch her, and she prayed he would keep his promise.

Time seemed to stand still, and she became aware of all the sounds. Her own labored breathing . . . and his. The scrape of his boot against the floor when he took a step. The pop of the fire in the corner fireplace.

She felt him lift her hair and move it to one side, as she had somehow known he would. She shivered.

Sloan felt that tiny movement to his bones.

Scars—old, old scars—crisscrossed her back. Sloan took a harsh breath. She had been savagely whipped, and the scars were as bad as any he had ever seen.

His gaze dropped to her bottom, the cheeks round and pale and lovely despite the one scar pointing raggedly toward her feminine cleft that was as different from his wife as day was from night. No birthmark in the shape of a lover's kiss on her bottom that his wife had. Not that he expected it any longer.

He had been so sure Jonah's broken story was a result of fever and exhaustion. He had found Charlotte with the Comanche, and she had died. Impossible. Charlotte was here, had been here for the last interminable weeks.

Except this woman was not Charlotte.

Abbey was at once more delicate and more rounded than his wife. No corset was needed to shape her waist into the fashionable contours Charlotte had wanted. Abbey's hips and breasts were fuller, her nipples bigger and puffier. His attention fastened on her thigh where someone had branded her. He stared at the obscene mark, trying to place why it was so familiar.

162

Then he recognized the symbol—the Flanders family crest. Sheer will kept him from touching her, except for her cool silky hair within his grasp.

Her posture was so rigid, he had the feeling she might snap. Her fear had shamed him . . . her courage held him in awe.

He searched for something—anything—he could say to her. *I'm sorry* was a pitifully small thing, and it couldn't make things right. The blistering things she had said to him that very first day echoed through his head. *A chicken intended for tonight's dinner would be treated with more kindness than you've given me.* And then he had kissed her in anger and frustration, and when he had felt her tears against his face, he had been so sure she— Charlotte—was simply playing out one of her elaborate games. He had given her every reason to be afraid that he might rape her. Good God, how could he ask for her forgiveness when he had done the unforgivable?

He let the curtain of her hair fall. Snagging a towel from in front of the fire, he handed it to her, then stalked from the room without a backward glance.

CHAPTER 12

Shaking from the force of her anger, Abbey stared at the floor. When she heard the click of the door's latch, she let the towel drop to the floor and sank back into the water.

Her thoughts much too chaotic to marshal into any order, she sat until the water began to cool. Only then did she realize her hair was floating in the water around her. She squeezed out excess water and stepped out of the tub. After she dried her body, she put on a nightgown and pulled a chair close to the small fire in the alcove where she began brushing her hair. Hours must have passed because at some point she recognized her hair was dry. As she plaited it into a loose braid, Miss Mary's oft repeated axiom of "God helps those who help themselves" marched relentlessly through her head.

Abbey couldn't bear another day here. Not a single one. Her glance fell to the dog who shadowed her so completely she sometimes forgot he was her guard rather than her companion. She scratched his velvety ears. He raised his head to look at her, his golden eyes reflecting in the firelight. As if sensing her distress, he sat up and rested his chin on her knee, his continuing regard of her so filled with sympathy that tears sprang to her eyes.

Had she ever loved anyone the way she loved this animal? Her grandmother, surely. Those memories were so faint they seemed but a distant dream. Had she loved Miss Mary? Abbey, like all the other children who had been gathered out of the bowels of war, had worshiped the woman who had rescued them, clothed them as best she could, tried to feed them during a famine, and sent them on their way when they were able to fend for themselves. Abbey would be eternally grateful. Was that love?

She shook away the melancholy of her memories and focused on formulating a plan. Somehow, she'd have to confine Silas and keep him occupied for a while. The large knuckle bone in the pot of broth would do quite nicely. She hoped.

To travel, she'd need warm clothes. Since a stage ran between Poncha and Denver, all she had to do was find her way there. How difficult could that be? She peered out the window and saw the night was bright with a full moon. Just as it had been when she arrived here. They had traveled at night then. She could surely do the same. If travel to Poncha took someone on horseback an hour or two, she could walk the distance in three or four.

This wasn't the time to dwell on her conclusion a few days earlier that to leave by herself was to invite disaster.

Opening the armoire, Abbey searched through the clothes. Loathe as she was to use any more of Charlotte's clothing, the two dresses Abbey had been wearing wouldn't be warm enough. She pulled out a riding habit, the woolen fabric a rich, dark brown. Examination of the garment revealed it had a split skirt instead of the tight garments used by women who rode side saddle, which Abbey supposed made sense as Charlotte was an expert rider. With a cloak, she would be protected in all but the coldest weather.

She glanced out the small four-paned window again. Tonight. She could leave tonight.

Going to the door, she placed her ear against it, listening for any sounds. All was quiet. As silently as she could, she unlatched the door and peered out. The door to the room across the hallway from hers was closed. And the front room was dark.

Her breathing suddenly fast, Abbey closed the door and leaned against it. She'd have to get the bone first, before she dressed. Wandering around in the middle of the night in a riding habit couldn't be explained away. Being in her night clothes could.

She cracked open the door again and peered out once more before stepping into the hallway. Her heart pounded harder each time the floor creaked beneath her feet. She hurried to the kitchen, Silas right with her, the ever-silent shadow. His interest became more intent when she pulled the bone out of the pot. It was far too hot to give to him. To keep from dripping broth on the floor, she set the bone in a pie tin. Even that sounded unnaturally loud. And the smell of the bone—would it waft into the room where Jonah and Sloan were, alerting them?

The instant she was back in the room, she closed the door, then leaned against it, her heart pounding. Silas sat in front of her, repeatedly licking, his teeth gleaming brightly in the dim light.

"In a few minutes, boy." She set the bone on top of the chest of drawers, well out of his reach.

Swiftly, she dressed in the riding habit and the moccasins. The extra fabric between her legs felt odd, and she considered choosing another gown. After a second inspection of the wardrobe, she decided the garment was warm and practical—a good choice for her journey.

She spread a shawl over the bed and laid the few things she thought she'd need in the center of it. Admitting she would need some way to pay for the stage, she opened Charlotte's jewelry box. Abbey had no idea which of the items within might be valuable, but she finally settled on a heavy gold chain. The theft gave her a moment's pause before she gathered the corners of the shawl together and tied them.

Through it, Silas watched her with accusing golden eyes and thumped his tail against the floor when she occasionally glanced at him.

Retrieving her ruined dress from the back of the armoire, she finished the job Sloan had started that day when she had first arrived—ripping the bodice away from the skirt. The tearing loud in her ears, Abbey fashioned the skirt into long strips that she tied together.

Then, she sat down on the floor with the dog and, while petting him, tied the makeshift rope around his neck. Still sitting on the floor, she tied the other end of the rag rope to one of the bed's legs. A corner of Abbey's mouth lifted as she contemplated the heavy wood—at last a practical use for Charlotte's excesses. The bed was heavy enough Silas would break the rope before moving the furniture.

Abbey doubted the rags would hold very long—but she didn't need a long time. And if he got involved with the bone, she might even have until morning. She could only hope. She petted the dog again, feeling like a traitor, especially when his regard of her was so accusing.

Taking a last look around the room, she gave Silas the bone. As she had hoped, he fell on it as though it were manna from heaven. She petted him one last time. Then she listened at the door, and she heard nothing. She cracked open the door and peered out. The house was dark except for a faint line of light shining from beneath the door to Jonah's room.

Abbey silently latched the door behind her, hoping Silas wouldn't sound the alarm. Swiftly she made her way down the hall. With each step her heart pounded, and she expected at any moment Silas would bark. At the heavy front door, she paused again to listen.

Still quiet.

She opened the door only far enough to squeeze through and

again silently closed it. She knew Sloan sometimes sat on the porch late at night, and dreading what she might see, she turned her head to the right. Nothing. To the left. Still nothing.

Shaking with relief and exhilaration that she might succeed, she stepped off the porch and hurried across the open space between the house and the barn, instinctively seeking the shadows that would hide her in the night.

At the barn door she paused once more, listening. Another decision to be made. Did she take a horse or not? That thought made her smile. The last thing she wanted was for Sloan to come looking for yet another woman who had stolen one of his horses. Even if she could ride, she was better off on foot. And she had another long open space to cross before she reached the gate.

Staying on the road was best, she decided. She was less likely to get lost. The road surely led to Poncha or to one that did.

"I wondered if tonight would be the night."

The soft drawl caught her midstep, and she whirled toward the voice.

A shadow separated from the corner of the barn. The man pushed his hat back. In the next second she recognized Caleb.

"Jonah is not a man to cross," Caleb said.

Abbey had no idea about that. "No, I suppose he's not."

"I thought you might want to leave once that redskin showed up. He hates . . . ."

His pause was long enough she was sure he was going to say "you." Her sense of alarm ratcheted up a bit.

He pushed the brim of his hat back, and she caught a glimpse of his face. He smiled. "He hated Charlotte most of all."

Once more reassured, she gave up her bundle when he reached for it.

"The horses are all saddled and waiting."

"They are?" Surprise made her come to a halt. "Why?"

"I thought you might need help." There was a smile in his voice when he answered. "And I know you don't ride, Miss Abbey, so I saddled the gentlest horse of the lot."

Miss Abbey. Relief shuddered through her. Still, how odd for him to be here at just the right time.

"I appreciate your offer. I really don't want to involve you. You know there is—"

"Going to be hell to pay. You're right about that, Miss Abbey." He emphasized her name as if to confirm he knew who she was.

"I cannot involve you in my problems."

"You're a woman alone. What kind of man would I be if I didn't . . ." His voice trailed away as though he were searching for the right word, then he added, ". . . offer my services."

That long pause once more worried her, but he was being gallant when he had no cause to be. Miss Mary had talked of a time before the war when men were chivalrous. Personally, Abbey had never seen such, and to find even a small bit of that right here, now . . . tonight . . . when she was most in need. In good conscience, she could not ask anything of him. That didn't keep her from imagining how it would be to confront Sloan Rafferty with a *See? See how to behave like a gentleman?*

"Perhaps you can point me in the direction of Poncha."

He came toward her. "Is that where you want to go?"

"Yes." He had pulled the brim of his hat back down, and she wished it didn't cast such a dark shadow over his face so she could see his expression.

"So you can catch the stage to Denver?"

"Yes."

"I'm at your service, Miss Abbey." He motioned toward the horse behind him before putting her small bundle inside a saddlebag. "Put your left foot in the stirrup, and I'll give you a lift up."

The feat was accomplished effortlessly, and Abbey found

herself sitting astride the horse, swamped with memories of the awful ride here when she had ridden double with Jake. Having this powerful beast beneath her with no one to control it except for her own inexperienced self was more than a little daunting.

Still, her overriding thought was she had been misjudging Caleb all these weeks, somehow reading malevolence into his kind actions. Maybe he really was like Sam, who bore her no ill will. She hadn't trusted Caleb, but now that she compared his treatment of her to the others, her conclusion seemed uncharitable.

"Ready?" Caleb asked, handing her the reins.

She nodded, but the horse didn't move forward when she gently pressed her feet against its sides.

As if recognizing the problem, Caleb smiled. "Since you're not much of a rider, how 'bout I hold the reins for you?"

Since she had only the vaguest notion of how to make a horse go in the direction she wanted, his suggestion reassured her. This way she had only to worry about holding on. And, he wouldn't have offered if he thought she were Charlotte, since everyone knew she was a skilled horsewoman. "That's fine. Thank you."

He stared up at her, the bright moonlight illuminating his startled expression, and she wondered what she had said that surprised him.

"Miss Abbey, I have to ask. Why do you look exactly like Miz Charlotte?"

"I truthfully don't know." She looked away, her gaze raising to the bright moon, which was partially obscured by streamers of clouds.

Rather than the night sky, the image in front of her, though, was Sloan when he had confronted her tonight, his dark eyes filled with revulsion and anger. He would never see her for herself, she realized. That somehow hurt far more than it should. Her breath caught on a ragged sigh, the humiliation of standing naked in front of Sloan so sharp she trembled.

"I can't bear to be here another day." She glanced at Caleb, whose face was once again hidden beneath the shadow cast by the brim of his hat. "He hates me, you know."

"And you hate him."

Abbey recited a verse she had learned from Miss Mary. "Love your enemies, bless them that curse you, do good to them that hate you, and pray for them which despitefully use you."

Caleb shook his head. "Pure foolishness, Miss Abbey. In my way of thinkin' it's another verse from that Bible of yours. An eye for an eye. The only thing turnin' the other cheek will get you is a second black eye."

Given all that had happened to her recently, she couldn't dispute Caleb's statement.

"Admit it, Miss Abbey. You hate Sloan Rafferty."

Did she? No other person in her life had made her as angry. If that was hate, surely she did, sin or no.

"Is the admission so important to you?" she whispered.

"Nah." Caleb vaulted onto his horse. "I wanted to know if you were sure you want to leave."

"I cannot bear it here."

He pulled on the reins for her horse. "Let's go, then."

She wrapped her hands around the saddle horn as Caleb led her horse across the compound and down the track toward the gate. And she discovered another sin within herself, this time envy. What she would give to have enough skill with a horse to be as comfortable as Caleb and the other men. Knowing how to ride would provide her with another layer of freedom.

She would learn, she decided. No more being this helpless. She, after all, was now a western woman, and adding this skill to her others, she had one more tool to make her way in the world.

For the first time in four long weeks, Abbey went through the gate of the Triple Bar S ranch. To her complete dismay, her eyes filled with tears. She was glad to see the ranch behind her. *She was.* She longed to return to the Haverlys' store in Plum Creek, and she didn't dare contemplate they might not want her back.

Soon the road forked, and Caleb took them left. In another few minutes they began to climb up a winding path. With each step the horse took, Abbey was half convinced she could fall off, so to keep from thinking about that, she imagined resuming her duties at the Haverlys' store.

They zigzagged through the timber and up the hill, and when Abbey looked down, she realized they had climbed quite a long way, the shadowy outlines of the ranch buildings barely visible below and far enough away they looked like child's toys.

As she had always assumed Poncha was somewhere in the valley, she was surprised they were ascending a rather large mountain.

"You have been to Poncha, haven't you?" she asked after they topped yet another rise.

"Many times," he answered.

"Oh, good. Otherwise I might be tempted to think we're lost."

"I'm not lost," he assured her with a laugh. "How did you manage to escape from that mongrel watchdog?"

"I gave him a bone."

"I hope he chokes on it."

"I hope not." This was the sort of statement by Caleb that always set Abbey on edge. She added, "Silas is a fine dog." She would feel terrible if something happened to him and it was her fault.

Caleb didn't answer, and as they were going up a yet another hill, Abbey devoted all her attention to staying seated on the horse.

The temperature fell, and Abbey pulled the cloak more tightly around her, once again comparing this ride to the one she had made with Sam and Jake. Winter was closer now than it had been then, the air much colder. Colder, in fact, by the minute.

After they had been riding for what seemed like hours, Caleb stopped with a, "Let's rest a bit."

Abbey slid from her horse, and she stood for a moment until her legs felt steady beneath her. Unlike that awful night with Jake and Sam, her legs held, and she was able to walk a few steps without any discomfort.

She looked into the sky, which was partially hidden by tall pine trees looking even more black than the sky. As she watched, she realized clouds had obliterated the stars and the moon she had been counting on to guide her way.

Once again, she remembered she had thought attempting the journey on her own would be foolish. Caleb's help was an unexpected blessing.

"I want to thank you. I'm not certain I could have managed on my own. The reverend said the stage comes to Poncha every Thursday, so I really wanted to be there before it comes."

"That it does," Caleb agreed, taking both horses by the reins and leading them away. "Good timing, since tomorrow is Thursday."

"Indeed," Abbey agreed. Once more she looked toward the sky, which no longer showed a bit of moonlight.

The complete black of the night seemed fitting somehow since she had been through her own darkest time tonight. Soon, though, dawn would break, and she would be on her way back to Denver. Ahead of her, Caleb and the horses were mere shadows, and she hurried to catch up with them.

"How much longer before we arrive?" she asked.

"We're nearly there," he called back.

She peered ahead and saw nothing but the black forest and

her own worst fears. She wished she saw the welcoming light from a tavern or even a house. Then, a squat building materialized out of the deep gloom, the shape reassuring her. Relieved, she smiled. The hour was late, after all, and a mountain town was unlikely to be big enough to have streetlights.

She heard the scrape of a gate opening, and as she came closer to Caleb, she saw he had tied the horses to the fence of a small corral—or at least she thought that's what it was since no distinct shapes were visible. From within came a nickering sound, a greeting the horse Caleb was riding returned. Another horse. So, this should be the livery even though the complete lack of light puzzled her.

And then she realized what had struck her as odd quite a while ago. There was no road, merely a path so narrow a pair of horses could not have traversed it side by side. It was far too late to remember a warning Miss Mary had taught Abbey long ago. "A wise man's eyes are in his head, but the fool walketh in darkness."

"This isn't Poncha, is it?" she asked. She glanced behind her, ready to run, but the utter black of the forest behind her left her uncertain about where the path even was.

Caleb came between the horses and snagged her hand. "No more pretenses, Miss Abbey." The emphasis was on her name, again, only this time she heard a sneer in his voice. He waved toward the dark outline of the cabin. "We met here many times, and you were always eager to see me." He pushed her toward the building. "The last time we were here, you said the same thing as tonight. That's how I knew it was you. You 'couldn't bear another day.' "

Utter shock froze her thoughts, but she dug in her heels. Like men always did, he used his size and his strength to make her go where he wanted, pulling her along as though what she wanted mattered not at all.

"Stop this," she commanded. "I've never been here with you. Stop at once."

"Now that's more like it, Miz Charlotte. You always were the one to be givin' orders."

"I'm not—"

"We both know that you are." He dragged her along an overgrown path. "There's nothin' more to be gained by lyin'."

"I'm not—"

"Ah, darlin'. Let's keep it honest. You hate your husband, and so do I. I want to know one thing. How did you escape from the Comanche?"

"I have no idea what you're talking about." Panic bubbled through her veins, making her shake. Comanche? A thudding roar in her ears made her sure she had heard him wrong.

"Buck was a greedy fool. I saw the money, Miz Charlotte, so I know he wasn't lyin' when he said he sold you and the mare."

She kicked at his feet, but her efforts didn't slow him down at all. "You're making a terrible mistake—"

"Fact is, it don't matter." He stopped at the open doorway of a squat structure. "What was it Preacher called you?" He pushed her inside, the musty room as dark as a nightmare, then followed. "Daft? Well, you surely are if you believe you're Miss Abbey."

Unable to see even her hands in front of her face, Abbey cried out when her shin connected with something hard.

"As for me, I don't much care whether you're a crazy woman or playin' one of your games." Behind her, light flared from a match, which he touched to the wick of a kerosene lantern.

Her eyes burned at the sudden light, and she looked away from the match. Her eyes adjusted to the illumination from the lantern, and she saw the cabin was as crude as the one where she had lived with Ma and Pa Hawkins. The single room was small, and her shin had connected with the frame of a bed.

175

Caleb casually grabbed her by one arm and looped a leather thong around her wrist. Frightened out of her panicked trance, she kicked at him, clawed at him, aiming for his groin and his eyes. She fought him with everything she had, sure this time her winning really did matter.

Through it, he cursed, filthy and vulgar words she last heard the night Miss Mary was raped. With strength borne of desperation, she pushed him away and somehow managed to slip out of his grasp.

That she was no match for his strength fueled her determination. Without thought, she grabbed the lantern and threw it at him. The lamp broke open, and the flame guttered out, leaving behind the stench of kerosene.

Abbey ran for the black doorway. Outside, she sucked in a huge breath of air and ran blindly into the black maw of night. She stumbled through brush. Only one thing mattered. Getting away from Caleb.

His footsteps crashed behind her. She ran faster and saw nothing in front of her.

The moon suddenly shone, and she dodged around a huge tree. Oh, God, if she could see, so could he. She didn't dare look behind her. His pounding footsteps sounded close. Too close.

The moonlight vanished once more, and once more she was blind.

Brush clawed at her clothes, and behind her, Caleb swore.

A boulder loomed in front of her, and she swerved.

In the next step, her foot didn't hit the ground at all. She screamed. Her balance lost, she tumbled down and down and down and down. Rocks gouged her shoulder once, then once more, then her hip. And she was sure she would die in this very instant. Only she didn't.

Instead, she slid. And slid while pebbles and rocks tumbled

down the steep slope with her.

And then it was all over. She lay there on her back and finally opened her eyes. Soft white shapes materialized above her, closer and closer. Were these angels, she wondered, come to get her? The first settled on her cheek, wet and cold.

Snow.

How very odd. Snow. Not angels.

Tears streamed out of her eyes, and she was so tired. Maybe she would lie here and rest for a minute. Above her, the snowflakes danced as if inviting her to get up. Only she was still crying. She couldn't decide if that was because there were no angels in heaven or because she was still alive . . . and there were no angels.

And she decided she wasn't dead because she was beginning to hurt everywhere. She wanted to sit up, to test her arms and her legs to see if anything was broken. Too frightened to move, she listened.

And heard nothing but the frantic pounding of her own heart.

She kept expecting to hear Caleb nearby. The idea he had tumbled down the steep ravine with her was terrifying, and she held her breath, listening for any sound, anything that would indicate where he was. She imagined he might be doing the same thing, listening for her, she had to bite back a sob.

Then, far above her she heard the crunch of brush, and she imagined she smelled something burning.

A flicker of light caught her attention, and she twisted her head to better see it. A torch, she finally decided, watching it move along the top of the slope. She couldn't judge the distance. Was he a few feet away? Or many? When she looked below her, she imagined she saw indistinct shapes there. How far to the bottom of the slope, she had no idea.

Above her, the light moved but seemed to be getting no closer. Still, if he had a light, he might be coming after her.

177

She turned over to her side, biting back a moan at the pain in her shoulder. A few feet away, a huge, dark object materialized, and she crawled toward it, not daring to move more than a few inches at a time for fear she would dislodge rocks and somehow reveal where she was. Finally, she reached it, discovering it was one of the many juniper bushes that dotted the hillsides.

Above her, she heard a slide of rock, then Caleb cursing. "Miss Abbey, if you can hear me, you better answer."

She shuddered. His voice was above her, but how far, she had no idea.

"You don't want to be left out here all exposed in the cold. Come on, Charlotte." A moment of silence passed. "You want me to call you Miss Abbey? I can do that."

Tears welled in her eyes. As if she would ever trust him again. Her only possible way of getting out of this alive was to make sure he couldn't find her. She prayed the ravine was too steep, too treacherous for him to safely attempt in the dark.

The snowflakes became thicker, and she imagined she was watching feathers from angel wings fall out of the sky. That was a much better thought than seeing snow. Snow was cold. Angel wings were soft.

"Think on it," Caleb called, his voice taunting. "And if you ain't dead, you will be soon. If the cold don't get you, maybe a cougar will. They can smell blood a couple miles off, Miz Charlotte. Now ain't that a fitting end for a hussy?"

CHAPTER 13

Sloan sat close to the bed. On a nearby table a kerosene lantern, with its wick turned low, provided a dim light. When Jonah's fever broke hours later, and he began to sleep more peacefully, the terrible constriction in Sloan's chest eased, at least where his brother was concerned. As for Abbey . . . The appalling wrong he had done her couldn't be made right by a simple apology or even by returning her to Denver.

The anger and confusion boiling in his stomach brought him to his feet. He paced while comparing the truth to his arrogant assumptions and growing questions. The bald truth was she wasn't Charlotte. Just as she had been insisting all these weeks. He was a damn fool for not seeing it. He had been so smug in his conviction that she was game playing.

Damn, how could another woman look so much the same? Charlotte had no sister that Sloan knew of, so the possible reason for them to look like twins was beyond the pale.

Tonight, he had really looked at her. Beyond the obvious similarities, there were subtle differences that, truth be told, he had chosen to ignore. Admitting he saw her cheekbones were slightly more pronounced or her lips were slightly fuller would have been the same as admitting he had made a grave mistake.

So here he was. Stuck in the middle of the most grievous wrong he had ever done another person. All in the name of his own arrogance. That thought weakened his legs and took him back to the chair next to his brother's bed where he clasped his hands and bent his head.

Too easily he had grabbed onto Preacher's explanation of things—his wife was daft. Too easily he had used the excuse of Charlotte liking the drama of her intrigues to explain away her most un-Charlotte-like behavior. She wouldn't have known the first thing about pruning trees or caring for an orchard. She wouldn't have bothered to befriend a little girl. And she certainly never would have taken on any work to ease Consuela's way.

"You look angry, Brother," came Jonah's voice, so deep Sloan first imagined he was conjuring the voice.

When he looked up from his folded hands, he found Jonah steadily watching him, his eyes clear. Immediately, Sloan lifted his brother's head and held a cup of water to his lips.

Jonah sipped, then grabbed Sloan's wrist with surprising strength for a man who had just had a bullet removed from his shoulder. "I may be injured, but I still see."

"You've always seen too much, Tami."

A smile lit Jonah's eyes at his childhood name. "I am your little brother in age only." He settled his head back onto the pillow. "You went to see her because you didn't believe me, am I right?"

Sloan nodded, knowing exactly which "her" Jonah referred to, his thoughts caught in that instant when Abbey rose out of her bath and his utter shock she was not Charlotte.

"And all she saw was your anger?"

Again, Sloan nodded.

"Ah, Brother. You have a very large, difficult mountain to climb this time." Jonah's eyes began to drift closed. "Perhaps you should seek her out and tell her you are a worm, undeserving of her forgiveness."

"No doubt," Sloan agreed, staring down at his brother. "How in the hell did you get shot?"

Jonah's eyes opened, and he pressed the flat of his hand

against his shoulder. "Came across a miner the other day. He had a wagon stuck in a creek and a bunch of scared kids sitting on the bank. His woman started screaming when she saw me." Sadness rather than anger filled Jonah's dark eyes. "Before I could offer to help him, he pulled out a rifle and shot me. I was close enough he had me dead to rights."

"Thank God he's a bad shot."

Jonah met his gaze. "Ask the question that most troubles you, Brother."

Sloan waited for the familiar anger to come that had ridden him all these months since Charlotte's disappearance. It didn't come. "Tell me how she died."

"I found her with Quanah Parker's band. I'd been tracking them for days, mostly avoiding the army patrols who were also searching for the band. The army didn't know where they were headed, but I had a hunch. My mother once told me she had spent summers on the Wahatoya when Quanah's father was still chief. He was a small child then, and now . . ." Jonah shrugged. "He will either be the doom of the people or he will be their savior."

"Enough of Quanah. What of Charlotte?"

"She said Caleb Holt helped her steal the Sun."

Sloan's heart suddenly, fiercely pounded. "What?" The name he had been wanting all summer. All summer he had dreaded one of his men had helped, and all summer he had wondered who. Charlotte had, to the best of his recollection, ignored Caleb. Sloan surged from his chair next to the bed.

Jonah motioned for Sloan to sit. "Before you go off half-cocked, Brother, hear all the story."

Sloan gripped the back of the chair.

Jonah's gaze was somber as he gazed up at Sloan. "The bastard double-crossed her. Instead of selling the horse like they had planned, he kept it, and he left her with Buck."

Sloan's throat dried. He didn't have to ask if Buck had raped his wife. He knew. God help him, he knew. And Sloan wished he had been the man to blow out Buck's brains.

"Buck was supposed to kill her. Only he didn't. After he was finished with her, Charlotte convinced him he could get the best of Caleb by letting her go. Only Buck by then had figured another way to make a profit. Dumb as he was, he knew enough to head south, and he found some of Quanah's warriors near Hardscrabble. He sold her for five dollars and a jug of whiskey."

Every word Jonah uttered sliced Sloan open a little more. At what Charlotte had endured, at the extent of her betrayal and the horrible price she had paid for it, at the involvement of men who worked for him. Odd pieces clicked into place. Caleb's frequent absences he managed to explain away, usually some high-stakes poker game somewhere.

"How did she die?" God help him, he had to know. He didn't want to know.

"She was sick. Chills, diarrhea, vomiting. They had her separated from the rest of the group when I got there, and so she hadn't been eating or drinking." Jonah met Sloan's gaze. "She said to tell you she was sorry."

Sloan was the one who should be sorry. And to the depths of his soul he was. He wished his assumption for her had been the one to come to pass—she had made her way home to Virginia. She had not. Instead, she had been raped and sold to the Comanches. Instead, she had died.

Sloan couldn't imagine what he was going to say in the letter that had to be written to her parents. Despite his urge to lash out at someone, anyone, for what had been done to her, the only man he could blame was himself. In the end, he had not loved her, but he hadn't wanted any harm to come to her, either.

Fierce emotion made his eyes burn. "Thank you."

"No thanks needed." Sleep overcame Jonah almost at once,

leaving Sloan once again alone with his dark thoughts.

To keep the ugly images of what had happened to his wife at bay, he concentrated on his brother, whose life was as precious to him as his own. It hadn't always been so. At first, Jonah had been a nuisance, and in Sloan's mind, no more than the bastard son born of a Comanche woman. At the time, Sloan had been an angry eight year old, filled with grief over his own mother's death. When his trapper father had returned to St. Louis for him, Sloan had been thrilled, imagining the life of adventure the two of them would share. His father had always been bigger than life, an adventurer who regaled them with fantastic tales of Indians and mountains and wide-open spaces. Going west with his father was exactly what Sloan wanted.

And then, he had learned his father had another life and another wife—a Comanche woman—and two other sons, an infant and a three year old. Sloan had hated Jonah on sight even though he was little more than a toddler. Only, Jonah had tagged after Sloan in the way younger brothers do. The day soldiers had stopped at their camp and labeled Jonah as a "stinking half-breed" was the day Sloan had become his younger brother's defender. After that they were inseparable.

Inseparable . . . until Sloan had married Charlotte. Upon her arrival at the Triple Bar S she had announced, "No filthy Indian is going to live in my house. I don't care if he's your brother." Sloan winced at the memory. He had begged his brother to stay, but Jonah had moved out, headed to New Mexico, and Sloan hadn't heard from him until about a month before Charlotte disappeared.

Now that Sloan had lived through his own loveless marriage, at least on his wife's part, he finally understood why Jacob Rafferty had turned his back on his wife in St. Louis and taken a Comanche woman. Between them, Sloan had witnessed genuine affection he had never seen between his father and his mother.

183

His thoughts led him to pace again, and several times during the long night, Sloan found himself standing outside Charlotte's—no, Abbey's—room. What could he say to her?

Since a man's actions spoke louder than his words—and not always to his benefit—Sloan eventually decided the best course was to take her to the stage stop in Poncha. Then what? Did he blithely send her away with no explanation? One part of his letter to Ben Haverly had been true. Abbey had been mistaken for his wife. He had white-washed the rest of it, making it sound like she had been wanted here. The enormity of the wrong he had done to her swept through him. Based on the scars on her back and the brand on her thigh, he wasn't the first to do so. Somehow, he would make sure she never faced anything like that for the rest of her life. He owed it to her to accompany her back to Denver and explain to her employer what had happened as best he could.

The thought of sitting on a stage for two days had him reconsidering once again. Perhaps if Abbey was up to riding, taking her back to Denver was best. Not that she had any reason to go willingly with him anywhere.

She had accused him of abducting her. To his complete shame, he had.

Then it occurred to him she might not even have a position to return to. If that was the case, he had the responsibility to look after her, even to ensure she had the resources she needed to move on to California in the spring.

A tangled web, and completely of his own making . . . a web that seemed to grow ever tighter as the long hours of the night passed.

Just after dawn, he heard Silas whine, and he immediately left Jonah's bedside. If the dog wanted out, the least he could do was let him out before he woke Abbey.

Sloan cracked open the door, and the dog slipped through

the narrow opening. In the dark hallway, the dog was nearly invisible except for his gleaming eyes. Sloan scratched his ears and led the way toward the front door, his footsteps sounding unnaturally loud in the quiet house.

He opened the front door, and Silas slipped outside.

Sloan nearly shut the door, but some sliver of awareness prickled at the back of his neck, and he followed the dog outside. The scent of snow was heavy in the air, which was bitterly cold. Though it was still dark, Sloan could see the dark outline of the bunkhouse and the barn and farther away the cabin where Consuela and her children lived. His home looked as it should, so what was bothering him?

Silas had headed to the opposite side of the compound as he usually did, but his nose was to the ground as though he was following a scent.

Sloan whistled for the dog, who glanced back in his direction, his eyes gleaming. Silas stood stock still, blending into the shadows. Finally, he trotted toward Sloan, something trailing around his neck. Quivering, the dog came to a stop in front of him and sat down.

And around his neck was a makeshift rope made of rags.

Awful premonition sliced through Sloan, and he ran back to the bedroom and pushed open the door so hard it bounced against the wall. Even in the dark he could see the room was as empty as his worst fear.

She was gone.

"God damn it." A length of rags tied together in a makeshift rope matching the length around Silas's neck was tethered to one leg of the bed frame next to a big knuckle bone. In two long steps, Sloan crossed the room and yanked on the rope. It tore so easily he instantly realized the dog could have broken free. Instead, his cooperation had been bought for the price of a soup bone.

Even though Sloan knew he wouldn't find her, he checked the small alcove that held the tub and flung open the armoire doors. Abbey had finally made her escape. Fool that he was, he had been convinced he had thought of everything, that he'd made her escape impossible.

For the longest half hour of his life, he divided his attention between the cabin where Consuela lived with her children and his injured brother. He couldn't leave Jonah alone, and in good conscience he couldn't barge in on Consuela since she had stayed so late and had her own family to be concerned with. The second she emerged from her house, Sloan hurried toward her.

"What is it?" Consuela asked as she hurried toward him, her baby held close to her breast. "Jonah, is he—"

"Better. But Abbey is gone."

"So she finally has you convinced of her lie."

"What?"

"Charlotte. Abbey?"

"Oh." He watched Consuela come up the steps. "Yes. Abbey." Sloan opened the door to the house and waited for Consuela to enter the house before he followed.

"You can be certain of only one thing. She'll tell any lie—"

"Charlotte's dead." Sloan closed his eyes against the images of what she had suffered. "Jonah found her, and she died." He turned around to look at Consuela. "I want you to look through Charlotte's things and tell me what Abbey might be wearing."

Consuela set the infant in the cradle, then led the way to Charlotte's room. Sloan lit the kerosene lamps on the dresser. Consuela opened the armoire, and the first thing Sloan noticed was Abbey had left behind the dresses she had been wearing since her arrival.

"She took the riding habit, the one with the split skirt."

186

Sloan only vaguely remembered it—a dark-brown woolen garment.

"And the cloak." Consuela pulled a coat from the closet. "Odd she didn't take this."

The garment in question was a royal-blue coat with a mink collar. That she had chosen a heavy cloak instead of a coat was yet another indication to Sloan she indeed was Abbey. Given the choice between stylish and practical, Charlotte would have chosen the stylish, including the leather boots in the bottom of the armoire.

At least she was dressed for the weather. Since she had talked endlessly about going to Poncha, he had to assume she was headed there. If she stayed on the road, she'd run right into it.

"You are going after her, aren't you?" Consuela closed the armoire doors.

"I have to." He turned the wick of the lamp down until it went out. "And don't tell me I'm making a mistake. I don't want to hear it."

When he went across the hall to the other room he found an awake Jonah, who smiled when his gaze lit on Consuela.

"I hope you're here to take pity on me. My evil brother has given me nothing but water."

"You must be feeling better." She pulled the blanket down and lifted the bandage on his shoulder so she could look beneath it.

"I am. Now, about some breakfast."

"Yours will be broth and perhaps a biscuit."

"With some apple butter?" Jonah asked.

Consuela tucked the blankets around his shoulders. "Next thing I know, you'll be asking me for a steak."

Jonah managed a grin. "Since my belly is gnawing on my backside, that would be—"

"Today you get broth." She patted his hand, then headed for

the door. "If you're asleep when I return—"

"I won't be," Jonah assured her with a scowl.

This sounded so much like the usual banter between them that Sloan smiled, the ache in his chest easing some more.

Jonah gave Sloan a direct look. "You look only a little antsy. What happened?"

"Abbey is gone." At his brother's raised eyebrow, Sloan added, "I don't know if she's been gone an hour or all night. And damn it, I should have known."

"Bah!" A bowl of steaming broth filled Consuela's hands. "Another twist of the knife." She came into the room. "I won't spare a single tear for her. Not after all that she did to my family. And I won't be changing my opinion of the other one. If they are sisters, the same blood flows through them both."

"And you," Jonah sat up and took the bowl of broth from Consuela, then stared at Sloan. "Is that the opinion you hold of Abbey?"

Image after image marched relentlessly through his mind of all that had happened since Abbey's arrival. Finally, he shook his head. "I've been blind where she was concerned."

Jonah's eyes lit. "That you have, brother. She's much prettier than Charlotte ever was."

Pretty? The instant he had pulled her off Jake's horse all those weeks ago flashed through Sloan's head. He had positively hated that her face had been bruised and that she had been hurt. Equally, he had been angrier with her—with Charlotte—than he cared to admit. And he remembered thinking that despite the bruises and the sunburn she was prettier than he had remembered.

Which was all a bitter reminder he'd been a damn fool.

Sloan headed for the door. "I've got to go after her."

"Remember what I told you last night," Jonah said.

"I remember." He crossed the compound and headed for the

bunkhouse to retrieve his coat and chaps. When he opened the door, he was met with the pungent aroma of coffee. Jake and Sam were sitting at the table, plates of beans in front of them.

"Snowing yet?" Jake asked.

"Not yet. Likely to be soon, though," Sloan responded, putting on the coat that hung at the end of the bunk where he usually slept and grabbing his chaps. Noticing all the bunks were empty, he asked, "Where's Caleb and Eli?"

"Eli's in the outhouse, or at least that's where he was headed. Haven't seen Caleb," Sam answered.

"All morning?" The knot in Sloan's gut tightened.

"All night," Jake clarified. "He probably took off for a poker game in Poncha or maybe Nathrop."

"Want some coffee, Boss?" Sam asked.

"No, thanks."

"Where do you want Buck buried?" Jake asked.

Feeling as though he had been punched in the chest, Sloan sat down on the bench next to Sam and began strapping on the chaps. Given the evil things that Buck had done to his wife, Sloan was half tempted to drag his body back into the hills and let him rot instead of burying him. It was no less than he deserved. Sure as he was sitting here, Sloan was positive Caleb had killed Buck. Unless the man confessed, proving that might be impossible.

"Anywhere except the family plot." Sloan checked for his gloves and a wool scarf in the pockets of his coat.

He glanced at the two men. Sam, still more boy than man, his expression revealing his thoughts. Jake, his friend who had come through the horrors of war with him. "I'm headed for Poncha. When Caleb shows up, I want you to tie him up and confine him."

"Sure, Boss." Sam set his spoon down. "What'd he do?"

"Just do it." Sloan opened the door, letting in a gust of cold air. There was no easy way to explain all Caleb had done. No point in even trying.

"I'll walk with you." Jake grabbed his coat. When they were outside, he added, "You could give the grim reaper a run this morning. How is Jonah?"

"He's going to be fine." Sloan pulled on his gloves, his gaze on the low-hanging clouds, his thoughts on the day Charlotte had disappeared last spring. "Charlotte told Jonah that Caleb helped her steal the Sun."

Jake was quiet a moment before he asked, "Well damn. So your brother found her, but not the stallion."

"Yeah."

"And since he didn't bring her back—"

"She's dead. And Abbey is gone, and I've gotta go."

Eli came around the corner of the building, his hat pulled low and his collar turned up. "Damnation, but it's cold," he complained as he stepped under the porch. "I wouldn't give you a pot of beans for this weather. Heard it's pert near like summertime all winter long down in New Mexico. Day like today makes a man think going there's worth the risk."

"What risk is that?" Jake asked.

"Apaches." Eli patted the top of his hat. "Like my hair just fine right where it is."

"You see Caleb this morning?" Sloan asked.

"No, siree. Last night he said it was a damn shame about ole Buck, but then he decided he'd ride into Poncha and play a little poker with a couple of fellers there."

"So, he never came back."

"Well, that's what I said, now, ain't it?" Eli stomped past them. "You two should come have some coffee and thaw out your ears." He slammed the door behind him.

Caleb was in Poncha, and Abbey was missing. Too easily, he read sinister implications into that. Odd that Caleb would take off the minute Jonah was back.

Sloan hoped Eli was right. Caleb was all consumed by a poker game. If he wasn't, Abbey was in terrible danger.

CHAPTER 14

Abbey awoke to a confusing gray dawn. Or perhaps she was dreaming, she decided, one of those where odd bits combined into things that made no sense.

The nightmare of Sheridan's winter siege of the Shenandoah Valley was long past. Wasn't it? Familiar hunger and raw fear coiled in her belly. She smelled smoke, but seeing where it came from was impossible since gray, cold clouds hung so low they smothered the trees. She peered through the gloom, sure she should be able to see the glow from the nearby farms that had been set on fire. No glow, not even the sound of men shouting or moaning in the distance. Only a gray landscape covered with a few inches of new snow and the occasional snowflake that drifted from the sky.

She couldn't fathom why she was outside or why she didn't hear Miss Mary's soothing voice or the cries of the younger children. So maybe she was dreaming because, if she were awake, she'd hear the younger children, and little Blanche would be clinging to her the way she always did.

Dear God, but she ached. Ached as she had never done so before in her life. Not even after Pa Hawkins had taken his whip to her. This was more like . . . jumping off a cliff into the pitch-black mouth of a nightmare and falling forever . . . because she was being chased.

Chased. She had run. Her heart began to pound. Run until she had no more breath. And then, she had fallen.

She twisted her head to look above her. The rock-covered slope was so steep it seemed to go straight up. And it was mostly covered with snow except for a bare patch of soil here and there where the ground was too warm for the snow to stick.

Or where someone had crawled. More bits of memory flickered through her head, too insubstantial to know if they were real or something she had imagined. Crawling. Hiding. Listening.

Afraid. So afraid Caleb would find her.

Caleb. Just that fast, the past dissolved.

This was no dream, and that awful winter of Sheridan's siege had long since passed.

Gradually she realized she was huddled beneath the meager branches of a small, straggly juniper, and she was much closer to the bottom of the ravine than she had imagined. She struggled to make a plan. Should she stay here? Or should she try to find shelter? She needed that, didn't she? Or . . . maybe a nice warm fire would be better.

Yes, that's what she should do. Build a fire.

Remembering she had carefully wrapped a few matches, she looked for the small bundle she had packed. Where could she have left it? she thought crossly. Of all the times to lose things.

She picked at the few pine needles under the tree with her and thought of how Billy Jackson had been able to make fire by striking rocks together. If Billy could, she should certainly be able to. Despite the ache in her shoulders and arms, she forced herself to sit up. She picked up one small stone, then reached for another.

A hot poker of pain in her shoulder stabbed her, and she screamed. Clapping a hand over her mouth, she looked wildly around, positive she had given away where she was, and any second Caleb would appear out of the gloom.

Since she could smell smoke, he had to be out there. Certain she was not strong enough to run and feeling unbearably exposed, she scooted as far as she could beneath the meager branches of the tree. Still, she reasoned, if she remained motionless, he'd have no reason to look for her beneath this one tree out of so many dotting the landscape.

She studied her arm. Something was wrong with the angle, but try as she might, she couldn't figure out what. One by one she flexed her fingers. That was good, she was sure. Her arm couldn't be broken if she could move her fingers. Or could it? She'd think about that some more when she wasn't so tired. Once more she lifted her arm, and as before blinding pain made her cry out and left her trembling.

Tears burned at her eyes as she searched the gloom. Snow sloughed off the branches of a tree at the bottom of the ravine with a loud swishing plop. The movement and the sound both made her jump. She listened, at first sure she had gone deaf because, except for that one sound, there was nothing. No . . . in the distance, the muted gurgle of water. The eerie call of an owl. The sound of her own shallow breath.

Her limbs felt weighted down, and she decided she'd feel better if she closed her eyes for a moment or two. Images of JJ lying on the dirt floor of the barn made her open them at once. Deciding her conclusion she hadn't broken her arm was wrong, she gently pressed against the bones up the length of her arm. None of that hurt, though. Simply her shoulder. She struggled to make sense of what the injury meant.

Except she was so sleepy. There would be time later to figure it out.

Some reason, though, she had to stay awake.

Oh, yes . . . Keep watch for Caleb. Through gritty eyes, she studied the gray landscape.

Against her will, her eyes drifted shut, and she dreamed of a man coming out of the gloom toward her.

An Indian. One of the short ones like had come to the ranch occasionally. Only this man was old with an unsmiling, wrinkled face, and he made her afraid. She cried out.

He murmured words to her she couldn't make sense of, his voice deep. He was telling her not to be afraid, she thought. Or maybe it was part of another dream. The fear was there, as it had been so many times when Miss Mary had urged her to be brave. She wasn't brave. She wasn't.

And she hid her eyes the way she had when she was a child, her worry pressing relentlessly against her chest. Later when she opened them, she didn't see the gray clouds anymore. Only the ceiling of the room climbing at an odd angle that didn't make sense. The air was warmer, too. Nice. Better than being so cold.

At some point, she became aware of the soft murmur of a woman's voice. Consuela? No . . . this voice was different somehow. Abbey longed to hear Miss Mary's reassuring voice, the one that promised everything would be all right. Except, it hadn't been.

Utter weariness once more caught up with her, and she let it claim her until she became aware of someone with fathomless, dark eyes. She tried to sit up but couldn't. Another face joined the first one, this one much younger.

"Please, I must go."

The older one answered in words she didn't understand, gently pressing her back down. The words made no sense, but she understood the tone because it was the same as Miss Mary's. *Rest. Just rest.*

She reached from beneath the blanket and grasped the woman's hand. "Please. I don't want to die."

She patted Abbey's head, once more murmuring the incomprehensible words.

Later, Abbey had no idea how long, the woman was back, this time with an old man whose face was deeply wrinkled.

They spoke with each other, pointing at her arm, pulling her from the warm cocoon where she lay. Before she could be anything more than alarmed, the old man pulled at her shoulder somehow. There was an instant of sharp blinding pain. After that, she drifted in and out of sleep, unsure whether seconds or hours were passing.

Through a dense fog that dulled her senses, she sipped broth held to her lips and felt her face being washed. She opened her eyes looking for Miss Mary, but instead found only the woman with dark eyes and kind hands.

Then she heard Caleb's voice.

"Have you seen her—Sloan Rafferty's wife? She's missing, and there's a reward."

Fear made her want to cry out, but the woman pressed a finger against her lips and shook her head. So close by—too close—another man spoke, the language filled with words she didn't understand, their tone a denial.

"Maybe I'll just take a look." The room became suddenly bright as though a door had opened, but all she could see was the back of the woman sitting next to her.

More words, this time angrier and more emphatic.

Abbey stilled her breathing, certain in the next second Caleb would wrench her from the warm pallet where she hid. Abbey stared at the structure above here and realized she wasn't in a room, but rather in a spherically shaped tent.

Once again, the room was plunged into darkness.

"Don't be getting all riled at me, old man." Caleb's voice again. "I don't care if your woman is sick. But know this, if you're hiding her, you're dead."

Instead of the discovery she feared, she heard the clop, clop of horse hooves that gradually faded away. The moment of danger passed, and once more she drifted asleep.

★ ★ ★ ★ ★

"Daisy Mae is gone," Sam reported when Sloan came to the barn where Jake was saddling their horses.

"At least she picked the gentlest one of the lot."

Sloan shook his head in frustration. "She made friends with my damn dog and a horse?"

"I never saw her around the horses at all," Sam offered.

"One of the saddles is gone, too," Jake said.

All this time, Sloan had envisioned her walking to Poncha, not riding a horse. Once more, he had underestimated her.

Jake checked the cinches on their two saddled horses, then handed Sloan the reins to his mount.

"I'm counting on you to hold down the fort," Sloan told Sam as he swung into the saddle.

"I've got it," Sam promised.

Sloan urged his mount into a walk. The cold leather creaked, and the cold bit into his thighs. Beneath him, the gelding sidestepped as though as anxious as his master to be on the way. Jake mounted his horse, which fell into step next to Sloan's as they left the compound and headed toward Poncha.

"Search," Sloan commanded Silas, who, looking like the wolves in his bloodline, immediately took off at a lope toward the gate.

Within minutes, snow began to fall, fine nearly-dry flakes that blew around them. As soon as the horses were warm, Sloan urged his into an easy lope that would shorten the ride into town by half. Ahead of him, Silas ran with easy grace, clearly following a scent. As Sloan had expected, the dog followed the road toward Poncha.

He cursed himself for his middle-of-the night cowardice. If he had tried to apologize sooner, he would have found her before she left. He would be hours closer to knowing where she was instead of this awful uncertainty that suffocated him.

Had he felt like this when Charlotte first disappeared? He couldn't remember, but he didn't think so. Mostly, he had been angry with her. Concerned, but not like now. Then he had been so sure she had gone back to her family in Virginia. Spring had been well on the way then, so he hadn't worried about her getting caught in a life-threatening storm.

Turned out he should have been worried. To have Charlotte's death on his conscience made him ache. To be responsible for Abbey's tore him open.

Ahead Silas veered off the road onto a trail—a trail that could have never been mistaken for the road into town.

A knot in Sloan's stomach tightened.

"Any chance your dog could be following a deer or—"

"He's following her." One more thing that should have alerted him Abbey was not Charlotte. Silas liked Abbey, which had been clear from the first day. He hadn't liked Charlotte.

At the fork where the trail took off, Sloan dismounted and studied the ground, which was covered by enough snow to turn the landscape white and varying shades of gray. Shallow imprints from shod horses were visible. Faint, but visible. His eyes on the ground, he followed the path. The trail led through a stand of aspens where no snow had reached the ground yet. Since Sloan had shod the horses himself, he knew the mark left by every shoe on his horses, and he recognized the telltale mark from one of his horses.

"Two horses," Sloan finally told Jake. "See the *V* in the track right here? That's Daisy Mae." He pointed to another track. Hair rose on the back of his neck. "And this one is from the horse Caleb Holt rides."

"Not good," Jake said.

"Nope."

Whether Caleb believed Abbey was herself or Charlotte, she was in danger, either way. He figured Caleb believed what they all had—she was Charlotte.

Sloan studied the tracks a moment longer. He stared at the intersect of the trail with the road. His gut was telling him that Silas was following Abbey's scent up the draw. What if the tracks weren't hers? One small herd of his cattle had summered up here, and he had sent Caleb back up here yesterday to make sure no strays were left behind. Could that be the logical explanation for Caleb's horse to be up this way? Maybe. There was no logical reason for the old mare to be with him.

Remounting his horse, Sloan looked at Jake. "I think we should split up. You head for town. I'll follow Silas."

"Sure you don't want to stick together?"

"We can cover more ground this way. And, if you find that son of a bitch before I do, hogtie him and take him back to the ranch."

"I will. Don't do anything stupid like getting yourself lost in this storm." Jake turned his horse back toward the main road.

"The same to you." Sloan urged his horse into a trot. The memory of finding Buck's body blazed in his mind, only this time he kept seeing Abbey's face.

A quarter mile later, the trail reached a creek and split off again. Sloan didn't see his dog, but the tracks were left behind. Instead of crossing the creek, Silas's footprints followed the trail that led inexorably up, parallel to the narrow creek. The banks were dotted here and there with abandoned mining claims, mounds of dirt and gravel somehow warm enough the snow wasn't sticking to them yet.

The forest was unusually quiet, the way it was during a storm. No birds chirping, no warning chatter from squirrels, nothing. Just the occasional plop of snow as it slid off the branch of a pine tree. Sloan saw movement across the creek, and he reined to a stop. A second later, a couple of does and a half-grown fawn emerged from the timber, picking their way downstream.

The clouds settled lower, and snow began to fall harder. Sloan whistled for the dog, who gave him an answering bark farther upstream.

At the first ridge overlooking the valley, the trail doubled back on itself and left the banks of the creek, and he slowed the horse to a walk as the trail climbed ever upward. Normally Sloan stopped when he reached the third switchback, which signaled he had reached the crest of the hill because he liked the view. Today, the clouds and snow reduced the view to a few hundred feet.

The trail straightened and headed straight across a meadow to a bank of nearly black pine trees. The tracks Silas left stretched out, indicating he was running.

As he reached the shelter of the timber, he heard a distant crack that sounded like a gunshot. Once more he came to a stop so he could listen. Whatever he had heard wasn't repeated, and so he had no idea whether he really had heard gunfire or simply the crack of dry timber somewhere close by.

Hours passed, and Sloan's focus narrowed to following the nearly invisible trail left by the dog and to his increasing worry for Abbey. The terrain was increasingly more rugged, and the storm was worsening by the hour. Usually the storms that came in late September were a tease for the more severe weather that would follow later in the winter. This storm, though, was a full-blown winter storm.

Finally, the outline of a small cabin became visible. Years ago, trappers had used it, and Sloan had been here with his father. Since then someone had built a small corral and a lean-to he didn't remember.

Ahead of him, Silas sniffed the ground in front of the cabin and next to the corral in a way that suggested to Sloan she had gotten off the horse and gone inside.

He dismounted and ground-reined the horse. Dreading what

he'd find, he pushed open the door to the tiny cabin. It was more squalid than he remembered. A wooden bedframe was on one side of the room and a rough fireplace on the other. Judging by the smell, he figured a weasel had been using the place as a den.

He went back outside, where the corral and lean-to were in better shape. And the tracks inside indicated both had recently been used. Keeping part of his attention on Silas, Sloan bent over the tracks and soon became frustrated trying to read them. Too much snow had fallen to determine how many horses had been here or whether any were the tracks he had seen leaving the road miles back.

Silas barked and took off at a run. Sloan climbed back on his horse and followed the dog . . . right to the edge of a steep talus slope that fell to the creek more than two hundred feet below. Whining, Silas paced back and forth at the edge of the ridge.

Sloan figured he might take a horse down the slope.

In broad daylight when the rocky incline was dry. Maybe.

If his life depended on it.

He didn't want to imagine going down the steep hill on foot, much less on horseback.

He studied the slope a while longer looking for any indication Abbey had climbed down the ancient rockslide. Scattered juniper trees had sprouted up here and there, clinging tenaciously to the steep slope. Of Abbey, there was no sign.

And then he smelled smoke from a campfire.

The only sensible choice was to double back a couple of miles to get to the bottom of the ravine.

"C'mon, Silas." Sloan whistled for the dog.

The reluctance with which the dog followed him increased Sloan's conviction that Abbey was down there somewhere. And he didn't like any of the images that came to mind as he contemplated her being at the cabin and then at the edge of the slope, much less at the bottom of it. The idea that he could find her body at the bottom of the ravine was enough to make him break into a cold sweat.

Another hour passed before he reached the bottom and found the trail along the bank of the creek. Silas stayed close as was usual until given the command to search. The smell of the campfire smoke gradually became stronger, and, when Sloan came around the end of a jutting ridge that marked one side of the talus slope, he found the source. A small band of Utes, no more than six or seven, were in the process of dismantling their camp. Travois were attached to three of the ponies. Two were loaded with supplies and the dismantled teepees, a pair of them, Sloan figured, looking at the outlines left on either side of the campfire.

"Stay," Sloan commanded his dog. Silas immediately sat, though objecting with a soft whine as he lifted his nose high into the hair, his nostrils quivering.

A gnarled old man watched Sloan's approach even as he motioned to a younger man—a boy, really—to keep working. Sloan recognized the old man, an elder from one of the Ute bands that hunted in this traditional summer range. The man himself was unremarkable, but his ponies had fine, clean lines and intelligent eyes.

"Hello, Little Skunk," Sloan said to him, speaking in the Ute language.

"Greetings to you, Sloan Rafferty."

Sloan remained on the horse, pulling the collar of his coat higher around his neck, waiting for the invitation that would come in Little Skunk's own sweet time. He glanced around at the busy activities, surprised they were preparing to travel even as the weather was growing worse.

"It's not a good day for travel," Sloan said.

"We are headed south. It will be better there."

"Are you meeting up with your brother Nashua?"

"Soon," the old man said.

It was clear he wasn't going to be invited to dismount. "I'm looking for a woman." He added a description of Abbey and what he thought she was wearing.

"You lose your woman?" Little Skunk returned with a biting laugh. "She run from you?"

"Maybe," Sloan agreed.

"Maybe you aren't so good for her, then."

Sloan nodded in agreement. "Have you seen her?"

"A man would remember finding a white woman in the mountains," Little Skunk said.

Was that a no, he hadn't seen Abbey answer or a yes? Sloan stared at the man a moment, then glanced around the camp. Only one way to find out for sure. Sloan whistled for his dog, who came running into the camp at full speed and made a beeline for a mound of furs beneath one of the pine trees close to the edge of the stream. His tail wagging, the dog nosed beneath the furs, and a pale hand appeared to pet the dog's head.

Sloan leveled an angry glance on Little Skunk as he dismounted and began walking across the camp. "Why the hell didn't you tell me she was here, old man?"

"She asked me to hide her." Little Skunk shrugged.

"Someone else came looking for her? A younger man about this tall with light hair and eyes?" Sloan indicated the height above his own shoulder.

Little Skunk nodded. "The other man said she was your woman."

"She is," Sloan agreed. If being responsible for her well-being made her his, then she was.

The older man motioned toward the towering pine tree. He crossed his arms over his chest. "I told you. A man would be remembering seeing a white woman in these mountains."

"And you, old man, would have let me leave without her."

Little Skunk shrugged. "Then I would have known you lied about her being your woman. A man protects what is his."

On that, they were in complete agreement.

CHAPTER 15

Abbey was shrouded beneath furs that had been tucked around her. Though Little Skunk and his small band had clearly cared for her, her face was damn near as white as the snow falling around them. When she opened her eyes, they were dark with pain. Relieved and afraid and guilt ridden, Sloan sank to his knees next to her. Bruises tinted the swelling on her cheekbone, and a scrape ran along her hairline. Good God, what had happened to her?

Her eyes opened, and she returned his intent stare, recognition of him in her beautiful dark eyes.

"I dreamed of you," she finally whispered.

"Did you?" A nightmare was more like it, given what he had put her through.

A ghost of a smile flitted across her face as her eyes drifted shut. "You finally saw me."

The dog nudged her hand with a soft whine. She softly murmured, "Silas, you're such a good boy," while her fingers sank into the dense hair of his coat.

Sloan swallowed the lump that choked him. A good thing she had closed her eyes because he would not have been able to hold her gaze.

"I do see you."

As she didn't respond, he wasn't sure if the words ever left his mind or if she had simply drifted off to sleep. Gently, he covered her head, protecting her from the falling snow.

"How injured is she?" he asked, speaking Ute to the woman nearby, who was efficiently tying together a bundle.

She glanced at Little Skunk as if asking for permission to explain. When he grunted in response, she pointed to her own shoulder. "Dislocated." She pointed toward another older woman. "We fixed it. She has many bruises." Again, she motioned, indicating far too many places on her own body. "The woman is frightened. Especially of the other man."

The other man. A traitor named Caleb Holt. Sloan glanced at Little Skunk. "Is that why you're leaving?"

The Indian shrugged. "It's time to go to our winter home."

Sloan looked back at Abbey, sure he didn't want to travel since she was injured, equally sure they couldn't stay here. If Little Skunk was worried enough to be packing up in the middle of a storm, he had some reason. Caleb? Or the jitters because of the anti-Indian sentiment that had intensified over the last few months?

The process of getting Abbey onto his horse and then mounting behind her went more smoothly than he had hoped, thanks to Little Skunk's able assistance. Sloan had the feeling the man cooperated simply to have them gone. Sloan settled Abbey across his lap, making sure her feet and legs were covered.

After thanking Little Skunk for his assistance, Sloan said, "If you need anything—"

"One of your cows?"

He nodded. "If you need the meat, then yes." He nudged the horse into a walk, turning back the way he had come. "Go to the ranch and see my brother Jonah. He'll take care of it."

Sometime after they left the camp, Abbey stirred. "Are we going home?"

"That's the plan." The word stuck in his head. She'd been his captive, judged for the sins of his wife, and she called the Double Bar home? How could she? Considering the vicious scars covering her back, what sort of home had she ever had? He'd gladly whip whoever had taken a lash to her. Whoever had branded her deserved even worse.

Snow was falling harder than it had been when they left the Ute camp, and he had serious doubts about trying to make it the whole way home. The clouds hung so low and were so dense, daylight was mostly a reflection of the falling snow. Night would be upon them soon, and he couldn't—wouldn't—risk Abbey's life by pressing toward the ranch during the night. Not when there was shelter a mile away at the old trapper's cabin.

At once he was struck with what had been at the back of his mind. This late in the day was a damn strange time to be breaking camp. He couldn't decide what to make of that. Had it been a ruse for whatever reason, or were they really leaving? If so, Little Skunk's band would be stuck with the same problems Sloan had—worsening weather and night coming all too soon. Could a threat from a single man make them skittish enough to leave?

"I'm going to California, you know." Abbey's simple statement was clear despite her voice being muffled by the robes covering her.

He glanced down at her, tipping his head a little so he could see beneath the hood of the cloak that protected her head.

"I remember."

"It's snowing like it did the winter the soldiers came."

"What soldiers?" he asked, mostly because talking would hopefully keep her awake.

"The Union soldiers," she said. "The ones who burned everything in the valley and took the food." She sighed. "I'm hungry."

Her statement was less a complaint than a resigned statement of fact, as though she had been hungry many times. He remembered how weightless she had felt that first day when he had lifted her off Jake's horse and how he thought she—Charlotte—had never been so thin.

"We'll stop soon." Sloan gazed at the sky above them, which was growing darker by the minute. They were nearly to the fork in the trail. Within the blanket and the deepening gloom, he could barely see Abbey's face. Traveling in weather like this by himself bordered on foolhardy. With Abbey, it was unthinkable.

"Were you with your parents then?" he asked.

"With Miss Mary," Abbey said. She uttered a soft sound of distress.

"Are you hurt?"

Against him, he felt her shake her head. "Just remembering. More children every day. Sick, hungry children. Every day, Sammy and I dug graves."

He regretted asking her anything that brought back memories of the war. He had known about the siege of the Shenandoah Valley because Sherman used the same tactics as Sheridan. Scorch the earth, and leave nothing behind for the enemy to survive, much less feed their soldiers. The autumn Sheridan had laid siege to the Shenandoah Valley, Sloan had been a teamster, driving wagons of ammunition in Sherman's army. After Sherman heard about the success of Sheridan's tactics, he copied them during the infamous march from Atlanta to Savannah. The orders had been to burn or destroy anything the army didn't need. And now, Sheridan had been sent west to handle the "Indian problem." The territorial governor, Edward McCook, had employed the same tactics during the war. Sloan figured that didn't bode well for the Utes, even though they had been promised fair treatment if they signed a treaty.

"Why are you going to California?" he asked.

"I'm planting an orchard." Her voice remained muffled within the blankets. "Abbey's Orchard. With apples and cherries. And peaches. I love peaches." She sighed again. "I'm still hungry."

"I know." The hardtack in his saddlebags would be all he could manage tonight. He wished he could give her more, even the peaches she professed liking.

If he was lucky, they could be to the trapper's cabin before it got completely dark. There he'd have shelter for the horse in addition to shelter for themselves. Wind came up as the falling snow grew thicker. Their travel slowed as the gloom of oncoming night deepened. They didn't reach the cabin until more than an hour after darkness fell.

During that long hour, he had kept Abbey talking and learned a woman named Miss Mary had taken in Abbey because she was orphaned, just as the woman had taken in a dozen of other orphans. Abbey had lived there until a couple of years ago, until she began her journey west. None of it explained the scars on her back, and he didn't have the courage to ask her. Two years represented a lot of commitment to make it from Virginia to Colorado. Sloan figured he owed her the rest of her journey to California.

At the cabin he climbed off the horse, then carried her inside. The musky smell from a weasel was still there, faint but unmistakable. He set Abbey down on the platform of the bed.

"Where are we?" she asked.

"An old trapper's cabin." Based on the crunch beneath his boots, he knew he had stepped on a pinecone. Lighting a match, he used the flare of light to look around and found dried leaves and pinecones scattered across the floor. Taking a handful of the kindling to the fireplace, he mounded it, then dropped the match onto it. "I've got to get some firewood, then take care of the horse."

When she sucked in a shuddering breath, he turned around.

Her eyes were wild within her pale face. She looked ready to bolt.

Crossing the room to her, he knelt next to her. "What happened? Are you hurt?"

"I've been here," she said, her gaze darting to the open door. "Caleb brought me here."

That confirmed what Sloan had thought all along—that she had left with him. "Did he—" Rape you? The red haze of his anger and his fear for her blurred her pale face. "—hurt you?"

She was trembling now. "I ran," she whispered. "And fell."

Since she had been found fully dressed, including her cloak, he hoped—prayed—she had escaped before Caleb had laid a hand on her. Too vividly he imagined what had happened as he recalled the zigzagging trail the dog had followed from the cabin to the edge of the ravine. Clearly, she had been running for her life.

With sudden strength, she let go of the blanket tucked around her and clutched his coat. "He came looking for me."

"I know." Sloan covered her hand with his own. "You're safe now."

"He'll come back." Tears filled her eyes. "He kept calling me Charlotte and telling me awful things." She raised her stricken gaze to Sloan's. "He wanted to kill me."

"I know." Sloan's voice sounded rough even to his own ears. Taking both of her hands within his, he leaned close, wishing with all his heart he could undo the events that had brought her into his life. "You're safe. He's not going to come back tonight. But I have to leave you for a few minutes."

The echo of that wish lodged in his throat. If he could undo the events that had brought her into his life, he would have never met her. That, maybe, was the biggest lie he had ever told himself.

Somehow, she had become so important to him that he

couldn't imagine not knowing her. This yearning for her felt like a great gaping hole that only she could fill. While he stared into her beautiful eyes, he wondered how he could have ever thought she was Charlotte, no matter how great the resemblance. In those few seconds, his life stretched out in front of him, this woman at his side through every minute of it.

He owed her the dream of the orchard in California. He would do well to remember that.

"Firewood. Your horse," she said.

With effort, he recaptured the last thing he had said to her. "That's right."

She moved as if to stand. "I can help."

Gently he pushed her back down. "You can help me best by staying here." He cupped the side of her face with his hand, her skin soft and cool beneath his palm. "You're safe, Abigail Wallace. No one is going to hurt you. I promise."

Abigail. He had called her by her name. Tears filled Abbey's eyes as she gazed up at him. His simple words were an answer to her prayer.

Only, she was afraid to really believe him, afraid to let him go. A sudden gust of wind shook the walls of the cabin, and a swirl of snow came through the open door.

"I'll be back in a shake." And just like that he was gone, disappearing through the door like the apparition she was sure he had been when he came to the Indian camp. The wonder of it filled her with warmth. He had come for her. Finally, he had seen her for her own true self.

Clutching the cloak and a blanket more firmly around herself, she looked around the room. She didn't remember it except for the pungent odor of some animal that had made it home. The kindling was nearly spent, so she stood, intending to add more pinecones to it before the fire flickered out. Instead, she felt so light headed she immediately sat back down. Silas was right there, nudging her hand and letting her know she wasn't alone. As had been the case for a while, the dog felt like her friend rather than her guard. She eased her hands into his dense coat, her fingers immediately feeling warmer.

She stared into the dwindling fire while disjointed memories of the last weeks floated through her mind. Sloan was at the center of those. Fair with his men . . . affectionate with the children . . . kind to Consuela. Abbey's eyes burned. As always, she had been the outsider. Drowsiness began to claim her, and with her relaxation came another memory from the day the bull had chased her. Had he been afraid for her?

The next thing she was aware of was looking at the fire and marveling it now was burning as a proper fire should, with logs stacked in such a way as to burn slowly and thoroughly. Light flickered across the ceiling, oddly comforting. Sloan's concerned face appeared in front of her vision, and she decided she must be dreaming. How could the man be so concerned after being so harsh for so many weeks?

She closed her eyes as sleep once again beckoned. Oh yes, she remembered now. He had called her Abigail. Abigail . . . Yes. Finally, he had seen her, just as she had dreamed.

The next time she awoke, she was ravenous. If she was this hungry, the smaller children would be, as well. When she didn't hear any of their cries, a stab of fear sliced through her, and she threw the covers back and sat up.

Instantly she was light headed.

"Not so fast." Gentle hands touched her shoulders, and she looked into dark, compassionate eyes. Sloan Rafferty. He'd been like that with JJ and Pearl. She remembered wishing he would look at her in the same way. And now that he was . . . her breath caught, the memories of the children at Miss Mary's house fading like mist under a warm sun, the present more firmly in her mind.

No children. The war was long over, and she was in Colorado. In the next instant, the rest of it flooded back. Her misplaced trust of Caleb. Her blind run into the night. The terrifying fall. The surprising rescue by the Indians and Sloan's arrival. The snowstorm.

"Is it still snowing?" she asked.

"Not since this morning."

"This morning." Struggling to make sense of that, she glanced around the room. A saddle was positioned near the fireplace as though it had provided a backrest. A rifle was propped near the doorway. And a cast-iron pot hung from a hook over the fire. Silas lay on the floor, his head resting on his paws, his golden eyes gleaming in the firelight. More than any other thing, seeing the dog reassured her.

"I kept smelling stew in my dream."

"No dream." Giving her shoulder a gentle squeeze, he moved away. "Think you can stay awake long enough to eat this time?" A second later, he tacked on, "You've been telling me for a couple of days that you're hungry, but after two sips of broth you fall asleep."

She latched onto the one part of the sentence that made even less sense than all the rest. "What do you mean a couple of days?"

He returned with the bowl. "Just that. Tonight will be our third night here."

"And it's been snowing all this time?"

"Yep. A good three and a half feet," he said.

"We're snowed in?"

"For the moment." He held the spoon out to her. "Can you feed yourself or . . ."

She took the spoon from him and then realized she was wearing only her shift.

Remembering all the times she had helped Miss Mary care

for sick children through cycles of fever and chills, Abbey had a very clear idea of the care she had received over the last three days. Three days.

"How sick have I been?"

He shrugged. "It could have been a lot worse. I've been afraid you'd develop pneumonia."

She shuddered at that thought. Too often she had seen the illness that was usually a death sentence. Sloan must have thought she shivered from cold, though, because he wrapped a blanket around her shoulders.

"You're not going to get all huffy because I undressed you?" He held her gaze a moment. "If there had been another way . . ."

She stared at him a moment, trying to put a name to the feeling coursing through her. The knot in her stomach didn't have the familiar pull of fear. Anger was part of it, she finally decided, but not so much at him as at her own inability to take care of herself. Embarrassment that he undoubtedly had a familiar knowledge of her body. Every time the man had touched her, his hands had been warm. The notion those hands had touched her intimately . . .

Unfamiliar heat coiled deep in her belly, which fractured her concentration while she continued to look at him. He held her gaze so steadily, his dark eyes unreadable. What had he asked, she wondered. Oh, yes. Was she going to be angry? She didn't know what to name this feeling pulling through her, but it certainly wasn't anger.

"No. I'm not . . ." she paused and searched for the word he had used. "Huffy."

The corner of his mouth lifted. "Well, then, maybe you're hungry."

"I am," she announced.

He held the bowl up, the aroma of the broth making her

214

mouth water. Her stomach rumbled, and he chuckled, the smile lighting his face and warming his eyes. "Then I'd better feed you."

She held out a hand for the spoon, which he immediately gave to her. Her fingers shook as she dipped the spoon into the broth and attempted to bring it to her mouth. Instantly, his were there, gently supporting hers as she attempted to get the broth into her mouth. Some of it dribbled onto her chin. Without a word, he took the spoon from her, filled it, then held it in front of her mouth.

"I want to do this myself." To her great annoyance, that sounded like a whine rather than a command.

"Tomorrow." A warm smile lit his eyes. The one she had longed for and hadn't known just how much until this moment.

Tears burned at the back of her eyes, but she opened her mouth.

One bite, then another. She trembled with the effort to stay seated, and he noticed that, too. He had been sitting across from her, his long legs crossed as he fed her. He put down the bowl, reaching for her. He lifted he as though she weighed nothing and settled her on his lap and wrapped his arms around her. Once more, he reached for the bowl. She found that, with his arms and chest supporting her back, she could feed herself. Almost. Maybe, if she hadn't been so aware of the feel of him against her back and bottom. Maybe, if he hadn't been so warm. Maybe, if she hadn't felt his breath next to the side of her head. Maybe . . . She sighed, sure she wasn't supposed to like this so much and sure she didn't want to be anywhere else.

After a few bites, she tipped her head back, her neck supported by his strong arm. The question she wanted to ask—why are you being kind now?—never left her lips when his dark gaze met hers. She couldn't have broken that connection if her life had depended on it. She remembered thinking his dark eyes were cold, but they weren't now. This close, she became aware of his lashes and a small scar mostly hidden by one of his eyebrows. Her hand crept out until she could touch it.

"Where did you get this?"

His expression softened even more. "My brother hit me with a big stick when I was about nine. Since he was four at the time, I couldn't hit him back even though I wanted to."

"Jonah?"

He shook his head. "No. Isaac."

His voice was so sad, she became sorry she had asked, after remembering Isaac Rafferty was one of the names she had read on a headstone in the family cemetery. That didn't keep her from saying, "Jonah is an Indian."

"A Comanche, to be exact."

"He's your brother."

She realized Sloan was holding the spoon in front of her mouth, so she took another bite.

"Yep." He was silent a moment. "When I was seven, my mother died. It was a year later when my father showed up, and my grandparents, who thought I was a heathen, were all too glad to let him take me. He was a trapper who always seemed huge to me when he'd bring his furs to St. Louis. He'd carry me on one of his big shoulders, and I remember thinking he was a Greek hero like Hercules. I thought we'd have a grand adventure, just the two of us. He didn't tell me I had two more brothers until we got to Bent's Fort or that he'd had a Comanche wife for most of the time he had been married to my mother."

He fell silent, and Abbey supposed she ought to have been shocked that Sloan's father had an Indian woman—a wife, Sloan had said, not mistress—in addition to his white wife. Sloan was so matter of fact, she found herself thinking about the odd assortment of people at the ranch and how they all seemed to fit somehow. This was so different from her Methodist upbringing, filled with rigid rules about people and their relationships to both one another and to God, but at the same time filled with caring for others. With Sloan, there was the caring, but more acceptance of differences in people, too. He had a brother from a different mother without seeming bothered by it. Had it always been so, she wondered?

He had left a lot out, she decided, in the way he had glossed over the year after his mother had died. "Do you remember your mother?" she had to ask. Of her own, she didn't have a single memory.

She stole a glance at him and found him staring into the fire, those dark eyes reflecting the firelight. She had the feeling he was remembering things he couldn't put into words. She knew about that.

Then he surprised her by answering, "My mother died one winter, and, before that, I don't remember much. I was mostly taken care of by a nanny who had also taken care of my mother."

"Your daddy was a fur trapper?"

"When he and my mother met, he was a teacher. But he had wanderlust. When I was about a year old, he took off and came back only when he had furs to sell. Almost a whole year passed after she died before he came back. He was one of a kind. Could skin a beaver while quoting Lord Byron and William Words-worth." The spoon appeared in front of her lips again, and she took another sip while Sloan resumed talking. "At first, I hated Isaac and Jonah and their mother, Two Doves, but somewhere along the line, we became a family. They are my brothers, pure and simple."

"I saw Isaac's grave. And your father's."

Sloan grunted a "Yep."

She didn't blame him for not wanting to talk about that any since she didn't like talking about the graves where she thought her mother and grandmother were buried.

They were silent for a while as she continued to eat, his only comment coming when she protested she was full. "Three more spoonfuls, and the cup will be empty." And so, she ate, whether to please him or because she was hungry, she didn't know. She only knew this was somehow as comforting as anything she had ever felt in her entire life, her back nestled against his broad chest and his arm easily supporting her. The fire crackled cheerfully, illuminating the room in a golden glow.

"Why do you look so much like Charlotte?" he asked sometime later.

"I don't know," she confessed, a hazy memory of seeing a dark-haired girl dressed in white drifting through her mind. "I may have seen her once when I was very small."

"Tell me about that." His voice was so gentle it sounded like an encouragement rather than the commands she was used to from him.

"I lived with Ma and Pa Hawkins, but I knew I wasn't their child. They were probably sharecroppers, but I don't really know. There was an old woman who lived in this huge house I always dreamed about. I'd watch for her, and she would always be so glad to see me. I knew it had to be a secret. Once there was this big party on the lawn, and everything was so white and clean and beautiful. I knew I wasn't supposed to be there, but a girl with dark hair and beautiful curls saw me. She screamed." The rest of the memory loomed but was too dark to grasp. Still, she trembled. Something about that day . . . Pa had surely whipped her though the memory of that particular beating remained in the misty recesses of her mind. She shifted against Sloan so she could look up at him. His stare left the fire and rested on her. "The old woman is the one who gave me the brooch."

"But you don't know who she was?"

"I think she was my grandmother, but do I have any proof? No." Abbey sighed. "After the war was over, I found her grave. Her name was Martha Flanders Wallace—I remember her telling me I was a Flanders when she gave me the brooch. She was buried next to Francis Wallace." The emotion filling Abbey that day came to the surface, and her voice clogged while her eyes burned. "She was the daughter of Martha and the mother of Abigail." Her voice caught. "That's me. Pa taunted me with being crazy like my mother. And then, he'd whip me, and he'd make me recite a verse from the Bible about a whip on the back of fools."

Chapter 16

The anguish in Abbey's voice ripped through Sloan as did his fury at the man who had taken a lash to her. He knew firsthand such cruelty existed. But toward a child?

He expected that her voice would break, but it did not. Instead, her voice was unbearably sad when she added, "After Miss Mary taught me to read, I found the verse in Proverbs. 'A whip for a horse, a bridle for a donkey, and a rod on the back of fools.'" Then her voice did break. "The preacher said it meant Satan was inside a fool, and the only way to get him out was . . ."

He drew her closer, tucked her in next to him, and whispered against her hair, "He was wrong." When she looked up at him, he repeated, "He was wrong, Abbey. Satan was never inside you." If Satan had been anywhere, he was inside men who could imagine such evil within a child.

She turned her head away, and thankfully, she once more relaxed against him. He watched the fire for a long while, sensing she was doing the same because, occasionally, she would sigh.

As surely as they were sitting here, Abbey's past was all tied up somehow with Charlotte's. Flanders—Charlotte's family name. If what the old woman had told Abbey were true, she and Charlotte were at least cousins.

"Do you know William Flanders?" he asked, naming Charlotte's father.

"No. If I had ever heard his name before the night Preacher read his letter to you, I don't remember it."

"If you're a Flanders, you and she are somehow related."

Abbey made a soft, involuntary sound of distress. "I don't know if I like that. She's . . ." Her voice trailed off.

"Not you." As happened too often for his peace of mind, he didn't like knowing he had judged this gentle woman for the sins of his wife. "I know."

She didn't say anything, which was no surprise. She was once more staring into the fire, so he couldn't see her face, only feel the tension in her body. Until now he hadn't thought about what it might have been like for her to be unable to prove to anyone she was not the person she had been mistaken for.

If his guess about her age was right, she'd be within a year of Charlotte, who had been eighteen when they had married three years ago.

"What happened to them? Ma and Pa Hawkins?"

"They both died soon after the war started."

So . . . she had been alone, an orphan, for years.

She was quiet for such a long time he thought she might have gone to sleep, but then she asked, "You do believe me now? That I'm Abbey?"

He looked down, trying to see her face. She was staring at the fire, and, though she still rested against him, her body wasn't as relaxed as it had been moments earlier.

"I believe you." That somehow sounded angry, which figured, since he vividly recalled the night he had stormed into her bath so damn sure Jonah had to be wrong. He couldn't have made such a colossal mistake. Only he had. He should have known it without waiting to see the scars on her back or the brand on her thigh.

He'd be a long time atoning for that particular sin.

He wasn't much better than the other men in her life who

had abused her. Especially since he was now remembering those moments when she had stood bare before him, her expression defiant, and her body more lovely and alluring than he had imagined. These last three days, he had drawn upon every ounce of discipline he'd ever had to keep his desire for her at bay when he had cleaned her and taken care of her most personal needs. And now she was recovering . . . and here, willingly, within the circle of his arms . . .

He sighed deeply, at once wishing he didn't want her and wishing she wanted him as badly.

She twisted in his arms once more to look at him, and it was all he could do to hold her gaze. Just as she had been the first day she arrived at the ranch, she was bruised. This might not have been by his hand, but he was as responsible as if he had hit her himself. A man protected those under his care, and he'd done a damn poor job of taking care of this woman who, by no fault of her own, looked like Charlotte. Except, when he looked at her now, he didn't see his wife. Truth was, he hadn't since a day or two after her arrival at the ranch.

Truth was, he was an idiot, which his brother would agree with.

"That night . . ." For the life of him, he couldn't finish the sentence. "I'm sorry."

He didn't like regrets, and he damn well didn't like doing stupid things he had to apologize for.

He wanted her forgiveness. Wanted it badly, in fact.

"If I could do things over, I would. I shouldn't have barged in on you." He touched the bruise at her temple and the scrape along her hairline. "My fault you were in Caleb's path."

She shrugged slightly. "It was my choice to leave." She laughed softly, a sound so sad it pierced right through him. "Miss Mary was strict with all of us. She'd say, 'You may have had no say in what happened to you before you arrived here, but you are in charge of what you decide to do about it.' "

"She sounds wise."

"I loved her, and she broke my heart the day she told me she thought I was eighteen, therefore an adult, and she couldn't take care of me any longer."

"She threw you out?"

He felt Abbey's head move against his chest. "No, though it felt that way at the time. She told me I had a month, and then I'd have to leave. I had this flier about the Homestead Act I'd been carrying around for years, dreaming of having my own place. So, I decided. I'd head west and homestead an orchard."

He had no idea how to respond. When he'd been that same age, he was surrounded by his father, his Comanche mother, and his brothers, and he'd had the naïve notion they'd be together forever. Instead, he'd gone off to war where he had driven ammunition wagons for the Union army. His father and Isaac had died trying to hold onto the ranch. Jonah and Two Doves had returned to the Comanche. Unlike Abbey, he'd had a family and had known where he belonged. Finally, Jonah was back, and Sloan hoped Two Doves would return, as well. Far safer for her to be with him than with Quanah's band. He had belonged and knew it. And Abbey had been isolated and alone. Even more so after being at the Double Bar.

She had among the rarest of qualities he'd found in anyone. She didn't blame others for her lot in life.

"What happened to Miss Mary?"

"I don't know. She's never answered my letters, but I don't know if that is because they haven't gotten to her or for some other reason."

One more loss, Sloan thought. "I'm sorry." The apology came easier that time.

"For what?"

"For too many things to count." This time he laughed, a

sharp sound with his anger directed inward. "For your not knowing who your family is. For misjudging you. For believing you were Charlotte. For barging into your bath."

"Thank you," she murmured softly.

Her lips remained parted, and all he had to do was bend his head a little. Just a little. And he'd be able to feel their softness against his. His wanting was a palpable thing, pulsing right there beneath the surface, so strong he could practically feel it. And, he feared she would push him away. She had every reason to distrust him, and yet, here she was within the circle of his arms and close enough to kiss if he only had the courage to lower his head a fraction.

Courage be damned. Only a cad would take advantage of a woman in as vulnerable a state as she was.

Her breath caught, and this moment stretched into the next. Her head raised a tiny amount until he could feel her breath against his face. In the next instant, her lips brushed his, the pressure light as a falling snowflake and as potent as a shot of whiskey. His blood thundered in his ears as he held himself very still, waiting . . . waiting . . . waiting for more.

And it came once more. Those soft, soft lips grazing his. She sighed, and his restraint fractured.

He kissed her back, the pressure of her lips enough that he could touch his tongue against the seam of her mouth. She didn't draw back as he feared she might but instead sighed, a small movement granting him access to where he wanted to be. Her shy tongue touched his, and heat speared through him like a first shot of sunrise at a jagged horizon.

That sweet dance of the kiss lasted for seconds—lasted for eons—and he never wanted it to end, except he wanted more, so much more. All of it. Her naked and willing beneath him. For this moment, he needed her trust most of all. Her budding exploration made his heart feel as though it would burst. So, he held himself in check. His own need be damned. He'd let her guide how much, how long, however she wanted.

At some point, his iron resolve dissolved into accepting this for what it was—a shy, sweet fusing of their mouths likely to go nowhere. And, so, he gave himself over to the moment, simply absorbing her into the depth of his being and admitting he had never enjoyed anything more than this not quite chaste kiss.

When she pulled away enough to break the contact, she stared at him with huge, beautiful eyes, her lovely mouth moist and swollen. "So that's what the fuss is about."

He laughed. It ended as suddenly as it came as the meaning behind the simple words sank in. This was her first kiss. No . . . not her first if that brutal kiss he had given her the day she had arrived at the ranch counted as a kiss. Once more, regret sliced him open.

"I wish . . ." He cleared his throat. "I wish our first kiss had been as sweet."

Confusion clouded her eyes for a second before she frowned. "I had forgotten about that."

He didn't believe her. "Those things I'm sorry for. There's another one."

One of the logs on the fire settled suddenly, the pop drawing his attention to the sparks that burst a few feet into the room and landed harmlessly on the hearth.

"I should get the fire banked for the night, check on the horse, and take Silas out." He removed his arm from around her, the chilled air penetrating where the warmth of her body had been. He stood and took a step away from her, mostly to prove to himself he could. "I fixed up a . . . um . . ." He pointed in the direction of the makeshift chamber pot he'd found for her so he wouldn't have to take her outside. Though she had been delirious with fever, he'd helped her several times. Not that she would like to be reminded now.

Her gaze followed his pointing finger, a flushing rising from her neck as though she had realized how intimately he had come to know her body over the last few days. She'd been so ill then he had mostly been able to ignore that she was lovely and female. "And, there's warm water in the pot over the fire." He pointed again, this time at the fireplace.

He took a few steps toward the door, his need to escape—mostly from his own arousal—suddenly urgent. Then he stopped suddenly and turned back to her. What was he thinking? She had been weak as a newborn kitten, unable to hold her own spoon steady. "I'll help you."

Slowly—and he could see the effort it cost her—she stood. "I can do this on my own."

The blanket slid from her shoulders, and, even though she was in shadow, her body was silhouetted within the sheer shift. With her bare legs and feet and her dark hair tumbling to cover one breast, she somehow seemed more vulnerable than she had the night he had seen her completely undressed in her bath.

"You're sure?"

Somehow, she smiled as she made a shooing motion with her hand. "No. But I'm determined."

He watched her a second more, then nodded his head before snapping his fingers to Silas. "C'mon, boy."

He snagged his coat from a peg near the door, jammed his hat on his head, pushed through the flimsy door, and followed the dog outside into the cold night. His breath turned to a cloud of steam in front of him. Overhead, the Milky Way lit the sky. Once more, he had a memory of Abbey as she had emerged from the cabin, staring at the night sky. Now, as then, he wondered what she had been looking for.

Silas headed to the edge of the clearing in what had become a routine for him and an assurance for Sloan. Nothing in the dog's behavior pointed to anyone or anything else being in the area. Except for the dog's deeper tracks and a rabbit's lighter ones, the snow in the middle of the clearing was untouched. From beneath the lean-to, the horse nickered softly. Sloan went to the animal. He broke the film of ice that had formed over the water that he'd left for the horse. Silas might not be sensing anyone here now, but the place had been used a lot recently, a fact that had nagged at Sloan since he'd brought Abbey here.

He had concluded Caleb had deliberately brought her here and had been planning to do so for a while. Sloan had found a bag of grain at the back of the lean-to. The cabin might have been in rough shape, but the lean-to showed evidence of recent repair. That and the grain bothered him every time he came to the paddock. Some piece of the puzzle was beyond his grasp. The deep shadows of the lean-to provided no answer, and his attention returned to the brilliant sky, his thoughts about Abbey once more pushing away everything else.

She was in there washing and doing the other things needed in preparation for bed. A bed he had shared with her. These last nights he had reasoned he needed to keep a close eye on her, needed to keep her warm. The truth was more elemental—he liked holding her, loved holding her, if he were honest with himself. His need for here tonight had nothing to do with ensuring she was safe and well. He prayed he had enough discipline to remember she was alone and vulnerable. He was a man, not an animal, and this unrelenting desire for her could be managed, if not wholly ignored.

He patted the horse a last time, crossed the paddock, and made sure the gate was latched behind him. Silas was nearly back to the buildings, his nose alternately to the ground and in the air. Sloan waited while the dog made its way toward him.

"Anything out there to be worried about?" he asked, more of himself than the dog. As soon as the snow melted a bit more, they needed to head back for the ranch. And, by then, someone looking for them would have an easier time of it, as well.

The dog looked up at him as though it had understood the question, an impression further emphasized when he shook his head. Sloan chuckled. "One of us has lost our mind."

Together, they walked back to the cabin, and Sloan picked up a few logs of firewood he had split and stacked next to the door. He knocked on it before opening it. Silas slipped in, heading for the warmth of the fireplace.

"You doing okay?" Sloan asked, following the dog and deliberately keeping his gaze away from Abbey, though he could see her from the corner of his eye.

She was sitting on the pallet he had shared with her and wondered how she would feel now that she was better. "I feel like I've walked ten miles."

"Not surprising. You had quite a time of it." He stacked the firewood before turning to face her. "You'll get stronger."

She had found the bar of soap, because the aroma of it wafted across the room to him. He allowed himself to look at her. She had arranged her hair into a loose braid, and some of the tendrils around her face were damp, and one of the blankets was around her shoulders, shawl style.

She looked away from him, her color suddenly a vivid pink. As much as he wanted her, her blush reminded him that she was an innocent under his care. He didn't dare forget.

"While you were outside, I realized something."

"Yeah." He took off his coat and hung it next to the door, along with his hat.

"All of the blankets to keep warm are here."

He looked at her then and found her smoothing a finger over a worn spot on the one around her shoulder.

"To ask where you've been sleeping would make me sound stupid." Then her clear gaze met his. "I thought I had dreamed it. Your holding me and keeping me warm."

"No dream." His voice felt like gravel abrading his throat.

"I . . . umm . . ." She held his glance, though doing so was clearly uncomfortable. "It's different now."

Slowly he crossed the room toward her, then dropped to his knees in front of her. "I like holding you. You keep me warm, too, you know?"

"I do?"

"Hell, yes. You were running a fever." He captured one of the loose tendrils of hair between his fingers, intending to brush it away from her face. Instead, he wrapped it around his finger, struck with the notion that it held him as tightly as any noose. "I promise I'll hold you and keep you safe, and I won't take advantage of you."

Some fleeting expression chased through her eyes—disappointment, maybe, but he doubted that.

She didn't say anything but scooted to one side of the pallet and lay down. His erection pushed insistently against his pants, which would be damn uncomfortable to sleep in. He went to the fire, banked it, and turned back to Abbey. Thankfully, her eyes were closed, though he knew she wasn't asleep. He loosened the belt and shucked out of his pants and shirt and prayed the ties on his drawers stayed put.

He slid under the covers, which were cool to the touch and made him even more aware of the warm woman next to him.

"Are you all right?" he asked.

Her soft "yes" was accompanied by a sigh.

Giving into his need to hold her, he turned to his side and tucked her back against him. "It will be warm soon," he whispered.

"I'm not cold."

Neither was he, but he didn't dare follow that train of thought.

She turned slightly, looking at him over her shoulder, her face in deep shadow. "Would you . . . kiss me again?"

He let out a short bark of laughter. "Not a good idea." To demonstrate, he wrapped his arm more firmly around her waist, pulling her soft bottom toward the erection that was demanding he let go of his conscience and his control. "I'm doing my best to remember all the reasons why I should wrap you up like a cocoon and sleep in my coat on the other side of the room."

"I wouldn't mind if you did more."

CHAPTER 17

"I would." Sloan allowed himself a kiss against her hair, gentle despite the bone deep arousal in response to her invitation. "You've been ill, and so you're not as strong as you should be. You're alone, and I'm responsible for your care."

"I'm responsible for me," she insisted, shifting so she faced him. The determined expression on her face was the same one she always had with him. The arousal demanded he ignore his conscience. He couldn't—wouldn't—do that.

Instead of disagreeing with her, because he knew how important her assertion was to her, he edged closer to her. "One kiss before we sleep." Her eyes instantly lit. "And after you can walk to the corral and back, then . . ."

"You will do this—join with me? This ache makes me feel—"

He pressed a finger over her lips, stunned by the blunt honesty of her statement, the need to act on her invitation clamoring for relief. "That's why I should be way over on the other side of the room and why chaperones are needed."

"We don't have one." Her cool fingers touched the scar at the corner of his eye. "And you're right here."

"One kiss," he said. "Don't ask for more. Not tonight."

"Not tonight," Abbey agreed on a heart-felt sigh, wanting the feel of his mouth on hers more than she was sure was allowed. And, yet, this wanting somehow had a will of its own, and she didn't want to resist it. She lifted her face toward his, slightly astonished at how much she liked this especially since she had been so leery of him—afraid even, if she were honest with herself. As if sensing her deepest desire, he closed the last little bit of distance between them, capturing her mouth with his and giving them both the long, penetrating, ardent kiss she wanted.

This was, she decided a moment later, just about perfect. His body settled onto the pallet, and his arm came around her, careful of her injured shoulder. The heat of his body was as warm and inviting as the fire at the hearth. Somehow her fingers found the bare skin of his back, which was as smooth as a satin ribbon she'd had once. For the merest instant, her awareness was pulled back as she remembered the scars on her own back and knew if he were to touch her as intimately, her own skin wouldn't be as pleasing to touch.

Then, he sighed, the sound reminding her of a cat's purr, and she flattened her hand against him. She was rewarded with him resting his big hand on her curve of her waist, the heat and weight of it bringing alive sensations she hadn't imagined possible. Her skin felt prickly and hot, and this longing to have him closer—much, much closer—made her press herself even closer to him until . . . finally . . . her breasts were pressed against his chest, only the thin fabric of her shift separating them. She loved that, but somehow it didn't help because this need for more bloomed into a more urgent yearning.

And, through it all, the soft sweep of his tongue against hers, the sensations so sweet, so sharp, she could only marvel at them as she greedily gathered them in. She couldn't breathe, but she didn't care. The only thing that mattered was this deepening hunger and the feel of his rock hard muscles beneath her hand.

Her body was nearly as hot as it had been during her fever. Only now, she faced him, her thin shift and his drawers the only things separating them. The thought of being completely bare so all her skin was touching him at once shocked her and thrilled her. Perhaps that wasn't allowed. That kept her from slipping her hands beneath the waistband of his drawers.

She sank more fully into the kiss, feeling more alive than she had ever been. Unfamiliar and entirely welcome sensations flooded her body. A part of her wanted to be thinking and concentrating and taking in every moment of this bliss, because it surely couldn't last. This hard man whom she had watched all these weeks was this man kissing her so sweetly and using his strength to take care of her? In the midst of the kiss, she had a fleeting image of Ben Haverly kissing his wife the first night she had been in their home, his hand resting lightly on the mound of their unborn babe. At the time, she hadn't understood the intimacy, though she'd had the sense of glimpsing an unspoken bond between them.

No wonder a woman wanted more. She hadn't understood until now. All these sensations she had never imagined made her want to be even closer to Sloan. She kept her mouth locked with his, which through some law of nature made the rest of her tremble and ache to be even closer to him. Her skin became ever more sensitive, making her aware of the pressure of his body where it grazed hers, the abrasion of the fabric of her shift against her breast, and the heat—the incredible heat—that reminded her of a warm bath, only better. And, with it all, she had the recurring thought this would be too fleeting, a moment to be grabbed lest she never have it again. One more memory to take with her, one more feeling to be savored and tucked away.

That thought made a tear seep from beneath her lids, and a sob caught in her throat.

His mouth lifted. "Abbey?"

Oh, the sound of her name within that deep voice. She opened her eyes and found him looking intently at her.

She touched his cheek, which felt like raspy sandpaper beneath her fingers. He turned his head slightly, until he could press his lips against her palm. Another sensation to be remembered.

"Are you ready to sleep?" he asked.

She managed a tremulous smile. "That was a goodnight kiss?"

The corner of his mouth lifted. "Yes."

"And tomorrow night?"

He brushed a strand of hair away from her face. "Kissing . . . often leads to more." Those dark eyes searched her face. "And you're alone and in my care."

"You keep saying that."

"Because it is true."

"I know my own mind."

Those dark eyes lingered on her mouth before raising back to meet her gaze. "Do you?"

She nodded, wanting to say something, do something to prove to him she wanted everything that came after the kissing. The touch of his body against her most secret parts.

"Then, tomorrow, we'll see. If you can walk out to the corral and back—"

A bubble of pure happiness expanded in her chest. "Yes."

"Twice."

"I can." If she weren't so warm and her limbs weren't so languid feeling, she'd leap out of bed right now and show him.

That surprising smile lit his eyes, their warmth so different than the icy regard he'd had for her in the beginning. "And maybe stay awake for more than an hour at a time." His hand went to her shoulder. "Does this hurt?"

"Only when I try to lift my arm."

"Then we'll have to see that you don't lift it."

She let her head fall against his arm, which was a surprisingly comfortable pillow. "You're bossy, you know?"

"So I've been told." He laid his own head down, remaining on his side, his gaze intent on her.

She watched him, sleepiness gradually overtaking her, but a delicious ache remaining in her body. "Promise," she whispered.

"Promise what?" he whispered back.

She let her eyes drift closed, because confessing what she wanted without looking at him was easier. "That you'll kiss me tomorrow."

"I promise."

"And more. All of it." When he didn't answer, she turned on her side until she faced him, her hand sliding around his waist. "Promise me."

"God help me, I promise."

The echoes of his promise stayed with Sloan the following day as Abbey insisted upon standing without help and going outside to relieve herself. He was at once happy she was feeling better and would be well enough for the "more—all of it" and acutely aware he was about to take a tumble over a precipice every bit as dangerous as the one a few yards beyond the cabin. He had a list longer than his arm of reasons to keep his distance, a list that began and ended with one thing. She was under his care, and, therefore, he had a responsibility—more than that, a moral-bound duty—to do the right thing. And that sure as hell wasn't bedding her. Even though he had promised, and even though his body hardened every time he allowed himself to think about how much he wanted to do as she had so innocently asked.

The day began with sunshine and was warm enough Sloan thought about packing them up and starting back to the ranch.

"A gorgeous morning," Abbey said from the doorway.

Sloan—who was stomping down the snow to create a trail between the cabin and the lean-to, not because he needed it, but because he remembered making her promise she would walk that short distance today—looked over his shoulder. She was the beautiful one, he thought. More radiant than the sun sparkling on the snow.

As if realizing the temperature was cold, she disappeared back inside, reappearing a moment later with the cloak in her arms.

He came back toward her, took the garment from her, and settled it around her shoulders so she wouldn't have to lift her arm.

"Thank you." Her eyes were wide with invitation as she gazed up at him.

He thought about lowering his head to kiss those parted lips and figured if he did, he didn't stand a chance of talking her out of the promise he'd so rashly made last night.

"You made a trail for me." She lifted her skirts, exposing the moccasins she always wore, and stepped across the threshold. "I can't believe how deep the snow is."

"It's packed down a lot from what it was a couple of days ago."

As if somehow sensing she had been ill, Silas walked along beside her, close enough to touch, which she often did. No wonder the dog stayed so close, Sloan thought. Now that he had felt her hands on his face, he was as hungry as the dog to have her hands on him.

It didn't take her as long to reach the corral surrounding the lean-to as he thought it would. Once there, she leaned against a rail and lifted her face to the sunshine while her gaze wandered the clearing, her eyes darkening a bit as she took in the way the land suddenly ended and a steep hill rose on the other side of a canyon. When she met his gaze, she waved a hand in the direction of the precipice. "I want to walk over there."

"Since the snow is deep, that's going to be a hell of a walk."

"I know." She took a couple of steps in that direction, clearly determined. "I need to see where I fell."

"You remember?"

"Yes." Another step took her into snow that came to her knees.

Two strides carried him to her, and he swept her into his arms and headed for the big pine that clung to the edge of the slope.

"I said I'd walk."

"I know."

"I want to get stronger."

"I know that, too, and you will." The truth was, he liked having her in his arms.

She fell silent, and her body relaxed subtly within his arms. That simple trust had him once again at war with himself. He'd do the right thing and get her back to the ranch as untouched as she was right now. He'd shelter her body tonight with his warmth, and he would somehow make her forget his rash promise. Except, holding her like this made him as hard as stone and made his resolve as threatened as the deep snow under the bright sunlight.

Too soon, they came to the edge of the slope. Silas sat next to her, and she patted the dog's head, a gesture so automatic, Sloan knew she had done so many times.

She took a step forward and peered down the slope. Not as much snow covered it, leaving some of the boulders exposed. Little Skunk had said they had found her near the canyon floor. Sloan too vividly imagined the horrifying fall. Terrible bruises covered her body, and he'd be a long time in forgiving himself for putting her in Caleb Holt's path that night.

"What happened the night you left?" he asked.

She closed her eyes briefly, and when she opened them, all the color had drained from her face. "He intended to rape me, then kill me." That flat comment shattered him because he knew it was true. She swallowed, then added, "I was running. The night was pitch black, and I couldn't see anything. I just needed to get away." Her breath caught, and she spread her arms wide. "And, then I was flying." She shuddered.

He noticed for the first time torn rips in the heavy fabric of the cloak. Damn little protection. "I wish . . . ." He had no words for the depth of his regret.

"You weren't to blame."

He shook his head. "I was—I am." He took off a glove and touched her cheek, her skin soft and smooth beneath his fingertips. "It's a pitifully small thing, but I am sorry."

She raised her hand and clasped his, pressing it more firmly against her skin. "I know." She looked away, then, her voice husky when she repeated, "I know."

"I'm glad you're better."

"I am, too." Her attention remained focused on the steep precipice that fell away at their feet. "I have to confess, though, I don't ever remember being as sore as I've been these last few days. I keep wondering if this is what it's like to be a hundred years old."

"It's only because you're covered in bruises."

Her head came up, and she looked at him, her eyes brilliant. "I keep forgetting . . . you would know."

"Please don't be—" What . . . He floundered for the right word. Angry? Her privacy had been violated, and he knew things about her body even a husband might not know. Embarrassed? He could imagine she was. "I didn't take advantage of you. I promise."

"I never imagined you had." She steadily held her gaze. "I know you're an honorable man."

"Except for thinking the worst of you and refusing to believe you."

"Well, yes." She smiled. "Except for that." She looked back toward the cabin. "You made a good enough trail; I believe I can walk without sinking in snow up to my knees."

"Maybe." He placed one arm under her knees and the other under her back and picked her up. "You'll still get soaked, though, so how about we stick to the original deal?"

"Two back and forth walks from the cabin to the lean-to?"

Unspoken but clear as the clouds sweeping in from the west and chasing shadows across the land was the rest of it. That he would make love to her.

"Yes."

She patted his chest. "I've done one already."

"Half of one," he teased. "You've walked from the cabin. Not back."

"I will, though. As soon as you put me down, I'm ready."

He set her down, his arms immediately feeling empty. This was the perfect moment to tell her that he couldn't—wouldn't—make love to her. Only the words remained stuck in his throat as she went back to the cabin, the dog trailing in her wake. When she reached the doorway, she turned around, a wide smile on her face.

"I hope there is still soup left. I'm hungry."

He followed her, too focused on another intimacy—eating out of the same cup and sharing the same spoon. By the time he came through the doorway, she had filled the cup from the pot hanging over the fireplace. "The only thing missing is one of Consuela's biscuits."

The mention of biscuits had him wishing the soup consisted of more than the rabbit, hardtack, and broth. A pure wonder she wasn't complaining about the meager fare.

She lifted the spoon of soup to her mouth, then offered it to him. "You keep watching the sky."

"Keeping an eye out for the weather."

"We have to leave soon, don't we?"

Her perception was another clue she was feeling a lot better. "Soon," he allowed. She was right, but he hated the idea of getting caught in a storm with her. If he'd had only himself to look after, he would have already headed for home.

"Soon." She looked at the dog. "He doesn't say much, does he? And here you are, getting thinner by the day."

"We'll head back tomorrow if it doesn't snow."

"And if it does?"

"I'll have to hunt and find us something more to eat."

"Maybe roasted rabbit instead of soup?"

He chuckled, since her tone of voice echoed his own thought. "Sure."

After they finished eating, they went back outside, where the sky was no longer blue and where the misty clouds obscured the forest on the other side of the canyon. The smell of snow was in the air. Sloan hoped squalls, not a full-fledged storm, were all they would have.

Abbey seemed determined to prove not only was she stronger, but she could pull her own weight. She found the pile of logs he had split. Despite the sling that kept her shoulder immobilized, she carried one of the logs back to the cabin with that trip, and the three more that followed. He watched without saying anything, liking her determination and admiring her grit. Maybe too much, because she kept watching him with hungry eyes. Everything in her expression suggested she remembered what had happened between them last night, and she wanted more as much as he did.

"I have a plan for this wood," she told him a while later.

"A bigger fire?"

"Yes." She led him to the corner of the cabin and pointed at a large galvanized tub hanging from the exterior wall. "And a bath."

"It's not big enough."

"Bigger than what I had when I was a child at Miss Mary's.

And we'd fight over who got to be first because that was the only time the water would be hot."

"You offering to share?" The instant the words left his mouth, he wanted to snatch them back.

"Of course," she answered simply, without picking up on the more intimate sharing that had seared his brain.

He lifted the galvanized tub down. To his surprise, it was cleaner than he figured it would be, no bird's nest or anything else inside. It was also small enough it would have been better for a child the size of Pearl Mae. Still, Abbey beamed.

"A bucket of hot water, and this will be about perfect. Thank you." She followed him into the cabin. "I half expected you to argue with me."

"I know how much you like your baths." That fast, the memory of his confrontation of her that last horrible night at the house was back. "This won't be much of one."

"It will be fine."

He carried the bucket to a miniscule stream behind the lean-to and filled it with icy water he figured would be warm by tomorrow morning. By the time he had returned to the cabin, though, Abbey had banked the fire, creating a nest of coals for the bucket. The cabin seemed warmer despite the snow that was beginning to drift from the sky. He figured his thoughts, not the fire, were the reason.

"You can manage by yourself?" he asked.

Abbey nodded.

"Then you need some time to . . ." He tipped his head toward the door. "I'll go . . ." The truth was, he had no idea what he was going to do for the next little while except have the image of her seared in his mind. "Holler if you need any help." Before offering to give her help she didn't need, he went outside and stared across the clearing, the sunshine completely obscured by the lowering clouds and the huge flakes of snow drifting from the sky.

Abbey stared after him, bemused he was at a loss for words. He'd been acting nervous all day, and she couldn't decide what to make of that. She was nervous, but then she'd never lain with a man before. She had seen animals mating and knew the rudiments of what would happen between them, but that wasn't the same thing as this quivering anticipation that had made her too aware of her body ever since he had kissed her.

Sometime during the night, she had concluded this might be the only time in her life she would know a man. If it was, she wanted it to be right, though she had no idea what that entailed. She might not be able to wash her hair, but she wanted to be rid of feeling weak and ill.

She tested the water and found it had warmed a lot. She imagined it sensing her need to hurry, a thought that made her smile. Nonsense. Water was just water. What she wanted touching her were Sloan's hands.

She set the galvanized tub close to the fireplace, then lifted the bucket out of the fire and poured it into the tub. Steam rose from the water. Before it could cool, she quickly removed her clothes, then knelt inside the tub. The cool air of the room and the warm water of the bath made her once conscious of her body in a way she had never been before. Despite her sore shoulder and tender bruises, getting clean felt good.

It was hours before nightfall, and she couldn't wait for the sun to set.

A gust of wind rattled the door to the cabin, making her shiver. She reached for one of the blankets and stood. The door swung open, and Silas came into the room, shaking snowflakes off his coat and heading for the fireplace. Behind him, Sloan stood, framed in the door, his gaze transfixed on her.

"It's snowing?" Though the blue sky of morning had disappeared behind another heavy blanket of clouds by the time she had come into the cabin, she hadn't anticipated snow would fall again.

"Yep." Sloan shook his head as if to clear it, then came through the door, latching it behind him. He took off his coat, and, to her surprise, his chest was bare. Too many impressions to process at once crowded into her mind. He was bigger, somehow, without his shirt than he was with it. His muscular chest was covered with dark hair that narrowed into a *V* at the waistband of his trousers. What struck her most, though, were the sharply defined ropes of muscle of his arms. His skin was red and dripping with water.

"You bathed in the stream?" she asked, immediately deciding that was a stupid question, since he clearly had.

"You weren't the only one feeling a little grimy." He stood there, his hands clenched around the coat. "Damn cold, though."

"I would have shared the bath."

"I know." He hung his coat on the peg and came toward her, reminding her she was wrapped only in a blanket. He came to a stop so close to the fire she could see the goosebumps on his skin. Holding his hands out to the warmth, he looked over his shoulder at her. "You're not the only one thinking about tonight."

Those simple words reignited the sweet fire low in her belly.

"You're beautiful." His voice was so low, so deep, she had the notion she had imagined, rather than heard, the words. Pleased as she was that he thought so, she shook her head in denial.

He took a step toward her, reaching for the blanket, which he pulled closer around her shoulders, and somehow pulled her within the circle of his arms. "Would you mind if we didn't wait until tonight?"

CHAPTER 18

Totally aware of his bare chest that would brush hers if she leaned into him at all, Abbey realized she hadn't thought this through. She wanted him . . . or at least a satiating . . . of these feelings that made her feel too small for her body. But him . . . bare like this, the strength and power of his body surrounding her. Touching her. Heat bloomed again, this time making her cheeks feel as though they were on fire. Not just her cheeks. The hunger and the deep empty aching at the apex of her legs encouraged the shocking notion of moving so close her breasts would touch him.

"Now?" She had the feeling her voice had squeaked, and she repeated, this time barely a whisper, "Right now?"

He tipped his head toward the door. "It's snowing again. Silas is ready for a nap. Things are buttoned up as well as they can be." His hand covered one of hers that was holding the blanket in place. "You're here. I'm here."

"You'll be able to see me."

His eyes gleamed in the firelight. "I hope so."

"But . . ."

He tipped her head gently up with a large knuckle. "I've been dreaming of seeing you again."

"Since I was ill." Of course, he had seen her body then, but she hadn't known. Hadn't wanted to think about it too much, truth be told.

"No." He pressed a soft kiss against her temple. "That doesn't

244

count. Since the night I came to your bath." His breath became ragged as he pressed his lips against her cheek. "You were the most beautiful thing I had ever seen."

He thought she was beautiful? Her certainty that she was not unraveled within the need in his deep voice. She wanted to look at him but dared not meet his gaze. She swayed towards him, which brought her against his thighs. "The scars."

He grasped the blanket and unwound it from around her, turning her so her back was exposed to him. Terrible, blessed anticipation pinned her in place. The fire's warmth seeped through the thin blanket held against her chest, or maybe it was the heat from her own body scorching her. His feather-light touch was on the scar at her nape, then his lips. She shivered at the scorching, tender touch. His breath, even hotter than her skin, narrowed her awareness to this moment as his mouth followed the length of the scar to her waist in an endless, searing kiss. The touch singed her in a healing benediction that made her feel cherished as she never had in her life. She trembled beneath his touch, his large hands at her waist, gently holding her in place. He repeated the caress with each scar. In the wake of all those kisses, sensations danced across her skin, each one joining the others, the pleasure of it all more than she had ever imagined possible. When she felt his kiss on the swell of her bottom, she realized he had dropped to his knees behind her, and he had wrapped one of his arms around her waist. She was trembling so badly, her legs feeling as though they'd stop supporting her if she let her body relax in the tiniest bit.

"Please don't be afraid of me," he murmured, his voice deeper than she had ever heard it. "I promise, I won't hurt you."

"I'm not afraid." Not of him, at least. What terrified her was her own body, alive with all these vibrations filling her with a fine, unfamiliar trembling. Things she'd been told flitted at the edge of her mind, then vanished like a thin fog on a warm morning when she felt his lips on her bottom.

He must have sensed she was about to fall because, in the next moment, he turned her, and she sank to the floor until she was eye level with him. The fabric of his pants chafed her bare skin while her hands came to rest on his chest. It was covered with dark hair that felt surprisingly soft beneath her fingertips.

When her gaze drifted down, she realized the blanket was gone, and her legs were splayed across his lap, resting on either side of his waist.

She suspected she would be embarrassed later, but just now, being like this with him felt right. Perfect, in fact.

"Ready for more?" The question came with the brush of his lips against her bare shoulder.

In answer, she flexed her hands against his chest, absorbing the warmth of his skin.

"I like that." And then his mouth found hers. Until this very instant, she hadn't known this was what she had wanted all her life. This, she though dazedly, this was the meaning of those verses she hadn't understood. *I am my lover's and my lover is mine, he browses among the lilies.*

All the impressions she had savored last night returned, even more intense than they had been then. All that was left was to feel, and she surrendered to it as he drew her closer, then closer still. At the touch of his warm skin against hers, she would have stopped time if she could have. If nothing else but this happened, it would be enough—cradled in his arms like this, his sweet kisses devouring her, and the heat of his body surrounding her.

"Are you all right?" he whispered against her hair.

"Yes."

His fingertips brushed lightly down the center of her body, making her shiver. With each stroke, his touch became a little more intimate, all of it making her burn. At last, his warm palm covered her breast, and she sighed, her head falling against his shoulder.

"You like that, hmm?"

"Yes."

And then he repeated the same caress with her most intimate flesh, and that felt even better. She wrapped her arms around him, all thought gone, all her focus on the feelings effusing her body, some shimmering thing sliding ever closer until it speared through her with a dazzling shaft of feeling that made her convulse against his hand. She trembled at the wonder of it, her gaze seeking his.

She had a glimpse of him smiling; his eyes hot and filled with longing were a mirror of her own. He kissed her, then, laying her back on the pallet and covering her body with his. Somehow, his pants were gone, and he was there, all heat and gentle strength surrounding her. And then, he pressed forward, filling her with himself and sensations she had never imagined. The invasion stretched painfully, but mostly the pressure felt . . . right. Complete. The muscles of his shoulders beneath her fingertips were tense and hot.

He rested his forehead against hers, his gaze holding hers. "Are you okay?"

The expression in his eyes at once tender and fierce. She remembered thinking his eyes were cold. She'd been wrong. They were hot with the breath of life.

"Yes." She kissed his cheek, needing this connection more than she had ever needed anything. He began to move then, and the friction was unbearable—the initial pain giving way to more pleasure than seemed possible, certainly more than she had ever imagined. He drew her even closer in his arms and kissed her. Then, she shattered into a shimmering dance of fire that burned from their joining to the tips of her fingers. She clutched at him, then collapsed boneless against him. With wonder, she recognized the same thing had happened with him, his deep groan of release sounding like the purr of a huge cat. He rolled to his side, bringing her with him, so they remained clasped within each other's arms.

She liked everything that came after, as well—the focused tenderness within his fierce strength that she would remember forever. The first time, she didn't know what to expect, but when he came to her twice more during the night, she learned her touch pleased him, as well. In between, they slept. Each time she awakened, his body was cradled around hers, making her feel cherished and protected for the first time in her whole life.

Another few inches of snow had fallen overnight, Sloan noted when he emerged from the cabin well before the sun came over the horizon. Though clouds hung low in the folds of the mountain on the other side of the canyon, the overhead sky was clear. In the corral, his horse nickered in greeting. While Silas bounded across the pristine ground, shoveling his nose into the fresh snow, Sloan fed the horse and broke the crust of ice off the water bucket.

The time had come to head for home—in fact, they should have done so yesterday. Much as he liked having Abbey to himself, he could no longer use the weather as a reason to stay.

His gaze went to the cabin door. Inside, Abbey was asleep. Now that the weather had cleared, it was only a matter of time before Jake came looking for them. There was far too much going on at the ranch even if he wasn't determined to find Caleb Holt and make sure the man paid for what he had done to Abbey. He stared unfocused across the clearing. Abbey. To think of her by that name first without any stuttering qualification that began with "Charlotte"—he realized it had been that way for weeks.

Though he was horrified that his actions had set into motion the events leading to Charlotte's death, Sloan couldn't deny that his deepest anger was over what Caleb had done to Abbey.

Sloan shook his head, and his vision cleared. For months, he had been consumed with finding Charlotte because he had figured she would lead him to the stallion. The Cimarron Sun hadn't been in his mind once since leaving the ranch in search of Abbey.

Once more, his gaze lost focus as he contemplated that. He had built dreams of wealth and status around the acquisition of the stallion. Neither of those seemed so important this morning. True, he liked training horses more than running cattle, but the fact was the ranch needed cattle to survive. There might not be wealth like he had seen around Charlotte's family, but everything was in place for a good life.

Behind him, he heard the door to the cabin open, and he turned around. Abbey stood there with the cloak wrapped around her shoulders, her gaze on the sunrise that would spear over the top of a peak on the other side of the canyon at any moment.

She smiled when she saw Silas who was still romping in the snow. When her gaze found him in the shadow of the lean-to, her smile became even wider, and she waved at him, calling, "It's a gorgeous morning."

She disappeared inside again, then came back out a second later, this time without the cloak and this time heading toward him.

"It's not as cold as I was expecting. The snow will melt fast in this temperature."

"It will," he agreed, his gaze intent on her. He wasn't sure what he had been expecting their conversation to be after spending most of the night in each other's arms, but it wasn't this ordinary one about weather.

Her color was good, and though she still had her arm in the sling he had rigged for her, she looked as though her shoulder was no longer bothering her as much. The bruises on her face were fading, and her eyes were bright.

"We need to head to the ranch today."

She smiled once more. "I never thought I'd say this, but I can't wait to get home."

Home. Had she really said that?

As if she suddenly realized the same thing, she added, "Back to the ranch."

When she realized he was staring at her, she met his gaze with that direct way she had, her expression going from happy to more somber.

"You're very quiet."

"No more than usual."

"Well, that may be true, but you're back to scowling at me." She poked him in the middle of his chest. "You're not regretting what we did?" A deeply pink blush rose from her neck and suffused her cheeks as though she remembered exactly what they had done.

"I'm responsible for you, and I took—"

"Good care of me," she interrupted, taking his hand and clasping it against her chest. "I couldn't bear it if you regretted it." She took a shuddering breath, then rushed on as though she had been thinking. "I know I'll always remind you of Charlotte—"

"You—"

"Let me finish." He eyes were wide and dark as she stared at him. "I don't expect . . . or want . . . anything from you, except . . ." She swallowed and looked away then. When her gaze came back to his, her eyes were even brighter with unshed tears. ". . .

to go on my way as soon as can be managed."

Of course, she wouldn't want anything from him. He had judged her as badly as anyone, and he might not have beaten her, but he hadn't treated her any better than the men who had.

"You have my word." His voice felt dragged out of his heart, which figured since that's exactly how the promise felt.

She didn't say anything but nodded once as if satisfied. And then she surprised the hell out of him by leaning into him and putting her arm around his waist. She felt good there—comfortable and welcome. He wrapped her in his arms and stood there with her for a moment, wishing she had come into his life some other way. His surprise deepened when she put her arm around his neck and tugged his head down. Then she kissed him, her lips so soft and warm against his that she felt like his deepest dreams realized.

"You're a good man, Sloan Rafferty. Now. If we're leaving, what can I do to help?"

"Think you can stay on the horse riding behind me?" he asked after the horse was saddled and they were all packed up.

"There's not much other choice than walking," she returned.

"Then it's settled." He mounted, then walked the horse to a good-sized boulder than would give her an easier lift.

She understood immediately what he had in mind, climbed on top of the rock, and grasped his arm as she slid on behind him.

"Put your arm around me."

Abbey did, remembering the long, long ride with Jake and Sam when they had brought her to the ranch. Then, she had ridden in front of Jake. Then, she had hated the ride and equally hated him. Now, the warmth of Sloan's back invited her closer. Since she had a sling on her other arm, she found a grasp on the back of his coat. This would work fine, though she admitted she wouldn't mind riding in front of him, his arms protectively around her. That idea sent a rush of warmth and longing to have a repeat of last night. A wish for the impossible, however, and she was far too practical for that.

She couldn't decide what she felt about that. Probably best to not think about Sloan in that way at all. Even if he had finally seen her for herself, her resemblance to his wife would prevent him from returning the growing affection she had for him. She chided herself for her romanticized longings. All she had to do was remember her goal to have a home of her own where she was in charge of her own life.

Her orchard. In California.

She held onto him as he turned the horse in a circle, as though giving the area a last look.

She scooted a little closer to Sloan, and he pressed a gloved hand over her smaller one.

"You holler if there's any problem."

"I will," she promised. As he had done, she gave the small clearing a long last look.

The snow-covered world looked brand new to her. Except for where Silas plowed ahead of them, the snow was a smooth surface, sparklingly white in sunlight and softly gray in the shade. Occasional tweets from birds filled the air along with the plop of snow as it slid off the branches of pine trees. Snow had never been like this anywhere else, and she was enchanted.

Her most vivid memories of snow in the Shenandoah were associated with the winter of Sheridan's siege. Mud, cold, and hunger had been a constant plague, leaving behind misery and death. Nor had the snow been pristine like this in Kentucky, where she had spent the first winter after leaving the Shenandoah, or Lee's Summit in Missouri, where she had spent last winter.

This was a wonderland that somehow promised new beginnings with none of yesterday's hurts or memories tainting today. The anticipation of it made her shiver.

"Cold?" Sloan asked over his shoulder, patting her cool hand with his gloved one.

"No. I've never seen anything more beautiful than this."

"Wait until we get back down to the valley and you can see the peaks. Now that is something."

The going was slow. A couple of times, Sloan dismounted, leading the horse across dangerous looking precipices that provided a view of the valley below, which was also cloaked in white. They passed a copse of cottonwood trees where some branches had broken off from the weight of the snow and their golden leaves that hadn't fallen yet. The day warmed, tempting Abbey to forget she had ever been cold.

They traveled ever downward, sometimes the trail so steep that she wondered if this was the way she had blindly followed Caleb that fateful night. If it had been, she couldn't imagine she had been so trusting as to have ever thought they were on a road leading to a town.

Nearly four hours after leaving the trapper's cabin, Silas barked. As if answering, a horse whinnied.

Sudden apprehension swept through her, making a falsehood of her earlier idea that she'd left the past behind. Caleb, who wanted her dead, was still out there somewhere.

Sloan patted her hand. "I see Jake."

She couldn't see over Sloan's shoulder, but she heard Jake call to them a moment later.

"I'm sure glad to see you," he said when Sloan's horse drew alongside his. He tipped his hat to her. "You, too, Miss Abigail Wallace of the Shenandoah Valley. Looks like you found a place to weather out the storm."

She didn't know if he'd ever called her by name before, but if he had, he would have been mocking. Now he sounded utterly sincere. She couldn't decide what to make of him.

"Remember that old trapper's cabin at the top of the ridge?" Sloan asked.

"It's still standing?"

"Yep. Turned out to be a good shelter."

"Had to hogtie your brother to keep him from going out to look for you," Jake added as the two horses walked side by side across a clearing.

"Any damage from the storm?" Sloan asked.

"Nah. Everything is fine. At least with the ranch."

"What do you mean 'at least with the ranch'?"

"Well, a lot is going on." Jake held up a finger. "First, Consuela has had us all busy packing. She figured she'd better be ready to go as soon as this storm broke, or she'd be here for the winter. Said she'd promised her father she'd be there before winter set in."

"She might be too late on that one," Sloan returned, his answer punctuated by the plopping sounds of snow sliding off the spruce trees close by.

Jake shifted in his saddle. "Figured you wouldn't mind if me and Sam took her."

Sloan didn't immediately answer, his thumb absently stroking the back of Abbey's hand.

"That's a good idea. What's the second thing?"

Jake snorted, a sound of pure irritation. "Preacher showed up the first night you and me were gone with a visitor in tow. And, you're not going to like this." He paused for dramatic effect, reined his horse to a stop, and resettled his hat on his head. "He had a Mister William Flanders with him."

Beneath her hand, she felt Sloan's sudden tension.

She had also forgotten about that—the man's veiled accusation that Sloan might have been responsible for Charlotte's disappearance last spring.

Sloan's horse also came to a stop while the single cloud in the sky scuttled across in front of the sun, momentarily casting shadows across the meadow they were crossing. He urged the animal back into a walk.

"How did he take the news of Charlotte's death?"

"Nobody has told him."

Once more, Sloan's tension vibrated beneath her hand.

"He's run Consuela ragged—acts like Sam and her are his very own slaves."

"He's staying at the ranch? Not in Poncha?"

"He wouldn't hear of it. Said you had invited him." Jake expelled a heavy sigh.

"I wasn't at all sure he'd show up, but I sure never expected—"

"He's here, all right, making all sorts of accusations, and having a fit he has to sleep under the same roof with a heathen Indian."

Sloan shook his head. "Trying to get on my brother's good side and afraid of losing his scalp, huh?"

Jake laughed. "Yep."

She became so lost in her thoughts that she lost track of the quiet conversation between Sloan and Jake until Sloan said, "Hope someone thought to grease the axles of the wagon and make sure it's sound."

"We did," Jake said. "Sam and I spent the better part of a day going over it with a fine-tooth comb. Preacher thought Abe Venters has a pair of draft horses for sale."

"Then, we need to make sure Poncha Pass isn't snowed in and closed for the winter."

"Preacher already promised to find out, and we'll probably have word tomorrow."

They rode in silence then for quite a while. Once, Abbey would have been glad to see the back of Consuela, but her leaving meant JJ and Pearl Mae would also be gone. And, as for the possibility of meeting William Flanders—everything about that filled Abbey with dread and a bone-deep apprehension that chilled her.

She must have shivered because Sloan asked, "You doing okay? Need to stop and rest?"

She shook her head, her cheek brushing against his back. "I'm fine."

At last, they reached the valley, where the snow was a fraction of the depth it had been in the mountains. In fact, snow had melted enough that the road they followed was muddy, and the going was slow. Long shadows stretched across the valley by the time they reached the gate marking the entrance to the ranch.

Someone must have been watching for them because Sam and Eli met them before they reached the barn, where the doors stood wide open for them.

"Ain't you a sight for sore eyes." Eli took the reins to Jake's horse as soon as he dismounted but addressed Sloan. "Let me tell you, your brother is as cross as an old bear. He'll be glad to see you."

"Maybe things will settle down some now that you're back," Sam said. "That gent has sure raised a ruckus."

"So I hear. You doin' okay?" Sloan dismounted his horse, then reached for Abbey.

"Aw, I'm fine." Sam's usual grin failed to reach his eyes. "I can take whatever he dishes out, even when he calls me Darkie and pretends I don't have a name."

She expected Sloan would set her down, but he didn't. Instead, he secured her more firmly in his arms and strode across the compound, carrying her as though she weighed nothing.

"I can walk, you know."

"No doubt," he returned. "You can work on that tomorrow. I figured this way, I'd get you inside and closer to the hot bath you've been hankering for."

The man had somehow read her mind. She could only imagine how dirty and grimy she looked since that's how she felt.

He climbed the steps to the porch and shouldered open the door. Inside, the air was heavy with the odor of cigar smoke, to the point Abbey immediately coughed.

Worse, it was the aroma that had haunted her nightmares, and it chilled her to the core. A tight knot of fear slithered out of her belly and froze her fingers. She moaned against the onslaught of nightmares.

"What the hell?" Sloan set Abbey on her feet, waved a hand through the blue haze and pulled open the door he had kicked shut behind him. "Consuela!"

"She's not here," came a heavy southern accent from near the window.

Her eyes watering, Abbey's gaze sought the speaker. She had seen him, she realized, or at least men like him. His attire was that of a wealthy man who expected others to work while he— what? She wasn't at all sure she even knew what men like this did. He wore a maroon and brown brocade vest and snowy white shirt tucked into wool trousers that were, in turn, tucked into black, shiny boots. The man had brilliant blue eyes and dark hair whose color was impossible to discern through the gray haze of smoke. He sat at the chair by the small window, papers and an ink well at the table.

"William." Sloan strode across the room toward the man. "Despite your letter, I wasn't sure you were actually coming."

The man ignored Sloan's outstretched hand.

This was Charlotte's father? Abbey thought. This man somehow conveyed he was superior. Except, Sloan carried an authority even more potent, though their clothes clearly delineated the differing stations in society.

"You've taken long enough to return." Flanders pulled a pocket watch from his vest, clicked open the cover, closed it, then returned it to the pocket. "I've been here five interminable days and subjected to the least hospitality a man could possibly be given. Not one person from your Mexican maid to your boy to that heathen half-breed will tell me where my daughter is."

"You could have stayed at the inn in Poncha."

Abbey couldn't see Sloan's face since his back was to her, but his voice was deeper somehow and had that deceptively even tone he used when he was angry. She was acutely aware he hadn't answered the most important question—where was Charlotte?

William Flanders simply sat there, an ankle hooked over the other knee, acting like this was his home, not Sloan's.

"That so-called inn is a half step above a pig sty. I wouldn't recommend the accommodations as suitable for even a vagrant." He took a puff from the cigar, then set it on the dish he was using as an ashtray—one of the tin plates from the kitchen. He expelled the smoke, the horrible acrid aroma rushing across the room in a smothering veil. That voice and that smell . . . both filled her with such dread she trembled.

Sloan picked up the plate and carried it outside. "My home is not a smoking club. If you want to smoke, you'll be needing to take it outside."

"In my home—"

"Which this isn't," Sloan interrupted.

Abbey slid the hood of the cloak off her head, her attention fixed on William Flanders. The urge to run, to hide skated through her. Somehow, her feet remained stuck where Sloan had set her down. Her heart pounded so hard she thought she would choke.

258

"I will not be relegated to some—" The man's gaze lit on her, recognition in his eyes. "Charlotte? Praise God." He came toward her with his hands out, then abruptly halted a scant two feet from her. "You!" His expression of welcome hardened into a disdain-filled mask, and his upper lip curled. "You were supposed to be dead." Then he raised a hand, as if to hit her.

She flinched, expecting the blow. This man had hit her before. She knew it, though when or how eluded her. Instead, his hands grasped the fabric of her split skirt, pushing up the hem and exposing her leg.

"Stop!" She batted his hands away.

Suddenly, Sloan stood between her and Flanders. His hands were no longer on her, and the folds of her riding skirt fell back into place.

"This woman is an imposter. She is not my Charlotte, and I can prove it." Flanders aimed a finger toward her. "She has a burn scar on her thigh."

"And how would you know?" Sloan's voice became even more deep, even more flat.

"This, sir, is not about me. What should be concerning you is this imposter."

"How do you know?" Sloan tucked Abbey behind him, offering himself as a shield between herself and Flanders.

That simple act shattered Abbey. Not once in her entire life had anyone protected her.

Not ever.

Her legs trembled, and black spots danced in front of her gaze.

"Since you've taken her to your bed, you obviously know whether she has a scar or not. This woman is no more my daughter than your Mexican maid."

"I never said this was Charlotte. In fact, I know for certain she is not. How do you know she has a scar?"

259

"It was the only way to tell the two of them apart."

"We're twins?" Abbey asked, stepping from behind Sloan. "That woman is my sister?"

"No, you are not twins," Flanders sneered. "Your mothers were, however. And yours was the insane one, a demented harlot who accused me—William Flanders, her cousin who had cared for her since we were small children—of fathering her bastard. That would be you. A spawn from Satan." He smiled then, a sly grimace of bared teeth clamped around his cigar. "Like mother, like daughter."

The words roared through her head echoing and piling like heavy rocks that could bury her. Bastard child . . . her . . . the insane one . . . Had Pa Hawkins been right? Had he really been whipping the devil out of her—for the unpardonable sin of being a bastard? The rest of Flanders's accusation feathered through her head in disjointed bits . . . fathering a bastard . . . Oh, dearest heaven, did that mean this horrible man—

Abbey's legs went weak, and when she thought she might fall, Sloan guided her toward the chair where Flanders had been sitting.

A sob caught in her throat, and her gaze fixed on Sloan, who had never looked more forbidding.

"The number of reasons a man could know anything about what a woman's body looks like are damn few." His voice was as cold as she had ever heard it. "What did you mean—it was the only way to tell them apart?"

Flanders didn't immediately answer. Sloan stood with his legs spread and his arms folded over his chest, all his attention focused on Flanders.

"This isn't a hard question, William."

The man gave a negligent shrug. "When a man in my position owns property, he knows a great many things."

"You're not suggesting she was ever your property?"

"Of course, she was my property, my responsibility. Everything on the farm either belonged to me or was someone I was responsible for."

"And which of those categories does Abbey fall into?" When Flanders didn't immediately answer, Sloan added, "Property to be branded? Or someone under your care?"

"So, you have seen it."

"Yes, and the scars on her back. I suppose you wouldn't know anything about that?"

William's gaze slid to Abbey, and he smiled, but the expression was cruel. His gaze fastened on her, and she flinched while raw recognition poured through her, scalding her.

This man and Pa. He had come saying she had pretended to be Charlotte, had taken her clothes. The clothes had been given, not stolen. Pa had marched her off to the woodshed, this time without the other children who before then had been forced to watch—she was example to keep them from committing her sins. This time, the fear had made her fingers clumsy while Pa had waited with his whip coiled in his hand while she stripped. He hadn't yelled at her, but the whip was new, and the silence had been worse by far. This man had watched, a half smile on his face and a wicked gleam of anticipation in his eyes. His attention had fastened on her chest, no longer the flat one of a child but budding into womanhood. Pa had roughly tied her, yanking her arms above her head. This time, she had not been able to retreat into a numb, dark place because this time it was a lash, not a rough length of rope. With each stroke, her skin was sliced open, her own warm blood dripping down her legs. And, *he* had puffed on his cigar, watching and watching, the gleam of evil on her destruction. Then, he had taken off his ring, held it against the tip of his cigar and . . .

CHAPTER 19

Abbey screamed, all the hurt and anger and terror she had felt that awful night erupting through the long-ago past to this moment right now. She lunged at Flanders. "How could you?"

Before she could strike him, Sloan captured her in his arms and folded her close. She fought him, kicking and struggling to get away, furious once more that her strength and size were no match for a man. Holding her close, he dragged her with him as he went to the open door. And, she was sure he was going to throw her off the porch like so much trash, the way it had happened so long ago, the way she had sworn would never happen again.

Her fury turned on Sloan, and she fought him with every ounce of her strength. Her efforts were futile, and she hated that most of all. "Let me go."

"Sam!" he bellowed, and to her, his voice dropped to a hoarse whisper. "Oh, Abbey. Please, stop fighting me."

The anguish in his voice reached through her fury, and she stilled.

"You're safe. He can't hurt you."

Through her tears, she watched Sam emerge from the barn.

"Get the buckboard," Sloan yelled. He set Abbey on the bench and brushed a hand across her cheek. "You're safe," he repeated. "Wait here."

And then, he was gone, and she sat there shivering, tears continuing to slide down her face. She scrubbed at them, ready to get up and do battle. Except, Sloan had promised she was safe. That promise stuck like a wisp of cotton to a bur. Did she dare believe him?

Sloan, for whatever else he was, kept his promises. Still, she hated this—being at the mercy of what someone else thought she should do.

She heard Flanders say, "Good riddance. A man who has come to his senses."

"Oh, I've come to my senses, all right." There was the sound of a crash followed by Flanders's outraged howl. "That's for insulting Consuela."

Then, the man somehow was on the porch, stumbling and grasping for balance. He toppled to his knees, then stood.

Sloan appeared in the doorway, one long step putting him within reach of Flanders. Sloan punched Flanders in the jaw, and the man stumbled backwards off the steps and landed on his seat in the mud.

"And that is for Sam, who is more of a man than you will ever be." Sloan followed as though he had all the time in the world, and when Flanders stood, Sloan hit him again, this time landing a blow to the middle of the man's ample, brocade-covered stomach. "And that is for Abbey, who was a child—an innocent child—when you branded her."

Flanders gasped.

Abbey was sure she had, as well. If what William Flanders had said was true, Francis was her mother. Abbey didn't remember her, but the memories of Martha, the grandmother who had rocked her so tenderly when she was a tiny child, were right there at the surface. The truth of it was on the headstones. *Like mother, like daughter.* Her eyes filled with tears. A bastard who hadn't been worth keeping. The knowledge wasn't new, but the reality of it slammed through her. Pa had beat her, chanting she was the seed of evildoers, forever banned from heaven.

She started when she felt a movement next to her.

Jonah sat beside her, close enough their shoulders touched. He tipped his head slightly toward her, his eyes warm when she met his gaze.

"I'm glad my brother found you," he murmured, his voice nearly as deep as Sloan's.

The instant Flanders made it to his feet, Sloan hit him again, and this time the man fell to his back. Abbey could see his eyes were wide open. For one awful moment she had the notion he was dead. Then, his eyes blinked.

Sloan loomed over him, his anger palpable. "Get up, you son of a bitch."

Flanders struggled to his feet.

Sloan grasped him by the collar and leaned close. "I ought to brand you."

Flanders blanched, and with a mutter of disgust, Sloan struck him again. The man's head snapped back, and he slumped. Sloan let Flanders fall to the ground. This time, he remained there.

Abbey couldn't take her eyes off the man, images from the long-ago past overlaying the present.

Sloan heaved a sigh, removed his hat, and slapped it against his thigh. His gaze briefly met Abbey's, and then he looked away at the sound of Consuela's greeting.

She held the baby, and Pearl Mae skipped along beside her. Farther behind, JJ hobbled toward them, his progress hampered by crutches.

Consuela's dark gaze took them all in, lingering a long moment on the man lying in the mud. For once, her dark eyes were not filled with hatred when she looked at Abbey before addressing Sloan. "Señor, I see you are home."

"And glad to be here." He tipped his head toward Flanders. "Since this son of a bitch was acting like my house was his, I'm assuming he came with a trunk."

She nodded. "He will be leaving?"

"Yep."

"It is a very large trunk."

"I figured he planned to stay the winter," Jonah offered.

"Sam will be along in a minute to help you pack Mr. Flanders's things."

Consuela's gaze lingered on the crumpled man who lay unconscious in the mud, her mouth tightening. "The mud is a better place for him than the house."

"Abbey?" Pearl Mae dashed up the steps and threw herself against Abbey. "You're back. I'm so happy to see you."

Sudden tears at her eyes, she brushed the fine hair away from the little girl's face. "Not nearly as much as I am to see you."

"It snowed lots and lots"—Pearl Mae waved in the direction of the pasture—"and JJ and me, we made a huge snowman, but it's mostly melted now."

Her innocence amid all this madness made Abbey's throat catch on a sob, this one near laughter. "I would like to see it."

"Later." Consuela came up the steps and held out her hand to her daughter, her gaze cool when she met Abbey's. "You can help me," she said to her daughter.

"I should help, as well." Abbey stood.

"You should sit," Sloan commanded while Consuela said, "There's no need."

Feeling a little put out, she sank back down to the bench. Jonah smiled at her. "Give it time." As though understanding her unspoken thought, he added, "She knows you're not Charlotte."

From the ground, Flanders said, "I'm assuming if I stand, you'll hit me again."

"That's right," Sloan agreed.

"You'll never get away with this," Flanders said, as though he somehow thought he was still in control. "She is a strumpet. I don't know what she's told you about—"

"She's never said one thing about your daughter. Except to wonder why they look so much alike."

"I demand to know where my daughter is. Likely as not, that imposter is responsible for her disappearance."

Sloan exchanged a glance with Jonah while Flanders sat up.

"Not my place to tell him." Jonah shrugged, then in a flat voice said, "Me, Injun. Stupid savage not fit to speak to white man."

Flanders glared at Jonah. "He's a bloody heathen."

"This man is my brother," Sloan stated emphatically, looming over Flanders. "This ranch is his home. And your daughter, sir, is dead."

His statement dropped like a stone, freezing the moment. Then, Flanders shuddered.

"Dead!" His face paled, and his lips pinched into a tight line of denial. "No. You must be mistaken."

"No mistake," Jonah said. "By the time I found her, she was sick."

"And?" Flanders demanded.

"And, she died," Jonah said, his voice somehow sad.

Abbey knew there was more, much more, Jonah wasn't saying. Flanders sat in the mud, his gaze fixed on the ground. At last he stood, straightening his vest and flicking bits of mud off his shirt. A myriad of emotions chased across his face before settling into a scowl of deep anger.

"If my daughter is dead, you two are undoubtedly responsible, and I will see you hang. Both of you."

"What happened to her," Jonah said, "she brought on herself."

Sam came out of the barn driving the buckboard. Behind

him, Jake emerged, leading his saddled horse. When the buckboard came to a stop in front of the house, Sloan said, "Go give Consuela a hand. Mr. Flanders is returning to Poncha."

"If you're going to insist on this madness, I can pack myself," Flanders said as though he was still in control. His cheekbone was red and beginning to swell, as was the corner of his mouth. Sloan simply stood there with his arms folded over his chest. When Flanders took a step toward the house, Sloan blocked his way.

"You are not welcome in my home."

Jake looped the reins for his horse around one of the wheels of the buckboard. "I'll give you a hand." He and Sam climbed the steps and went into the house.

A silence, so thick and tense it raised the hairs on the back of Abbey's neck, settled over them, her memory once more sliding back to her childhood not long after she had been taken to the shack where Ma and Pa Hawkins lived. She remembered often standing in road, staring at the big house off in the distance, wanting to be there so badly and knowing she would be beaten if she tried to go there. This day, a horse and buggy had galloped toward her, and she was sure she would be run over. She hadn't been, but she remembered feeling frightened and lost.

Sloan stood between Flanders and the porch, his attention on JJ. "Looks like those crutches need some adjustment so they're easier for you to walk. How is the leg feeling?"

"It don't hurt. Not so bad as it did, anyway." JJ hobbled up the steps and went into the house.

Abbey realized Flanders was once more staring at her. There was a malevolence in his eyes that chilled her and pinned her to her seat.

"She's damaged goods, you know." Flanders continued to stare at Abbey. "Barely fit for even a brothel, which is where you should deliver her to."

With every bit of willpower she had left, she raised her chin and met his gaze head on.

"No one will ever believe she isn't tarnished, especially after spending all this time here with you while she pretended to be my daughter." His gaze shifted to Sloan. "And, I do remember how smitten with Charlotte you were. No matter the protests of her mother or me, you couldn't wait to seduce and steal my daughter, who was worth a thousand times more than this one." He pointed at Abbey with his cigar. "She's—"

"Don't say a word," Sloan warned, "unless it's to apologize."

"No apology is in order." Flanders straightened to his full height.

The word was barely out of his mouth before Sloan hit him again. Once more, Flanders went down, this time with a howl of outrage.

Sam and Jake emerged from the house, carrying a large trunk between them. The packing had clearly been done in a hurry since a shirtsleeve hung down the side from beneath the lid.

"It ain't real pretty, but it's all in here. Every bit of it." Sam and Jake set the trunk on the back of the buckboard.

"I've got his hat and coat." Jake took the items off the top of the trunk.

Sam and Sloan hauled Flanders to his feet, and Jake held out the coat. Flanders made a point of brushing off the sleeves of his shirt before thrusting his arm into the coat sleeve. When it was clear he wasn't steady enough to sit on the bench with Sam, Sloan lifted him and put him on the back of the buckboard next to the trunk.

"You won't get away with this," Flanders said.

"Don't come back," Sloan advised, his tone as cold as the words.

"I'm thinking I should ride along." Jake took the reins from around the wagon wheel and mounted his horse. "Figured Sam would like some company."

"Good idea," Sloan agreed.

Sam tipped his hat to Abbey and climbed onto the wagon and flicked the reins against the horse's rump.

"Jake," Sloan called.

When he brought the horse to a stop, Sloan went toward him and removed a coin from his pocket and tossed it to him. "Maybe you and Sam should spend the night at the inn. Make sure Mr. Flanders is all settled in."

Jake easily caught the coin and pocketed it. Then, Sloan leaned against Jake's horse while he leaned down, their extended conversation so quiet Abbey couldn't hear a word of what they were saying until Jake said, "You're sure that's the way you want it?"

Sloan nodded.

"Consider it done."

Sloan stepped away and stood there watching the buckboard head toward the gate.

"Well, that's about enough excitement for one day," Jonah said.

Sloan came up the steps and squatted in front of Abbey. "Are you okay?"

She nodded.

"He won't ever bother you again." He briefly touched her cheek with his thumb, then stood. "You stay here and get acquainted with my brother while I help Consuela get things squared away inside."

"I can help."

He pointed a finger at her. "Rest. Your shoulder has to be hurting after being jostled on the back of a horse all day."

She would have liked to have denied that but couldn't.

Next to her, Jonah chuckled. "There you go again, big brother, bossing everyone around and assuming they'll do your bidding." He slanted a glance at Abbey. "He's always been like that. Even to me, his wiser brother."

Sloan slapped his brother on the back without comment and went into the house.

"I feel like I should be doing something instead of sitting here."

"All the more reason to rest while you have the chance."

Jonah didn't seem any more inclined to talk than she was, and the silence that fell between them was surprisingly comfortable. She stared across the yard to the valley beyond and the mountain peaks in the distance, but her thoughts were caught in a churning maelstrom whose center was the awful thought William Flanders might be her father. Everything about that tied her into knots.

With effort, she shut those images away and focused on patches of snow remaining under the trees. Except for the occasional rustle of the breeze that carried a chill, the air was as warm as it had been before the storm. Little by little, her breathing slowed, the sense of panic ebbed, and she turned, as she always did to remembering what Miss Mary might have advised. Since the only book in her house had been a Bible, they learned to read from that, and the advice was always sourced from that. Peace, she finally remembered, I leave with you. Let your heart not be troubled. The notion made her smile. She was likely to be troubled, but she still felt better. Comfortable. Grateful she could sit here in the silence with Jonah, who seemed to expect nothing from her.

On the other side of the compound, a wagon was parked in front of Consuela's cabin. A canvas tarp covered a sizable mound suggesting it was mostly loaded. "She really is leaving," Abbey murmured. Even though Sloan and Jake had talked about it, seeing the partially loaded wagon brought home the realization.

"Yep. JJ was no bigger than little Sarah when she first got here."

"Changes." As before, she found herself thinking about a home of her own where she hoped the changes would be fewer, or at least more gradual. That thought led to the orchard she hoped to have one day and the seeds in a trunk in Denver that she wasn't sure she would ever see again.

"I hope the snow didn't do any damage to the trees in the orchard." A stupid thing to be concerned about, she decided, since she wasn't likely to see the trees bloom.

"It looks the way I imagine Pop hoped it would someday. Pearl Mae told me you've spent a lot of time out there. Your hard work shows."

"It gave me something to do and kept me out of Consuela's way." She looked at Jonah. "She told me Charlotte had seduced her husband."

"Yep."

"Your brother is—" She broke off not at all sure what she wanted to say about Sloan.

"My brother didn't intend to bring home a bride. He'd gone to see Flanders because he had fine horses to sell. Charlotte seduced him, and he did the honorable thing—he married her, which, it turned out, she didn't want."

"I had wondered how—"

"He made such a mistake?" Jonah shook his head. "He saw what he wanted to see, and then it was too late."

"And she really is . . . dead?" Asking filled Abbey with dread. She had known there was a little girl who lived in the big house that had been the farm's center. She had even known they both had dark-brown hair. Never once, though, had it occurred to her they were related.

As she had done, Jonah stared across the valley, but his dark gaze was somehow turned inward, and his expression was somber. Finally, he looked at her. "I'm sorry for what happened to you."

Abbey didn't know how to respond. These last weeks had been sometimes upsetting and sometimes surprising. Then, it settled over her that she still had her life while Charlotte had lost hers. Death had been all too common for most of Abbey's life, so hearing of Charlotte's hadn't been all that surprising even though the news was unexpected. Miss Mary had taught Abbey everyone's soul had a chance at redemption, no matter how wicked during life. All she could think of was maybe there would be some measure of peace for all the people Charlotte had hurt.

Jonah stood, his tall frame much too thin. The way the muslin shirt hung loosely from his shoulders, it was clear that he had lost a lot of weight.

"You're recovering?"

He smiled. "Yes." His gaze lit on her feet, then his smile grew even wider. "You're wearing the moccasins my mother made."

Abbey stuck her feet out in front of her and looked at them. "They were all I had after Jake threw away my shoes." She clapped a hand over her mouth, then added, "That sounded ungrateful. They've been a blessing. Charlotte's feet are—were—smaller than mine, and without these, I would have been a barefoot orphan." She stood and faced him. "I'm also very thankful you have recovered."

He laughed. "You've proven you couldn't be Charlotte. She would have been the first to dance on my grave." He waved toward the door. "I think I'll go see what I can do inside."

She watched him go, struck by how much he sounded like Sloan and how little he sounded like anything she imagined an Indian would. Since she remembered Sloan's father had been a school teacher before becoming a trapper, it made sense Jonah would have been schooled, as well.

272

She found herself prey to her own tumultuous thoughts, the internal peace of a few moments earlier gone. Eliza, one of the older girls at the orphanage, hadn't been right in her mind. Abbey wondered if that was how it had been for her mother. A woman not in her right mind. Miss Mary had caught a man pawing at Eliza, who had mistaken the attention for flirtation. Had it been that way for her mother?

Abbey shuddered at the thought, then dropped her face into her hands, more and more certain William Flanders was her father. Nothing else could explain why she and Charlotte looked so much alike. Mothers who were twins and the same father. The haunting echo of her grandmother's words echoed through her mind. *You're a Flanders no matter what anyone says.* Only her name had been Wallace, the one Abbey had adopted as her own.

Once more the vile accusations Pa had chanted as he beat her echoed through her head. Tears came, and she buried her face in her hands, her heart feeling as though it might break open.

Then she felt an arm come around her, and she started.

"Shhh," Sloan said against her hair. "I'm right here."

He pulled her closer, and she burrowed against him, his strength and warmth flowing through her. As happened every time he held her, she felt comforted, cherished, and as though she had come home. Except this wasn't her home, no more than Miss Mary's house had been. She clung to the idea of a homestead in California. This one dream had kept her going for years now. Only, when she got there, she would still be alone.

She didn't know how long they sat like that, but twilight was creeping ever closer.

"Do you want supper first?" Sloan asked, his voice deep. "Or a bath."

"A bath," she murmured promptly.

He laughed. "I figured that would be your answer." He lifted her into his arms and stood. This time, when they came into the house, it smelled fresh like the sage and cedar sometimes did in the early morning after Consuela had cleaned.

He didn't set her down until they were in the bathing alcove, where a fire burned cheerily in the corner fireplace. The tub was already filled with hot water. He set her on her feet and unbuttoned the cloak, which he hung on a peg near the doorway.

"Thank you."

"For what?" Sloan stirred the fire, then added another small log to it, determined the room would be as cozy and warm as he could make it.

"Until you, no one . . ."

When her voice trailed away, he faced her, finding the color in her cheeks a rosy pink. While he watched, she pressed her lips together and nodded her head once as though gathering the courage for whatever she needed to say. She met his gaze, then looked away.

"No one ever stood up for me before."

Her words echoed through him, reinforcing what he already knew about the brutal treatment she had suffered as a child. Somehow, she had forgotten his own judgment of her had been as harsh as anyone's. Truth was, he hadn't stood up for her until he had been forced to. To be thanked for not taking a lash to her or branding her or turning her out made him angry. She deserved far better than he had given her.

"Take your bath, Abbey." He stalked out of the bathing alcove.

When he looked back at her, she stood watching him, looking more lost and unsure of herself than he had ever seen her. He would have given a lot to see the righteous fire she'd had in her the day she arrived here. Not trusting himself, he pulled the curtain across the opening and left the room.

He found Consuela and Jonah on the back stoop where she

was vigorously scrubbing the sheets they had taken off the bed. The two wooden tubs—one for washing and one for rinsing—were filled to the brim.

"That man burned holes in the linens with his cigars." She held one of them up for his inspection, then lapsed into Spanish as she often did when she was upset. The litany provided Sloan with a vivid picture of how miserable William Flanders had made everyone from the moment of his arrival. "It's so late, they won't dry before dark."

She made that sound like a major transgression, which made Sloan grin. "If they hang on the line overnight, it will be fine."

JJ and Pearl Mae sat on the edge of the porch playing checkers, though everything in JJ's posture suggested he'd rather be doing something else.

"You doing okay?" Jonah asked Sloan.

"Yep." Sloan studied his brother. "You don't look too much worse for the wear. Maybe as skinny as that old nag Pa used to have. How's the bullet hole?"

"Healing, thanks to Consuela."

She was still muttering about William Flanders's many faults but looked up when she heard her name mentioned.

"And you." Sloan directed his attention to her. "Are you okay?"

She nodded once, her attention still mostly on the washboard.

"From the looks of the wagon, you must just about be packed up and ready to leave."

She nodded again, but this time her hands slowed. "It's time." Her gaze went to the two older children, then to the baby, who was awake in the cradle but seemed content to watch all of them as though they were fascinating.

"You don't have to go." In fact, he was pretty sure the place would fall apart without her.

She shook her head. "My mind is made up. And Jake will

take me as soon as we know that Poncha Pass is cleared."

She dumped the heavy sheet into a basket, clearly intending to carry it out to the line. Sloan picked it up and followed her, then held onto the heavy sheets while she attached the clothespins to the line. Her dark eyes met his.

"Jonah says he was with your wife when she died, but I still see her when I look at . . . the other one."

Sloan understood. Consuela had paid a bigger price for his wife's wickedness than anyone else on the ranch.

"I can't forget. Or forgive."

"Abbey is not Charlotte." The refrain sounded old, and he realized how frustrated Abbey must have been all these weeks.

"I know." A heavy sigh followed as she fastened the last clothespin. "It makes no difference."

Sloan didn't like it, but he also understood. "I won't try to change your mind, but I'm sorry to see you go."

She gave him a sharp nod, picked up the empty basket and headed back to the house.

Instead of heading for the barn where a couple of dozen things required his attention, he took the trail leading to the family cemetery, the trail barely visible in the deepening gloom of evening. The gravestones were barely visible, only because he knew where to look for them. His father and brother who had been laid to rest on a day not unlike this one. Nearby were Consuela's infants, too briefly here. Joey, the most recent addition and the mound of earth over his grave more settled than the last time Sloan had been here.

They had been so much in love with each other Consuela had defied her father to be with Joey—a man whose dreams of breeding bulls would give rise to fine, healthy herds of cattle, and who had died far too soon. That she was going home meant there was healing, or at least the possibility of it, with her father. A good thing, Sloan reminded himself, even though he had no idea how he was going to manage without her.

The end of this day marked one of those pivots in life. The certain end of any ties to William Flanders. The regret over Charlotte's death. The huge hole that would be left when Consuela and her children left. The change in his relationship with Abbey. That one filled him with anxiety and hope she would change her mind about leaving.

CHAPTER 20

When Abbey awoke the following morning, hungry, undoubtedly because she had been unable to resist the allure of the bed
last night after her bath and had missed supper. Everything last
night had been clean and filled with the scents Consuela put in
the soap—cedar and lavender—no trace of William Flanders's
cigar smoke or the rose scents Charlotte had left behind. Sleep
had come easily, and if she had dreamed, it was of being held
by Sloan.

She opened the armoire in search of something to wear. The
blue dress she had worn for so many days hung there, clearly
washed and pressed since the last time she had seen it—another
unexpected kindness. She put it on, then left the sanctuary of
the room, automatically stopping at the door and waiting for
Silas. Only the dog wasn't there.

Nobody was in the kitchen, and, in fact, the house appeared
to be empty except for herself. She was reminded of her first
day here when she had been a stranger, and everyone had been
so sure she was Sloan's hated wife.

Abbey went through the kitchen door outside, finding the
temperature warmer than she had expected. Patches of snow
beneath the deep shade of the trees at the edge of the yard were
the only evidence of the recent snow storm, though the pasture,
dotted with the cattle brought from the high country, was
greener than she had seen it.

Movement at the edge of the porch caught her eye. JJ sat on

a bench against the wall, his crutches as his side.

He regarded her warily. "Ma says you're not Miz Charlotte, and I'm supposed to be nice to you."

"I see."

"Don't know how one body can look so much like another and not be the same one."

She smiled at his vehemence. "I don't know, either." She looked around the yard. "Where is everyone?"

"Sam and Jake ain't back yet. Everybody else is with Mama." He pointed toward the small dwelling on the other side of the compound. "Deciding about how to get everything she wants to take into the wagon."

"So, you're really leaving?"

"Yep." Without warning, the boy's chin trembled.

Realizing he wasn't as nonchalant as he wanted to portray, Abbey crossed the porch and sat down next to him.

"This has always been home?" she asked.

"I was borned before we came here, but I don't remember." He slid her a glance from the corner of his eye. "Why would you care?"

"Every time I go someplace new, I'm scared," she admitted without adding each move as a child had been by force. Until she had been taken in by Miss Mary, those moves had never been for the better.

"You don't act scared." He swung his leg not in a splint back and forth. "Mama says you're uppity."

Cutting as the remark had probably been when made to JJ, it made Abbey smile. She tipped her head toward the boy and whispered, "That's how you know I'm scared. It's my way to keep others from knowing."

This odd conversation refocused her energies. Now that she was no longer forced to stay here, she needed to find her way back to Denver and the Haverlys. Hopefully they still had her trunk. Somehow, she would once more be on her way west, toward the homestead that seemed more out of reach than ever. Like every place else she had ever lived, this was a temporary stop along the way of finding her own home.

"It's a small comfort now because you're leaving everything familiar to you. You will find new friends."

"How would you know?" he challenged.

"Because I was taken away from my home and given away to strangers when I was about Pearl Mae's age. Then the war came, and I went to live with Miss Mary. She took care of me and other children who had no family. Since then, I've lived in Kentucky and Missouri and, finally, here. Every place I've been, I've made new friends."

"You don't have friends here."

"Perhaps not." There was no point in arguing with the boy, especially this one who was hurting and who was determined to see the world in his own way. She had a certain satisfaction in knowing JJ's sister and Silas had been her friends. After others realized she wasn't Charlotte, she hoped there would be others.

Her hope was renewed. She had survived Caleb. All she had to do was keep working toward the home she had always longed for. Abbey's Orchard.

Voices coming across the compound reached her ears, and she looked up to see Sloan coming from the direction of Consuela's cabin. With him was Preacher. Seeing him was a surprise.

"Good morning," she called when they were closer.

She was aware of Preacher's smile, but her attention was mostly on Sloan. She couldn't read anything of his expression, but those eyes she had once thought to be cold were soft. Alluring.

"You're looking better."

"I feel better."

"You're not wearing the sling."

She moved her shoulder experimentally. "It feels better today."

Preacher climbed the steps of the porch, and when she stood, he clasped her hands within both of his.

"You look fine, lass. I hope you'll forgive this foolish old man for not being willing to believe you were telling the truth."

Unexpected tears burned at the back of her eyes. "There's nothing to forgive."

Her gaze sought Sloan's, who looked different. Then, she realized someone had trimmed his dark hair, which no longer fell over his collar. And, he was wearing a white linen shirt—a Sunday go-to-meeting shirt—that had been ironed and was buttoned to the neck. He was also clean-shaven, which left the angles of his face in sharp relief. At her examination of him, he flushed, and he looked away, ruffling JJ's hair.

"Well," JJ said, "when is the wedding going to be?"

Sloan and Preacher exchanged a look.

"What wedding?" Abbey asked.

Once more, Preacher and Sloan gave each other a long stare without speaking. Then Preacher nodded at the boy. "JJ, why don't you and me go check on your mama and sisters?"

Sloan watched them go while Abbey watched him. "What wedding?" she repeated when he looked back at her. A balloon of anticipation, or perhaps dread—she wasn't sure which—filled her.

"Ours."

That made her take an involuntary step backwards, and she bumped into the bench where she and JJ had been sitting. Her legs gave way, and she sat down.

Sloan squatted in front of her, his expression wary. He took both of her hands within his, the hard warmth of them igniting memories of their lovemaking.

She swallowed against this awful burgeoning of confusing

hope filling her chest.

"William had a point yesterday. You've been an unmarried woman here for weeks without a chaperone. Living under my roof while everyone thought you were my wife." Something in his expression shifted, his eyes becoming softer. "I have ruined your reputation. So, we should get married. It's the only way I have of doing right by you."

"That's . . . I don't—You want to get married?" The confusion vanished.

"Yes."

"Because I'm ruined." Her hope burst.

"Yes."

"Because of what we did on the mountain?" Once again, she was someone's duty. Never mind her own free will.

"Yes."

Anger bubbled up in a sudden rush that numbed her lips. She pulled at her hands, needing to put some distance between them. His grip tightened, once more proving he was stronger than she, once more at the mercy of someone else's will.

"Let me go." When he did, she stood and stepped to the edge of the porch.

"Abbey, this needs to be done."

"No." At last, the crisp linen shirt and his trimmed hair made sense—he thought they would be married. "I will not be a duty—a responsibility—a *thing* that needs to be handled all in the name of propriety."

"Damn it, Abbey, I want to do right by you."

"Do you love me?"

He froze, to the point he didn't seem to breathe.

She glared at him, her stance equally still because she had shocked herself by asking. Of course, he didn't love her. Holding herself as rigid as she could so she wouldn't tremble, wouldn't show him that she loved him—oh, sweet merciful heaven, how had that happened?—she loved him, which was the most foolish thing she had ever done in her life.

She lifted her chin and somehow held his gaze though doing so cost her everything.

"I thought not," she whispered. "And how could you?" She gestured toward her face. "How could you not be reminded every single day of her?"

"I don't see her," he said, his voice so deep she more felt it than heard it. "I haven't for a long time. I see you, Abigail Wallace."

He reached for her hand, and when she stepped out of his reach, he sighed.

All her life, she had lived with the whispers and the sometimes subtle, often overt glances directed at her. All her life she had never had any value even though she had spent much of it as someone's duty. And now this. What he proposed would surely be living hell.

She closed her eyes against the burning intensity of his gaze. How could he not see Charlotte when he looked at her, no matter how he protested? Of course, he couldn't love her. But she wanted him to. Wanted it badly, in fact.

Her imagination raced ahead to years in front of them, and she concluded such a marriage would be worse than anything she had endured so far. Everything she had learned of Sloan since she had been here assured her that he was a man of his word, so he wouldn't pawn her off the way the Mr. Flanders had. He was a man who stood by his duty, but she too well remembered how frightened she had been of him those first few days. She wouldn't subject herself to that, but more . . . she couldn't do that to him, either. Such a life would be equally a hell for him.

"No," she said, straightening to her full height, which still left her looking a long way up at him. "Thank you for your concern, but no."

"What do you mean, 'no'?"

"You've already done quite enough for me. More than I had any right to expect, in fact. You kept me safe even when you believed I was the wife who had betrayed you. You rescued me from Caleb. And, you protected me from Mr. Flanders. I will not be your burden to bear for the rest of our lives because of some misguided sense of honor."

"What the hell are you talking about?" He leaned toward her, his eyes fierce. "A man protects those under his care, and I didn't protect you."

"I am not your responsibility."

"You damn well are while you're under my roof."

"I'd appreciate it if you'd stop swearing at me."

"Abbey, please."

"As for being your responsibility while I'm under your roof . . . that can be remedied. I can leave, and then you won't have to be concerned with 'ruining me,' as you put it, nor will I be your responsibility." She made her voice as firm as she could and was relieved it didn't shake. She did need to make her escape soon because she was on the verge of crying. She'd die rather than have him see how affected she was. "I appreciate your offer more than you can possibly know."

She was tempted to extend her hand for a handshake like she had seen men do. He stared down at her, a muscle in his jaw so clenched it stood in sharp relief. And those dark eyes she had once thought cold burned. She had a far greater desire to touch his cheek, to assure him everything would turn out for the best. Except she had never touched him except for the night he'd held her in his arms, and they had made love. To ensure she kept her hands to herself, she clasped them together.

"What if there is a babe?" he asked.

The mere thought made her eyes burn. She shook her head in denial.

"You can't know for sure."

A baby. She would be lying if she denied thinking about it, but her focus had mostly been on the wonder of the pleasure they had shared. Nothing had seemed more important than being joined with him. She stared into his dark eyes, finding them as intensely focused on her as they had been when they made love. Her cheeks burned at the memory and at the knowledge she wanted him as much now—nay, even more, because now she knew how wonderful he had made her feel.

"A baby of mine will be raised by me."

His emphatic statement brought her back to this moment, and once more she shook her head. She swallowed the lump in her throat, then blinked to relieve the burning of her eyes, praying no tears would fall. None did, but her composure was so thin she wasn't sure how much longer she could withstand his scrutiny. A part of her wanted him to swoop her into his arms and declare his love for her whether they had created a child or not. A foolish thought found only in Miss Mary's tales of chivalrous knights and fair maidens.

The moment shattered when Preacher appeared at the corner of the house, then came toward her. "Are we set for a wedding?"

"We are not." Sloan threw up his hands and stalked off the porch and toward the barn. "Maybe you can talk some sense into her," he said over his shoulder.

"She hasn't agreed to marry you?"

"No."

Abbey went back into the house, wanting to escape and knowing none was available when Preacher followed her inside and closed the door behind him.

"Well, I wasn't expecting that." Preacher pulled a chair out from the table. "Come. Sit."

She stood uncertainly for a moment, wishing with all her heart she could escape and give into the unshed tears burning her eyes. After Preacher patted the table, she sat, and he took a chair across from her.

"Sloan—Mr. Rafferty—did ask you to marry him?"

"He did. And I thanked him and refused his offer."

"Why?" Preacher set his hat on the table, his attention wholly focused on her. "Surely you can see the sense in the proposal."

She sighed, stared at her hands, and wondered how to make her position clear. "He sees marrying me as a duty—a way to redeem my reputation." She managed a small smile. "I'm a woman without any social stature. Surely my reputation can withstand what has happened here."

"What about Sloan's reputation?" Preacher asked. "You'll be long gone if you follow your plan to go to California, but he'll be here, tied to this community and what people think of him. Would you have him appear to be less than the honorable man he is?"

"A man doesn't have the same constraints as a woman. Within a short period of time, I'll be that unfortunate woman who had the bad luck to look like his dead wife."

"You are correct. A woman is expected to be more chaste and more circumspect. A man lives and dies by his word. When others learn Sloan Rafferty hadn't treated you as he should, they'll judge him for it the next time they do business with him. They'll wonder if he'll do right by them."

"Surely, not," Abbey protested.

"There is a more compelling reason." Preacher fingered the brim of his hat. "William Flanders came to see me last night with serious accusations." He let the silence between them stretch, the added, "He would see you in prison for impersonating his daughter, and he'd see Sloan and Jonah hang for her death."

Abbey's chest constricted. "That's not what happened."

Preacher shrugged. "We may think so, but he's a wealthy, connected man who claims to be friends with Governor Mc-Cook. Facts can be twisted, and I have a hunch Mr. Flanders is an expert at arranging the truth to serve what he wants."

"Wouldn't it look worse if Sloan married me?"

"You have many witnesses who know you have been insisting from the beginning that you're Abigail Wallace. His accusation about that will never hold water. The account of her disappearance and her death . . . those may be in question."

"Don't you see?" she leaned forward. "What if I do something that makes him doubt me? Building a life together in a loveless marriage . . ." She surged to her feet. "I can't do it. I can't."

"Love grows, lass, so I wouldn't be too troubled. You begin with respect and commitment. Sloan Rafferty has demonstrated that and more."

Somehow, she didn't think it was all as simple as Preacher made it sound.

"Charlotte wasn't well liked, as you know. And, most folks would be thinking he did the right thing by marrying you. If you're not here, those same folks will never have a chance to know you, and they might be thinking Mr. Flanders could be right—you're a loose woman of immoral character, another of the less than desirable people Sloan associates with. Many of those same folks think Sloan is too tolerant of the Utes and their thievery of the occasional cow, so things could go against him. They might not want to buy his beef, and they might come to believe lies masquerading as the truth. In an investigation, someone could use that as a reason to think the worst of him."

She shook her head. "You're asking me to believe I'll be hurting Sloan if I don't marry him?"

"I believe it's the truth, lass. The man is in a bigger bind than we could have imagined."

She pressed a hand against her forehead, which was beginning to ache. "I need a while to think about this," she finally said.

"And perhaps a good prayer would be in order, as well," he added.

She nodded and headed for her room. There, she closed the door and leaned against it. All the emotion she had been holding in seeped out, first in tears washing down her face, then in shuddering sobs that brought her to her knees. How could she choose her own wants over hurting another? If she did the right thing, her dream for a home and her own place where she truly belonged would be forever lost. If she did the right thing, she would be binding herself to a man who did not—and probably never would—love her. She would be taken care of, but at what cost? Easier by far this decision would be if she did not love him. The right thing . . . how could she be sure what was?

Her greatest fear loomed ahead of her—what if he banished her one day the way her mother's family had and the way Miss Mary had after Abbey had turned eighteen? What if the place where she truly belonged—that was truly her own—was forever lost to her?

CHAPTER 21

"Well?" Sloan demanded when Preacher came out of the house, meeting him halfway between the house and the barn. Jonah, who had been trying to distract him by talking about the need to visit the livery in Poncha to find a pair of draft horses for pulling Consuela's wagon, trailed behind him.

"She wants some time to think. And, given the circumstances, you can't blame the lass." Preacher settled his hat more firmly on his head, his regard somber. "This wedding you want, though, might be the least of your worries given Mr. Flanders's accusations."

"Which don't hold water." He had hoped William Flanders had taken the morning stage back to Denver.

"That Caleb Holt fellow—"

"What about him?"

"He's been seen in town, and the story he's telling is a tall one."

Sloan stared at Preacher, wishing he'd get to the point.

Preacher took off his hat and fingered the brim. "He's doing a fine job of stirring people up. Has been going on about how you're so friendly with the Utes when everyone knows they'd scalp you in your sleep. He's claiming if you have any cattle missing, it's because you sold them in secret." Preacher paused and settled his hat back on his head. "He claims you took Charlotte into the mountains and killed her right before the storm hit."

"What?" Jonah's sharp exclamation was an echo of Sloan's.

A dawning realization bloomed in his chest. Sloan looked at his brother. "He doesn't know."

"Know what?" Preacher asked.

"Charlotte really is dead," Jonah said. "I found her."

"You mean to tell me Caleb knows Miss Abbey is not Charlotte?"

Sloan shook his head. "No, he thinks she's Charlotte, all right. As for the taking her to the mountains and killing her—that's exactly what he did—or at least what he intended."

The rest of the story followed with all that had happened since Jonah's return until Preacher nodded with an, "Ahh. I understand." Preacher looked at Jonah. "Folks might not take your word about what happened to Charlotte."

"William Flanders knows Abbey isn't Charlotte." Sloan was still stung that William had seen the differences between Abbey and Charlotte right away while he hadn't known for sure until the night when he had confronted Abbey in her bath. As happened every time he remembered that night, he cringed. However much their faces might resemble one another, their bodies did not—even without the scars.

"And, he's made other accusations. You're responsible for his daughter's death," Preacher said, even as he raised a hand in assurance, "which don't mean I'm accusing you of anything." He looked at Jonah. "You said you found her with a Comanche band. How did she die?"

"She was sick." Jonah's gaze went from Preacher to Sloan, and his eyes were filled with regret. "She had been sold to them, which made her nothing more than a thing to be used until they were done with her . . ." His voice trailed off, and he shrugged. "After she told me what had happened, it was as though she didn't have any reason to hang on."

Sloan's chest tightened, the horror of what she had endured

too terrible to think about. Rape. Being their slave to be used and abused. He had learned to hate her, but he'd never wished her harm. When she had disappeared last spring with the Cimarron Sun, to his shame, he had been more concerned with the stallion than with her.

Preacher cleared his throat. "You're telling me Caleb helped her steal the stallion, then double-crossed her with your other ranch hand—"

"That's right—Buck," Jonah said.

"And, he was supposed to kill her but sold her to the Comanche, instead?" Preacher added.

"That's what she told me."

"Buck is also dead," Sloan added. "He's the one Jake and I found up on the ridge a couple of weeks back."

"Caleb is tying up loose ends," Jonah mused. "He probably killed Buck, then had to kill Abbey since he thought she was Charlotte, so she couldn't betray him."

"Only she didn't die," Sloan said. "And, if Caleb crosses paths with William Flanders before he leaves town, he's going to know Abbey is who she says she is." He surged to his feet. "She's still not safe. I need to go find the son of a bitch before he strikes again."

Preacher patted the seat. "I'm advisin' you as the probate judge, you need to lay low and keep your head."

"My brother didn't give the man half of what he deserved," Jonah said. "Did Flanders tell you he branded Abbey so he could tell her apart from Charlotte?"

Preacher's eyebrows short up, then he scowled. "He insisted Miss Abbey had been impersonating his daughter." He cleared his throat, looking down while he continued to run a finger along the brim of his hat. "He's sent a telegram to the territorial marshal, who can't very well ignore accusations."

"Accusations are one thing," Sloan said. "The truth is another."

"Abbey and Charlotte . . . I take it they're related?" Preacher said.

"Charlotte's mother and Abbey's were twin sisters. Based on what we learned yesterday, I'm pretty certain William Flanders is Abbey's father."

"Oh, my." Preacher took off his derby, then patted his bald head with a handkerchief before putting the hat back on. "My advice is the same—lay low and watch your back." He paused and looked from Sloan to Jonah. "Hate to say it, but with folks all riled up as they are about the Indians, they aren't likely to believe your account of what happened to Charlotte—convincing the territorial marshal of the facts about Charlotte without a body might be impossible. The whole Comanche nation could show up to repeat your story word for word, Jonah, and they wouldn't be believed. As for what happened last spring, that's a problem since there were no witnesses except for Caleb, maybe, and your dead cowhand. The only thing going in your favor is you don't have the stallion, and everyone knows it."

Sloan scrubbed a hand over his face. "A helluva mess, that's for sure."

"She's pretty dead set against marrying you."

"Yeah." He'd been so certain that he could protect her best if she'd take his name.

The door into the house opened, and he turned toward it, finding Abbey in the doorway. Her eyes were red as though she had been crying, but she was composed, her chin lifted high the way she often did when she had something on her mind.

She stepped off the porch and came toward them, her demeanor as regal as anyone he had ever seen. Sloan knew her well enough, at last, to understand her rigid posture. She was hanging onto her composure by a thread. He didn't like knowing he was once more the reason.

Jonah smiled at her. She brushed past Sloan, heading for the barn. There, she took a seat on the bench by the wide door that he and Jonah had occupied while waiting for her and Preacher. She arranged her skirt, crossed her feet at the ankles, and waited for them to approach. Sloan felt a lot like he had when he was certain the confrontation with his father was going to result in a whipping.

Nothing in her posture was relaxed, from her clasped hands to her straight back. Nothing in her expression gave him a hint as to what she planned to say.

He wanted to say something—anything—to tell her that he hated how badly he had misjudged her, how much he wanted her forgiveness, and how he'd take care of her whether she agreed to marry him or not. Only the words remained stuck in his throat.

"I've decided . . ." Her voice was too soft, and she cleared her throat, then looked at Preacher. "I've decided to accept Mr. Rafferty's proposal."

A balloon of relief expanded through Sloan's chest.

She looked at him. "As you know, I have no clothes of my own. I will not be married wearing one of your wife's dresses."

"We need to get this done as soon as possible." He wondered what the hell difference it made. Clothes were clothes. "Today. Preacher is a busy man."

"Perhaps. I've made up my mind. Is there a mercantile in Poncha?"

"Sure is," Preacher said. "And they have pert near anything you could ask for."

"Ready-made dresses?" she asked.

He scratched the side of his nose. "Well, to be honest, I never paid any attention."

"Maybe Consuela can help," Jonah offered. "She's a fine

293

seamstress."

"Anything on your mind besides a dress?" Sloan asked.

She managed a small smile. "Many things. A marriage changes everything for me."

"I wish there were some other way," he returned, admitting to himself that was a lie. Fact was, he wanted her bound to him, wanted her to be part of him and this place. In these few weeks, she had invested more of herself in the well-being of the ranch than Charlotte ever had. She had lent a helping hand to Consuela too many times to count without complaining about the rebuffs she continually faced. She had worked so diligently in the orchard it at last resembled the one his father had imagined. Sloan hoped to hell that was the last comparison he ever made. However much they looked alike, Abbey was nothing like Charlotte.

"Preacher assures me there is not." She met his gaze and lifted her chin. "And so, we shall make the best of it."

She made it sound like marrying him was about as appealing as going toe to toe with an angry bull. "You won't be changing your mind—after getting a dress?"

Something in her eyes hardened, making him immediately regret the question.

"You must be mistaking me for someone else. If we have any chance at all of living peaceably with each other, you won't make that comparison again."

Since her comment was an immediate echo of what he had been thinking, he flushed.

"Well, now." Preacher clasped his hands together. "Sounds like there won't be a wedding today, after all."

"Is that what you and Jake were talking about right before he left yesterday?" Abbey asked as if the thought had just occurred to her. She crossed her arms over her chest. "A wedding today?"

Once more, he felt his face heat.

"Without talking to me?"

"I talked to you," he gruffly said.

"Hmph."

Sloan looked at Preacher. "When will you be coming back?"

He took off his hat and ran the brim through his fingers. "That depends on the dress for Miss Abbey now, don't it?"

Sloan looked back at Abbey, her simple request gaining monumental proportions. What did he know about women's clothes or how they came about them?

As if catching his thought, Preacher said, "I'll drop by Nate and Katherine Long's place on the way to town. With all their daughters and two recent weddings to boot, plus Mrs. Long being a fine seamstress, I bet there's a solution right under our noses."

Sloan could only hope.

"I think we can get this all settled in a couple of days. I'm betting you can plan for Mrs. Long to pay you a visit before you know it. Maybe Sam should come along with me so he can report back to you."

"The sooner, the better," Sloan said.

"Maybe by Sunday." Clearly liking the idea, Preacher beamed. "That gives us all week to plan for the celebration. You can bring Miss Abbey to the church, and we can have the wedding there. I can perform the ceremony right after the morning service. It's as good a time as any for her to meet your neighbors."

"Thank you," Abbey said as though it was all decided. "I must ask. Mrs. Long—what makes you so sure she will help?"

Preacher laughed. "She'd take a strip of my hide if I had this sort of problem and didn't ask. Don't you worry, Miss Abbey. She didn't cotton much to Charlotte, but I figure she'll like you fine."

Sloan hadn't given any thought to being in a church or guests in attendance. This thing was getting out of control at the rate of a stampeding herd. He'd imagined a simple ceremony right here in the front room with his brother, Consuela, and the hands as witnesses. That was enough to bind a man and a woman together. This was about doing right by Abbey, not inviting the whole Arkansas Valley to a wedding.

"You're still likely to end up wearing a borrowed dress. Maybe even an ugly hand me down."

"You're missing the point, brother," Jonah said. "She doesn't want to wear anything that might make you think she's Charlotte."

Sloan stared at Abbey a moment, not seeing anything of Charlotte in her features. Sure, the physical resemblance was there, but truth was, he no longer thought about Charlotte at all when he looked at her. "You can stop worrying that I see her when I look at you."

Pink pulsed from her neck to her forehead. "How could you not?"

He took a step toward her, then reached for her hand and found it icy. Resting her palm against his, he smoothed the top of her hand with his own. "I promise you. I don't see Charlotte when I look at you. I haven't for a long time."

"I've got to be goin'," Preacher said, moving toward the barn and calling to Sam. He tipped his head to Abbey.

Sam emerged, riding his own horse and leading Preacher's mule.

"Washed your face, I see," Preacher said to Sam, climbing into the saddle.

Sam's smile was on the sheepish side.

Sloan grinned. "I know you're sweet on . . . which one?"

Sam glanced at his boots. "Ursula. Not sure she would give me the time of day, though."

"She would if she had any sense," Preacher said. "Lad, I like your ambition to one day own your own property and have a family. I figure those qualities are the ones that count."

Abbey looked from the minister to Sam and back. Though she didn't think about the color of Sam's skin, she hadn't imagined how he might find a suitable woman.

Preacher must have caught the gist of her thoughts because he said, "Don't look so surprised, lass. We're either all God's children, regardless of color, or none of us are." He tapped his chest. "You judge a man by his deeds, not by his looks."

"Yes." Abbey remembered Miss Mary had taught the same thing, and no child had been turned away from her door.

"Well, come home without dawdling," Sloan said. "There's a lot going on here, and we need you."

Sam nodded his agreement, and the two men headed toward the gate.

The exchange pierced Abbey. A whole community of people lived beyond the confines of the ranch, busy doing the things people did. Falling in love, if Sam's discomfort was any indication. Despite Preacher's assurances, she worried about meeting Mrs. Long and her daughters who might see Charlotte.

She met Sloan's serious gaze, realizing her hand was still held by his.

"Everything is going to work out," he said.

She was far less confident than he sounded. She glanced down and found him staring at their still-clasped hands. He cleared his throat, then released her—reluctantly somehow. She had no idea what to make of him or the fact that he seemed unsure of himself. He surprised her even more when he tipped his hat and strode away from her without speaking.

CHAPTER 22

"Why, you must be the bride," a tall, robust woman called from her wagon the following morning. Curly, gray hair surrounded her round pleasant face, which was creased with a wide smile. The time was early, just as Sam had reported was the plan upon his return last night. "I'm Katherine Long, and these are my daughters. Olivia—I bet she's about your age. She's betrothed to Adam Kuttler, so we'll be having another wedding come November. And this here is Ursula, and my youngest, Victoria." By then, she was out of the wagon and moving toward Abbey with the grace and speed of a racehorse despite her size.

Jake and Sam came across the compound, offering their hellos.

"Good morning, Sam." Ursula's smile lit her eyes. "It's nice to see you again today."

Sam, his eyes gleaming, smiled and removed his hat. "Miss Long, glad to see you."

"You two gents carry the trunk into the house," Katherine commanded, her big smile making the order seem more like a request.

She followed the men inside, as did Abbey and the daughters, who continued to chatter and giggle with one another.

"Set it right there. I always liked this room, I did, though Nate always insisted a sitting room on a ranch was a waste." Katherine pointed to where she wanted the trunk set. "Now, gents, you've served your usefulness. Out."

"Aw, Missus Long, I could stay and keep you ladies company," Jake teased.

Abbey looked sharply at him, his transformation from the quiet, brooding man to this more carefree one a surprise among all the others of the last couple of days.

"I'm sure you would," Katherine returned with another laugh but shooing him and Sam out of the house. She closed the door behind them. "Now, then, let's have a look at you." She somehow managed to open the trunk and coax Abbey close all at the same time. Two of her daughters continued to talk over her, mostly teasing Ursula about Sam.

"Thank you for coming to help me." The truth, but she was at a loss for words, the women's chatter at once familiar and foreign because it had been so long since she'd had any semblance of this.

"Don't you think a thing of it," Katherine said. "My, but you're a little slip of a thing, even smaller than my Victoria, and she's not yet full growed." Without asking for permission, she curved her hands around Abbey's waist as though taking a measurement. "What is it with these men wanting a wedding in six days? Are you in a family way?"

"No." The blunt question shocked Abbey, especially when Katherine's daughters giggled, bringing home the reason Sloan was insistent they marry. She was a woman alone living in Sloan's house. Why the same didn't appear to be true of Consuela was a mystery to Abbey. Did her status as the widow of his foreman really make so much difference? All fine logic, if she kept her mind away from the intimacies she had shared with Sloan not even two full days ago.

"Are you sure, girl? If you're going to be needing a midwife, there's none better than Gertrude Draper. She has delivered most of the babies in this valley over the last ten years."

"I'm sure." Abbey confessed her courses should begin in the

next day or so. A week ago, she would have been able to truthfully say she had never lain with a man. The notion she couldn't now made her heart pound and her face heat.

Once more, Katherine's humor surfaced in another laugh. "Men. Thinking they can control the world with their planning and their schedules. Your new husband may be in for a surprise on the wedding night."

Wedding night! Oh, my. Abbey's face heated. Come a wedding night, there would be all those lovely intimacies. Intimacies she had longed for last night after she'd gone to bed. These last many nights, she had slept in Sloan's arms, which had been the sweetest of her life. A wedding night . . . foolish of her not to have thought about that sooner.

As if by magic, all sorts of colorful piece goods were draped over the open lid of the trunk, all of it carrying the scent of lavender. A length of pale pink ribbon drew Abbey's attention, and she couldn't resist running her finger over the silky surface. She was reminded of the sewing days at Miss Mary's house. Abbey's sewing skills were measly, at best, but Miss Mary had possessed the knack for creating lovely things out of bits of fabric and leftover lace. She had the feeling Katherine Long was the same way.

Katherine pulled a white dress whose skirt had yards of fabric from the trunk, seeming oblivious to Abbey's soft gasp of pleasure. "Let's get you down to your shift and see what we're working with."

Before Abbey could draw breath or protest she could dress herself, the three daughters were there, unfastening tabs and pulling away her clothes, leaving her standing in the middle of the front room in nothing but her shift.

"You don't wear a corset?" Katherine clucked her tongue. "Those bosoms of yours will be sagging to your waist if you don't keep them supported all nice and proper." She laughed then, pointing at her own. "Of course, nursing five babies don't do them much good, neither."

"My corset was lost."

"Go see what Missus Charlotte left behind," Katherine ordered Victoria. " 'Course, knowing her, hers might be bright red."

Victoria went into the bedroom while Katherine continued to survey her, turning her this way and that.

Abbey knew for a fact there was no red corset in the dresser. "I really don't want to wear her clothes." The statement struck her as suddenly absurd since Charlotte's clothes were all she had been wearing since her arrival. She giggled. "But, then, I have none of my own." The giggle ended on a sob. A corset was one of the garments that separated an impossibly poor woman from one who was better off, and she no longer had even that.

"Well, my goodness. However did you manage to arrive here without your own clothes?"

"Jake and Sam mistook me for Charlotte and brought me here." Abbey paused, too aware that any further revelation would cast the two men in a terrible light. Finally, she added, "Without giving me any chance to bring my things."

"And Sloan Rafferty didn't send for them?" Katherine held a petticoat against Abbey's waist while she talked. "Men can be the most obtuse creatures. Mules and men—I sometimes wonder if the Good Lord didn't get one mixed up with the other when He set them on the earth."

The image made Abbey laugh softly.

"Well, now, that's more like it." Katherine patted her arm. "I was afraid I was going to make you cry there for a minute. Don't mind me. I'm a little blunt around the edges."

Consuela came into the room still carrying the baby as Victoria emerged from the bedroom, her arms filled with lingerie.

Victoria came up behind Abbey, then gasped. "Look at those

horrible scars."

Katherine turned Abbey's back toward her and clucked her tongue. "My goodness. I've never seen the like. Why, someone took a whip to you."

Consuela also moved behind with the other three women. Abbey stood there with her head bowed while all sorts of conflicting thoughts raced through her mind. She had lived with the scars for so many years, she hadn't thought about them much until the last few days. Yet here she was, once again under scrutiny for something that happened so long ago.

"I saw this once," Katherine said. "Years and years ago when we still lived in Kansas. A woman who had been stolen by the Sioux who was returned by soldiers."

"You escaped from Indians?" Victoria asked, clapping her hands together in childish glee while managing to also look horrified.

"No," Abbey said, then added, "Indians didn't do this."

"Does Mr. Sloan know about this?" asked Consuela.

"He does." Abbey turned her head to meet the other woman's gaze.

Consuela's lips tightened. Shaking her head, she moved back toward the kitchen door. "He must not have known until after Jonah returned. You would have saved everyone a lot of heartache if you had shown these to him right away."

Katherine planted her hands on her hips. "What was the girl supposed to do? Strip so he could see?"

"Yes!" Consuela's voice was vehement. "Something like that . . . All you had to do was show Señor Sloan this. You would have saved me weeks of renewed agony."

Katherine must have read something of Abbey's dismay in her expression because she patted her hand and asked, "Who beat you, lass?"

"Pa Hawkins."

"Well, I hope he's long dead," Katherine said. "An eye for an eye, as the good book says. A man like that don't need to be walking around on this earth."

"I don't remind you of Charlotte?" Abbey wasn't sure why she had to ask, but she kept having the feeling if just one person besides Pearl Mae could look at her and know for certain, it would somehow make a difference.

"Oh, a little, maybe, when I first got out of the wagon." The older woman rummaged through the open trunk. "You're thinner."

"Not to mention nicer," Olivia said. "I wanted to be friends, but she acted like—"

"You know the rule," Katherine said. "If you can't say something nice, don't—"

"Say anything at all," Olivia finished, her sisters chiming in. She shrugged. "We did try. All of us. And, after a short while, we stopped trying."

"Consuela, do you have a corset Miss Abbey could borrow?" Katherine asked.

"No. I don't." Consuela met Abbey's gaze, and there was no softening of her expression. Abbey was certain Consuela saw Charlotte, not herself, and she couldn't blame her.

"I'll manage without," Abbey said.

"You won't have to," Victoria said. "I found all sorts of lovely things. Mama, look at this." She held up a corset, one Abbey had marveled at the first day she had arrived here when she had wondered how one person could have so many changes of clothes. The garment in question was snow white, trimmed in pale-blue lace.

"Perfect," Katherine announced, wrapping it around Abbey and tying the top lace.

"It's Charlotte's."

Katherine untied the top lace and began examining the garment as though the stiches would reveal some secret. Then she sniffed at the garment.

"I don't think this has ever been worn. The stitches and fabric don't show any wear at all, and there's no aroma of soap or perfume."

Victoria held up a second corset, this one a pale pink and edged in lace. Katherine dismissed it with a wave of her hand. "Definitely has been worn." She held the first one up to Abbey.

Recognizing she was being given a choice, Abbey finally nodded. Gorgeous as the garment was, and much as she had thought about putting it on when she first saw it, this was a special item—the sort of unmentionable a woman would wear on her wedding day. And, though she had been determined she wasn't going to think about the intimacies she would share once again with Sloan after the wedding, the fact was right here, impossible to ignore. Since this corset laced in the back, she wouldn't be able to take this off by herself.

The sound of the exterior door to the kitchen opening and then closing made Katherine call out, "No coming into the front room."

"Good morning," Consuela said to whomever had come into the kitchen.

"I've been talking to Sam and Jake," Sloan said. "They tell me the only things left to go in the wagon are a few personal belongings."

Abbey couldn't hear Consuela's answer, only that her tone seemed to be one of agreement.

Then Sloan said, "Abe Venters at the livery has a fine pair of draft horses that would be more reliable to make the climb over Poncha Pass. Assuming he and I can come to an understanding, you could leave anytime. As soon as day after tomorrow, if you wanted."

"Yes. Soon. Before another storm." Consuela's voice carried

over the chatter surrounding Abbey.

"Sloan Rafferty, you can't be coming in right now." Katherine blocked the doorway to the kitchen, her ample form filling the opening.

"I'm not," he assured her. "Just talking to Consuela."

"I heard, but you're not to hang around here."

Sloan laughed, a warm sound Abbey wasn't sure she had ever heard from him before. "Why, Mrs. Long. You're kicking me out of my own house?"

"I am," she returned firmly. He evidently went back outside, because Abbey heard the door close. Then Katherine asked Consuela, "You're going back to your family?"

"My papa has asked me to come home. It seems like the right time."

"I'm going to be real sorry to see you and your youngins go," Katherine said. "Your husband was a fine man. Didn't deserve what became of him. Who's taking you to Santa Fe?"

"Sam and Jake."

As soon as two more days, Abbey realized, her gaze lighting on the cradle where Sarah often slept. Surprising tears burned at her eyes. She would miss them—Pearl Mae most of all.

As soon as the daughters had laced Abbey tight into the corset, Katherine ordered Abbey to sit in a chair. And, she felt as though she would immediately suffocate.

"Too tight." Katherine pulled her to her feet. "We can't have you passing out." She loosened the ties a bit, though not as much as Abbey would have preferred.

After the corset was laced to her satisfaction, Katherine settled the white dress over Abbey's shoulders. It slipped off Abbey's shoulders and left her feeling as though she being smothered in a fragrant, white tent.

"My goodness. You are much smaller even than I thought." Katherine pushed the dress off Abbey's shoulders, and it pooled around her feet. "Olivia, hand me the pink one—the one you outgrew last year."

The dress lifted from the trunk was far simpler than the white one, but Abbey immediately liked it better. To her surprise, it was too short, reminding her of the time in her life when she had sprouted to her current height.

"Well, my word," Katherine muttered, rummaging through the trunk. "Who would have ever thought I wouldn't get this right by the second try?"

She pulled a third dress from the trunk, this one a pale lavender, and Abbey admitted to herself she hoped this one would be the one since she liked the color even better than the pink one.

"This may be too old-fashioned." Katherine shook it out, revealing a full skirt accented with bows in a deeper shade than the dress. "Oh, it was the height of fashion before the war came."

Olivia helped Katherine put the dress over Abbey's head. The bodice fit around her as though it had been made for her.

"It's too long, Mama," Ursula announced after straightening the skirt.

"Easier to fix than too short. I think this is the one. Do you like it?" Katherine asked Abbey.

"I do." Abbey was surprised at how much she did. She smoothed a hand across the soft fabric. Much as she liked it, she felt compelled to add, "Since your daughters are taller, are you certain about hemming this to fit me?"

Katherine laughed. "Take another look at my girls. Even Victoria, who isn't full growed yet, is too big in the bosom for this dress to ever fit." She patted Abbey's shoulder, then added in a whisper, "Bessie Newell gave me the dress—wanted it out of her sight after they had to marry Henrietta off in a hurry because she was in a family way. She didn't want any reminders around of the shame the girl brought to the family." Katherine pulled at the sleeves, adjusted the neckline, and continued to flutter around Abbey, making this adjustment and that, then standing back to survey the dress. "This one was made for you."

Abbey took in the long length of the skirt. She would trip on if she attempted to make a step. "Except for it being way too long."

Katherine laughed. "Or for you being too short. This is not a problem, lassie."

She sat on the floor, and by some unspoken agreement, Ursula sank to the floor with her, a pin cushion and tape measure in hand. "Get the chalk out," Katherine told Olivia, "and mark the sleeves."

Abbey would have insisted they were all right until she saw the sleeves trailed onto her hands, reminding her of the too-big shirts the boys at the orphanage sometimes wore.

"What about shoes?" Katherine asked, then added, "Victoria, go see what is in Missus Charlotte's wardrobe."

Even though Abbey already knew the shoes in there wouldn't fit, she didn't say anything. She was already going to have far more than she deserved by having this fine dress. Wearing the moccasins wouldn't be so bad, especially since she had grown used to them.

Victoria returned a few minutes later, carrying several pairs. Abbey halfway hoped she had overlooked a pair, but all the shoes were ones she had tried on before.

"Thank you for looking," she told Victoria, "but all those are too small."

The girl smoothed her hand over one of the pairs, made of kid and white satin. "These are so pretty that I would be willing to mash my feet into them."

"I bet after an hour, you'd be begging to take them off." Ursula continued to mark where the dress needed to be cut off, while Olivia pinned up the sleeves to the correct length. The two of them turned her as though she were a doll, each of them focused on reaching some part of the dress.

All of it left Abbey feeling a bit like a scarecrow in the middle of the orchard. Still, all the activity reminded her of wonderful times in Miss Mary's kitchen. She hadn't known until right now she missed the companionship quite as much as she did.

At last Ursula and Olivia were finished. Katherine clapped her hands together. "Now, to get you out of this without poking you with any of the pins."

Katherine turned Abbey again, continuing to insert pins in the hem. "Are you and Missus Charlotte somehow related?"

It was a question she was likely to be asked a lot, Abbey thought, searching for an easy way to explain what she believed to be true. "Cousins," she said after a moment. "Her mother and mine were identical twin sisters." Better than admitting the bitter truth—that she and Charlotte were most likely sisters, as well.

"I bet that was fun when you were little," Victoria said. "Playing together and—"

"I didn't know her," Abbey interrupted. "We were raised apart. The last time I saw her, I was a small child."

"That was quite a blow last spring when she and the stallion disappeared," Katherine said. "Sloan was sick with worry."

When she paused, Abbey searched for the appropriate response, then settled for, "I can imagine."

"He has been through too much, I'll tell you. What kind of foolhardy man would go off to war and then volunteer to drive ammunition wagons? If you could have known him before the war and before he came home with the other one. He was a lovely man then, he was. They all worked so hard to make this place into a fine ranch, not the rundown hovel it was at first. Sloan's daddy, God rest his soul, won this place in a poker game, and most everyone figured he was as foolish as the drunk he won it from when he decided to make a go of raising cattle."

As if realizing she was rambling, Katherine looked up at Abbey. "Do you know this story?"

Abbey shook her head, which she would have done even if she had heard it before, because she was suddenly hungry to know everything about Sloan.

"Well, this is a good one." Katherine continued to pin the skirt while she talked. "Sloan's daddy was a trapper, and he was well known in these parts a good long while before they ever came to have this place. Everyone thought well of him, even though they held he was a bit on the odd side seeing how he was a teacher before he took up trapping." She sighed. "He had the most wonderful way of speaking, which took folks by surprise, seein' as he let his hair grow long enough to wear Indian braids.

"And, of course, he had a Comanche wife, which folks looked down on, but out here people are more forgiving of such things than they are in some parts. And then there was Charlie Isenholt."

The part of the name Abbey heard was "Holt," and she had to ask, "Charlie Holt?" Could he be related to Caleb?

"Isenholt," Katherine repeated, emphasizing the first syllables, then continued, "He claimed this land, and started mining back up on the hill. All he ever found were hot springs." She shook her head. "Didn't see much use for those, and rumor was the man had never had a bath. He lost everything except the shirt he was wearin' in a poker game with Sloan's daddy. He and his boy took off. They weren't seen again until after the war. Sloan had been away all those years, sending money for improvements and stock. After the war ended, he worked as an iron man for the railroad, you know, like my youngest brother."

"An iron man?" Abbey asked.

"Why, they're the fellas who drive the spikes into the ties as the rails are laid. Hard work, swinging a sledge hammer all day, but the best paying job, too. When he came home, he had Sam, who wasn't much more than a half-starved kid. They all worked hard to make a go of things. 'Bout that time, Charlie came back, and after the rewards of hard work, he started singing the song he'd been cheated out of this fine ranch."

"What was the son's name?" Abbey asked, still wondering if Charlie had anything to do with Caleb.

"I don't think I ever knew." Katherine turned Abbey around every now and then so she could reach a new part of the skirt. "By the time it was over, Sloan's daddy and the middle boy, Isaac, were dead. 'Course, Charlie Isenholt was, too. That didn't stop Sloan none. He just got back to work, saying miners needed to be fed, and he was going to raise the beeves to do it. 'Course, he made a mistake marrying a young woman who had never lifted a finger in her life." Once more she patted Abbey's hand. "He must have been blind to have thought you were her."

"They look alike." Victoria sighed. "She had the most beautiful hair. I practiced until I could do mine with all those pretty ringlets. I could do yours up just the same, if you wanted."

"No." The idea horrified Abbey. Every time she went into the bedroom, the first thing she saw was the portrait of Charlotte, her hair all in those very ringlets. "I don't want to look like her at all."

Victoria drew in a sharp breath. "Mama, I need some fresh air." And she flounced outside, shutting the door firmly behind her.

"Consuela and Victoria are wrong." Katherine looked up at Abbey. "Miss Charlotte always looked like she'd just eaten a green apple. A surface resemblance. Nothing more."

Abbey felt her eyes well with tears. "You're very kind."

"Psshaw! Kind ain't got nothing to do with it." Katherine stood, then stepped back, surveying her work. "Time to get out of this dress so we can cut off some and get it hemmed up." She headed for the kitchen. "I could sure use a cup of your fine coffee, Consuela."

Abbey had forgotten about the laughter and the companionship of being around other women. Three long winters since leaving Miss Mary's house, yet she had not known she missed it until now. This felt like the beginning of a friendship where . . . hopefully . . . she wasn't abandoning her dream to have a place where she belonged.

CHAPTER 23

Sloan was in the middle of saddling his horse when Jonah came into the barn.

"Going somewhere?" He came to a stop in front of the stall where his own horse stood.

"Yep. Jake told me about a pair of draft horses Abe Venters had. Need to see if he might lease them to me for a couple of months."

"He'd be smarter to sell them." Jonah reached for the harness hanging next to the door of the stall. "Figure I should go with you."

Sloan glanced over the top of his horse to his brother, who was leading the big bay out of the stall. "No point in asking if you're up to the ride."

His brother's dark eyes gleamed as he brushed his horse. "None at all, Brother. Besides, you remember Preacher's advice. Lay low and watch your back. Well, since you're heading to town, you're not laying low. Figure it's up to me to watch your back since Jake, Sam, and Eli are loading Consuela's wagon."

Sloan's attention moved from his brother to the activity in front of Consuela's cabin. The pace of change was like an itch in the middle of his back. He didn't like it, but all he could do about it was let it happen.

Easier, not to mention more familiar, to pick on his brother. "I think you're going stir crazy and don't have enough to do."

"Maybe," Jonah agreed, hefting his saddle over the back of

his horse, proving he was stronger than all his weight loss suggested.

They finished saddling the horses, mounted, and left the barn, taking a detour toward Consuela's cabin, where they came in on the tail end of Eli's explanation about JJ benefiting from the wisdom of his grandfather.

"That don't sound right," JJ said.

"Doesn't." Sloan and Jonah looked at each other, then grinned with the shared memory of similar corrections their father had given them when they were JJ's age.

"Well it doesn't," JJ asserted. "If my grandpa was so smart, how come didn't he like my Pa? And how come he waited all this time to ask Mama to come home?"

"Pride, probably," Jonah said, his statement an echo of Sloan's thought. "It's a powerful thing and can get in the way of a man's good sense."

"Ain't that the truth," Eli said.

Jake and Sam came out of the cabin, carrying a large trunk they set in the wagon.

"No point in telling you to stay here, I s'pose," Jake said.

"I won't stay here hiding," Sloan said. "If Flanders wants me, he knows where to look."

"It's not him I'm worried about," Jake returned. "Don't you be going off to find Caleb Holt without me."

"We're just going to see about some horses."

"Uh-huh. Well, since there's no talking you out of goin' . . . if you're not back by supper, Sam and I will come lookin' for you."

Jonah grinned. "When did you get to be such a nag?"

"Oh, I dunno." Jake pointed to Jonah. "After you got yourself nearly killed." Then at Sloan, "After you disappeared in a blizzard for five days."

They said their goodbyes, but that didn't keep Sloan from

looking at the house one last time where the Longs' wagon was still parked in front of the house. Preparations for a wedding were sure nothing he had imagined when he had sent for Preacher.

"You're looking as dejected as an old cow missing her calf," Jonah said to him as they headed toward the gate. "You having second thoughts about the wedding?"

"Nope." In fact, though, he was. Not the marriage, just the process of getting there.

Somehow, he had to convince Abbey staying was good for her—better than a homestead in California. Still, the name of her place—Abbey's Orchard—and his promise he'd help her get to California weighed on him.

Jonah's thoughts had evidently gone back to Consuela and her children because he was saying, "I think she's happy her children are going to be able to know their grandparents. This is a good thing, Brother."

Maybe. His grandfather had been a stern disciplinarian who seemed not to know what to do with a grandson who dreamed of becoming a trapper like his father rather than a successful merchant in St. Louis. He remembered the wealth, though, and a fatal lure when he had purchased the Cimarron Sun.

"I bet I can still beat you, Brother." Jonah grinned at him, then touched his heels to his horse's side. The horse surged forward into a gallop. "C'mon."

The taunt was irresistible, another reminder of years gone by. When he had first come west with his father, he was as much of an outsider as he had felt in his grandparents' home after his mother had died. Isaac and Jonah were proof his father had another life that hadn't included him at all. They might have been younger, but they also had the skills he had desperately wanted for himself. His shock at not fitting into the life he had dreamed of had erupted in jealousy of his brothers and rage at their Comanche mother, who somehow made space in her heart for him anyway. A mess, but they had cobbled together a family. He had learned a valuable lesson, which had allowed him to make the same space for Sam that he'd once been given. It gave Sloan hope he and Abbey could do the same thing.

As ill as Jonah had been these past weeks, he was still a better rider than Sloan. Much as he loved his brother, he still hated being beat, but he grinned at the exhilaration of the run even as he worried the pace would somehow break open Jonah's healing wounds.

They gradually slowed the horses into an easy, ground-eating canter as they approached the outskirts of Poncha, They brought the horses to a walk and rode into town side by side.

"Before we go see Abe, I want to see whether Flanders took the stage to Denver," Sloan said.

Despite the sunshine, the afternoon was brisk, and no one was outside. They tethered the horses to the hitching rail in front of the inn.

"I'm going to head over to the trading post," Jonah said. "Burnett knows more about what's going on than anyone else."

Though he was right, Sloan figured the real reason was innkeeper Niles Edwards had accused Jonah of being a savage last spring when the anti-Indian sentiment was being whipped up by the *Rocky Mountain News*.

Sloan watched his brother continue down the street before going into the inn. Behind the counter closest to the door, sat Niles Edwards. He looked up and smiled.

"Haven't seen you in a while, Rafferty. How have you been?"

"Doing fine. Did William Flanders get checked in all right?"

Niles's smile faded into a frown. "Yep. Not without his opinion being expressed, however. He's anxious for the next stage to Denver and not at all pleased it won't be until Tuesday."

"Tuesday? I thought there was a stage today."

"There was supposed to have been, but one of their wagons has a broken axle." He nodded toward the swinging door leading to the dining room. "Mr. Flanders has taken up residence in the dining room and has been bending Lem's ear all day. At least until that Holt fella showed up."

"Caleb Holt? He's here?" Finding the man couldn't be that easy. Sloan strode toward the dining room, which turned out to be empty.

Niles followed him to the doorway, where he waved at the open windows letting in chilly air. "Thick as thieves, those two. Sat in the corner all morning, smoking cigars. With them gone, I can air out the place. God knows why, though, since he'll stink the place up again when he comes back." He gave Sloan a considering glance. "Caleb Holt has been talking up a storm about you and the Utes. In fact, Burnett kicked him out of the trading post and told him his talk was going to get someone killed. Some folks might be swayed by all that nonsense, so you be watching your back."

The advice was getting old, Sloan decided. "Where did they go?" The fact that Caleb had been talking to William Flanders was interesting—one man convinced Abbey was Charlotte and the other convinced she was an imposter, and neither of them wishing her well.

Niles waved toward the door. "Mr. Flanders has decided he needed a buggy while he was here and didn't like the wagon Abe Venters offered him. Abe says the Widow Davis over in Nathrop has one for sale, and so likely that's where they went."

"He's leaving on Tuesday, but he needs a buggy?" Jake said. "Sounds like the man has more money than sense."

Nile grinned. "Ain't that the truth?"

"Holt and Flanders went together?" Sloan asked.

"Nah. Holt was braggin' he had a good job lined up with Hutchinson. You just missed him." Nile waved toward the road.

"Hard to believe Hutchinson is hiring this time of year."

Sloan agreed. Over the winter, there was precious little need for extra cowhands. All the ranchers in the valley were more likely to be letting help go than hiring, the sad state of being a seasonal cowhand.

"Preacher told me you're getting hitched right after the Sunday service," Niles said. "A lot going on with you—your wife disappearing and then finding out she died. And now a wedding." The last ended as a question, inviting Sloan to fill in the details.

"Yep." Sloan figured he should have known news would travel fast. He had wanted to do right by Abbey but hadn't given a bit of thought to how things would look to others. He didn't want her to be the object of gossip and speculation. "Hope you and Mrs. Edwards plan to be there."

"Wouldn't miss it. Your new bride is some sort of relative of the old missus?"

Sloan had a quick flare of annoyance followed by the realization that Preacher, in his own way, was probably doing his best to fill in answers to questions people were bound to have. "That's right. Cousins." Too soon they would all see how much alike the two looked.

Once more Niles shook his head, this time with a wry grin. "You're sure a man courtin' trouble with Mr. Flanders. I don't know I'd like having him as a relative, even by marriage." Then he laughed.

Sloan hadn't considered Flanders would still be his father in law, at least by blood. Not that the fact mattered one whit to him. Taking care of Abbey and ensuring she never again suffered at the likes of men like Flanders—that was the only important thing.

Niles chatted a bit longer, relating the rumor folks were leaving Oro City in droves because the gold was played out. Sloan knew for a fact this was more than rumor since his last order for beeves was half of what it was a year ago.

"With all the trouble of the last year, lots of folks here in the valley are talking about leaving," Niles said.

"We're staying," Sloan said. "Gold or silver will be found in some other mountain between here and Oro City. I figure if folks like Charlie Nachtrieb are putting down roots and investing the way he did with the grist mill, the grass will be just as green here as somewhere else." This was something he knew for a fact after driving ammunition and supply wagons during the war and laying iron for the crawl of the railway across the Great Plains. To his way of thinking, no valley anywhere was prettier than this one, and living here suited his plans just fine.

Niles followed him outside, both looking up and down the street. His gaze lit on Jonah, who was sitting on his horse in front of the inn. "Heard you were shot, but you don't look too much worse for wear."

"Not much." Then to Sloan Jonah said, "Caleb Holt was kicked out of the trading post yesterday."

"That's what Niles told me."

"Mad as a hornet, too," Niles offered.

"We have one more reason to go see Abe," Jonah said. "He bought a mare from Caleb—a pretty chestnut with a white star."

Ice pooled in Sloan's gut. His brother had described Charlotte's horse, which had gone missing the same day she and the stallion had.

Sloan tipped his hat to Niles. "Hope to see you on Sunday." He mounted his horse, following Jonah, who was already headed down toward the livery at the sound end of town.

Abe Venters's son, Zeke, a boy of eleven or twelve, lounged on a bale of hay outside the door. When they drew closer, Sloan saw the boy was reading a dime novel, which he dropped behind the bale as soon as he realized he was being watched.

"Came to see your pa." Sloan didn't let on that he knew Abe had taken William Flanders to Nathrop, a community even smaller than Poncha.

"He ain't here, but he left me in charge."

"He still have a pair of draft horses?"

"Yep." The young man stood and motioned them to follow him through the barn. "Says he thought you'd be wanting to buy them. A good thing, too, since he said he'd be lucky to get rid of them before they eat the supply of hay he had set aside for winter."

The lament, which diminished the value of the animals, though Zeke didn't seem to notice, made Sloan smile. The boy was clearly repeating his pa. He followed the boy through the stable to the corral behind the building.

The two draft horses, a well-matched pair of black Percherons, were there, along with a couple of other horses. One of them was the chestnut that had been Charlotte's horse. He ducked through the corral and made his way toward her. She watched him with dark, curious eyes, her ears perked forward, her nostrils flaring.

"You remember me, girl, don't you?" She shook her head but didn't step away from him. Her skin quivered a bit as he rested a hand on her neck, then ran it down her withers to her flank. The brand—a simplified version of the Flanders family crest— had been marked over by a simple *X* and *O*, effectively masking the original brand. The XO brand was the sloppy one of a too cool iron that would have been painful for the animal. This one showed evidence of scabbing over, then festering.

He glanced at his brother, who had joined him and was also inspecting the brand. "Crude, but effective." He came to the mare's head, scratching between her eyes. The horse groaned with pleasure and dropped her head against him. "The way the brand was done, it's a wonder she's letting us touch her."

319

"She's a beaut, isn't she?" Zeke called from the fence.

"She is," Sloan agreed, lifting her leg and examining her foot. Her hooves had been cleaned, which said a lot about the livery's operation and good care of their animals but left him with no clues about where the animal had been before Abe purchased her.

"My pap says she's a good one that some cowboy down on his luck should have never sold."

Sloan gave the mare a last pat.

"You act like you know this horse," Zeke said.

"Yep," Sloan allowed. "When will your pa be back?"

"Dunno. He wasn't happy about making the trip over to Nathrop—thought it would take all day and then some, but that Mister Flanders fella is going to pay Pap for taking him."

"Anybody else go with them?"

"Nah," Zeke returned.

"How much does your pa want for the draft horses and the mare?"

The kid flushed. "He's the one to talk to."

Sloan shook his head slightly, meeting his brother's gaze. Abe Venters may have left his son in charge—for a day's rental of a saddle horse or to make sure the animals were cared for, but nothing else.

"Tell your pa to bring the three of them out to my place tomorrow. I'll make him a fair deal."

Zeke nodded. "I'll tell him."

He and Jonah mounted up. They had walked the horses back through town on the way back to the ranch before Jonah said, "If Caleb Holt had the mare, he's got the Cimarron Sun."

"More than likely," Sloan agreed. "The question is where." He now had a good idea of where they had been—the old trapper's cabin where he and Abbey had weathered the storm.

CHAPTER 24

Abe and Zeke Venters arrived early the following morning with the two draft horses and the mare. They hooked up the draft horses to the partially loaded wagon, made a couple of adjustments, then drove them around the compound and out onto the road. As Sloan had hoped, the horses were well trained and knew what was expected of them. They handled a steep incline on the road heading north, which assured Sloan they would do fine traversing Poncha Pass before dropping into the San Luis Valley and crossing into New Mexico.

After they came back and the horses were unhitched, Sloan inspected their feet, discovering they were freshly and expertly shoed. Only a minor adjustment was needed to the harnesses, which meant the next step for Consuela being able to leave was taken care of. Sloan turned the animals into the corral and became aware Abe was staring toward the house, where Abbey had emerged with Pearl Mae.

They were chattering a mile a minute and holding hands as they made their way off the porch.

When she was closer, Sloan introduced her. "Miss Abigail Wallace, this is Abe Venters and his boy, Zeke."

"I'm pleased to make your acquaintance," she said while Abe tipped his hat.

"Though I was seeing a ghost," he said.

Abbey's smile faltered a bit. "So I've heard."

"The pair of Percherons are going to work out fine," Sloan said.

"Why, look it there," Pearl Mae exclaimed. "It's Lady G'diva."

At the name, the mare in the corral with the two draft horses looked up, her ears perked forward.

"Lady Godiva?" Abe echoed.

"My wife—Charlotte's—mare." Sloan watched Abbey and Pearl Mae approach the corral. The mare recognized the little girl, came close, and dropped her head so she could have her ears scratched.

Abe, like Sloan, watched the two. Then he lifted his hat, then resettled it on his head. "Caleb Holt showed up a few days ago with her. Gave me a long song and dance about how he'd traded with the Comanche for her." He tipped his head slightly. "The brand was obviously all wrong, but he swore she was like that when he got her."

"Traded?" Sloan shook his head.

"I didn't believe him—except for your brother, no Comanche have been around here in a couple of years. Said he was hard up for cash. She was filthy and full of burrs. Took Zeke and me a while to clean her up. She's a well-trained little gal—didn't fuss much at us while we did what needed to be done. Didn't realize she had a white star in the middle of her forehead, either, until we cleaned all the mud off her." He met Sloan's gaze. "Don't seem right to be asking you to pay."

"Neither does leaving you holding the bag for an animal you bought in good faith. I'll pay you whatever you paid for her."

"Sure you want her back?"

Sloan nodded, having the same feeling about the mare he'd had when he first saw her . . . and the other horses William Flanders had bred and raised. "I think she'll drop real pretty foals."

"If you had your stallion back," Abe said dryly.

"Yeah, if I had the Cimarron Sun," Sloan agreed. Truth be told, he was still coming to grips with how little he had thought about the stallion over the last six weeks. "Don't suppose Holt had anything to say about that."

Abe returned Sloan's rueful smile. "Nope. With everyone knowing he was stolen, no buyer would be so dumb."

His gaze followed Abbey, who had her arm in a sling again this morning.

"Preacher told me what happened to your wife. Damn shame." Abe lifted his hat once more, his gaze also on Abbey. "Have to say, that Miss Abigail Wallace is the spitting image of your wife."

"They are cousins," Sloan said, keeping to the easy part of the story. "Their mothers were identical twins."

"Huh," came Abe's comment.

"Hope you and the family will be there on Sunday," he said. "I imagine Preacher told you there'd be a wedding after the Sunday service."

"He did."

Their conversation turned back to the draft horses, and, when it became apparent Abe wasn't the least interested in renting them, Sloan agreed to the purchase for a price he considered more than fair, especially since it also included Charlotte's mare.

"I took Flanders to buy a buggy from Widow Davis yesterday," Abe said when their business was concluded. "There's a man who drives a hard bargain. Tried to pay her a third of what it was worth, and he might have haggled her into it if I hadn't been there." Once more he lifted his hat and resettled it, a gesture indicating he was organizing his thoughts. "He sure asked a lot of questions about you and this ranch—how long you had owned it, how many hands you have, and what your daddy did and why you have a brother who's an Indian. He might be leaving soon, but he's a gent filled with too many plans and too many ideas about revenge. He seems to think he can talk the governor into stringing you and your brother up to the nearest cottonwood without a trial."

A corner of Sloan's mouth kicked up. "You trying to tell me to watch my back?"

Abe nodded with an answering grin. "Heard that advice before, huh?"

"Yep."

"Well, then." Once more he lifted his hat, then called out to his son, who was with JJ. "Let's go, boy. The day ain't gettin' any younger." He mounted his horse. "You know where to find me if you need anything."

"Same goes," Sloan returned.

He joined Abbey and Pearl Mae at the corral. "I see you're back in the sling. You doing okay?"

"I thought I had healed more. Turns out, I'm going to be no good hanging up the clothes Pearl Mae and I washed."

"You should have asked for help," His own gaze followed hers to the clothesline. Next to it was a basket filled with wet clothes.

His tone must have been sharper than he intended because her chin came up the way it did when she was challenged.

"It's not easy for you, is it?" he said. "Asking for help."

Her eyes widened in surprise. "To be honest, it never occurred to me."

"I'd hang the clothes," Pearl Mae informed him, " 'cept I'm too short."

Sloan grinned and ruffled her hair. "What about me?"

"You're not short," she agreed but added in a doubtful voice, "Do you know how?"

"I can probably figure it out."

"Okay." She grinned and took his hand. "C'mon. Abbey and

me, we can teach you."

Still smiling, he allowed himself to be led to the clothesline. Granted, the job wasn't as neat or as fast as it would have been with Consuela's expertise, but he got it done.

"We'll want to leave as close to daybreak in the morning as we can," Sloan told Abbey as they worked. "If everything goes smoothly, we can make the summit before nightfall. We'll spend the night, and then we'll head back here the next day. We can hitch up the small buckboard so you don't have to ride, which will be more comfortable for your shoulder."

"You want me to come, too?"

"I sure as hell don't want to leave you here." That had him worried. Leaving her here—mostly alone. Only Jonah and Eli would be here. "You're safe." He wasn't sure whether he was trying to convince her or himself. Safe, but not safe enough until Flanders was on his way back east. Not yet. "So . . . what's it to be? Do you want to ride in a wagon or on horseback?"

Abbey had finished putting on her nightgown and washing her face when a knock at the bedroom door interrupted her reverie. To her surprise, Consuela stood there, the usual annoyance in her expression in place. She glanced down the short hallway that led to the front room, firmed her lips, and stepped inside the room, closing the door behind her. She folded her arms over her chest, her expression changing slightly as she sniffed the air. She crossed the room to the wash bowl, lifting the bar of soap sitting next to it.

"You use this?"

"Yes." Abbey stared at her, the question about the soap surprising. Weeks ago, she had put away the soap heavily scented with roses. She didn't know what herbs scented the soap she had been using, but it was a clean one reminding her of the outdoors. "Actually, I like how it smells."

Consuela made a sound of annoyance.

"What do you want?" Abbey asked.

Consuela stared at the floor a moment, then met Abbey's gaze, her expression more fierce than ever. "I don't want you to come with us when we leave tomorrow. Señor Sloan has his mind made up, and you need to change it. I will not have my last hours here nor the first part of our journey tainted by you or any memories of your presence."

Hatred dripped from each word and hit Abbey with the force of a gale, and she suddenly sat on the chair next to the dresser. She didn't intend to ask, but somehow the word, "Why?" came out, anyway.

"It's very simple," she said. "I don't know how Jonah was fooled into thinking he had found you, and I can't imagine how you came by the scars on your back. You are Charlotte. I would bet everything I ever hoped to own—even the love of my own dead husband—that your father will be back here tomorrow, and you will go away with him. I hope, in fact, that happens. The sooner you leave, the sooner Sloan will be free of you and all the evil you have brought into our lives."

Abbey stared at the other woman, no coherent thought forming. Her mind and her lips went numb beneath the waves of loathing directed toward her. She shivered.

"*¿Comprende?*"

Understanding and understanding *why* were two very different things.

"I don't care how you do it or what you say to him. But tomorrow morning, you are to stay here."

"And if I don't?"

The smaller woman's eyes gleamed. "My grandmother taught me long ago, '*El salario del pecado es la muerte.*' Yours will not be at my hand, though I often dreamed of it."

The meaning conveyed through Consuela's tone was clear

even though the only word Abbey had understood was *muerte*—death. She didn't doubt for a minute Consuela wanted hers. What she asked was a small thing, really. To have those last hours with the family she had known here to herself without the intrusion of someone she hated.

Sweet Pearl Mae's face was right there before her, and Abbey's chin trembled. "Please don't deny me being able to say goodbye to the children—to Pearl Mae."

"As you wish." Consuela nodded sharply. "I don't do this for you, but for my children."

Evidently satisfied she'd had the last word, she swept out of the room.

The bustling activity before dawn the following morning reminded Abbey of the first leg of her trip west, when she had secured passage with a minister and his family who were moving from Virginia to Kentucky. Now, as then, the children's emotions on display ranged from anticipation on Pearl Mae's part to resignation on JJ's. The temperature was cold enough her breath was visible as she made her way toward the wagon where the two draft horses were already hitched. The buckboard was also hitched with its horse, and Sam's horse was tethered behind the wagon.

She hadn't spoken to Sloan yet this morning who seemed to be everywhere all at once with a dozen things on his mind. He was making some sort of adjustment where the tongue of the wagon joined with the front axle, a bucket of grease in one hand. He waved, then went back to his task.

Consuela came out of the cabin with a bundle she tucked behind the seat. She didn't say anything to Abbey though she had clearly seen her.

Jonah and Sam emerged from the cabin a moment later, carrying yet another trunk between them. Like Sloan had, they both waved at her. They stowed it away, then dropped the canvas over the back of the wagon and tied it. Jonah came toward her.

"You look terrible," he said without even saying good morning, then yelled, "Sloan, get over here."

"In a minute," came the answer.

Jonah stripped off a glove and held his palm against her forehead. "You could be running a fever."

She managed a smile and batted his hand away. "Maybe you have cold hands."

He grinned back. "And dirty feet."

"And no sweetheart," Sloan finished, joining them. His gaze roamed over her face, and, as Jonah had done, he took off a glove and touched her forehead. Then he cupped her cheek. "You look like a stiff breeze would blow you over."

"About how I feel," she returned, which was mostly the truth. She supposed she had finally slept, but if she had, it had been a fitful one where she had been chased by phantoms. One thing about crying—it had made her throat sore and her nose clogged to the point where she really did feel as though she was coming down with a cold. She sniffed, then wiped her nose with a handkerchief.

"She's going to be miserable riding." Jonah glanced at the sky. "And, it's only going to get colder as you get to the summit of the pass."

Sloan shook his head. "I don't like leaving her here—"

"Stop!" Realizing how sharp her interruption had sounded, she put a hand on Sloan's arm. "Please. I'm right here. Talk to me."

He took off his hat, worrying the brim with his fingers a moment, his gaze intent on hers. She smiled at him then, absorbing the warmth and the concern in his dark eyes.

"I know you want me to go with you. Jonah is right. I feel terrible." She looked past Sloan to Pearl Mae, who was skipping toward them, a baby doll tucked under her arm. "The idea of riding in a cold wagon all day . . ."

"Understood." He settled his hat back on his head.

"Are you coming, too?" Pearl Mae asked, skidding to a stop in front of her.

"Sadly, no," Sloan said. "Abbey's under the weather this morning."

"But yesterday, you told me you would. And, you promised to tell me stories, too."

Abbey knelt so she was at Pearl Mae's height. "I know I did. I just didn't know today I'd have the sniffles and feel like my head was as big as a pumpkin."

"So, we have to say goodbye now?" Pearl Mae's chin quivered, and Abbey felt her own control slip.

She held out her arms. "We do. I promise, I'll write you letters."

"I don't know how to read yet," came her muffled reply against Abbey's shawl.

"Then you'll have something to look forward to. Maybe your mama or your grandfather can read them to you."

"Maybe." Her answer can on the heels of a shuddering sigh, and Pearl Mae wrapped her arms around Abbey. "You'll take care of Tabby Cat?"

"You know I will." The promise made Abbey's voice break since, in truth, she was bound to break it because she still half expected Sloan to change his mind about marrying her.

"And you won't forget me?"

"Never." Abbey squeezed her tight, then lifted her up. "You are possibly the best friend I ever had."

"Me, too." Pearl Mae leaned back in Abbey's arms so she could look at her, then she looked back toward her mother before whispering, "I love you."

"Oh, I love you, too." Abbey carried her to the wagon, where

Sloan was waiting to lift her up and set her on the seat.

She saw they had rigged up a support for JJ that would make riding with his broken leg easier. He was already in the seat, and his lips were tightly pressed together though his chin quivered. Since he was leaving behind the only home he remembered, Abbey understood.

There was a place for the baby right behind the seat, where she would be protected from the weather.

Almost at once, they seemed ready to leave, and a feeling of loss once more swept through Abbey. Jake was mounted, and Sam was on the wagon with Consuela and the children.

He urged the horses into a walk, and the wagon moved forward.

Sloan came back to Abbey and took both of her hands within his, his hat once more off.

"I'll be back tomorrow afternoon. The day following at the very latest."

"You'd better be," Jonah said. "Otherwise, you're going to miss your own wedding."

Sloan brushed the side of Abbey's cheek with his thumb. "Not a chance in hell I'm going to miss that." He dipped his head then and kissed her.

She leaned into him, all the remembered heat and sweetness from before flooding her and making her cling to him. Tears seeped from beneath her closed eyes even though she had resolved she would remain dry eyed.

He lifted his head and gazed down at her before jamming his hat back on his head and striding across to his horse. He swung himself into the saddle, tipped his hat to her, then followed Jake and the wagon out of the compound. Silas loped along beside him, looking like an extension of the man.

Jonah came to stand next to her, and they stood there watching until the wagon disappeared around the first bend in the road beyond the gate.

"Well." Eli came out of the barn. "I could sure use a cup of coffee."

"We all could." Jonah extended his hand toward the house. "Coming, Abbey?"

She tore her gaze from the empty road and followed the other two men toward the house.

CHAPTER 25

"Are we there yet?" Pearl Mae's voice was the whiney one she used when she was bored and tired. "We've been riding forever."

Consuela's patience was wearing thin, as well, because her answer was sharp. "We wouldn't still be riding if we were, would we?"

"Soon," Sloan said to her. "And we might even be able to make a snowman if there is still snow at the summit."

The day had been a long one even though they had made good time and would likely reach the summit of Poncha Pass before nightfall, as he had hoped. He had been told a way station had been built since the last time he'd been over the pass. As the altitude increased, the temperature dropped. The breeze that came off the mountains had a sharp bite of approaching winter. Snow remained on the ground where the pines cast their deepest shadows.

He and Sam had traded off driving the wagon a couple of hours ago since Sloan had been expecting deep ruts in the road. They, thankfully, were absent, an indication of the good maintenance Otto Mears's crew had done on the road—a good thing since the toll was a bit steeper than Sloan had figured was fair.

The new road zigzagged through the mountains, somehow following a more gentle grade than the old path he had remembered the last time he had been this way.

"I'm cold." Pearl Mae placed one of her small hands on the

back of his, bringing his attention back to this moment. "Feel my hands."

She was right. They were cold.

"Are your mittens in your pocket?"

Her answer was lost beneath the loud crack of a rifle report and Sam's shout.

Sloan pulled the team to a stop, alarm thundering through his veins. Being held up had been dead last on the list of concerns he had for this trip.

Another loud crack of gunfire echoed through the trees.

He set the brake on the wagon, thankful they were on a level stretch of road. "Stay here," he commanded, as he leapt off the wagon. When Silas followed him, he commanded the dog, "Stay. Guard."

"Señor," Consuela said, while Pearl Mae said, "I'm scared."

"Stay put. Silas won't let anyone near." He lifted a finger toward JJ. "I'm counting on you."

JJ nodded.

Sloan retrieved his horse from behind the wagon and swung into the saddle, releasing his rifle from its sheath as he urged the horse into a fast walk.

He came around the bend and didn't see anything except a huge pine tree blocking the road. "Jake?" he called. "Sam?"

Neither one answered, but a second later, he saw Jake wave. He had dismounted, and he was using another large tree as cover.

Another gunshot sounded. A bullet whizzed past Sloan's head. He dropped out of the saddle and swatted his horse's rump, sending it back toward the wagon. Jake fired, and whoever was above them immediately fired back. Sloan used an outcrop of rock for his own cover. From here, he couldn't see a thing, nor did he have any way of moving forward.

Where the hell was Sam?

Sloan peered around the rock. Another shot, this time with a splat of dirt spraying him when the bullet hit above him.

"Who are you?" Sloan shouted. "What do you want?"

Another shot, which struck near the last one.

"I've got your stallion," came the returning shout. "Come and get him."

Caleb Holt. Those words made Sloan's stomach clinch. He peered around the other side of the outcropping to see Jake motion at him again, indicating he had eyes on and warning Sloan to stay put.

"That you, Caleb Holt?" Sloan shouted back.

"Isenholt." The announcement was followed by a laugh. "All these months, and you never figured out I'm Charlie Isenholt's son."

Isenholt. Holt. Isenholt. How the hell had he missed the connection? Not once had he connected the names or the obvious similarities.

The odd accidents and mishaps had plagued the ranch for months. The Utes blamed for cattle theft that didn't fit their usual pattern. Charlotte's disappearance without a trace. Bad luck the barn caught fire. Worse luck with Joey's death in a freak accident. More recently, Buck's murder. Sloan's perspective shifted, and too easily, he saw Caleb's hand in all of it. Sloan took a deep breath, then another. He needed a clear head, free from the rage bubbling in his veins.

"Give it up," Sloan shouted. "You can't win this."

Another shot rang out, followed up by the splat of dirt ten feet away from Sloan's position. Either Caleb didn't know where he was, or he wasn't that great of a shot.

"Come on out. Let's talk."

Another shot, this one landing a few feet above the previous one. "I'm in charge, Rafferty. Anything you've got, I can take away. Your wife." Gunshot followed. "Your stallion." Another gunshot. "Your ranch." One more gunshot. "Your life." Another gunshot, and this one hit a rock close enough to Sloan that his cheek was struck by the splintering stone.

"You're a coward." Sloan lifted high enough to fire a shot toward where he hoped Caleb was hiding, then rolled from behind his hiding place and sprinted toward the timber. Jake fired, giving Sloan much needed cover while he scrambled across open ground.

Sloan reached the next cover, a little higher on the hill and behind a bigger pine and a couple of huge boulders. Jake fire a couple more shots. From his new vantage, Sloan still couldn't see Caleb, but he could see Sam, who was flattened behind a log. He was so still Sloan feared he had been wounded. Or worse. He also didn't have enough cover to be safe.

Jake signaled he wanted to move, so Sloan fired in the direction the shots had come from. Jake moved up the hill while answering shots spattered around him. He disappeared as he found better cover. A second later, he waved, then was on the move again.

There was another gunshot, this time from Jake's new position. Sloan used the moment of Caleb's returning fire toward Jake to make his way toward another set of boulders. This time when he looked, he could see a pair of horses tethered back in the timber. One of them was the Cimarron Sun. He left his head up too long because Jake yelled, then fired just as another gun shot hit inches from Sloan's shoulder.

He ducked, then settled more deeply behind the outcropping, his attention now on Sam.

"Sam!" he called.

Another gunshot, this one splaying dirt close to his prone figure.

Then, he heard Jake shout, "God damn it, no!" Two more shots rang out, followed by the high, agonized scream of a horse.

Then, Caleb's head appeared over the top of the trees. Sloan took his shot, and with the second report, realized Jake had done the same thing from his vantage point. Caleb disappeared.

No more gunfire. Just the screams of a horse in agony.

Sloan ran forward, reaching Sam. He rolled over the young man. Relief flooded him when Sam opened his eyes. "Figured playing dead was the only way to keep from being dead."

"You hurt?"

"Got the wind knocked out of me pretty good."

From farther up the hill and through the timber, Sloan saw Jake, who used his rifle to wave at Caleb's position.

Caleb lay on the ground, blood soaking his jacket. Jake had kicked his rifle aside and taken his revolver. Twenty feet behind them, the stallion was down. It writhed in pain and struggled to stand while blood poured from a wound in its neck.

Despair and horror hit Sloan in the middle of the chest.

He ignored Caleb and went to the stallion that had represented everything he had hoped for since the end of the war. The best horses to work cattle that money could buy. A prosperous ranch that raised beef to feed the growing population. The stallion was all tangled in his anger over Charlotte's betrayal. Even down and in pain, the animal was magnificent. Those intelligent, dark eyes glazed over in agony.

The Cimarron Sun released a deep shuddering breath and bloody foam appeared in its nostrils. The stallion was dying.

He knelt next to the horse, laying a hand on his neck, his regret swamping him. No animal deserved this. The horse violently twisted his head toward Sloan, his massive teeth bared, his eyes wild.

"I did it," Caleb called. "He's mine now."

"That's a damn shame," Jake murmured, laying a hand on Sloan's shoulder.

"Yeah." Grief and necessity poured through him in equal

measure. He took his revolver from the holster, placed it against the stallion's temple, and did what needed to be done to put the animal out of its misery.

At the sound of the gunshot, Caleb cried out, and Sloan would have sworn it was a sound of triumph.

He went back to the man, whose eyes were wide open between slow blinks.

"I won," he taunted between labored breaths. "I got it all back. Your wife. Your stallion. Your ranch. Everything you've got—it's all gone." Blood trickled from the corner of his mouth, and he coughed.

"You're going to die a failed man." Sloan glanced back at the dead stallion, then at Caleb.

"Nope." A smile of satisfaction leaked into Caleb's grimace of pain. "Flanders will see to it. You and your half-breed brother will hang, and the ranch will be ash. I did my part, and he's doing his."

His breathing became more labored. Sloan caught Jake's gaze while ice pooled into his gut. Abbey and Jonah were there alone except for Eli. Alone.

CHAPTER 26

After the wagon with Consuela and her children disappeared around the bend beyond the gate, the day loomed as a long one and lonely one. Abbey, Eli, and Jonah set about taking care of chores that had been ignored while getting Consuela's wagon ready to pack. Eli and Jonah disappeared into the barn, and Abbey decided it was a good day to wash the bed linens. Since hot water was readily available, the chore was not the daunting one that it usually was. The challenge came with hanging the laundry since she couldn't lift her arm over her shoulder. Jonah showed up to help, as though he had been keeping an eye out.

He turned out to be surprisingly good company, telling her about the years before the war when his dad had been a trapper.

They ate the midday meal on the porch with Eli despite the chill in the air. The two men conversed about a cow with a limp and a plan for her treatment. As for Abbey, she marveled that it was warm enough to eat outside when only a few days ago she and Sloan had been stranded because of the snow. After the meal, Jonah and Eli disappeared in the direction of the barn again.

Abbey cleaned up the kitchen after the meal, taking time to become more familiar with where things were kept. She kept expecting Consuela would come bustling in at any moment and scold her for interfering. This had been her domain, and Abbey had been tolerated rather than welcomed. Still, the house was decidedly quiet without the activity of Pearl Mae and JJ or Consuela as she went about her activities. Consuela had hummed while she worked, Abbey realized, one more reason the house was so silent.

She went back outside, where she began taking down and folding the dried sheets. The task required she take her time since her shoulder was still tender and prevented her from lifting her arm as high as she needed to do the job. The crisp, clean scent of the laundry made her bend her face into one of the sheets as she folded it. She inhaled more deeply. She thought she caught the aroma of smoke, and she looked over her shoulder, expecting to see a curl of smoke coming out of the chimney of the house, which would be odd, since a bank of coals was all she had left there. No curl of smoke.

She went back to the task of taking down the next sheet without letting it touch the ground as she folded it and set it in the basket. She thought she heard Eli or Jonah shout, possibly at the cow they were treating. She continued with the task of folding the sheets, then carefully picked up the basket to carry it back to the house.

The smell of smoke became suddenly stronger, and she looked toward the barn.

It was on fire.

She dropped the basket and ran across the yard. Smoke billowed out of the door, and she could see the flicker of flame at the back of the barn.

"Eli! Jonah!" She didn't see either of them, but the cow in the enclosure next to the barn was running in a panicked circle. She hurried to the gate leading to the pasture and opened it. The bellowing animal ran past her, its hooves thundering.

She ran back to the door of the barn and called again.

The smoke shifted and heat from the fire rushed toward her. It crackled and hissed. At last, she heard a shout. And she rushed inside.

"Go back!" In the next second, she saw Eli next to one of the stalls. His ever-present battered hat was missing, and blood covered the side of his face. He hung onto the top of the gate, his leg twisted.

She rushed toward him. The milk cow was in the stall next to him, which she opened. She shooed the cow outside, and it ran past her.

"Go back!" he repeated as she skidded to a stop next to him. "We've got to get out of here." She reached for him, put her shoulder under his, and dragged him away from the stall. Straw on the floor caught fire and licked around them. "Come on."

"Jonah," he groaned.

"I'll find him." For a short wiry man, Eli was heavy and awkward, and by the time they cleared the door of the barn, Abbey felt as though she had run miles instead of a few yards. When she looked over her shoulder, the flames reached to the loft. So much fire so fast!

How was this even possible?

As soon as she was away from the barn door, she let Eli fall to the ground, and she ran back to the barn. Smoke billowed as though a fire-breathing monster.

At last, she saw Jonah. His arms were tied around the upright of one of the stalls at the back of the structure. He was slumped as though unconscious. The fire licked closer.

"No!" she rushed forward while smoke rose from the straw around his feet.

She reached him. The knots in the rope were wet, and they didn't come loose. She sobbed in frustration. "Wake up, Jonah."

His head remained slumped against the post.

Somehow, she remembered he usually wore a knife at his waist, but it wasn't there.

She tugged harder at the knots, frantically looking for

anything she could cut the rope with. And then she saw the knife laying in the straw behind them, straw beginning to smolder that would erupt into flame at any second.

She dove for the knife. She sawed at the rope, praying and crying and hurrying because the fire was hotter and licking ever closer.

At last one of the strands of rope loosened, and she pulled with all her might. It suddenly came loose, and Jonah slumped to the ground.

"Come on." She lifted one of his arms and jammed her shoulder into his middle. He groaned, but he came to his feet. They staggered toward the door. Behind them, the fire burned hot. The flames crackled with burning breath and chased them to the door.

Outside, she urged him forward, each step a struggle, each step still too close to the inferno behind them. At last she reached Eli, who lay in the dirt where she had left him. His eyes were closed, and blood from his wound had pooled under his head.

The growl of the fire became suddenly more intense, making her turn around. The barn was fully engulfed. Flames leapt from the roof, and charcoal smoke billowed into the afternoon sky. Jonah's legs suddenly gave way, and she fell to the ground with him.

As she rose to her knees, another awful whoosh of sound caught her attention, this from the house.

Like the barn, it was also on fire.

And William Flanders sauntered toward her.

A cigar was clamped between his teeth, and the big pistol in his hand was pointed at her. He changed the aim to Jonah, who lay on the ground, his cheek pressed into the dirt.

"You should have left him where he was." Flanders cocked the pistol.

"No." Abbey surged to her feet, hitting Flanders's arm as the gun fired.

It spun out of his hand and tumbled to the ground.

Surprise and fury curled his lips in a snarl, and he raised his hand to hit her. "I always win."

She ducked, and his blow glanced off her back. She dove toward the gun while he grabbed at her skirt. It tore. She had a single thought.

Not this time! Never again was a man going to use his size and strength against her.

She kicked at him. He grunted and grabbed her ankle. She wrenched away, kicking at him. He gripped a fistful of her skirt, and it ripped as she struggled to reach those final few inches. At last, her fingers closed around the gun. She lifted it, and as she had seen him do, she cocked the hammer and pulled the trigger.

The gun fired with a tremendous boom and knocked her backwards.

Flanders's hands went to his chest, pure surprise in his expression. A bright bloom of blood pulsed from the front of his shirt. He looked down at his bloody fingers, then raised his gaze to Abbey. Disbelief filled his eyes. He opened his mouth, as if to speak.

He rocked back on his heels and sat heavily, his eyes not leaving hers while a spot of blood appeared at the corner of his mouth and dribbled down to his chin. He blinked, his gaze refocusing on her.

Something in his expression softened. "I was so afraid I wouldn't find you. And here you are."

He fell over then. And his eyes fixed on the sky that rained down ash from his destruction.

Behind her, the fire from the barn heated her back unbearably, while the roof of the house in front of her collapsed. Things needed to be done, but she couldn't stop shaking, couldn't focus her thoughts. The apparitions of her nightmares writhed within the smoke and flames, paralyzing her with memories as searing as the fire.

Today, it wasn't snowing. That day, snow had fallen with the ash. The stench of the dead had clogged her nostrils and lodged in her throat. She took in a shuddering breath. Today, she smelled only the fire and the dissipating scent of gunpowder.

Ashes drifted down, settling on the prone bodies. When one fell on William Flanders's sightless eye, she supposed she should do something. At least close those dead eyes. Instead, she simply sat there, anchored by old memories as desolate as she felt.

And then, she felt warmth along her hand. Long fingers curled around hers, and her gaze fell to their clasped hands. Jonah. Then she met his gaze, his dark eyes bright even though he didn't lift his head.

They hadn't moved when Preacher showed up, though how much time had gone by, Abbey didn't know. A while, because both the barn and the house had collapsed, and the inferno of the fire had settled into a steady burn. She had intended to get up and somehow take care of Jonah but hadn't been able to summon the energy.

He wasn't alone. Two other men were with him, and their actions blurred together. At some point, she realized someone had draped a blanket over her shivering shoulders.

Snatches of conversation surrounded her, little by little becoming more clear as she stopped shivering.

"What brought you this way?" Jonah managed to sit up, though he was supported by a grizzled bear of a man who had a scar in the shape of an *X* high on his cheekbone.

He waved vaguely toward the house. "Smoke. Ran into Preacher who was headed here anyway. Figured I'd tag along in case you needed help."

He managed what Abbey supposed was a smile, though his heavy beard made knowing impossible.

"Sure glad we won't be digging a grave for you today."

Jonah let out a ragged sigh. "That makes two of us."

Another man knelt in front of Abbey, leaning down until she met his gaze. His warm eyes were familiar, but she couldn't summon the energy to know why.

"Are you all right?" Like his eyes, his voice was also familiar.

Her gaze left his to take in the destruction of the barn and the house. The basket of clean sheets by the clothesline looked out of place. The two cows she had shooed away from the barn were grazing on one of the final patches of green, also ordinary. William Flanders still lay a few feet away, though someone had put his hat over his face. She shuddered.

"Miss Abbey" came that kind voice again.

Once more she looked at him. Abbey. Not Charlotte. And said so surely. At last recognition dawned. "Mr. Haverly?"

He smiled. "Sure looks like you've had a time of it."

"I . . . How . . . Harriet and the new babe?"

"They're doing fine." He measured a space in front of him with his hands. "Little Evan is growing like a weed. Healthy. And Harriet, too."

Somehow that news brought tears to her eyes. "I'm so glad." She looked once more around the compound, surprised that Jonah was now standing, huddled with Preacher and the other man over Eli. Her gaze returned to Ben. "How did you get here?" It wasn't what she really wanted to know, but asking about Eli was too painful to face.

"Well, Mr. Rafferty had written to me to let us know you were here, and he asked about your trunk. Even sent me money to have it shipped to you. And, as it happened, I was able to make a deal with a shipper who had goods for the trading post in Poncha, so figured I'd kill two birds with one stone—deliver your trunk so I could make sure you're all right and to finally meet Kenneth Burnett."

All the information piled into an incoherent jumble in Abbey's mind. Sloan had written to Ben all the while refusing to send her letter? Or had he? She couldn't now remember when she had last seen it on the sideboard in the front room. Once more her gaze went to the still-smoldering ruins of the house. Ben had her trunk? With the seeds she had feared were forever lost to her? Odd, she thought, as her gaze once more took in all the destruction.

Seeds and destruction.

Somehow, another of Miss Mary's axioms surfaced, something about out of the ashes a new birth, though now she couldn't remember the whole verse.

"Can you stand?" Ben asked. "Are you hurt?"

She stood without accepting his hand, mostly to prove she was uninjured. Her shoulder hurt like fire once more, but when she tested it, it seemed merely strained, not dislocated as it had been. The huddle around Eli dispersed.

Preacher's expression was somber as he came toward her, his gnarled hands fingering the brim of his derby. He shook his head slightly before meeting her gaze. As Ben had done, he asked, "Are you all right, Miss Abbey?"

She nodded slightly. "Eli?"

"Told us how brave you were. Dragging him from the barn and then getting Jonah out. How he was sure Flanders had killed you all." He paused and looked around the yard. "When I told him it hadn't turned out quite that way—Flanders was dead and you and Jonah were alive—he sighed, then smiled, and said he was mighty glad. His last words, lass."

Time blurred for Abbey as did her thoughts. Eli was dead. A man as old as he should have been able to peacefully die in bed, not murdered.

Ben Haverly was here. Though she remembered he had explained, the connections remained elusive for her. She listened to the men making plans, and the next thing she knew, she was guided toward one of the wagons with Preacher saying they were headed for Poncha with a stop along the way to see Nate and Katherine Long. Another marvel—she was once more leaving the ranch.

This time, she felt sorrow and couldn't keep herself from turning around to look at the still-smoldering ruins of the barn and the house. Two men dead and so much destruction. She supposed she should be glad to be on the outside of the gate, but she was not.

CHAPTER 27

The sound of voices woke Abbey from a fitful sleep. The unfamiliar sensation of someone in bed with her—Ursula Long—plus the unfamiliar scents of the bedding immediately grounded her and reminded her of where she was. The Longs' farm, where Preacher had delivered her shortly after sunset. The room was still dark, so not yet morning.

She couldn't make out what was being said but recognized Katherine Long's voice, then the less familiar one of her husband. Then an even deeper voice—Sloan's. Her heart clutched.

She slipped from the bed, crossed the small bedroom, and flung open the door. He looked up, and those dark eyes lit when they met hers. A second later, he caught her in his arms, and she was unsure of whether she had run to him or he to her. He was big and solid and here. Nothing in her life had ever felt as good as being caught within his tender embrace.

"You're here," she said against his neck.

"And you're all right." His voice was a rumble she as much felt as heard.

"Yes."

His arms tightened around her, lifting her off her feet. He kissed her then, a claiming so complete and filled with so much longing that she trembled. She kissed him back, her worry and fear pouring through her. And love. So much love. So overpowering and humbling and overflowing. Her lips clung to his and

347

tears seeped from beneath her eyelids.

When the kiss ended, she found his warm gaze fastened on hers.

An enormous lump rose in her throat as she leaned back to look at him. "The ranch . . ."

He let her slide to the floor. "I know."

"Jonah?"

"Is fine. He's with Preacher in Poncha."

"I'm so sorry."

"You?" He cupped her face toward him. "No. I shouldn't have left you alone."

"You couldn't have known Mister Flanders—"

He pressed a finger against her lips. "Flanders made it clear he wanted revenge. And I didn't—"

This time she pressed a hand against his mouth. He immediately kissed her palm before taking her hand in his. She swallowed a lump in her throat. "I'm still sorry about the ranch and Eli and Jonah."

"Jonah's going to be okay. You're unhurt." As if to reinforce the statement, he brought her fingers to his mouth again, pressing a warm kiss against her knuckles. "The whole way back, it was the only thing I could think about."

"Consuela and the children?"

"Are fine," he said. "We made it to the summit." He cleared his throat and glanced beyond her.

She turned around, remembering Katherine and Nate Long were behind them. And she had run from the bedroom without any thought except seeing Sloan. To the point she had forgotten all she wore was one of Victoria's long cotton nightgowns.

"We did run into a bit of a problem." Taking her hand, Sloan led her to a chair near the fireplace and urged her to sit. When she did, he dropped to one knee so they were eye level.

"A bit of a problem?" she echoed. His comment was so vague

she was immediately alarmed. "The children?"

"They're fine." A ghost of a smile flitted across his face. "They are driving Consuela to distraction. Riding long hours is far more boring than the fine adventure it sounds like."

"What problem, then? And you weren't supposed to return until tomorrow."

"I was worried about you being alone."

"What problem?" she repeated.

Katherine answered. "An unfortunate incident with a tree blocking the road."

"That's right." Sloan's look of relief at her explanation did nothing to reassure Abbey.

"Thankfully, they were almost to the summit, and after they got the road opened, they decided to spend the night there instead of going the last few miles to the summit."

Katherine, again, which made no sense to Abbey; why she was explaining instead of Sloan?

"Pearl Mae and JJ and Sarah are all okay? Consuela, as well?" She knew the question was a repeat of her earlier one but had to know. "Why did you come back?"

"I was worried about you." His hand cupped her cheek once more. "With reason, it turns out."

"You were?" That somehow came out as a whisper as she relived those awful moments of escaping from the barn with Jonah. Sloan's statement was also characteristic, the way he had been from the beginning. A man who saw the care of others as his sole responsibility. Since she had never been on the receiving end of that . . . not once in her whole life . . . she didn't quite know how to receive this level of concern. Tears filled her eyes.

"Don't cry."

She sniffed and used the sleeve of her gown to blot her cheeks. When her vision cleared, she noticed a trunk next to the door. A big, battered . . . familiar . . . trunk. She moved out of Sloan's loose embrace and crossed the room. More memories from the day crowded forward. Ben Haverly had been at the ranch with Preacher, which hadn't made any sense to her. Still didn't make any sense.

"My trunk."

His warm hand folded around hers. "Yes." He stroked the back of her hand with his thumb, then cleared his throat. "I wrote to him—Mr. Haverly—right after you got—" His voice trailed away. "He came with Preacher today—"

"So I did see him."

"You did. And, he brought your trunk."

"I wasn't sure I'd ever see it again."

"I know."

Katherine and Nate had sat down at the table, their quiet conversation and concerned glances at Sloan once more making her certain something awful had happened despite all their reassurances.

"Anyway, I wanted you to have this." He gestured toward the trunk. "And, I need to get back to the ranch. Nate and some of the other neighbors are going to come tomorrow and help get a temporary shelter built for the milk cow and the horses."

"Don't forget: a wedding day after tomorrow," Katherine said from across the room.

Sloan once more looked at Abbey, his expression so somber, she couldn't help but press her palm against his cheek. He turned his head enough to press a kiss against her palm. "There's a letter for you."

He stepped away from her and began buttoning his coat. "See you in a couple of hours, Nate."

"I'll be there."

Then, he was gone, a rush of cold air coming through the door as he left. Abbey stood there, becoming aware of the cool floor against her bare feet, but her attention still focused on Sloan's expression and his lack of response to Katherine that their wedding was a day away. Had he changed his mind? Then she saw the envelope tucked beneath the leather strap. Her mouth dried as she reached for it, then realized there was a folded sheet of paper tucked beneath the envelope.

"The light is better over here." Katherine motioned toward the fireplace.

"And warmer." Nate touched Katherine's shoulder in a gesture of familiar affection while he stood, then took his coat off the peg near the door. He went through the door, which let in another gush of cold air while Katherine urged Abbey to sit.

She sank into the chair next to the fireplace, fingering the two papers—dying to read, but also somehow certain her life was about to be turned upside down once more. During her life, there had been few letters, so few, in fact, they had been saved and were inside the trunk. Those with bad news and good news were about equal.

Finally, she unfolded the sheet of paper, where the handwriting was bold and precise—easy to read. And from Sloan. "Dear Abigail, Ben Haverly and his wife are fine people, and I can see what a good employer they are. His coming all this way to deliver your trunk is proof. If you would like to return with him to spend the rest of the winter in his employ, you are free to go. He has assured me that you are both welcome and wanted. If you would like to stay here for the winter then continue with your journey to California in the spring, you are welcome here. Either way, I will pay the fare for your transportation so you can fulfill your dream of an orchard."

Tears sprang to her eyes as she read, blurring the rest of the page. She closed her eyes again, her breath caught in her throat. Exactly what she had wanted all these months. Exactly what she had prayed for all those days before she ran away and ran into

351

Caleb Holt. She bent her head into the crook of her arm where the fabric of her gown absorbed her tears. She continued reading.

"No one deserves a chance at happiness more than you do," Sloan had written. "My offer of marriage stands, but you need to choose for yourself what will make you happy." His name was signed at the end, as precise as the rest of the note. Since his penmanship was better than her own, she had a sudden image of him as a boy practicing to perfect his letters in much the same way Miss Mary had insisted for her and the other children.

She carefully refolded the letter, her thoughts a total jumble. She stared at the flickering fire, aware Katherine was bustling about. She pressed a mug into Abbey's hand. The tea felt good as she sipped, warm and laced with honey. Katherine scooted a chair close and sat.

"Bad news?" she asked gently.

"No." Abbey took another sip of tea. Once more, tears burned her eyes. Marriage, but no mention of love. Freedom to be on her way, just as she had wanted. No love there, either. So, what did she do with this gaping hole in the middle of her chest? The one where love had taken hold for the first time in her life.

"Can I do anything to help?"

The simple question was Abbey's undoing, and she sobbed.

"Oh, lass." She took the cup from Abbey's hand and then, somehow, enveloped her in a nurturing hug. Abbey was undone and had no words to explain her confusion, her relief, and her sense of loss caught up in this cauldron of chaotic thought.

"Shhh," came the reassuring murmur from Katherine, who stroked her arms.

She allowed the comfort that Katherine gave so freely as they rocked, taking her back to her earliest memories and the old woman on whose lap she had sat as a very small child. She needed to make sure she had a chair like this, she thought, even as she recognized it was an odd one that had no bearing right now.

"Did you know Mr. Haverly was my employer before I came here?"

"You mean before you were brought here against your will?" was Katherine's tart response. "Yes."

"You know about that?"

"The last few hours have been very enlightening. Sloan Rafferty is not the man I thought he was."

Abbey sat up and took her seat back on the chair facing Katherine's.

The older woman frowned as she took a sip of her own tea. "If I had known you were here against your will, I wouldn't have been helping Preacher to get you married off. I don't abide by that." She fell silent and, like Abbey had, stared into the fire. Finally, she said, "He gave his word. You can leave with Mr. Haverly."

Once more, she was overwhelmed. She could leave. As overwhelming was her realization she could stay. From the day she had been taken to Ma and Pa Hawkins to the day she had left Miss Mary's house, the choice had never been hers. Not during the war when the farm and all the buildings had been burned and she had been abandoned, not after Miss Mary had announced she was an adult and needed to leave. And thus, her journey had continued as she had traveled west, knowing each stop was temporary, knowing she was an outsider whose presence would soon be forgotten.

Katherine picked up the letter and envelope that had fallen to the floor and gave them back to Abbey. When she opened the envelope, she found the letter to be from Harriet.

"Dearest Abbey, we were so relieved to receive Mister Rafferty's letter and learn you are safe and well. I am pleased to report young Evan, who is eight weeks old as of this date, is a happy and healthy baby. We are both thriving.

"As it happens, Ben and Kenneth Burnett have been cor-responding for some time, and they have become friends. Mr. Burnett has invited Ben to visit, which provides him with the opportunity to learn if all is as Mr. Rafferty has reported. To have been mistaken for someone else must have been so frightening. Ben hopes to deliver this letter and your trunk directly to you. Please know this, dearest Abbey. However, we want you to know you are welcome in our home any time. I am most anxious to hear from you, so please write and send a letter back with Ben.

"Wishing you every blessing and God speed."

The letter was signed "Harriet." Abbey was filled with so many emotions that thinking coherently was beyond her. Clearly, Sloan knew she could return with Ben, so they had talked. She handed Katherine the two letters. "I don't know what to do."

"You want me to read these?"

"Yes. Please."

Abbey was drawn across the room to the trunk that she had never again expected to see. She unlatched it and lifted the lid. The scent of lavender wafted up. The list of contents she had neatly written so long ago was still there, a little wrinkled along the edges. At the top neatly tied together were the packets of seeds she had been collecting for years, each one identified by type and date. Beneath them was the heavy volume of *American Pomology: Apples.* Her relief ballooned in her chest and once more brought tears to her eyes. So many hopes and plans had been tied to this one idea. And now, here she was, more uncertain than she had ever been. Did she choose Sloan and this valley or her long-held dream for Abbey's Orchard?

His sudden appearance here at the Longs' house still made no sense to her.

"Why did he come back early?" she asked Katherine.

The older woman sighed. "I'm sure he will explain."

"So you know what happened." Abbey crossed the room and sat back down.

"The man who kidnapped you—"

"Caleb Holt?"

"Yes. He ambushed them when they were almost to the summit of the pass."

"Oh, dear God."

Katherine patted Abbey's arm. "Everyone is okay. Well, almost. He's dead."

Her throat tightened. "Sam? And Jake?"

"They stayed with Consuela and will take her to Santa Fe."

"What made Sloan come back?"

"Evidently Caleb bragged he could take away everything Sloan had ever loved—the stallion, of course, but also his ranch. You." Katherine sighed.

Abbey had forgotten about the stallion. "The Cimarron Sun—"

"Is also dead. Caleb shot the horse when he realized he was going to lose. Revenge."

"Is mine, sayeth the Lord," Abbey said. Sloan hadn't talked much about the horse, but she understood enough to know this was the death of one of his dreams, as well.

"I admit it: I don't understand that man sometimes," Katherine said, "but, he came home when he realized the jeopardy you were in. He did the right thing."

The door to the bedroom Abbey had shared with Katherine's daughters opened, and the three of them emerged, their chatter taking over. The easy conversation and companionship made Abbey homesick for Miss Mary's house, which had been even more noisy in the mornings. Even though they included her, another wave of sadness swept through her. She was an outsider, and she feared she might always be an outsider. And what if she finally had her homestead and there was no one to share it with? She closed her eyes against that thought, consumed with the memory of meals at the SR Double Bar with a different kind of cobbled-together family with Consuela, her children, the ranch hands, Sloan, and his brother. All these people with their relationships—she wanted this for herself.

The allure of Sloan's embrace and the sweet kiss he'd had for her a little while ago made her think she might have that here. Did she dare hope? Or was it better to hang onto her familiar and cherished dream?

Katherine said, "Sloan said Mr. Haverly will be along later today."

"Yes." According to Sloan's letter, Ben would take her back to Denver with him if she wanted. She had been so sure that was exactly what she wanted. Except, she would never see Sloan again . . . or be held by him.

Katherine handed Abbey back the two letters with a murmured, "Give yourself some time. You'll know what you want to do."

Abbey was less certain about that. She set the letters in the trunk and closed the lid. Abbey's Orchard had been her deepest desire ever since she had first seen the flyer for homesteading in California. At first, it had been a distant dream, and then, little by little she had forged a plan. She saved enough for the first leg of the journey, worked hard, saved again, and repeated as she worked her way west. For years, those two words—Abbey's Orchard—represented her future. A place that would be hers, a place where she truly belonged.

For her whole life, she felt as though she had been swept along by currents beyond her control. The notion of giving up Abbey's Orchard carved out a giant ache in her chest. Only, she had given her word to Sloan, this hard man she had come to love. He would be bound by his own sense of duty, but did she dare trust that she wouldn't one day be cast aside?

Give up Abbey's Orchard? Give up Sloan? Tears burned her eyes and heart, then spilled down her cheeks.

CHAPTER 28

Abbey might have been uncertain whether there would be a wedding, but the flurry of activity in the Long household assumed there would be. Katherine insisted on a final fitting of her dress, and Abbey had to admit she loved it. She had never had anything so fine or felt so beautiful. She also had the odd sensation of being in her own clothes once again, thanks to the return of her trunk.

They were all at work in the kitchen assembling ingredients for a cake that was to be served after the wedding. Abbey hadn't imagined the wedding beyond the actual ceremony, a notion Katherine put to rest with a, "Of course there will be a celebration. A proper welcome to our community. Besides, it will be one the last opportunities for a party before winter sets in."

She was also shocked to learn the Longs were immediate neighbors of the SR Double Bar though their property did not have as much acreage as the ranch.

"By the road," Katherine told her while they poured the cake batter into a pan, "it's about four miles." She pointed her wooden spoon in a different direction. "Go beyond the wheat field in that direction, and it's a walk of less than a mile. You have to hike over the hill and cross the creek. Could be snow up there, but probably not."

"There's a trail?" Abbey asked.

"Yes, so no chance of getting lost. As soon as you get to the top of the hill, you'll be able to see Sloan's ranch." Katherine gave Abbey an assessing look. "You're not thinking of going over there, are you?"

Until that moment, Abbey hadn't considered it. Though she shook her head, she kept thinking about it while they worked. All this time she had been convinced the ranch was so isolated she was miles from the nearest neighbor, but here they were, within walking distance of one another.

"I wish I'd known sooner you were so close," she confessed.

"Sloan Rafferty is a scoundrel who should have told us weeks and weeks ago you were there." Her comment came with a forceful slap to the bread dough she was kneading.

The home scents of baking seemed suddenly more intense. "Why are you doing all of this when I don't know whether I'm going to stay."

"I saw how you kissed the man, lass. Walking away from a love like that . . ."

When her voice trailed away, Abbey swallowed and gave voice to the idea lodged in her mind: "For my whole life, I never got to choose. And I never belonged."

"Are you sure?" Katherine patted the ball of dough and dropped it into a large bowl that she covered with a towel. After wiping her hands on her apron, she faced Abbey. "About not choosing. What about your determination to come west all alone, regardless of what anyone else thought?"

"I had to leave Miss Mary's house. That wasn't so much a choice, but a necessity."

"Most women would have looked around for an eligible man to marry, not followed an advertisement to homestead land on the far side of the continent. Most men don't have the confidence to do such a thing, much less a woman. A young woman."

"There weren't many men to marry." Abbey's memory was drawn back to the utter destruction of the valley after the war.

The few men who remained were either old or broken.

"You could have settled for what was in front of you."

That had not occurred to Abbey. Miss Mary had told her she had to leave. She was an adult who had to make her own way. What else could she do but pursue the dream for a place that could not be taken from her? She had the advertisement for free land, free to anyone who was willing to make the claim and work it. And she knew how to work hard. And she had the seeds she had been collecting since she was a child. Until Jake and Sam had brought her here, she hadn't considered any other possibility for herself.

"I just took the next step," she said.

"A choice, by any other name." Katherine set her hands on her hips. "And, now, you get to choose again."

The next set of chores took over, but Abbey kept thinking about that as the day passed. Had she really been choosing all this time when she simply had thought she was being swept along by the next thing that came her way?

Ben arrived with Nate at suppertime, and, when he saw all the preparations that had been made for the wedding, he seemed to have the same assumption that everyone else did—she was staying. After dinner, though, he did draw her aside.

"Sloan Rafferty seems pretty sure you'll be leaving with me tomorrow."

Abbey had no idea how to respond to that.

"Maybe the better way of putting that is the man is scared to death you'll be leaving with me."

"Scared?" The man always was so resolute, she had a difficult time imagining him scared.

"It's clear he wants what is best for you, to the point he's trying to put aside his own feelings."

Abbey shook her head. "He seems concerned about my reputation is all."

Ben snorted. "A man doesn't go to the lengths he has if reputation is all he's concerned about."

"A guilty conscience, then," Abbey said.

"Maybe. I think it's more." He paused, waiting for Abbey to look at him. When she did, he added, "I've seldom seen a man work harder than he did today—not on the stuff needed to take care of the livestock, but of cleaning out Consuela's cabin and making sure it will be nice for you." His attention went beyond Abbey to the chore of doing dishes and straightening the kitchen that was going on behind them. "You could have a good life here, much as it pains me to say it since Harriet and I were looking forward to your help over the winter."

Abbey turned around to look at Katherine and her daughters who, as usual, were talking over each other. She liked them, and she easily imagined shared time together, especially since they were neighbors. Or would be, if she stayed.

Ben stood and reached for his hat on the hook near the door. "Tell you what. I'll be back here in the morning. If you want me to take you to the church, I will. And, if you want to go back home with me, we can do that, too."

Once more, a choice. Had they all been, she wondered.

Ben said his goodbyes, then left for town saying it would take him only a half hour to get there. One more indication the ranch was not so isolated as Abbey had imagined all this time.

As soon as it was light outside, Abbey got up and dressed. Before she chose, she decided, she needed to see the ranch. Would she see it as a prison or a home?

Since Katherine had told her it was within walking distance and she was sure to see it from the top of the hill, she set off.

Katherine was right. Abbey reached the top of the hill about the time the sun peeked over the top of the eastern hills and spilled light into the valley. The charred ruins of the barn and the house were clearly visible. There was new construction, too. A lot of it for a mere day's labor—a large three-sided shed that would provide at least some shelter for the milk cow during the storms. From here she could see the squat stone bunkhouse and small cabin where Consuela had lived with her children, which were still standing. Fleetingly, Abbey wondered how Mr. Flanders had missed burning them since he had been so set on destroying everything. The orchard was there, too, along with the milk cow grazing in the adjoining field. It was all surprisingly normal despite the amount of work needed to rebuild.

She made her way through the trees, and a path became more pronounced as she descended from the crest of the hill. She found herself at the family graveyard where the children had led her the very first day. A fresh mound of earth marked a new grave.

Eli. Sadness welled within her for the old man who so often had a twinkle in his eye to match his vivid language. He had been limping more lately, and he'd announced his bones told him when a storm was on the way long before any changes to the weather.

Tears filled her eyes, and a prayer filled her heart as she stared down at this newest grave. Another life among all the others that were the high price of living on this ranch. She thought about her dream for Abbey's Orchard and suspected she would be naïve to imagine the price paid for her own land would be any less high. Imagined people she had not yet met, but their possible loss made her sink to her knees with a sob. She hadn't known Sloan's father or brother or Consuela's babies, but her tears were equally for them.

Another of Miss Mary's axioms filled her mind. To everything there is a season, and a time to every purpose under the heaven. She had seen how seasons of hope followed those filled with despair, so knew it was possible. Especially with the one thing

Miss Mary had relentlessly beat into their heads—God helps those who help themselves.

Abbey knelt there, feeling the cool earth seep through her skirt while she whispered a final prayer for Eli.

She rose and followed the trail through the trees toward the ranch. At the edge of the grove, she stood there, absorbing the joy expanding through her chest. This place looked like home, felt like home. Not some far off land, but here. As she had done so many times before, her steps took her toward the small apple orchard. The branches of the trees were bare, but in her mind's eye she imagined them blooming next spring. To everything there was a season. She hoped her own season of blooming would be here. The realization made her steps slow once more. Here. Not some far off land, but right here.

Her slowed steps halted completely when she saw movement at the edge the orchard. Not the bull that sometimes appeared in her nightmares, but Sloan, who was pounding a stake into the ground.

Then, he moved, and she could see a sign attached to the stake: Abbey's Orchard.

The name in big, black letters against a board that had probably been part of the barn, since one of its edges was charred. The letters were a little crooked, and the sign nailed to the stake was, as well. Crooked or not, it was the most beautiful thing she could imagine.

Tears came to her eyes.

"What are you doing?" Her question came out as a whisper that he evidently didn't hear, because he continued tapping the top of the post. She cleared her throat, and he whirled around.

His eyes were wary and a little bloodshot, as though he hadn't gotten enough sleep. A big mallet hung so loosely in his grasp that it fell to the ground. His worried expression smoothed into the implacable one he wore to hide what he was feeling.

"What are you doing?" she repeated, her slow steps carrying her closer to him as she gestured toward the sign.

Abbey's Orchard. A lump rose in her throat, and she couldn't have said anything more if her life had depended upon it.

"I . . ." His voice trailed off while he turned around to look at the sign. He gave his head a single shake, then took those few steps that separated them. "I wanted you to know that you could have it all if you came back here with me." He came to a stop in front of her. "Had it all planned along with a fine speech."

"What plans?" She wanted to reach up and touch his jaw where a muscle bulged, but she didn't. "What speech?"

"Plans." He nodded in the direction of the compound. "How we'd be okay this winter despite not having a barn. That Consuela's cabin would be comfortable enough for us."

"Those sound like good plans." Abbey took a step closer. "But that doesn't tell me about this. Abbey's Orchard."

"I know how important this is to you." He reached for her hands. "Everything I have or ever hope to have is yours."

That came too close to sounding like she was a duty or an obligation, but "everything" covered a lot of ground. She stepped closer and pressed a hand against his chest. "What about your heart?"

His gaze was so intent as he stared down at her that her courage faltered. What if this huge thing she felt for him was one sided? What if this thing with the orchard was merely a way to sweeten her up? Could she settle for that?

He bent his head toward hers until their foreheads touched. "My heart is yours, too, Abbey. The idea of you leaving just about kills me—"

"I love you." She stood on her tiptoes and turned her face enough to kiss his jaw.

He shuddered, then gathered her close. His heat surrounded

her while he pressed kisses against her cheeks and hair before finding her mouth. As happened with her every single time, she lost all coherent thought except for one. This was home. Wherever he was would be home.

"You're sure?" he asked.

"That I love you?" She leaned back to look at him. "What kind of question is that?" Despite wanting to sound playful, the question was too important.

"Sure that you want to stay."

"I choose you." Her throat clogged. Another choice, this one consciously made. This one feeling more right than any since she had embarked on her trip west.

"I love you, Abbey. So much." His voice was so deep, it sounded as though the words had been dredged up from his soul.

"I know."

He must have heard the smile in her voice because his own smile began to crack through his usual somber expression. "How?"

"Because you were willing to let me go."

He shook his head slightly. "Glad that I don't have to prove that I could have."

"It's all right here."

"What?"

She squeezed his hand with one of her own and waved across the valley, encompassing the orchard, the remaining buildings of the ranch, the snowcapped peaks beyond the valley. It was all so beautiful that she had to blink to keep her tears at bay.

"Abbey . . ." His voice cracked, and he pressed their clasped hands against his heart. "You belong. You have from almost that first day."

Her tears did spill then. He cupped her face with both hands and wiped them away.

"That's all I ever wanted. To belong, really belong."

"You do." He laid his forehead against hers, then pressed his cheek against hers. "I promise."

She kissed him then, that sense of being at home so complete her heart filled to bursting. When he lifted his head, she met his warm, dark eyes. "I think it's time for you to walk me back to the Longs' house. We have to get ready for a wedding later today."

EPILOGUE

Sloan ran a finger beneath his collar, which was starched to the point it felt like a board. With every movement, the collar chafed his neck. He and Jonah stood at the back of the church, dressed in their Sunday best and waiting for Abbey's arrival. The church was already filled with a couple dozen of his neighbors.

Abbey's promise to see him in a couple of hours after they had walked back to the Longs' house should have reassured him. Maybe she had come to her senses and decided she would be better off without him. A burned-out ranch wasn't much to offer a bride, yet here he was.

Preacher came through the door, and he smiled when he saw them standing there. "Stop worrying."

Sloan didn't like that he was so transparent.

Jonah nudged Sloan's arm with his shoulder. "This is what tired looks like."

Preacher smiled and shook his head. "Nah. I recognize worried when I see it." He slapped Sloan on the back. "Happens with about every groom. Had breakfast with Ben Haverly before service." Preacher evidently read something in Sloan's expression because he said, "He was leaving for the Longs' place right after."

Remembering the man had promised to stick around until Abbey made her decision tightened the knot in Sloan's stomach another notch. "I'll see you in a couple of hours," she had promised.

Preacher went into the church, stopping along the way to chat with people inside.

"She'll be here," Jonah said. "But I can ride out to the Longs', if you want."

Sloan shook his head. "Won't change the outcome."

"True. But, it could put you out of your misery."

A wisp of dust arose from the road at the bend, and a second later a wagon appeared. Nate Long was driving the team, and so many people were with him that Sloan couldn't see if Abbey was one of them. Katherine spotted him and Jonah, and she waved. The wagon slowed. The passengers were all the daughters and their new son-in-law. No Abbey.

Sloan's knot tightened some more.

And, then, another wagon came around the bend, this one at a bit of a faster clip than the Longs' wagon, which had now come to a stop. Nate's family spilled out, all of them talking at once in the usual way for the family. Sloan's attention, though, was on the other wagon, this one driven by Ben Haverly. And Abbey was with him.

The knot loosened a bit. Was she here to get married or say good-bye?

"Come on, you," Katherine commanded, taking Sloan by the arm. "It's bad luck for you to see the bride before the wedding." She steered him inside and down the aisle. "You, too, Jonah. Somebody has to keep your brother in tow."

"A job I can do." He grabbed Sloan's other arm.

Evidently satisfied they were following directions, Katherine bustled toward to the door.

Sloan looked over his shoulder, desperate to see Abbey, who was now surrounded by Katherine and Nate's daughters. Ben caught his eye and saluted with a wide grin as Jonah pulled Sloan away.

He found himself standing at the front of the church with

Preacher and his brother. His neighbors sat there, some smiling at him and some turned to see the bride's entrance.

Movement at the back of the church caught his eye, and he looked up. Ben Haverley had slipped into a seat at the back of the church. Katherine and one of her daughters came through the door, big smiles on their faces as they took seats near the front of the church.

Then, Abbey appeared in the doorway. Her face paled a little as she took in the room filled with people who were suddenly silent. Her gaze finally landed on him. She looked so alone and uncertain.

There was no one to give her away. It shouldn't be like that. And so, he went to her, his steps as slow as they would have been if he had been approaching a skittish mustang.

She had never looked more beautiful to him. Her hair was braided as she often did but somehow wound around her head so it looked like a crown. The dark blue of her eyes were luminous and so beautiful. The smattering of freckles across her cheeks and nose should have alerted him the very first day of who she was . . . and was not.

"Abbey, you're so beautiful." He touched the sleeve of her dress, the lavender a muted color of an early morning sunrise. "Are you okay?"

Her wide gaze caught with his, then slid toward to the people watching them. His own followed hers, and he supposed they seemed like a lot after the isolation of the last weeks. He frowned since that was his fault. One more thing to make up to her.

"We're in this together." He offered her his arm. "Are you ready?"

"Yes." Instead of taking his arm, she slipped her hand into his.

That felt right, too, and he gently squeezed hers in reassurance. They walked side by side the way he hoped they

would for the rest of their lives. Abbey, his beloved, who was no
longer a stranger.

ABOUT THE AUTHOR

Sharon Mignerey has been a voracious reader all her life, which she credits to her mother, who read to her before bedtime almost every night. Sharon says she came out of the womb telling stories, and she likes romance best—the stories of a woman pursuing her dreams and goals, being the hero of her own journey, and earning a well-deserved happily-ever-after with a man worthy of her.

Sharon's great-grandfather was a circuit-riding Methodist minister in Colorado who later settled on a ranch on Grand Mesa in Colorado. The character of Preacher in this novel is a tribute to him.

Sharon is a long-time member of Rocky Mountain Fiction Writers and holds an M.F.A. in Writing Popular Fiction from Seton Hill University. She is the author of eleven other novels.

For additional information, see sharonmignerey.com.

The employees of Five Star Publishing hope you have enjoyed this book.

Our Five Star novels explore little-known chapters from America's history, stories told from unique perspectives that will entertain a broad range of readers.

Other Five Star books are available at your local library, bookstore, all major book distributors, and directly from Five Star/Gale.

Connect with Five Star Publishing

Visit us on Facebook:
https://www.facebook.com/FiveStarCengage

Email:
FiveStar@cengage.com

For information about titles and placing orders:
(800) 223-1244
gale.orders@cengage.com

To share your comments, write to us:
Five Star Publishing
Attn: Publisher
10 Water St., Suite 310
Waterville, ME 04901